# a shot of
# PRETTY
# POISON

## USA TODAY BESTSELLING AUTHOR
## KELSEY CLAYTON

Copyright © 2023 by Kelsey Clayton

All rights reserved.

No part of this book may be reproduced in any form or by any electronic or mechanical means, including information storage and retrieval systems, without written permission from the author, except for the use of brief quotations in a book review.

Editing by Kiezha Ferrell at Librum Artis
Proofreading by Tiffany Hernandez

*To my editor, Kiezha*
*Thank you for always being such a goddess.*
*Anyone else would've fired me by now,*
*but you deal with my crazy.*
*It's appreciated more than you know.*

**CONTENT WARNING**

This book deals with sensitive topics that may not be suitable for all readers. As some readers have said they find descriptive trigger warnings to be spoilers, I have provided a link to where you can find all of the trigger warnings for each of my books. Please read safely.

**For trigger warnings:** Please go to www.kelseyclayton.com/triggerwarnings

# Hayes
# CHAPTER ONE

The pain of heartbreak is all consuming and love is nothing but a parasite. I should've stuck by my own rules—kept her at arm's length. But instead, I let her take up residence inside my chest, gave her everything I had to give, and when she left, she took my heart with her.

I'm cold.

I'm empty.

I'm a broken shell of a man.

And her? Well, I'd guess she's God-knows-where, living out her life like we didn't spend the summer falling in love with each other. Little did I know, she could fly.

But I hit the ground.

*A Year and a Half Later*

## Chapter 1

Let it be known that twenty-two is far too young to take on the world. No matter how strong you try to be, there's always going to be something that breaks you. But what happens when you refuse to even bend?

I wear my skin like a shield of armor, and I'm pretty sure I'm too numb to feel anything anymore. It's as if my nerves shut off in an effort to protect me, because the day she walked out of my life was only the start of the downward spiral that has become my new normal.

Getting out of my truck, I check my reflection in the window and hold my head high. I don't have the luxury of anything else. Letting myself break isn't an option. Not when she's depending on me.

*New Horizons of Calder Bay.*

The sign on the door looks way too happy for what this place represents. There haven't been many times where I left here with a smile on my face—not when I know she'll never make it out of here alive. The hope of that died six months ago. And I'm guessing that this meeting is only going to confirm my darkest fear.

*My mom is dying.*

I walk into the conference room with a level of confidence they can't tell is just me faking it until I make it. It's the only way to survive anymore. The director of the nursing home sits at one end of the table, surrounded by a few of my mom's doctors and a nurse from the local hospice organization. It's been something we've tried to avoid. The word feels like giving up, and none of us have been willing to do that yet, but there's only so much that can be done before that becomes the only option.

"Mr. Wilder," the director greets me. "Thank you for coming. Is your sister here as well?"

I shake my head. "She's away at college. But as my mother's sole Power of Attorney, it shouldn't be an issue."

## Chapter 1

"Very well." He nods once. "Dr. Chen, would you like to begin?"

Dr. Chen is my mom's oncologist. She was assigned to my mom in the hospital, when the cancer that inhabited her brain was found. And the kindness she has shown my sister and me over the last year has earned her my respect. But the grave look on her face gives me no hope for good news.

"Unfortunately, Hayes, the chemotherapy and radiation no longer seem to be working," she tells me. "We've tried upping the intensity of the treatments, but I'm afraid if we continue to do that, it will jeopardize her quality of life."

*Fuck.* "What about the clinical trial we talked about?"

She frowns. "Once the cancer spread to her kidney, she became ineligible."

"So, I'll give her one of mine. Book the surgery and I'll be there."

Dr. Chen reaches out and puts her hand on mine. "H, I'm sorry. The clinical trial is not an option we have anymore. And you know she would never let you give her an organ. Even if that were a solution, she'd block it before we got started."

She's not wrong. My mom is nothing if not protective of her kids. She didn't even tell us about how she hadn't been feeling well. We had to find out through a doctor at the hospital. There I was, hoping and praying the symptoms she was experiencing weren't early onset dementia, and the reality was so much worse.

I swallow down the lump in my throat as I let the wall that I've built around myself block out the pain. "Okay. Where does that leave us?"

"Well, we could continue what we're doing," she suggests. "But there's not much chance of it starting to work after this long. And we have reason to believe that's not something your mom wants."

## Chapter 1

"What?" My brows furrow. "No. My mom is a fighter. She wouldn't give up like that."

They all look to Dr. Tracy, my mom's therapist, and she gives me a sad smile. "She's tired, Hayes. You're right, she is a fighter, but she's very tired. I think the only reason she's still trying to beat this is because of you and Devin. But she's exhausted."

I drop my head, holding back the tears as the pain finds its way through. My mom has always put us first. I can't remember a time where she didn't. And deep down I know Dr. Tracy is right.

"So, what we're getting at here is you all recommend she stop treatment and begin hospice. Am I right?"

The representative from hospice wouldn't be here otherwise. We've had plenty of meetings since it was first recommended, and she wasn't at any of them. Everyone in the room stays quiet, as if none of them want to be the one to confirm to the man young enough to be their child that his mother is dying, but that's all the confirmation I need.

"If you don't mind," I begin, standing up. "I'd like a chance to talk to my mother before I make any decisions."

"Absolutely," the director tells me. "Take your time. We'll be here when you get back."

Mumbling a quiet *thank you*, I walk out the door and head toward my mother's room. It's small, with bland gray paint on the walls and a TV mounted in front of the bed. The room itself is definitely not worth the nine grand I pay each month for her to be here, but the care they provide her with *is*.

When this horrible journey started, only seven months after I woke up to find out my wife was gone, my mother insisted if she reached a point where she couldn't care for herself, she wanted to be put somewhere that could. During her years as a nurse, she had seen too many instances of family members having to endure the emotional hardship of

## Chapter 1

having to take care of their sick loved ones. She knew I would do it. I would take on that burden and care for her even if it killed me, but she doesn't want that for us. So every day, I stop by and spend time by her side, and then I leave, feeling like I'm abandoning her.

And I know the feeling of being abandoned.

Let me tell you, it's hell.

"Hey mom," I greet her.

She lights up as she sees me, the same way she always does. "Hayes! My baby."

I walk over to her bed and kiss her forehead. "How are you feeling?"

"Oh, you know. A little of this, a little of that."

She plays it off well, the whole *I'm totally fine and you don't need to worry* act, but I know her well enough to see right through it. Grabbing the chair and sliding it up next to her bed, I sit down and take her hand in mine.

"Mom," I say softly. "I need you to tell me what you want."

"Hayes," she whines, trying to pull her hand away, but I don't let her.

"I'm serious. Don't worry about me or about Devin."

She gives me a look that could shoot me dead. "I *always* worry about you and Devin."

I chuckle. "Yes, Gladiator, I know. But right now, I need to know what *you* want. Do you want to keep fighting this? Keep getting treatments and going through scans? Because if that's what you want, I'll do it. I'll continue to pick you up and bring you to every single appointment. I learned how to roll a joint for you—which is so fucked up to say, by the way."

She giggles, and I know there's going to be a time where I miss that sound.

Smiling at her, I exhale slowly and let the grin fall from

## Chapter 1

my face before I say the words that will hurt me a million times more than they hurt her. "But if you want to just stop and enjoy the time that you have left, that's okay, too. I'll understand. You've spent your life working your ass off for us. It's hardly a stretch to say you deserve to rest."

A tear escapes and slides down her cheek, and I gently wipe it away. My mom lets out a wet laugh and does the same for me. I didn't even know I was crying. But then again, for the last year, I've zeroed all of my focus in on making her happiness my first priority.

My own isn't even on the list.

"Who is going to look after you and Devin?" she asks.

"I've got Devin. Don't worry about her."

Her other hand comes over to rest on mine that's holding hers. "Yes, but who is going to worry about *you*?"

Images of Laiken flash through my mind, and I immediately push them away. When she left, I didn't know what to do with myself. And right there by my side was my mom. But what she doesn't know is a part of me blames myself for how long it took for the cancer to be found.

She was a nurse. She knew the warning signs of things like that. But she was so concerned with taking care of me that she neglected herself. And I was too wrapped up in my own shit to notice something was wrong.

"I'll be fine," I tell her.

Her eyes roll. "Please. I'm a woman. We basically changed the definition of the word *fine*. No one is ever fine when they say that."

Okay, so maybe she has a point. But I'm not selfish enough to make her go through more torture for the sake of my happiness.

"Mom," I say. "It's okay. What do you want to do?"

Her chest falls as she lets out the air in her lungs. "I want to see the sunrise on the beach. And I want to have dinner

## Chapter 1

with my kids. And I want to look forward to the next day and not worry about if I'll be too nauseous to hold down my lunch."

*There it is.* I hold back all of the emotions that flood through me at the sound of her words. If there's any time that I need to get her to believe I'm okay, it's now. And she looks scared until I force a warm smile on my face.

"Okay," I agree. "I'll sign the paperwork. As of today, you'll be able to rest without worry."

There's relief in her eyes. The kind you see in a young child when they finally get the comfort of their mother. It's that moment when they know that everything is going to be all right. They're safe. They're warm. They're protected.

And now I have to sign a paper that means all of that will be ending soon for me, for the sake of giving it to her.

"I love you, Hayes," she says. "I love you so much."

I stand and kiss her forehead once more. "I love you too, Mom."

The second I leave her room, I need to grip the railing against the wall for support. When I woke up this morning, I knew this meeting was going to be hard. It doesn't take a rocket scientist to figure out where all of this was going. Happy news normally doesn't require a conference room. But there's no way to mentally prepare for having to sign a document that officially ends all lifesaving treatment for the woman who raised you.

The woman who loved you even when you didn't feel lovable.

The woman who helped you pick up the pieces of your broken life. Multiple times.

There's no way to get through that without it completely ripping you apart.

Dr. Chen keeps a comforting hand on my shoulder as I sign and initial on all the necessary lines. If I'm honest, it

## Chapter 1

feels a lot like giving up, but this isn't my battle to fight—no matter how much I wish it was. Once I'm done, the notary stamps it and hands me back my license.

"There are different levels of care options," the hospice rep says. "I'll leave this paperwork with you. I've highlighted the one I believe best suits her, but look that over and let me know."

I shake my head. "No need. Just do whatever is going to make her the most comfortable."

She and the director share a glance, but it's him that explains. "Mr. Wilder, each level of care comes at a certain price bracket. And her insurance won't cover it past thirty days."

*Of course it won't.* "I understand, but my answer remains the same. Her comfort is what's most important to me right now. Do what you need to do."

They both nod. The question that conversation raised lingers in the air, but it's not one I'll ask. I don't want to know how much time she has left, or when I'll have to say goodbye to her. All she wants is to enjoy the time she has, and I'm going to give her that.

"Thank you for all you do for my mother," I tell everyone in the room. "Now, if you'll excuse me, I have to get to work."

Shaking each of their hands, I feel the vomit creeping up the back of my throat. I leave the room with as much calmness as I can manage, but the minute I'm out of sight, I book it to the bathroom.

If I thought coffee tasted gross in general, there's no way to explain how repulsive it is when it comes back up. But as I crash onto the floor after emptying my stomach, that's the least of my worries.

There's something to be said about those who can carry the burdens of the world on their shoulders. The ones whose

## Chapter 1

knees don't buckle under the pressure of it all. I try to be that guy—for my mom and for Devin—but sometimes I can't help but wonder the one thing I never should.

*Would it be any easier if she were still here?*

*If I had her to lean on at night, would the agony be any less intense?*

Problem is, I'll never know. So, I push the thought of her away once more, like the trained professional I am, and I pick myself up off the floor.

Because if I don't, no one else will.

**THE BAR IS STARTING** to pick up, with the summer months approaching. Not that the rest of the year is slow by any means. The laid back environment and the beachy feel that the place has earned us the title of Best Bar in the County last year. Though while I wish that was responsible for our success, it's not.

Our barmaid, Riley, posted a TikTok of Cam that went viral. Apparently, there's something attractive about a bartender who can mix a drink and shotgun a beer, all while the saltwater is still in his hair and his wetsuit hangs halfway off his body. Since then, we've had people come from all over just to get a glimpse of Cam.

And while you'd think he would eat the attention up, he's

# Chapter 1

more focused on the business than the flirting—especially after what went down between him and Mali.

But that's not my story to tell.

As I walk in, Cam is standing behind the bar, getting it ready to open. He glances up at me for a second.

"Hey," he drawls. "How'd it go?"

I shrug, not really wanting to talk about it. "Okay, I guess. Nothing really new."

Okay, so maybe it's stupid. If there's anyone I could count on with this shit, it's him. He's always been there for me, even when his own sister was the cause of my misery. But there's a part of me that likes living in denial. Where I can ignore all the shit going wrong in my life and pretend like everything is fine.

Like my world isn't being held together by tape.

And not even the strong duct tape shit. I'm talking about the tape that can hardly hold a poster on the wall because it's designed not to leave a mark behind.

"Is this today's mail?" I question, looking at the pile sitting on top of the bar.

He nods. "Yeah, I grabbed it before I came in."

"Thanks, man," I say as I take the envelopes. "Let me bring this shit upstairs and I'll be down in a bit."

"Sounds good. And don't forget about tonight!"

My brows furrow. "Tonight?"

He looks at me like I've just broken our most sacred rule. "It's the third Friday in May."

*Shit.* "Right. The first bonfire of the season."

"Fuck yeah!"

I force a grin on my face, one that immediately disappears as soon as I start heading up the stairs.

It's no surprise that I'm not as excited for bonfire season as I used to be. Just like last year, it only reminds me that it's been that long since I heard Laiken's confession spill from

## Chapter 1

her lips—when the feelings I put in a box at fourteen-years-old broke out and demanded to be noticed. That night was the start of it all. The beginning of the only meaningful relationship I've ever had. And no matter how many days go by, I've yet to break my vows.

The ones that still apply because we're still married—whether she's here or not.

If elective amnesia were a thing, I'd like to think I'd be the first one in line. Anything would be better than this mess of emotions I drag around day after day. I'm just as angry as I am hurt. There's no justification for what she did.

But my heart will always belong to the girl who made me feel for the very first time.

I take a deep breath and sit on my bed, opening the mail and feeling my anxiety build with each one. The words *past due* and *final notice* in bright red stare back at me, taunting me as they threaten to take away the only dream of mine that still remains intact. But my mom's care is more important.

The little voice in my head reminds me that I need to tell Cam. And I will. I just need to figure out how. It's not exactly easy to tell someone that we may lose vendor contracts and possibly the bar itself because I was selfish and fucked up by paying for my mother's nursing home instead of the bills at the bar. It has to be done right, and at the right time, or he'll hate me.

Who am I kidding? He might hate me anyway.

I put the bills into a pile and shove them into a desk drawer, where they'll stay, mocking me, in the way I deserve. A stark reminder of what a fucking failure I am.

Can't be a husband worth staying with.

Can't save my mom.

Can't even keep a bar running that was basically handed to me.

*My life is a fucking mess.*

# Laiken
## CHAPTER TWO

I'VE NEVER UNDERSTOOD THE SAYING *misery loves company*. Whoever came up with that must have confused misery with being a vindictive bitch, because when I'm miserable, I just want to be alone. There's no one I want near me. Nothing can make it better. Just let me lie there in the aftermath of the chaos I caused.

I deserve to be this broken.

There's nothing that can rid me of the feeling that came when I left. It's there, staining every inch of my life. And no matter how happy I should be, those feelings don't exist for me.

Not anymore.

Not since him.

The artist's voice rings through the studio as she belts out the song I wrote, and it's beautiful, but it's just not it. There's something missing. Something keeping it from being as strong as it should be.

"Stop her," I tell the producer.

Getting out of my chair, I step into the recording booth and look at the innocent-eyed up-and-comer who still thinks the world is beautiful and life is full of roses and rainbows.

"I don't feel it," I say simply.

She looks confused. "Feel what?"

## Chapter 2

"The pain. The absolute *agony*. This song is about real heartbreak. The kind that makes it so you can't take a single breath without feeling like someone cut open your chest and ripped your heart right out your body. It's the kind you don't recover from, no matter how much time passes or how many times you convince yourself that you did the right thing."

I nod for her to move, and she steps out of my way. After I slip the headphones on, I rest my hands on the microphone. The faded *H* on my ring finger stares back at me—the one thing that constantly reminds me what we had was real.

The tune of the chorus starts to play in my ear as I belt out the lyrics with the conviction they deserve.

*Left my heart on the floor,*
    *As I walked out the door.*
    *Do you still think about me?*
    *Please don't think about me.*

*Cause I don't deserve you,*
    *After what I put us through.*
    *I need to set you free.*
    *Please don't think about me.*

The producer grins as he presses a button and stops the music. I look over at the freshly signed artist, and her eyes water. At first, I don't understand why, until I feel a tear slide down my own cheek. Swatting it away like it never existed, I hand her the headphones.

"Try it again."

She agrees, and I leave the recording booth. The producer

## Chapter 2

waits for her go ahead, playing the music once he gets it, and then turns to me.

"Are you sure you don't want to sing this yourself?" he asks. "No one seems to be doing it as well as you do."

I listen to the way she screams the lyrics, like speaking the words are actually painful for her, and the hint of a smile forms on my face. She's a quick learner. And when she extends that last note, goosebumps rise across my skin.

"I'm sure," I answer with finality. "She's got it."

**WALKING THROUGH THE FRONT** door, I drop my keys into the bowl we have by the door and kick off my shoes. The cold tile chills my feet as I go through the foyer and into the kitchen. Honestly, this place is a little too big for my liking. I've always preferred having my own little oasis. But I didn't pick this place.

Nolan had it long before I moved in.

It's a mansion by all accounts. The ceilings are so high not even a ladder could help me reach them. And the doors are twice the size of me. The whole thing just *screams* expensive, and I always feel like I'm going to break something valuable. It's been my place of residence for over a year and a half, but it's never had that feeling of home.

I look through the house, finding each room empty until the last one. Nolan lies face down on the massage table, letting the masseuse work their magic on her back—as if she

## Chapter 2

does something worth working out. Leaning against the doorway, I clear my throat, and my roommate lifts her head to look at me.

"You're home!" she says excitedly. "How was it? Did she totally crush it?"

My head tilts from side to side. "Eventually."

Meeting my heiress of a roommate was a blessing I didn't see coming—one that confirmed I was making the right decision and karma was rewarding me. I was staying at a hotel and trying to figure out who was behind the texts that led to me leaving Hayes. I was trying to find someone who could help me, someone powerful or well connected, so I went to a club. One of the exclusive ones where the guests are some of the most influential people in the area.

Problem is, I was only nineteen.

Enter Nolan and her magical methods of persuasion.

She not only helped me get into the club that night, but we managed to hit it off—despite the mental breakdown I had that resulted in a mix of snot and tears ruining her shirt. She wanted me to meet her the next day, *because every girl needs a fake ID*, and when she found out I was living out of a hotel, she insisted I come live with her. I tried to refuse, but when she whined about being alone in such a big house all the time, I caved.

Was it reckless moving in with someone I've known for only a matter of a couple days? Definitely. But when your only plan is to leave to save the life of the guy you're in love with, you tend to make some shitty choices.

Luckily, this one worked out.

Everything I have, including my job, is because of her. She was there for me while I cried about things she still doesn't know about, and she distracted me from the times where I wanted to just take my chances and go back home. She even

*Chapter 2*

had her dad pull some strings to get my foot in the music industry door.

No one will *ever* compare to Mali, but Nolan's a pretty decent alternative.

She sits up, with her tits full on display and zero shame, and I look away as I chuckle. That's the thing about her. Modesty just isn't in her vocabulary.

"You're free to go," she tells the masseuse. "Unless Laiken would like a massage."

I stare up at the ceiling as Nolan puts her shirt back on. "Nope. I'm good."

She snickers. "You're such a prude. What would you ever do at a nude beach?"

"That's the thing. I'd never go to a nude beach."

I look back down to see that she's clothed now, and her lips are pursed. "You really should. I could call Daddy and have a jet ready in an hour. We can be in Ibiza by tomorrow."

Pinching the bridge of my nose, I groan. "Babes, how many times do I have to tell you that every time you call him *Daddy*, it sounds like you're talking about a *sugar* daddy?"

She cringes the same way she always does. "Right. Gross. My *dad*."

"I appreciate the offer," I say through a small laugh. "But I have work tomorrow. We still have four more songs to record before the EP is ready."

Her shoulders slump. "That's no fun. It would be so much better if you would just travel the world with me."

It's the same disagreement we've had many times over, and one I'm not going to budge on. "I want to work."

She narrows her eyes at me. "No one *wants* to work."

"That's not true."

Sure, maybe people don't want to work at a job they hate, but I've seen plenty of people love what they're doing while

## Chapter 2

they're working. And I genuinely love my job. It's all I've ever wanted to do.

I just wish I had Hayes to share it with.

The day I sold my first song, all I wanted to do was call Hayes and tell him about it. When everyone else laughed at my dream and told me I was being unrealistic, he believed in me. He listened while I sang the same three lyrics over and over as I tried to figure out what wasn't right about it. He celebrated with me every time I finished one. But he wasn't there.

And that's all my fault.

I laid in bed that night and imagined all the things we would have done. He probably would have taken me out to dinner and whispered in my ear how he knew I was going to make it happen one day. There would have been flowers and champagne, with the stipulation that no one knows what a romantic sap he can be. And of course, the night would've ended with him making me scream as I came more times than should be possible, because that's the only music he ever wanted to hear.

When that song was released, I wondered if he heard it. Or if he knew it was about him. Because he's the subject of all my songs—with the exception of one I wrote just to release my anger at anonymous life-ruiners, but that one will never see the light of day. It would only come back to bite me in the ass anyway.

I haven't heard anything since the day I left, when I texted them and told them I did it. That I walked out on the love of my life in the middle of the night, shattering his heart and mine in the process. There hasn't been a single message. A single note. It's been radio silence, but the fear they're still waiting for me to fuck up hangs over my head like a guillotine, keeping me away from my hometown.

But if I could, I'd go back in a heartbeat.

## Chapter 2

"Laiken?" Nolan softly asks, and I realize she's halfway down the hall. "Are you coming?"

"Where?"

"To eat. I'm going to have Pierre cook something up."

Mm-hm. "You're going to sit there and watch his muscles, aren't you?"

She smirks. "What can I say? I'm a horny girl."

"You mean you're a *hungry* girl."

"I said what I said."

Jesus Christ. Nolan's crush on the French chef her father let her hire is the worst kept secret in history. I mean, the girl practically drools every time she looks at him. She's anything but discreet, and while usually I'd find it comical, I'm just not in the mood today.

I fake a yawn and stretch my arms over my head. "I'm actually pretty beat. I'm going to get some sleep."

She tsks at me. "See? Work is sucking the life out of you. You should quit."

"Goodnight, Nolan," I say warningly.

"Night," she singsongs, skipping down the hallway to the kitchen.

It's not like I lied. Not really, anyway. I *am* exhausted. We were in the studio for twelve hours, listening to the same song over and over until we felt it was right. That gets tiring faster than you think. It's not an easy job, but hearing my words come to life makes it worth it.

I retreat to my room and climb into the bed that is entirely too big for one person. No matter how comfortable the mattress is, or the way the fluffy comforter basically swallows me whole, it's never enough. I crave the feeling of Hayes's bed. *Our* bed. I want to lie beside him as he wraps his arms around me and mumbles nonsense in his sleep.

Taking out my phone, I go for the self-destructive route and open Instagram. The date on the calendar stared back at

## Chapter 2

me all damn day, reminding me of what today is. I used to get just as excited as Cam would for this. Bonfire season was everything to us—the start of summer, the end of isolation, and the best Friday night of the year.

Owen is the only one to not suspect anything when I followed him from my pseudo-account. One that has barely any pictures other than a few of Nolan's cats and one of the pool. He probably didn't even notice, and if he did, just assumed it was a girl who thinks he's hot or something.

*Gag me.*

The most recent post is from an hour ago, with the caption KICKING OFF BONFIRE SEASON RIGHT! It's four pictures within a slideshow. The first one is him and a beer—his one true love. The second is of the fire in front of him, but my stomach hurts when I see Cam in the background.

Hayes wasn't the only person I left that night, and I miss my brother more than most would in my situation. He was always my rock growing up, and I really could have used that support when I left, but I knew that if I reached out, he would tell Hayes where I am. I just couldn't risk it. So, I lost him, too.

I swipe to the next picture and chuckle as I see Owen and Lucas looking like drunken idiots, with Owen smiling at the camera and Lucas smiling somewhere else. There's never really been a good picture of the two of them. One is always managing to screw it up.

It's the last picture that does me in. It's of just Hayes, flipping off the camera with one hand and a beer in his other. He looks so damn good, the same way he always has, just a little older. I've tried to avoid seeing pictures of him as much as I can. It's tempting enough to go back even without being reminded of what I lost. But there's something about the sadness in his eyes that no one else seems to notice. Like he's desperate to escape his own life, even if only for a moment.

## Chapter 2

And I get it because I feel it, too.

Tears fill my eyes as the pain in my chest intensifies with each second. There aren't enough words for how much I miss him. How badly I wish that I could go back to that horrific night and do things differently. But there's also the part of me that's relieved to see he's still free. He's not rotting away in a prison somewhere.

He's got his bar and his friends, and he's sitting by a fire and drinking a beer—his favorite way to spend a night. I just wish I could be there, sitting on his lap and making Cam and Mali complain about how disgustingly in love we are. Because we were. We were *so* insanely in love. I still am. That feeling is never going to go away for me.

And as I cry myself to sleep like I've done so many nights over the last nineteen heartbreaking months, I let the pain of missing him eat me alive.

If only it would consume me.

# Hayes
# CHAPTER THREE

THE FEELING OF BEING HUNGOVER HAS BECOME far too familiar. There's a lingering taste of alcohol on my tongue that makes me feel nauseous, but the headache keeps me from getting up to do anything about it. I blindly reach over to grab my phone and see I'm an hour late for opening the bar. I'd say Cam is going to kill me, but he's probably just as fucked as I am.

Swiping my phone open, my eyes go wide as I see Laiken's name. But the hope that she tried calling me dies a painful death as I realize it was *me* who tried calling *her*.

Twenty-seven times.

Thankfully, it doesn't belong to anyone else. But technically, it doesn't belong to her either. Her parents transferred the number to my account when we got married, and I would rather pay for it than cancel it. At least that way I can still hear her voice when she doesn't answer.

I know, it's pathetic. Most of the time, my anger overpowers any feelings of missing her and being upset she's gone. But when I'm drunk, all bets are off. Either I don't care at all, or I call her—twenty-seven times, apparently.

"You alive up here?" a familiar voice asks.

Groaning, my head slumps to the side as Mali comes upstairs. "Fuck. Cam's here, isn't he?"

She smirks. "He is, and you're in trouble. The bar was

## Chapter 3

supposed to be open over an hour ago. There are some thirsty people on the beach."

"It's ten in the morning," I grumble. "Their alcoholic asses can wait."

"Funny you mention alcoholic asses..." She steps closer, and I instantly regret my words. "Are you doing okay?"

Surprisingly enough, Mali has become one of my closest friends since Laiken left. Don't get any ideas. She's like my sister. But we leaned on each other while Cam self-destructed. I don't think any of us took her absence well, but Cam was hanging by a thread. And when Mali tried to rein him in, it didn't go well.

"What are you getting at?" I ask tiredly.

She puts the glass of water and two Advil down beside me. "I'm just worried about you. That's all. You've been drinking a little excessively and being as alcoholism runs in your family..." Her voice trails off and she sighs. "I'm just making sure you know what you're doing."

This is not a conversation I'm willing to have. Not now and not ever. I never understood why my father gave up his family to be drunk all the time. If I had a choice between the two, I'd pick Laiken without an ounce of hesitation. But I didn't get the opportunity to do that like he did.

Grabbing the pills, I toss them into my mouth, swallow them quickly, and then push myself out of bed so I can get in the shower. But first, my gaze locks with Mali's.

"The difference between him and me is that he left his family. Mine left me."

She frowns, sympathy all over her face, but I turn away before acknowledging it. I've tried to hide my pain from everyone around me, other than my mom. Though Cam knows my mom is sick, no one really knows *how* sick. And Mali doesn't know anything at all. She worries about me

## Chapter 3

enough. I didn't want to give her another reason to watch me like it's her job to take care of me.

It's not.

"Hayes," she says sadly.

"Tell Cam I'll be down in a minute," I call back as I go into the bathroom.

It's not the answer she wanted, but she's not about to argue with me right now. "Yep."

It's not the first time we've had a conversation similar to this—where she tells me that my actions and ways of coping are unhealthy. But what's *unhealthy* is being put through more shit in two years than some people deal with in a damn lifetime. And if drowning all my feelings in a bottle of vodka and a few beers manages to dull the pain of that a little, then thank fuck for whoever created alcohol.

I turn on the shower and direct the hot water to pour on my face as I let my mind wander back to when Laiken left. It's not somewhere I go often, but maybe I should, because every time I do, I get a little angrier.

For six months, I tried looking for her. Cam and Mali helped at first, tracking down any lead I could find on where she may have gone. We even went back to the hacker and paid him to try tracking her phone, but there was no luck. Every attempt we made came back empty. And then the day came where Cam's parents got a letter.

It was a few pages long, explaining that she had to leave to make something of herself and couldn't do that here. Granted, she couldn't tell them what had happened. That's a secret we will all take to our graves. But she apologized for leaving so abruptly and not saying goodbye.

That's the first time in my life that I've ever been jealous of her parents. They got a well written and fully thought-out letter, while I got three measly words scribbled onto the back

## Chapter 3

of our wedding photo. It wasn't fair. It still isn't. I gave her everything, and all I got back was pain and a shitload of tainted memories.

After that letter, Cam stopped looking, and Mali followed suit shortly after. Their main concern was that someone took her and made it look like she left on her own accord. But knowing that she was safe—that was enough for them to let her live her life and move on from the nightmare that torments every one of us.

But I kept looking, at least until that phone call came.

*It was six months after she left, and the number wasn't one in my phone, but the feeling I got when I watched it ring it told me to answer it. And I did.*

*It was quiet at first, with just the sound of breathing, but I knew it was her. It filled my chest with hope for the first time in months.*

*"Laiken," I said, my voice dripping with vulnerability.*

*But I was met by silence. I tried to make out the background noise, to maybe get some indication of where she might be, but I couldn't.*

*After a few minutes of quiet, I tried again. "Baby, talk to me."*

*I shouldn't have done that, though, because the words that followed will always be as painful as they were in that moment.*

*"You have to stop looking for me," she said, and then the call went dead.*

Six months of searching tirelessly for her, and she never wanted to be found in the first place. And if I thought the three words scribbled in her handwriting hurt, they paled into comparison to the way those spoken seven made me feel. I thought I was going to die. Genuinely considered it, because a life without her wasn't one that I had any interest in living. But somehow, I managed to push through.

## Chapter 3

And three weeks later, I stood in a hospital room while my mother was diagnosed with cancer.

You know what they say: *when it rains it pours.*

And I'm living in a perpetual monsoon.

**THE BEST PART ABOUT** the weekend is that when the bar is busy, it's easy to distract yourself. People come in after spending the day in the sun and want to get a drink to cool off. It's not even that hot out, but the sun can be brutal, and the ocean is still too cold to swim in.

Over the first few weeks of the summer last year, we underestimated the amount of bottled water we'd be selling. Needless to say, we corrected that for this year. At least half of our summer sales are non-alcoholic.

My mind wanders as I try to brainstorm ways to make some extra cash to cover the rise in my mom's expenses. Turns out, I should've looked at that paperwork. Not that I would have had a different response to what kind of care she should receive, but I would've been a little more informed of what I was agreeing to. A couple grand more per month might not be a lot to some, but to this broke bar owner who is already paying almost ten grand for her room alone, it matters.

The added bill won't be easy, but I'll figure out a way to make it work.

## Chapter 3

"That's a sick bike outside," the surfer that just walked in says. "That yours?"

I nod, smiling to look friendly. "Sure is."

"Sweet. I wanted a motorcycle, but there's nowhere to put my board." He extends his hand toward me. "I'm Finn."

"Hayes," I reply. "Yeah, surfboards and motorcycles don't make a good team."

"I know. Fucking sucks. But if a shark ever bites off one of my arms and I can't surf anymore, I'm getting a bike."

Mali looks up with a blank expression on her face. "If you're missing an arm, how the fuck are you going to ride a motorcycle?"

He checks her out, his eyes glossing over as he realizes he has the attention of a beautiful girl. "I'm Finn. And you are?"

"Someone who doesn't have patience for stupid."

She goes back to flipping through her magazine like she can't be bothered, and I'm not the slightest bit surprised by it. If I didn't know she was hopelessly hung up on my best friend, even after he fucked it up, I'd think she's asexual. But I've heard enough to know that's not the case.

"Mali," I say quietly as I step up next to her. "What did I tell you about insulting the customers?"

She hums. "Babes, you don't pay me enough to bite my tongue. Actually, you don't pay me at all."

She's right, we don't. She comes over to hang out and pretends like she's helping, when really, she's just bored on her days off. And after everything she went through, she doesn't trust anyone else. Not that I blame her. We all have our issues that stemmed from that summer.

Riley and Cam walk back in, laughing about something, and I don't miss the disgusted sound Mali makes. She and Riley have never gotten along, and she doesn't make a good attempt at hiding her disdain. At first I thought it was

## Chapter 3

because Riley may have had a thing for Cam. But that wasn't the case. Instead, it's because Riley has a thing for *me*. And Laiken might be gone, but Mali's love for her runs deep. She'll always look out for her best friend, even as I try to tell her that Laiken has no claim on me anymore—which we both know is a fucking lie.

I watch as her lips purse when she gets an idea, and I'm afraid of where this is going.

"Riley!" Mali calls like they're the best of friends. "This is Finn. Finn, this is Riley. You two would be great together."

Riley looks skeptical while Finn smiles at her. "What makes you think that?"

"You're both embarrassingly senseless."

Cam chokes on his water while I chuckle. "Way to sugarcoat it."

She raises her brows at me. "Do I look like Willy Wonka to you?"

God, she's going to kill someone with her sass one day. I just hope I'm there to see it. Then again, the person might very well be me.

Riley crosses her arms over her chest and glares at Cam and me. "Are you kidding me? You're not going to yell at her for speaking to me that way?"

Cam and I look at each other, then at Mali, who knows she could get away with just about anything in this place, and we both shake our heads, looking anywhere but back at Riley as we find busy work to do.

"Bitch," Riley grumbles.

If we were anywhere else, I'd be worried about Mali going after her, but she knows better than that here.

"That's *Miss Bitch* to you. Seniority, asshole."

Yeah, at some point they're going to end up going at it.

## Chapter 3

**AS I GO OUTSIDE** for a smoke break, I look at the bike Finn was admiring earlier. He's right—it is beautiful. It was an impulse buy after Laiken left—my own version of extreme retail therapy, if you want to call it that. I emptied my account and dropped it all on this babe of a motorcycle.

The deep red paint sparkles in the sunlight, and the exhaust purrs as I start her up. Mali accused me of chasing the adrenaline I felt when I was still with Laiken, and in a way, she wasn't wrong. This bike gave me the rush I was missing, and sometimes it still does, but not nearly enough anymore.

When it comes down to it, I could use the money more than I use the bike. It was fun for a while. And I enjoyed the whole *biker dude* persona that matched effortlessly with owning a bar. But sacrifices need to be made.

And if I get enough for it, I can catch up some of the bills for the bar before Cam even knows there's a problem.

## Chapter 3

**THERE'S SOMETHING TO BE** said about figuring out a potential solution to your problems. It has a way of boosting your mood and making you feel like everything might not be going to shit after all. It's not enough to rid me of all my problems, or even enough to make me not crave a drink, but it's something, and I will take everything I can get at this point.

The bar starts to pick up as the sun starts to set. Beachgoers filter in the door, ready to start their Saturday night. There's a DJ setting up his stuff on the small stage we built in the corner, and Cam lights the fire outside for people to sit around. But while I love all my customers, there's always one that's difficult.

"H," Mali says. "What the fuck is the Wi-Fi password?"

*What?* "How the hell would I know?"

She shrugs. "Bookish Barbie over there wants to do a last minute assignment on her computer and needs the Wi-Fi password, and you apparently advertise free Wi-Fi on your website."

"We have a website?" I chuckle. "For the love of fuck, who does work in a bar anyway?"

Mali laughs and walks away, leaving me to deal with it. I turn around just in time to see Cam walking toward me.

"Hey, do you know the Wi-Fi password?"

His brows furrow. "No, why?"

I nod to the girl with her face in the computer over in the back corner. "She needs it, and our website promises free Wi-Fi. Did you know we have a website?"

He rolls his eyes. "This place would crumble without me. It's upstairs. I'll go get it."

"Thanks."

Riley, Mali, and I manage the bar in the meantime, dealing with the "sunset rush," as we call it. Though, with

## Chapter 3

three of us, it's not too hard. Mali manages to not *accidentally* trip Riley, and Riley keeps all her nagging comments about Mali being behind the bar to herself. But when the girl from the back corner comes up, once again asking for the Wi-Fi password, I realize Cam's been gone for over a half hour.

"Mal, have you seen Cam?" She shakes her head. "Riley?"

But she hasn't seen him either.

I pass the beer to the guy waiting and head upstairs, wondering if he got stuck looking for the password or something, but the result is so much worse. He's standing in front of my desk, with the bottom drawer open and all the past due bills spread out across the top.

*Motherfucker.* "Cam, I can explain. Hear me out."

He looks mortified. "Dude!"

This is not how I saw this shit going. Well, that's not true. I didn't picture how it would go at all, because I finally came up with a solution.

"I know! I'm going to fix it," I tell him. "I'm selling my bike and—"

"Your bike?" he says in disbelief. "H, there's over fifty grand in fucking bills here!"

Jesus. I never added it all up. I was too afraid the number would only increase my anxiety and look at that—I was right.

"How the hell did shit get so behind?" he snaps. "We were doing well! We should be in the black! Do you know how many bars don't go into the black until five years in? How the fuck are we in the red?"

My head falls forward. "I haven't been paying the bills."

"No shit, you haven't!" He throws the few papers in his hands onto the floor. "What the fuck is wrong with you? I know this was your idea, but this isn't just *your* fucking bar! This is my goddamn livelihood!"

"What's going on?" Mali asks.

## Chapter 3

Cam huffs and rolls his eyes. "Of course, you're coming to save him. Unbelievable."

If anyone isn't afraid to talk back to Cam, it's her. "What the fuck is that supposed to mean?"

"It means he's ruining his life, and you're fucking letting him do it!" Cam roars then focuses his attention on me. "I know you're heartbroken over my sister, but it's been almost two years! Move the fuck on!"

Okay, fuck this. "This isn't about Laiken, asshole!"

"Oh, bullshit it's not! Why else wouldn't you be paying the bills? Is it drugs? Do I need to take you to rehab? Christ, it's bad enough you're drinking half the goddamn beer in this place. Now I have to worry about you tanking the entire fucking bar, too?"

"Cam!" Mali shouts, but it's too late to get him under control.

"Screw you," I sneer. "I'm not going to sit here and listen to you berate me like you're so much better than I am."

I turn around and head for the stairs, needing to get the fuck out of here, while Cam shouts behind me. "Like husband, like wife, right? Running when shit gets tough!"

Mali yells at him again, but I can't hear what she says as I book it down the stairs and out the door. Getting around the corner, I see my bike sitting right next to my truck and well, fuck it. If I'm going to sell this thing, I may as well get one last ride out of it.

Throwing my helmet on, I buckle it and listen to the bike roar to life. I back it up and turn to leave the parking lot just as Mali comes running outside. I'm sure she's screaming for me to stop, but there's nothing she could say that will keep me here right now.

The exhaust rumbles as I turn onto the street and open her up. There's a chill to the wind as it blows against my sweatshirt, but it feels good. It feels like something.

## Chapter 3

Something that isn't numbness but isn't pain either. And I'm living for it.

I don't know where I went wrong. There was a time I had it all. Everything I wanted was right in front of me, and I thought my everything wanted me too. Maybe I misread the look in her eyes or the honesty in her voice as she told me she loved me. Hell, I could've imagined the whole damn thing for all I know. But the moment she left, my entire life fell apart. It's like she was the glue holding it all together, and now karma is making me pay for all my wrongdoings, ten-fold.

Two years ago, I had it all, and now, the only thing I can do is stand by and watch as it's all getting ripped away from me.

The engine gets louder as I speed down the road, watching the beach pass me by, and I'm lost in a time where I felt like I could take on the world. For her, I would have. I wish I could go back and freeze time. I'd rewind to our wedding night and live it over and over again, because that's when we were the happiest.

When cancer wasn't slowly killing my mom.

When Laiken was in my arms.

When I was high on life and watching my dreams come true.

And now there's just...whatever the fuck this is.

I speed up a little faster, and a couple on the sidewalk catches my attention. His arms are wrapped around her, and she throws her head back, laughing like being in love is the greatest thing in the world. Little do they know that feeling is a falsehood. Just a bunch of chemicals in your brain meant to trick you into thinking it's going to last forever.

It's going to ruin them the same way it ruined me.

I turn to focus on the road again, but it's too late. The red light is too close, and even as I slam on the brakes and the

## Chapter 3

bike skids when I lose control, it doesn't help. The bike slides out from under me and I skid across the ground before the bike and I both crash directly into the SUV in the middle of their left turn.

And the pain doesn't even register before everything goes black.

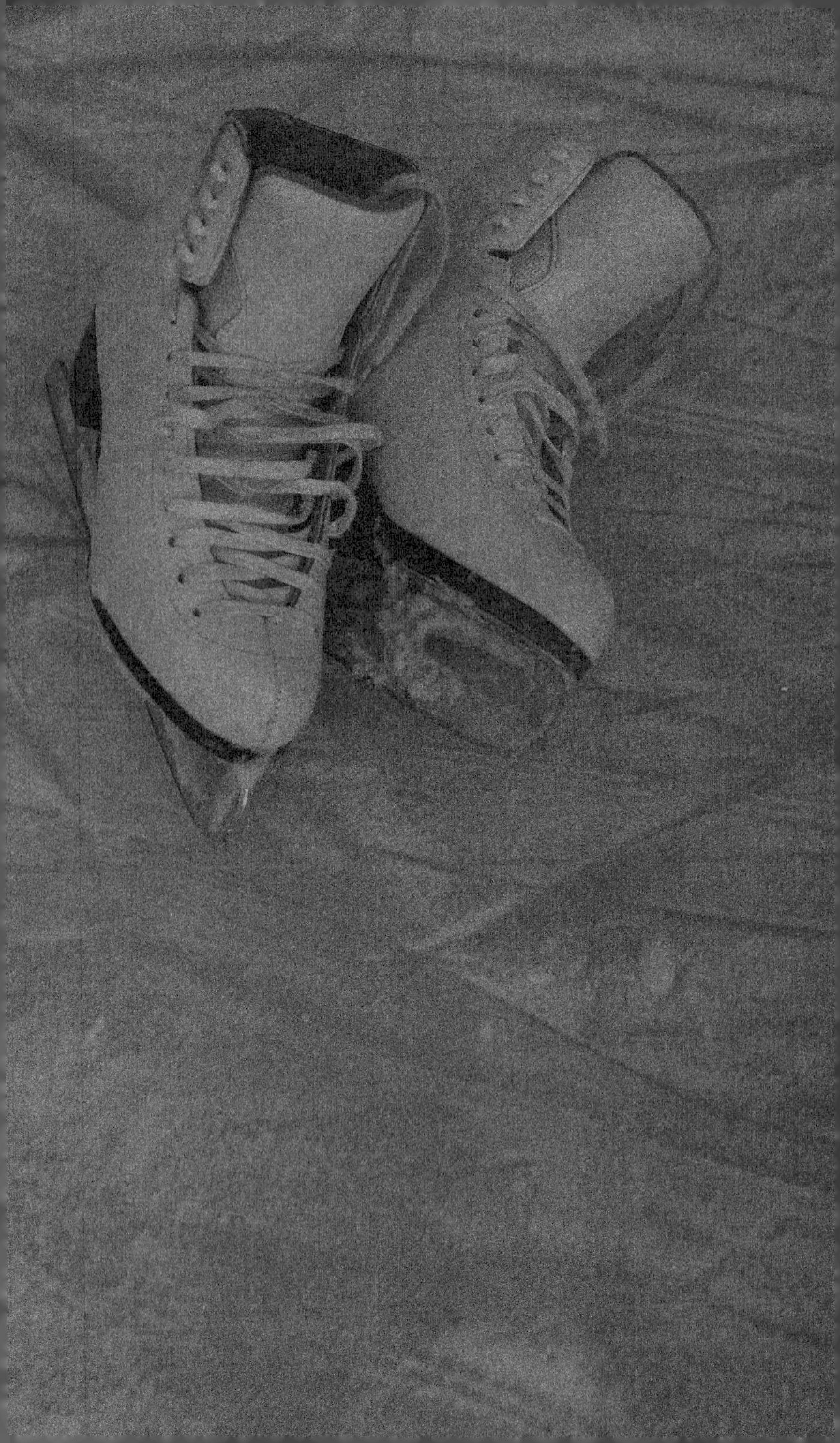

# Laiken
## CHAPTER FOUR

PANIC. CHAOS. EVERYTHING IS A BLUR AS I PRESS the gas pedal into the floor. The phone call I got an hour ago was my worst nightmare come to life. All of the words run through my mind on a loop.

*Motorcycle accident.*

*Possible broken ribs.*

*Possible swelling in his brain.*

*Too soon to tell.*

The pain of missing him is intense and constant, but the pain of not knowing if he's going to be okay is unmatched. It brought me to my knees, and as I hung up the phone, there was nothing I could do but be completely rocked by the panic attack that had one goal—to destroy me. Before I was fully able to breathe again, I was in my car.

Some of my clothes are shoved into a suitcase. I don't even know if any of it matches, and I didn't have time to zip it shut before I ran out of the house. Hell, I haven't even told Nolan where I'm going. I figure I'll text her when I get there, but right now, my only focus is getting to the hospital.

I shouldn't go.

I know that.

I was given strict instructions to stay away or I risk Hayes's future, which is why I haven't tried to return since I left. But right now, I don't know if he has a future at all now,

## Chapter 4

and I can't keep myself from rushing to his side—though I'm not sure he'll even want me there.

But I need to be there.

I need him to be okay.

*For the love of God, please be okay.*

**THE ANXIETY THAT GETS** triggered by the *Welcome to Calder Bay* sign pales in comparison to the nausea that creeps up on me as I turn into the hospital parking lot. Before I can stop myself, I throw my car in park and get out, rushing for the door of the emergency room. It's been a few hours, but I haven't received any updates yet, and I'm not sure if that's a good thing or not.

The moment I walk through the doors, all of the air is sucked from my lungs, and I stop in my tracks. Mali and Cam are standing in the corner of the waiting room, looking stressed, and Mali is definitely pissed.

"I fucking told you; you can't push him when he's like this. He's reckless and unstable. You know him better than I do. You should know there's more shit going on than either of us know about!"

"I know," he says, pulling at his hair. "Fuck, just let him be okay, and we'll deal with whatever comes after it."

She softens at the sound of his words. "He will be. This is Hayes we're talking about. He's going to come out of this like the Incredible Hulk, with an ego to match."

## Chapter 4

A doctor's voice catches all of our attention as he asks for the family of Hayes Wilder. I wince at the pain that shoots through me. The idea of him being in this place is too much to handle, and if he's not okay—

"Are either of you family?" the doctor asks Cam and Mali as they walk up to him. They shake their heads. "I'm sorry. Unfortunately, I need to speak to a family member."

Cam sighs. "His sister is away at college and his mom is in a nursing home. She can't—she's unavailable."

Mali's brows furrow at the same time mine do, showing that little bit of information is new to her, too. *Why is his mom in a nursing home?*

"Is there a way you can get his sister on the phone?" the doctor presses. "It's imperative that I speak with someone legally related to him."

*Fuck.* "I'm his wife," I pipe up.

Both Cam and Mali's heads whip toward me, and Mali's eyes water while Cam looks like he's seeing a ghost. I guess, in a way, he is. But right now, I can't deal with all of that. It can wait.

I need to know if Hayes is okay.

"Laiken Wilder," I say to the doctor, using my actual last name for the first time in a year and a half. "How is he?"

"Your husband is very lucky, considering the accident he was in," he tells me, and all three of us exhale. "Now, that doesn't mean he's injury free. He's suffering from a couple bruised ribs, and a very large abrasion on his torso, but his helmet is what saved his life. Being as he was unconscious for a worrisome amount of time, we want to keep him overnight for observation, but we'll run another CT scan in the morning to make sure there's no brain damage or severe concussion."

Holy shit. I didn't know it was possible to feel this relieved. Tears fill my eyes as I realize he's going to be all

## Chapter 4

right, and Mali seems to feel the same because I can hear her sniffling behind me.

"That's great news," I tell the doctor. "Thank you."

He nods once. "Would you like me to take you to him?"

I hesitate. Honestly, the best thing to do right now would be to leave. To get the fuck out of town before anyone ever knows I was here. But after the scare I just had, I'm not sure I'll be able to sleep until I see him. Until I can see with my own eyes that he's okay.

"Yes, please," I reply.

He starts to lead the way and I glance back, giving Mali and Cam a small smile before I follow the doctor. But just as we get to the restricted access doors, Cam calls my name.

I spin around just in time for him to crash into me, wrapping his arms around me tightly. The emotions of being able to hug my brother again, especially at a time when I *needed* a hug, are overwhelming. I let myself have this, hugging him just as tightly as he's hugging me.

"Fucking hell, I missed you," he murmurs quietly. "I am *so* mad at you, but I'll be even more mad if you leave again without talking to me. So, when you're done here, come find me."

Okay, that's to be expected. "I will."

It's a promise I intend to keep, because I missed him, too. So, fucking much that I almost don't want to let go. But Hayes is in here somewhere, and now that I've already come to terms with seeing him again, I need it more than I need the air I breathe.

Cam releases me and I follow the doctor through the doors, feeling both Cam and Mali's eyes on me through the window all the way until we turn the corner.

"His room is right down there. 12B," he tells me as he stops at the desk.

I nod. "Thank you."

## Chapter 4

My feet carry me down the hallway on autopilot, and my heart wants to run to him while my traumatized brain tells me to flee. Just being back in this town is a risk, and once I see him, I'm not sure I'll be able to leave again. It was hard enough the first time—when I stood at the doorway to our bedroom and watched him sleep soundly, wanting nothing but to get back in bed next to him where I belong.

As I reach his room, a part of me hopes that's what I'll see now. Him sound asleep, peaceful and oblivious to me being here. But as I turn into his room and his gaze locks with mine, my breath hitches.

Pictures have never done him justice, no matter how good the photographer. He looks the same as he did the day I left, only a little older. His hair is an inch or two longer, and the stubble on his face looks good on him. God, it hurts to look at him and know what I was forced to give up.

He's always been gorgeous—the kind of beautiful even the angels would damn themselves for—and at one point, he was mine.

But not anymore.

Any hope I had of him being happy to see me dies as he huffs out a dry laugh.

"If you came for a divorce, now's really not a good time," he spits.

I wince, even though I know I deserve that. "Are you okay?"

"Oh, so all of a sudden you care about my wellbeing? Where the fuck was that shit two years ago?"

He's angry, and I get it. He doesn't know about the text messages or the envelope that was left under the driver's seat of my car. He doesn't know anything except that I left.

"What are you even doing here, Laiken?" he growls.

I run my fingers through my hair as I sigh. "The hospital

## Chapter 4

called me. I'm still your wife, which makes me your next of kin."

He hums, grabbing his phone off his lap. "Hey Siri, set a reminder to remove Laiken from anything with an emergency contact." His phone confirms the reminder is set and he smiles darkly at me. "Don't worry. They won't bother you again. You can go back to your new life and forget all about me."

But that's the thing, I can't.

The feeling of knowing he hates me so much isn't a pleasant one. If I had to guess, I'd say this feels exactly like what I imagine hell feeling like. My heart hasn't been whole since the day I walked out the front door of the house we shared, but somehow, it's breaking a little more right now.

If I could forget about him, I wouldn't have this issue. I wouldn't wake up in the middle of a dead sleep in tears because I dreamed he was holding me and I never wanted it to end. I wouldn't replay all the moments we shared together in my mind when I'm feeling particularly self-loathing. I wouldn't be standing in the middle of a hospital in a town I'm not supposed to be in, desperately needing to know that he's okay.

But he's not okay.

He's broken...and I'm to blame.

Sure, I could tell him everything. About the texts and the threats I'm not allowed to mention. Really break every last rule I was given in just a few short hours and see what happens. But I can't. My being here is only making things worse, so as much as it hurts, I need to leave. He's already suffering enough; he looks like he's in pain every time he breathes.

"I'm sorry," I say, knowing it's not nearly enough. "Feel better."

He says nothing as he rolls his eyes and looks away, and

*Chapter 4*

God, I would do anything to go back to the time when he would stare at me like I was the only one who mattered in the world.

I keep my head down as I make my way back to the lobby, trying to keep the tears from coming, but the moment I see Mali still waiting for me, it's a hopeless feat. She smiles sadly as she sees my bottom lip quiver, and I walk directly into her arms.

"He hates me," I sob. "He hates me so much he can't even stand to look at me."

She sighs heavily and rubs my back. "He doesn't hate you. I don't think he's capable of hating you."

"You didn't see the way he looked at me. It was like I was the worst thing that ever happened to him."

I pull away to wipe the tears from my face with the sleeves of my sweatshirt, and Mali frowns, feeling my pain the same way she always has.

"I'm sorry. I shouldn't have called you. I just didn't know what else to do," she tells me.

I shake my head. "No. You did the right thing. I needed to know, because if he wasn't so lucky…"

My mouth can't even say the words. Losing Hayes the way I have is hard, but if I knew he wasn't out there somewhere, existing and rubbing how unfairly good-looking he is in everyone's faces—well, that's not a world I want to live in.

"I know," she says in understanding. "Do you think he knows?"

*Mali sits on my bed with me after what was probably the most intense argument Hayes and I have ever had.*

*"Let me ask you this," she murmurs. "Say Hayes* did *kill Monty intentionally…do you think he was in the wrong?"*

## Chapter 4

*It only takes a moment for me to answer.* "No one deserves to die, especially the way he did. But I don't miss him, now that I know who he was."

She purses her lips. "That's understandable. Honestly, I've felt the same way the past few weeks. It's not that I would ever wish death on anyone, but I feel like I don't even know him anymore, so how can I grieve someone I never really knew?"

"Exactly."

*I wipe away a stray tear as I think about the envelope that was left under my seat. My ultimatum of sorts. I can either walk away—leave everything I've ever known and loved behind—or I can stay and watch as Hayes's life gets ripped apart in front of a judge and jury.*

*How am I supposed to do nothing when he could end up spending the rest of his life in prison? And for an incident I practically caused, no less. If I hadn't been stupid enough to leave Hayes with Monty when I knew how much he hated him, chances are we wouldn't be in this mess in the first place.*

*He would do anything for me. I know that. But I can't let my shitty decision ruin the rest of his life. If anyone has to suffer, it should be me.*

*I take a deep breath and open the bottom of my nightstand, pulling out the envelope before looking at Mali pleadingly.*

"Mal, I need a favor…and you're not going to like it."

---

"No. I told him the hospital called me, being his wife and all."

"Oh, that's smart." The relief is evident in her voice. "I can't even imagine what he would do if he found out I've known where you've been this whole time. Or worse, if Cam found out."

*Honestly, I don't want to know.* "They won't. Trust me. I can never repay you for everything you've done, especially looking after him."

## Chapter 4

Mali shrugs. "It wasn't a hardship. I mean, he's a fucking handful. How you married him, I have no idea, but he's one of my best friends."

"He's lucky to have you," I tell her. "We both are."

She hugs me once more, and I missed her comfort. We've seen each other a couple times since I left, but it's hardly enough when you're used to spending almost every day together.

"I'm going to go see him, but Cam went back to the bar to close up. You should go talk to him."

Ugh, the pit in my stomach doesn't seem to be getting any smaller. "Okay, but if I go missing, this time it was not my own doing."

She chuckles. "I'll have the search party on standby."

"Much appreciated." I head to the door, turning around to face her as I walk backward. "Love you."

"Love you more," she calls back, and then she goes up to the front desk to get a visitor's pass to see Hayes.

There aren't many times I've been jealous of my best friend, but knowing she gets to see him, to spend time around him just talking and laughing, that definitely makes the list.

I hope my talk with Cam goes better than this.

I don't know that I could handle two of the most important men in my life hating me.

*Chapter 4*

**THE BAR SHOULD STILL** be packed, but the parking lot is practically empty as I get out of my car. I can remember how hard we all were working on this place. We couldn't wait for it to open. But unfortunately, I never even got to see it finished.

I knew they got around to opening it. Mali told me. It was a little later than scheduled, but they managed to complete the renovations. And from what I've heard, it's one of the best bars in the area.

Looking up at the sign, it's so Hayes. Made out of an oversized surfboard, with waves crashing against the name of it. It's everything I imagined it would be.

*Shore Break.*

I'll be honest, I was relieved when Mali told me they decided on a name that isn't ridiculously stupid. After hearing some of the ideas they tossed back and forth, I wouldn't be surprised if they made it sound more like a strip club than a bar. But this one I actually like.

I don't expect this to be a warm welcome, so I give myself a minute to prepare myself. When I feel even just a little ready, I force my legs to move and walk around to the front of the bar. I take in the fire pit they built on the sand in front of the bar, complete with a patio and chairs. I've seen it in pictures they've all posted, but seeing it in person gives me a chance to admire how good it looks.

Cam must have built it himself—he's always been good at that stuff.

He's closing up the bar as I walk in, in awe of how it looks all finished. But the way I immediately recognize the smell of Hayes's cologne has my eyes falling shut for a second while I catch my breath.

"Hey," Cam says, still sounding like he's in disbelief that I'm here.

*Well same, bro.* "This place looks incredible, Cam. It's

## Chapter 4

better than I could've imagined. I'm really proud of you guys."

He nods slowly, glancing around the place, but then his gaze locks on me. "Where've you been, Lai?"

Fuck. I was waiting for that. "You know…around."

"Around?" he repeats. "Not going to tell me where?"

My shoulders sag as I sigh. "I'm sorry. I can't."

It's not a lie. Meeting Nolan and getting to live with her was pure luck, and I have a life there, or as much of a life as I can have. My job at the studio and my place with Nolan are things I would trade in a heartbeat if it meant getting to come back here. But that's not an option. And telling Cam where I've been would make *that* no longer an option, too.

"You can't?" he balks. "Are you serious right now?"

"Please don't yell at me."

He scoffs. "No, fuck that. I'm going to yell at you. You just vanished, Laiken! Disappeared and couldn't bother to tell anyone where you were, or if you were even still alive! What the fuck is up with that?"

"I had to," I choke out. "I didn't want to, but I had to."

His hand pushes the hair out of his face as he rolls his eyes. "Oh, that explains it. Thanks for that."

"Cam."

"Don't!" he growls. "I was worried sick about you for weeks, until Mom and Dad finally got that letter. And Hayes? I don't think he'll ever fucking recover from what you did to him."

This is exactly what I was afraid of—him throwing the truth into my face. Mali has been good at only telling me what I need to know. She doesn't let me in on the things she knows will break me unless it's absolutely necessary. But Cam? He's not so nice. But he has no reason to be.

"You know, for someone who fought so damn hard for

## Chapter 4

that relationship, you sure knew how to fuck it up," he tells me.

My head drops as I look at the ground. "I know."

As if he can tell his words are getting to me, he takes a deep breath to calm down. "How was it when you saw him?"

I huff sarcastically. "He's really angry."

"Did you expect otherwise? I mean, you left in the middle of the night. I don't think that really warrants a warm welcome."

"No, I know."

I think about how if I had just waited a little longer, Mali would've let me know that he was all right. I wouldn't be risking his life by being in the one place I'm not allowed to be. But it's too late for that now. I just hope I can leave before our anonymous stalker realizes I was here.

"I didn't mean to make things worse," I say quietly. "But I had to know he was okay."

"How'd you even know he was in the hospital to begin with?"

I repeat the same lie I told Hayes. "They called me. We're still married which makes me his next of kin."

But while Hayes's brain might not be so clear after the accident, Cam's is sharp as a tack. "How did they have your new phone number?"

*Fuck.* "I gave it to them. Called after I left to update it, in case of an emergency."

His brows furrow. "So, you couldn't bother to tell anyone where you were going, but you thought to call the hospital in case *they* needed to reach you?"

Letting out a heavy exhale, I stare back at him. "It's not that I forgot to tell anyone where I was or was too lazy to. I purposely didn't tell anyone so none of you would come find me."

## Chapter 4

"How disgustingly selfish of you," he sneers. "Mom and Dad really raised a winner."

Well, this is fun. If I had known coming back here would be this painful, I would've done it sooner.

But the worst part is, I get it. I understand all of it. Every word that Hayes and Cam have thrown at me like knives—they're all things I've thought about myself. Just not for the same reasons.

They think I'm a selfish bitch for leaving.

But I'm a selfish bitch for not listening to Hayes about Monty in the first place. For honestly believing that Hayes was simply paranoid and possessive. If only I had listened to him from the start. I'd have the perfect life I still dream about from time to time.

"I'm sorry," I tell him. "Seriously, I'm really sorry for hurting you, and for hurting him. That wasn't my intention. But don't worry, I'm leaving tonight, and I won't come back again. My life here is gone. I know that."

He shakes his head, "That's the thing. You can't leave."

"What?"

"I need you to stay," he says, then corrects himself. "*Hayes* needs you to stay."

My eyes widen, and the hope that swells in my chest really needs to stop. "He couldn't even look at me earlier. What do you mean he *needs* me to stay?"

Cam comes around the bar and sits on one of the stools, rubbing his hands over his face. "He's spiraling, Lai. He's shutting everyone out and making reckless choices. I mean, he knew he shouldn't be going that fast on the motorcycle, but he did it anyway."

He looks so genuinely worried about him that it makes my chest hurt. "I heard you and Mali arguing at the hospital. You might lose the bar?"

He nods sullenly. "I found a stack of bills from recently,

49

## Chapter 4

all past due. Some are even threatening cancellation. The vendor contracts, the taxes…it's all in jeopardy. If I had to guess, I'd say he hasn't been paying the bills for about six months now. The taxes for longer."

"That doesn't sound like Hayes. Or at least not the Hayes I knew."

A hum vibrates in the back of his throat. "That's the thing, he's *not* the Hayes you knew. He's not the Hayes that *I* knew. And it wasn't until I called his mom on the way back from the hospital that I figured out why."

He starts to tear up, and there aren't many times I've seen my brother cry. He's an emotional brick wall. So, to see him so affected by this, I know it can't be good.

"She's dying, Lai," he tells me, and my chest cracks wide open. "She's had cancer for the last year, and I thought it was getting better. He made it sound like she was going to be okay, but she told me tonight that they put her on hospice yesterday."

My fist presses against my mouth as I start to cry. "No. She can't…"

He nods. "I know, but she is. He's trying to handle it all by himself, but he can't. It's too much. He may think he's superman or some shit but he's not. When she dies, it's going to break him. And I think you might be the only chance we have of not losing him completely to this."

I feel nauseous. Literally. Could throw up at any moment. "H-he doesn't want me here. Trust me, Cam, you didn't see the way he looked at me earlier. I'm the *last* person he wants to see."

But Cam isn't hearing any of it as he shakes his head. "He might think that now, but you're the only person he ever wants to see. He wouldn't have looked for you for so long if he didn't want to see you."

## Chapter 4

Right. The first six months I was gone. It's the reason I sent such a detailed letter to my parents. I was trying to assure everyone that I was okay, especially Hayes, and show him that he wasn't *meant* to find me. But he didn't let up. And the day finally came when Mali told me I needed to call him.

It was the hardest phone call I've ever had to make.

When I heard his voice, I almost couldn't do it. He sounded so desperate yet so relieved, and I didn't even have to say anything for him to know it was me. I let myself sit there for a few minutes, feeling connected to him in some way, and then I forced the words out of my mouth. The moment they were out, I slammed the payphone down before he could hear me break.

And fuck, did I break.

"Cam, I need you to trust me when I say that I *can't* stay," I tell him with as much conviction as I can manage. "I wish more than anything that I could. I really do. But the reason I left in the first place is the same reason I have to leave again. Staying will only make things worse for him."

He huffs, closing his eyes and raising his brows. "Unbelievable. Look, if you leave again, if you don't stay here to help him through this, then do us all a favor and stay gone."

Before I can say anything else, he gets up and storms over to the stairs. It's blatantly obvious that I'm not invited to follow him. He's angry, and he has every right to be, but the only way to fix that is to tell him why I left—which breaks rule number three.

Those rules are something I've lived by for the last nineteen months.

*Rule one: End things with Hayes and leave Calder Bay entirely.*

## Chapter 4

*Rule two: Zero contact. You're not allowed to see or speak to him at all.*

*Rule three: Do not, under ANY circumstances, tell him leaving was anything but your choice.*

*If you break any of these rules, I will see to it that Hayes is charged with the murder of Montgomery Rollins and spends the rest of his life in prison. I have enough evidence to guarantee his conviction. If you don't believe me, turn this over.*


Since the night I left, I followed the rules to a T—until tonight. Mali tried to point out that *she* could tell Hayes why I left without breaking the rules, but I don't think our stalker will take kindly to exploiting a loophole. It wasn't a risk I was willing to take. It still isn't. And that's exactly why I won't tell Cam. Because *he* would tell Hayes before it finished coming out of my mouth.

Knowing he's not coming back down, I hold back the tears and walk out the door. The message is clear; I'm not welcome here anymore.

# Hayes
# CHAPTER FIVE

LET THE RECORD SHOW, I AM NOT A PATIENT person. After being forced to spend the night here, despite my insisting that I'm *fine*, I'm anxious to be discharged. Ever since my mom got sick, hospitals freak me out. They're depressing and no one ever actually *wants* to be here.

I'm waiting for three hours to be discharged until I start to take matters into my own hands—starting with this fucking IV. They tape this shit on there as if you're going to go to war and it needs to stay in place, which means ripping it off is never a good time. To be quite honest, it feels like you're ripping off a layer of skin.

Just as I yank the thing out of my arm, using one of the napkins I had from the slop they call breakfast, the nurse walks in with my discharge papers. She gives me a look that tells me she's not amused.

"You're not supposed to do that," she scolds me.

I plaster an *I'm a good boy* smile on my face. "I was just trying to help you out."

"Mm-hm." She comes over and looks down at my arm. "Move the napkin before you get an infection and let me see the damage." As I do what she says, her lips purse. "Not bad. You'll have a bruise now, which you probably wouldn't had you just let me do it, but you're not going to bleed to death."

My eyes widen. "Was that actually a possibility?"

## Chapter 5

She shrugs and smirks at me. "You'll think twice before you do it again, won't you?"

I chuckle. "I'll do you one better and never get an IV again to begin with."

"Can't beat you there." She hands me a clipboard and starts going over the discharge papers. "You came in for injuries sustained by a motorcycle accident. You presented with two bruised ribs and a large abrasion on your left side. Your ribs will be sore for a few weeks, but make sure to follow up with your doctor. You're being prescribed Vicodin. Take it every four to six hours as needed for pain. It's important that you take it so that you don't stick to shallow breaths from the pain of your ribs. The road rash is already scabbing over, so light shirts. They'll hurt less. Any questions?"

"Just when can I get the fuck out of here," I murmur.

She rolls her eyes playfully. "As soon as you sign the papers."

I pull the pen out from behind the clip and scribble my name on the line, handing it back to her. She hands me my copy of the paperwork, along with my prescription, just as Cam walks in the room.

"Thank fuck," I breathe. "Get me out of here."

He looks me up and down before he smiles. "You going to wear that pretty gown out of here? Let your ass hang out and everything?"

"Yeah, you'd like that, wouldn't you?"

The smile drops off his face as I use his own joke against him. "Fuck you."

I snort. "In this gown, you probably could. Give me my clothes."

He chucks the pair of gray sweatpants and one of my shirts at me as the nurse giggles. She watches as I try to get up with a hesitant look on her face.

## Chapter 5

"You may need help," she tells me. "Your pain meds should be wearing off right about now."

I make a face like she doesn't know what she's talking about, only for the pain to almost knock me on my ass when I stand. I wince, groaning quietly at the pain before I mask it.

"See?" I say, failing at sounding normal. "I'm perfectly fine."

The nurse smirks, turning to Cam. "Good luck with him."

He hums. "Thanks. I'm going to need it, I'm sure."

It takes me longer than it should to get dressed. Each and every movement hurts like a bitch, and when my clothes rub against the road rash—forget it. Cam may have been kidding about me leaving in this gown, but for a moment, I actually consider it.

When I finally get out of the bathroom, he gives me a knowing look. "You good?"

I flip him off. "Can we go?"

"Say the magic word," he teases.

Nope. "Fuck it, I'll walk."

As I grab my phone and leave the room, Cam snickers as he follows behind. I try to walk normally. I can only imagine what he will say if I have to start taking my time. But as the pain becomes too much, I have no choice. My breath hitches as I grab the railing on the side of the hallway and slow my steps.

"You good, Grandpa?" Cam asks.

I roll my eyes. "Do I even want to ask how my motorcycle is?"

He winces. "No. You really don't."

Fucking great.

*So much for selling that.*

"Ugh, I loved that bike."

I know I used the wrong choice of words when his eyes

## Chapter 5

light up at the opportunity to mention Laiken. Sure enough, he jumps on it.

"Speaking of things you've loved," he singsongs. "See anyone interesting yesterday?"

"Nope."

He glances over at me but I won't meet his gaze. "No one worth mentioning?"

"Nope," I repeat.

We get to the front door and his Jeep is waiting for us right outside. "I know you saw Laiken yesterday."

I gasp in mock surprise, immediately regretting my choice as pain shoots through my chest. "No, really?"

He opens the passenger side door for me and watches as I struggle to get in. "I'd help you, but you just lied to me."

"I don't want your help," I say stubbornly. When I finally get myself into the seat, I turn to look at him. "And I didn't lie. Seeing her was not interesting or worth mentioning, as far as I'm concerned."

It's obvious that he doesn't believe me, but he also knows not to push it right now as he shuts the door and walks around to the driver's side.

To be completely honest, seeing her yesterday was a shock to my system. I never knew how I would feel if she were to come back. I mean, I suspected that I would be angry. After the way she left, I have a right to be. But I don't think I expected the way a part of me still lurched at the sight of her.

She looked so good—just as beautiful as I remember her being. I had hoped she would've gotten ugly. Aged horribly and let herself go or something. Maybe then it would have been easier to see her. But the universe doesn't like me that much.

Or at all, apparently.

Thankfully, the IV meds helped as I watched her walk away and relived that pain—only this time I saw her leave. I

## Chapter 5

wasn't sound asleep in my bed, thinking she was next to me. Though I haven't decided if that made it better or worse.

"Well, she's gone," Cam says as he puts the Jeep in first gear. "Left last night after she came to see me at the bar."

I press my lips together before letting out a huff. "Good for her."

*Yeah, I'm leaning toward worse.*

**I THOUGHT WE WERE** going straight back to the bar, but when Cam makes an unexpected turn, I realize that's not the case. I glance between him and the road in front of us, but he's trying his best not to give himself away. Instead, he's tapping his thumbs against the steering wheel to the beat of the song.

It isn't until he makes one final turn that I know where we're going.

My heart races as he turns into the nursing home parking lot. "What are we doing here?"

"Well, I figured you'd want to see your mom, since you were in a life-threatening accident yesterday and all."

He's right, I do, but I had every intention of coming alone once I got my truck—and a pain pill in me for that matter. This shit fucking hurts.

"Thanks, man," I tell him, opening the door. "I'll be out in a bit."

## Chapter 5

But he shuts off the Jeep and unbuckles his seatbelt. "Nah, I think I'll come with you."

Fuck.

He knows.

My head falls back against the seat and I sigh. "Son of a bitch."

"Don't talk about your mother that way," he jokes, but then his face turns serious. "Why didn't you tell me she was put on hospice?"

"I don't know," I admit. "I guess I just wanted to ignore it. Pretend it wasn't happening."

His brows raise. "Yeah? And how's that working out for you?"

"Don't be a jackass."

I'm not in a joking mood. Not when we're sitting in the parking lot of the place my mom is wasting away in. It's the one place where I can't block it out. When I'm here, I have to be strong for her.

"So, the unpaid bills for the bar?"

I nod slowly. "I've been paying for this place. Her insurance doesn't cover it, and she won't come live with me so I can take care of her. There was a place that would've just taken her disability check, but it was a shithole."

Cam rubs his temple as he exhales. "Why didn't you just talk to me about it? You know that I'll always do whatever I can to help you, don't you?"

"Yeah, I know." And I do. "I guess I convinced myself that I could handle it. That I was strong enough to do it all. At first, I figured it would just put us a little into the red but then the summer months would make up for it and it could come out of my half of the profits. But it got out of control. And now I don't even have my bike to sell to pay for it."

He looks out the window, letting it all sink in before he answers. "First of all, we don't do this shit. We don't lie to

## Chapter 5

each other. That's what we agreed after you admitted to fornicating with my sister behind my back for months, right?"

I can't help but laugh, wincing at the pain. "Fornicated?"

"It's the only word I can use without gagging," he growls. "Deal with it."

Fair enough. "Fornicating it is."

"I know you like to think you're this major hardass, but for the love of fuck, asking for help doesn't make you weak, H."

Fucking hell. This conversation almost makes me miss the hospital. *Almost.* "I know. I'm sorry. I should've come to you about it."

"You're damn right you should have," he agrees exasperatedly. "Look, it's not the end of the world. We just have to figure out how to fix it."

I shake my head. "It's not your problem to fix, dude."

"Yeah, fuck that. We're brothers. We take care of each other." He pauses, looking anywhere but back at me. "That's why I called all the companies we owe money to and paid them enough to keep shit running."

My head whips toward him. "You did *what?*"

He shrugs. "It's not everything. We're still in the red. But it's something for now."

God, I'm such an asshole. "Thank you. You didn't have to do that."

"And *you* didn't have to bail me out of jail a couple years ago," he points out. "This is what we do."

He puts his fist out and I bump it, feeling a little relieved. The future of the bar was weighing on me, and it still is, but it's less intense for now. And it helps knowing I'm not doing it alone anymore.

"Now we just have to figure out how to come up with the

## Chapter 5

rest of the money," he sighs. "You're right. The summer months will help, but I don't think they'll be enough."

I shake my head. "Nah, I have another idea."

It's something that I've been thinking about since last night, when Laiken stood in my doorstep looking every bit like heartbreak incarnated. For the first time, I stopped blocking everything out and started realizing everything she gave up. Everything she walked away from. And it became clear that I have to stop holding onto something that was never actually what I thought it was.

What we had is gone now.

It's time for me to let go.

"I'm going to sell the house."

**OKAY, SO THE NURSE** may have had a point—my medication is not optional right now. Trying to bartend with sore ribs and a scrape that covers half my side is challenging. And by challenging, I mean it's fucking torture. Every move I make feels like someone is slicing me open or stabbing me in the chest. But I don't want to be working while on painkillers. By the time I realized how badly I needed it, it was too late. If I took it then, I wouldn't be able to take it before I go to sleep.

Somehow, I manage to make it through. Cam and Riley head out, leaving me to close up, but that's nothing I can't

## Chapter 5

handle. They took care of the cleaning. The only thing I have to do is the register. Usually, I'd restock, but lifting heavy cases of beer doesn't sound like a good idea right now.

I'm finishing up when I hear the door open. Cam must have forgotten to lock it when he left.

"Sorry, we're closed," I call out.

But there's no response. I don't hear the door open, so I know they're still in here, but unless it's a fucking ninja about to rob me, they should still be standing by the door.

I spin around, being careful not to twist my body, but the pain comes anyway as I see Laiken standing there. I look her up and down, closing my eyes for a second as I commit the sight of her to memory, and then my walls go up.

"Maybe I didn't make myself clear yesterday," I growl. "You're not getting a divorce. So go ahead and do the little vanishing act you're so fucking good at because I'm not signing anything."

Her eyes glisten in the light, revealing that she's on the verge of tears, but I refuse to let myself care as her shoulders sag in defeat. "I don't...that's not why I'm here."

I shouldn't be so relieved to hear that. Frankly, I shouldn't be denying her a divorce at all. She's not mine anymore, meaning she's free to do whatever she wants with whoever she wants.

Yeah, never mind. Fuck that.

I'd still knock someone out for letting their eyes linger on her too long.

"I thought you left," I mutter.

She sighs heavily. "I tried, but I couldn't. Cam told me about your mom. I'm so sorry."

I scoff. "For what? For not being here when she was diagnosed, or for fucking me up so much that I was actually jealous of her death sentence?"

## Chapter 5

Her hand moves to her chest, showing my words hit their mark. "Hayes."

Yeah, I can't do this. Anything she has to say is too damn late. Besides, I'm in enough pain as it is. I really don't need her adding to it.

I walk around the bar and over to the door, pushing it open even though it physically hurts.

"Like I said, ma'am...we're closed."

She looks like I punched her in the gut as she tries and fails to hold back her tears. I wait for her to take a couple steps out the door before I close it, and we stare at each other through the glass as I lock it in her face.

This time, it's me that gets to walk away.

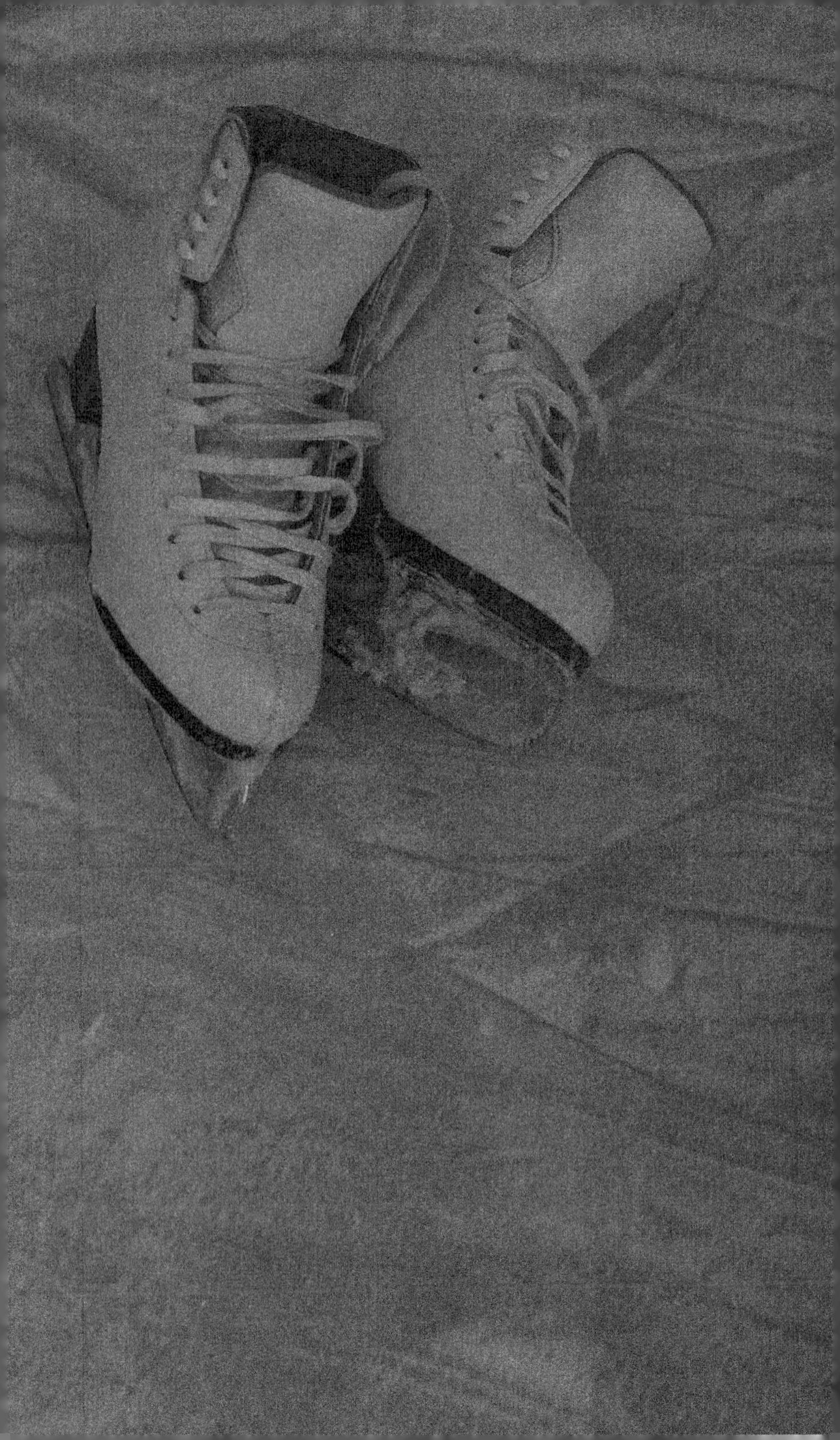

# Laiken
# CHAPTER SIX

I STAND IN FRONT OF THE DOOR, SOMEHOW intimidated by it. I never thought there would be a time when I'd feel uncomfortable in my own hometown. This place was always my safe haven. But after the last couple days, I don't know what to expect anymore.

It takes me five minutes just to talk myself into knocking, but only a few seconds for him to answer it. Cam's eyes widen and his lips purse as he sees me.

"You're still here," he acknowledges.

I nod up surely. "For now."

It's not exactly what he wanted to hear, but it's enough for him to open the door further to let me in.

Seeing Cam with his own apartment is strange. I mean, I knew he had one because Mali told me the day he moved out of my parents' house. But it's one thing to hear about it and another to be here. It's not the biggest apartment, but it's perfect for him. And I love the way he's made it his own.

"How'd you know where to find me?" he asks, going into the kitchen to pour another cup of coffee.

I glance around some more, a small smile splayed across my lips. "Mali."

He hums. "Yeah, that was a stupid question. I should've known."

## Chapter 6

My eyes land on a picture on the entertainment center. It's of Cam and Hayes, taken on the day they opened Shore Break. They're both grinning from ear to ear, and I hate that I wasn't there to see it in person.

Cam comes back out and hands me a mug of warm coffee, and I sigh in relief. "You're the best. Thank you. The motel coffee tastes like heated mud."

His brows furrow. "*Motel*? You're not staying with Mom and Dad?"

"No," I say immediately. "I don't think they would even let me in the door."

When I left the way that I did, it worried them too. I'll admit, it was selfish of me to disappear without saying anything to just about anyone. But in my defense, to say I wasn't in the right state of mind would be a massive understatement. My mind was a mess.

Still is, honestly.

Once I knew they got my letter, I gave them a week before I tried reaching out. There was no return address for obvious reasons, so it's not like they could have written me back. But within the first thirty seconds of the phone call, I knew they were livid.

I should've known they would be. Their beliefs when it comes to the sanctity of marriage have never been a secret, so of course, they lectured me about how wrong it was to leave my husband like that. They couldn't understand how I went from head-over-heels in love with him to running away, all within a six-week time span. But it's not like I could tell them why I left.

I had no choice but to let the blame rest entirely on me.

And over time, I've started to believe it does.

"Don't be ridiculous," Cam says. "You're their daughter. They're always going to want to see you."

I snort. "Yeah, you also told me Hayes needs me here."

## Chapter 6

"You saw him again?"

"Went by the bar last night after closing."

I'm not sure which was worse—the way he looked at me or the words he spoke. Quite frankly, both cut like knives. I knew he would be upset when I left. No part of me thought I was imagining the feelings between us. But I guess I thought he would bounce back eventually. That living without me would be better than spending the rest of his life in prison for murder—and that's if he wasn't given the death penalty.

Being who Monty's dad is, that's more than a possibility.

But I'm starting to realize I may have underestimated just how much he loves me.

*Loved* me.

"That doesn't sound good," he says, cringing. "Didn't go well?"

I sigh heavily. "Do you remember that time Dad was in a bad mood, and I didn't want to tell him they gave me the wrong size skates?"

"Yeah. They were like three sizes too small, and you tried using them anyway. Cracked your goddamn head open on the ice."

I nod. "It went kind of like that, only last night hurt a lot worse."

"Fuck."

"Mm-hm." Taking a seat at the small table he has in the corner, I put my mug down in front of me. "I don't care what you and Mali say. He hates me."

He leans back in his chair and stretches his arms above his head. "I don't know, Lai. That's a little extreme."

"Cam, he told me I made him jealous of his mother's terminal illness."

He looks surprised but only for a second. "Well, that's twisted. Doesn't mean he hates you, though."

## Chapter 6

I roll my eyes. "Right, because I tell everyone I care about that they make me want to die."

"Did you try apologizing?" he asks.

"Yes, but he wouldn't hear it. He basically kicked me out and called me *ma'am*."

That makes him chuckle. "I'm sorry to laugh, I've just never heard him call anyone ma'am."

"Yeah, I know." That's why it hurt so much, and I know that was his intention.

He looks like he's thinking for a moment before he finally gives in. "Okay, fine. Maybe I was wrong."

"You think?" I sass, but that admission shouldn't be as painful to hear as it is.

It's not like I didn't already know Hayes doesn't want me anywhere near him. I could see it in his eyes when I saw him in the hospital. If he could have physically thrown me out of there, he would've. But Cam knows him better than anyone, and a part of me hoped what he told me was true.

"I'm sorry," he tells me. "I didn't mean to be an ass and make things worse for you. I'm just worried about him."

"Me too," I say honestly. "But while I may have been the one who could save him at one point, I'm not anymore. He made that pretty clear."

He groans, and I can see how stressed out he is over it. "Fair enough. You can leave—go back to wherever it is you're living now—if that's what you want to do. But I think you should see Mom and Dad before you go. If they find out you were here and didn't at least make an attempt to see them, they'll be really hurt."

Ugh. I know he has a point. It's one thing if they never know I came back in the first place, but if someone has seen me and mentions it to them, they'll be heartbroken. Any chance I have at repairing my relationship with either of

## Chapter 6

them would die right then and there. And besides, it's not like I'm trying to hurt anyone.

I never have been.

"Will you go with me?" I plead.

He snickers. "Going to use me as a shield?"

"If I need one, maybe," I joke. "Come on. I used to play mediator for you. Not that you ever really needed it, but when you thought you were going to, I was there."

His head tilts to the side. "Didn't you actually get me in *more* trouble once?"

"Cam!"

I kick him under the table and he laughs. "Okay, okay! I'm going over there for dinner tonight. Six o'clock. Come then."

Dinner. Okay. I think I can handle dinner—as long as Cam is there. It's not like they'll censor themselves in front of him or anything, but he's never been afraid to take my side or call them out when they're being too irrational.

"All right," I agree. "I'll be there. But if I don't see your Jeep in the driveway, I'm leaving."

He looks away, pretending to be offended. "You have such little faith in me."

I flip him off before the two of us chuckle, going back to drinking our coffee. You can practically feel the shift in the air. It's more comfortable, more normal, than it was the other night at the bar. But I don't blame him for anything he said. He's right to be worried about Hayes. He's hanging by a single piece of thread. A strand of hair, even.

But while I wish I could help him—could be that person for him again—I can't. If anything, I'm only making matters worse.

"So, what are your plans for the day?"

I take a deep breath, knowing I need to do something even scarier than showing up at the bar. "That's the other

## Chapter 6

reason I'm here, actually. I need to know what nursing home Hayes's mom is at."

**TO MAKE UP FOR** steering me in the wrong direction with Hayes, Cam even tells me when he gets to the bar and sees H is still there. I'm grateful for it. This visit is going to be hard enough, but with him here, I don't see it going very well. Then again, the likelihood of this going well, even without him here, is practically null.

There's no way to mentally prepare for this. If I wait until I feel ready to face my mother-in-law after I shattered her son's heart, I'll never go in. My only option is to dive headfirst into the deep end and hope the water isn't secretly acid.

I force myself out of my car and head inside, going to the front desk. "Hi. I'm here to see Valerie Wilder."

"Is she expecting you?"

*Fat chance.* "Sure is. I'm her daughter-in-law."

Taking out my license, I pass it to her to show that we have the same last name. She smiles politely as she gives it back.

"Go to the right and then around the bend to the left," she explains. "Make your second left. She's in room 511."

"Thank you so much."

I repeat the directions over and over in my head. The last thing I want is to get lost in this place. I'd never find my way

## Chapter 6

out. Then again, playing bingo with a woman named Edna would probably be a better alternative than having dinner tonight at my parents' house.

The room numbers pass by until I'm standing outside her room. It's hard to imagine her in a place like this. She's only in her fifties. That feels far too young for her to be here, but knowing Hayes, he wouldn't have put her here if she didn't absolutely demand it.

Holding down the bile that rises in my throat, I take the few steps into the room. His mom is lying in the bed, watching TV, when she sees me. Tears instantly fill my eyes. She looks so fragile, lying there. The woman I've known for years was a force to be reckoned with. She worked her ass off for her kids, and being a single mother was no easy feat, but she did it. And now a cancer rips through her body like she's not the strongest woman I've had the pleasure of knowing.

"Laiken," she sighs, looking both relieved and surprised to see me.

I press my fist to my mouth and shake my head as I feel all the emotion. "I'm sorry. I'm so, so sorry."

His mother has every reason to hate me. Hell, *I* hate me. But she opens her frail arms and invites me in. I rush to her side, hugging her tightly and crying like a baby. I've spent the last two years trying so hard to stay strong, but I didn't even realize how easy I've had it. Meanwhile, she's been here, fighting for her life, while Hayes has had to watch her lose that fight.

I'm the fucking worst.

"Shh," she says calmly, running her fingers through my hair as if I'm the one dying, not her. "You're okay. You're all right."

I pull away and use my sleeve to wipe away the tears. "Cam told me the news. I had no idea."

## Chapter 6

She shrugs. "How could you? No one knew how to get a hold of you."

There's an underlying sharpness to her words, but honestly, she could be saying a lot worse right now. "I know. I'm sorry."

"So you've said. Does Hayes know you're back?" I nod and look at my feet. "I take it he hasn't been the most welcoming person."

Snorting, I shake my head. "No, but I deserve it."

She takes a breath. "His emotions are his own to deal with, yes, but no one deserves cruelty. You're young. Part of growing up is making mistakes. They're normally not *getting-married* level serious, but everyone makes them."

"No," I say seriously. "Marrying Hayes was not a mistake. I will never consider that a mistake."

"Interesting. Then why did you leave?"

There's no way I can explain this. Not in a way that doesn't risk her view of her son. I'd much rather her place the blame on me. After all, it *is* my fault.

"It's complicated," I answer. "Really complicated."

"It must be if it made you leave him after the way I saw you two look at each other," she says.

I smile sadly. "I still look at him that way. I think I always will."

"Have you tried telling him that?"

*Yeah, right.* "That would require him letting me tell him anything at all. He doesn't want me here, and I don't hold that against him. I know I hurt him."

She scrunches her nose. "I don't mean to make you feel worse. I really don't. But *hurt* is a bit of an understatement, honey."

My head drops. "Would you believe me if I told you everything I did was what's best for him?"

It's quiet for a second before she answers. "Surprisingly,

## Chapter 6

yes. I believe you love him, Laiken. That's never been something I've questioned. I think that's why I was so shocked when you left the way you did."

"I do," I confirm. "I love him. I'm always going to love him. I mean, it's been like five years of it. I don't think I remember what it's like to *not* love him."

"It's funny how that works, isn't it?"

God, I knew this would hurt, but this feels like a blowtorch straight to my heart. Or pouring salt in the wounds Hayes's words left on me last night. I hold her hand and hate the way her skin feels so much cooler to the touch than mine.

"I thought he would be okay," I admit. "But he's not okay."

She purses her lips. "How could he be? He's dealt with so much over the last couple years. He probably feels like the blows just keep coming. But even so, he's been my rock through all of this."

That brings a smile to my face. "I'm not surprised. He would do anything for you."

"He'd do anything for you, too," she tells me.

I shake my head. "Not anymore. There was a time he would have, but not after what I did. He made that very clear last night."

Her brows raise for a second as my words register. "He's stubborn. You and I both know that. But he loves you. He's just hurting. The pain he was in when you left...I've never seen him like that. So desperate and broken. You don't get over that kind of love, no matter what he says."

I wish I could believe her. I really do. It would make all of this so much easier. At least before I came back, I could let my imagination run wild—picture him catching me as I ran into his arms. I could convince myself that he would be happy to see me and relieved that I'm back. But the way he

## Chapter 6

looked at me last night was so cold. The hatred that burned in his eyes made me feel like I was personally responsible for every negative thing that ever happened to anyone.

"Do you mind if I ask why you came back?" she asks.

"I heard about his accident. That call ripped my heart right out of my chest and set it on fire. I couldn't stay away from him anymore."

"And what about now? What are your plans?"

It's a question I've been asking myself since two nights ago, when I pulled into the motel parking lot instead of turning toward the highway. There's a voice inside of me that's screaming for me to leave. That I shouldn't be here and that I'm only making things worse for everyone I care about. And after my talk with Cam this morning, I think it's probably best that I go. But there's still that part of me that wants nothing more than to stay.

"I'm not sure," I tell her honestly. "I mean, I think I should go, but…"

"But you want to stay for him," she finishes for me, and I nod. "You know, there's a chaplain that has been coming to see me a lot lately. Praying with me and just being a good friend. And the other day, when I officially started hospice, he asked me if I'm afraid to die."

The lump in my throat doubles in size, listening to her mention the inevitable outcome in all of this. "Are you?"

"No," she says with a smile. "I'm young, yes, and let's be honest, it sucks that my life won't be longer. There are so many more things I'd love to see and do. But the years I have lived, they've been so full of love and joy. I've gotten to watch my kids grow and even saw one marry the love of his life—something I had given up on, if I'm honest. He never seemed like the type until you. I've helped people feel better, and I've been there for some during their worst times. I know there's a place for me in heaven. One with a view

## Chapter 6

where I can watch everyone I love. And I don't have a single regret."

She reaches up with a shaky hand and tucks some hair behind my ear, smiling at me kindly, the same way she always has. I don't know how she's not holding my actions against me. If someone hurt my son the way I hurt hers, I'd probably give them valid reasons to take out a restraining order against me. But not her.

"Don't live with regrets, Laiken," she murmurs softly. "If my son is the one you want, then I think you should fight for him. Fight for your love, because I've seen it. I've *experienced* it. And it's so special. Somewhere beneath all of the hurt and the anger, he knows that, too. But only do it if you know without a doubt that he's what you want. You can't get him back just to walk out on him again. He won't make it through that."

The emptiness in my chest that yearns for him demands to be felt. "Trust me, it was hard enough to do the first time. If I thought for a second we still had a chance, I wouldn't even consider leaving. But I'm pretty sure he's done. There's no coming back from this."

She doesn't look convinced. "Think about it. He might surprise you."

We both take the opportunity to drop the touchy subject and move onto something less heavy. If it wasn't for the small physical changes and the scarf that covers her bald head, I wouldn't realize how sick she is. We talk about the list she and Hayes are creating of all the things she wants to do, and how he ruled out skydiving before it even finished coming out of her mouth. She tells me how much he hates Devin's new boyfriend, despite never meeting him. And she lights up with pride while she gushes about the bar. To anyone else, you'd think she has two sons, with the way she talks about Cam, too.

## Chapter 6

And I hang on every word she says, knowing how missed she's going to be when she's gone.

**WRAPPED IN LACE HAS** never been my favorite place to be. It always feels so awkward to me. I would never be able to help someone pick out something that is going to be sexually peeled off them later. But Mali? She has no shame. She'd sell a pair of crotchless panties to a ninety-three-year-old woman and personally show her the best position to get it on without hurting her hip.

"Thank you! Oh, and tell your husband I said you're welcome," she tells the customer with a wink as she hands her the bag.

The woman chuckles, promising she'll pass along the message. Once she leaves and the store is empty again, she turns to me.

"Honestly, I'm a bit surprised she didn't spit in your face," she tells me as she leans against the counter. "Or at least get you kicked out of the place."

When I told Mali that I went to see Hayes's mom, she choked on her drink. Literally sputtered the whole thing all over herself like a baby still learning how to swallow. Turns out, she didn't even know Hayes's mom was sick, let alone in a nursing home and on hospice. She knew something was up with him, but she never imagined it was something so serious. I think she's also a little mad he didn't tell her. That's between them, though.

"I wouldn't have blamed her if she had," I reply. "She has every right to hate me. But I'd be lying if I said it wasn't such a relief to know she doesn't."

"And she told you that you should fight for Hayes?"

I nod. "Yep. Though I don't think she realizes how much he hates me."

Her eyes roll. "I told you; he doesn't hate you. He can't. He might really dislike you right now but *hate*? Nah."

"The three of you are adorably naive," I tell her. "If looks could kill, he would have had *another* body to dispose of last night."

She throws a hand over her mouth, trying not to laugh, and I'm right there along with her. I can't believe I just said that, as if that night wasn't hell for all of us. But it's still true.

"Shut up," I groan playfully as she cackles. "You know what I meant."

Taking another sip of water, she closes her eyes to mentally shake it off. "Oh, that was so beautifully fucked up."

"Whatever."

Mali goes to the other side of the counter and hoists herself up on it. "Do you think maybe he wouldn't hate you if you told him *why* you left?"

"I thought you said he can't hate me."

She glares at me. "Use my words against me like that again and *I* might hate you."

A bark of laughter shoots out of me. "Okay, if there's anyone who can't hate me, it's you."

"And Hayes," she adds. "In all seriousness though, you *could* try telling him. You know, actually talk for once instead of fucking like a couple of nymphos."

Ugh. Images of all the times we spent wrapped up in each other run through my mind, reminding me of how he would

## Chapter 6

smirk as he made me scream. I can't help but press my thighs together as I clench around nothing. I've craved that feeling since the day I left.

"Oh my God, my point exactly," Mali whines. "Stop thinking about you two fucking!"

"Sorry," I mumble, but I'm not. Not really, anyway. "I get what you're saying, but I can't. You read what was on the back of that picture. I've already broken two rules. You want me to break the third?"

She shrugs. "I mean, you've been back here for three days now, and I haven't seen anything explode. Maybe they moved on with their lives."

"Or maybe that's what they want us to think."

"Could be. But if you leave now, you'll never know. And you can't tell me that there's not a big part of you that wants to do exactly what his mom said and fight to get him back. For that to even be slightly possible, he can't think you left because you didn't want to be with him. You have to tell him the truth."

A heavy sigh flows from my mouth. "As if that's going to make it any better."

"It might not," she says honestly. "But you'll never know unless you try."

**I SIT IN THE** driveway of my childhood home. The place I spoke my first words and took my first steps. And yet, now

## Chapter 6

I'm afraid to go inside. Even with Cam's Jeep right out front, showing me he's here like he promised he would be, I feel like I might throw up.

Barely speaking to my parents has been difficult to say the least. It's crazy how when you live with them, they drive you nuts. But when you're out living on your own, you wish they were with you. I think during the time I spent living with Hayes, before everything went to shit, I called my mom at least four times a day. Sometimes for the most meaningless things.

And then chaos struck.

Cam had a point, though. If they find out I was in town and I didn't come to see them, they'll be really hurt. And it's not like I don't want to see them. I'm just afraid of the judgment I know is coming.

For the second time today, I give myself a pep talk and force myself out of the car. As I walk up the driveway and see the detached garage, I remember when I stood here and watched Hayes storm past me—determined to tell Cam about us and show me that I'm the one he wanted.

*I would give anything to go back to that.*

Getting up the courage, I raise my fist and knock on the door. My heart pounds against my ribcage as footsteps come toward the door, but I relax when it opens and Cam stands on the other side.

"You actually showed up," he says, a little surprised.

"I told you I would."

"Yeah, I know. But I wasn't sure if you'd go all Houdini on me again." He opens the door further and I walk in, waiting for him to shut it behind me. "Mom, Dad! I have a surprise for you," he sings.

My eyes widen and I turn around to face him in a panic. "You didn't tell them?"

He smirks. "What's the fun in that?"

## Chapter 6

Ugh, fucking asshole. I should've known better. I very well may have walked into a damn ambush. Do I think Cam would let any harm be done to me? Of course not. But do I also know he's mad and wouldn't mind seeing me in an uncomfortable situation? Absolutely.

"Cameron, we love you, but we don't need another—"

My mom's voice cuts off as she gasps behind me. I turn around to find her hand over her mouth, tears already starting to slide down her cheeks. She looks at me in disbelief and shock all at once.

"Hi, Mom," I murmur quietly.

Her breath hitches, realizing I'm actually here and she's not seeing things, and comes toward me with open arms. I step into them willingly. Finding out Hayes's mom doesn't hate me earlier, when she has every right to—it helped. But finding out my own mom doesn't hate me either, that's a level of relief I didn't expect.

Maybe Cam was right.

My dad comes into view, with his jaw tense and an angry glint in his eyes.

*Okay, half right.*

"Laiken," he says sternly.

Dad was always the disciplinarian out of our parents, and I've spent my fair share of time being on the receiving end of it. But I don't think he's ever looked at me with this much disappointment before. It makes the little girl in me want to cower.

"You think you can just waltz back in here and expect everything to be fine?" he asks with brows raised.

"Dad!" Cam protests.

"No, it's fine," I tell my brother. "That's not at all what I expect. I know that leaving the way I did wasn't okay, and I'm sorry for that. If you want me to leave, I'll go."

His gaze stays locked with mine, as if he's actually

## Chapter 6

considering taking me up on my offer, until my mom's voice cuts through the uncomfortable silence

"Andrew," she scolds him. "Give your daughter a hug."

He glares at her for a second, but everyone in this room knows she has him wrapped around her finger. So it's no surprise when he sighs and pulls me into him.

"I missed you, kid," he tells me. "Still don't agree with what you did, but I missed you."

"I missed you, too."

We pull away and the four of us walk into the kitchen while Mom works on making dinner. It smells delicious. The tension still lingers in the air, but Cam sticks by my side like the protector he's always been for me.

"So, what's been new, Lai?" Mom asks. "Anything interesting?"

I'm basking in the nostalgic feeling of being here. "Not really. I've been working a lot."

"Another ice rink? Mr. Zimmerman was devastated to lose you," Cam adds.

*Add him to the list.* "No. Actually, I work at a studio. I'm a songwriter."

A smile spreads across my dad's face. "Is that so? Have you written anything I'd know?"

"Probably not. A lot of what I've written is just starting to come out now," I explain. "Making an album is a long process."

"That's amazing, sweetheart," Mom tells me. "I know that's always been a dream of yours."

Cam nudges me with his elbow. "Pretty impressive, sis."

It feels good, finally being able to share my accomplishments with my family. It's something I've wanted to do since I was younger, and the only people I've been able to tell about it have been Mali and Nolan. Not that it makes

## Chapter 6

it mean any less, but I'm proud of it, and I've always wanted to share that part of my life.

"All right," Mom announces. "Dinner is almost done so grab your drinks and sit at the table."

We do as she says, though it still irritates me a little that I can't grab a beer. My twenty-first birthday is coming up, but to them, I'm still only twenty. They may have ignored that we would drink when they're not around, but they still refuse to outright allow it.

Going into the dining room, my brows furrow as I realize it's set for five. My dad had added a place for me when I got here, which means it was already set for four. But that wouldn't make any sense, unless…

The familiar rumble of a truck comes to a stop right outside and then goes quiet. I feel like I might be sick. My head whips over to Cam and he acts like he doesn't notice me shooting daggers into him.

"What the hell did you do?" I whisper-shout.

He looks over at me, smirking. "Moi? I didn't do anything. I just invited you to dinner."

My mind is reeling as I'm trying to figure out my options. Should I hide? Should I leave? After what he said to me last night and the way he looked at me, seeing him again will take a level of preparation I don't have time for at the moment. There's no way he won't see my car in the driveway. Maybe he'll leave, since he made it clear that he doesn't want to see me.

But when I hear the door open, I realize I'm not that lucky —and I no longer have the option to run.

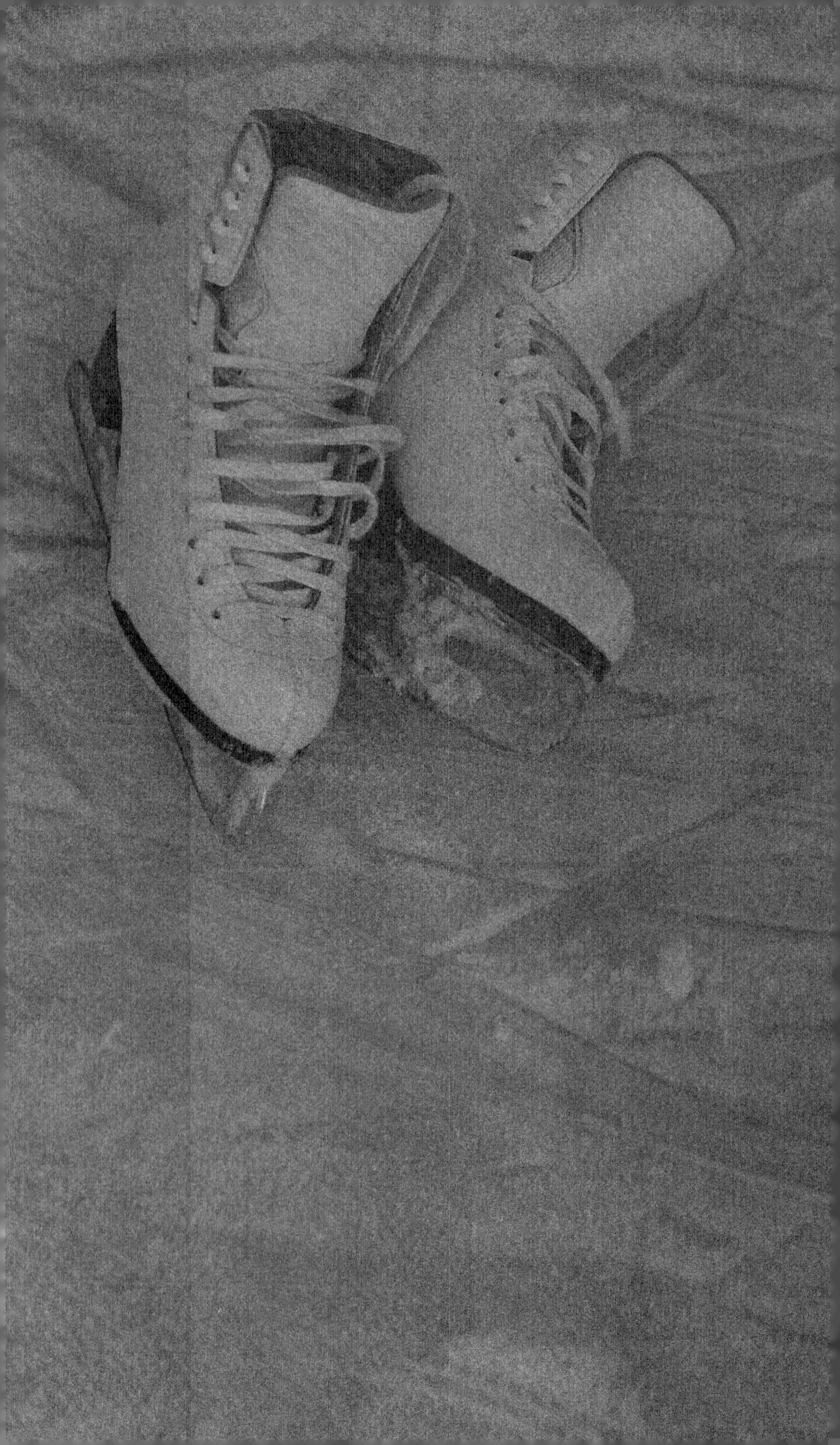

# Laiken
# CHAPTER SEVEN

IF MY HEART COULD JUMP OUT OF MY CHEST AND run out the door, believe me, it would. There isn't a single part of me that is ready to see him again. Not when I know he doesn't want to see me. But thanks to Cam, I don't have a choice.

The sound of Hayes's voice fills the house as his footsteps move through the living room. "It smells so good in here."

"Hayes," my mom greets him, sounding relieved. "Thank heavens, you're all right. I was worried sick about you, but Cam said I shouldn't come to the hospital."

He chuckles. "Please. I'm perfectly fine. It was like hitting a pillow."

"Punch him in the ribs and see how fine he really is!" Cam calls out.

I can hear him coming closer, and I brace myself for the impact of seeing him again.

"Fine, but that means I get to…"

His words die out as he steps into the doorway and his gaze meets mine. He lets his eyes rake over me for a moment. It shoots me right back to when I was a hopeless teenager crushing on her older brother's best friend. A time when I would have killed for him to be looking at me like that. But I know better than to think he's checking me out right now.

## Chapter 7

"Scoot," Mom tells him as she tries to get through.

He pulls his attention off me and steps out of her way. "Sorry, Ma."

*Ma?*

I hold my breath as he comes closer to the table and takes the seat straight across from me. *Fuck*. Cam snickers under his breath, and I swing my leg to the left to kick him.

"I'm so glad you came," my mom tells Hayes. "I needed to see that you're okay with my own eyes."

My head drops and I press my lips together, because I know the feeling.

"You know I'd never miss Sunday dinner," he tells her. "Thanks for moving it by one night for me. You didn't have to, though. I would've come yesterday."

"Nonsense. You needed your rest."

Judging by their conversation, I'm guessing this is a weekly thing they do, and before I can stop myself, I comment on it. "Y-you guys do this often?"

My dad grins smugly. "Yep. We started it after Cam moved out. Gets us all together. You'd know if you had been around."

I swallow, feeling like razor blades are sliding down my throat. This is starting to feel less like a family dinner and more like an ambush. Even Hayes glances at me for a second and there's a hint of sympathy for a second, but it quickly vanishes.

"You be nice," my mom says with a frown.

At least she has my back. Meanwhile, Cam is too busy putting food on his plate to even realize I need saving. Well, at least some things haven't changed. He always has been a human garbage disposal. You'd never be able to guess that by looking at him, though.

"I'm always nice," my dad protests with waggling brows. "Aren't I, darlin'?"

## Chapter 7

God, I wish Mali were here right now. At least then I wouldn't feel like I was so completely alone. But if I had the chance to leave right now, I don't think I would. Like I said, there's no way he didn't see my car outside, and yet, he came inside anyway.

Even though it shouldn't, hope swells inside my chest at that realization.

**DINNER IS MOSTLY SPENT** with them talking while I push the food around my plate. Let's just say I don't have much of an appetite anymore, even if the smell of my mom's cooking makes my mouth water. She tries to get me involved in the conversation, but I try not to bite. The last thing I want to do is rub my new life in Hayes's face. Not when he's been going through hell while I've been living in a mansion and working at my dream job.

It should be the other way around. I should be the one suffering while he's living his ideal life. Not to say I haven't had a hard time. I mean, it was months and took prescription medication before I was able to sleep through the night without Hayes by my side. But saying my problems compare to his is like saying a skinned knee is the same as a gunshot wound.

The hope he actually wanted to see me died when he started to avoid looking in my direction. There used to be a time when he couldn't look away from me. I was the center

## Chapter 7

of his attention, and I lived for it. Now, I'm nothing more than someone he used to know, and I hate it.

As soon as we finish eating, Hayes brings his things to the sink.

"Do you want help cleaning up?" he asks my mom.

She shoos him away. "The only thing I want is for you to take it easy so you can heal properly."

He huffs out a laugh and nods. "Okay, in that case, I'm going to head home. Get some of that rest stuff you keep referring to."

"Good!" She stops washing the dishes to give him a hug. "Please let us know if you need anything."

"I will," he assures her.

He comes into the living room and shakes my dad's hand before fist bumping Cam. The two of them are watching the baseball game, and I'm guessing Hayes would normally join them, but my being here throws a wrench into his plans. His eyes land on me and both Cam and my dad watch us like a soap opera to see what happens.

"Ma'am."

He nods at me as he passes, smirking, but not in the way I like. This smirk is more sinister, as if his words were meant to hurt me and he knows he hit his mark. My dad looks shocked while Cam cringes. I'm frozen in place, feeling like I'm about to break down but holding it back. The sound of the front door closing is my only indication that he left.

"Are you okay?" Cam asks.

I blink and a single tear escapes. "What do you think?"

He sighs, putting his beer down and standing up but the only thing going through my mind right now are the words that were said to me by two incredibly smart women today.

*Fight for him.*

*Fucking fight for him!*

## Chapter 7

Cam goes to hug me but I shake my head. "I have to..."

Without finishing what I want to say, I turn around and run out the door. Hayes is halfway across the front lawn when I get outside. His steps slow, like he knows exactly who just followed him.

"Hayes," I call.

He stops, throwing his head back as he turns around. "What do you want, Laiken?"

"What I've wanted since I was fifteen," I answer. "You."

My words catch him slightly off guard and his brows furrow. "That's the thing, Lai. You had me. I was *all fucking in*. But you threw that away."

"I know, but if you would just listen—"

"No," he cuts me off. "I was willing to listen before you left. Before I woke up to find you gone. All I wanted to do back then was listen. But now? I don't want to hear it. It's too late, Laiken."

I wonder if he knows how his words cut me like knives. Or if he even cares. Not that I would hold it against him if he didn't, but the guy I knew hated hurting me more than anything. And here he is, doing nothing but hurting me.

"Please," I beg. "Ten minutes. That's all I need."

"Ten minutes?" he asks, and I nod. "See, that's where we differ. You only need ten minutes with me, but I needed the rest of my life with you."

Before I can say anything, he turns around and finishes the walk to his truck. I take a couple steps toward him, but I know there's nothing I can do to stop him from leaving. He starts his truck and only glances at me for a moment before he throws it into drive and pulls away.

I run my fingers through my hair as my eyes stay locked on his taillights. I've never wanted to see someone hit their brakes so bad in my life, but it never comes. He drives off

## Chapter 7

into the night and leaves me here to feel the loss, just like I did to him.

Mom comes out shortly after I sit on the porch steps and takes a seat beside me, wrapping her arm around me and pulling me in. I rest my head on her shoulder as I cry.

"I don't understand, baby," she says softly. "If you still love him so much, then why did you leave?"

I hate how many times I've been asked that question, and how each time, the urge to tell the truth gets a little stronger. But if Hayes's mom wouldn't understand, there's no way my God-fearing mother would. She would drag all four of us to a confessional by our ears before dropping our asses off at the nearest police station.

"I don't want to talk about it," I choke out. "Please. It's bad enough knowing everyone hates me."

"Oh, honey." She kisses the side of my head. "You were wrong to leave the way you did, and I was disappointed, but none of us hate you. You're our Laiken. We could never."

"Hayes does."

"I can't speak for Hayes," she says. "But personally, I have a hard time believing that to be true."

Why does everyone keep doing that? Is it because they don't want to hurt me by telling me the truth? Because all it's doing is hurting me by stoking the fire that burns for him to keep it alive.

"Mali wants me to fight for him," I tell her.

Mom pulls her head away and tilts it so she can look at me. "Is that what you want?"

I exhale. "The only thing I've ever wanted is him, Mom. But mostly, I just want him to be happy, and I don't know if I'm the person to make him happy anymore. Not after I broke him the way I did."

"Lai, marriage is hard. It takes work. The honeymoon

## Chapter 7

stage ends and that person is still there. You're going to fight, and hurt each other at times. There's no way around that. But that doesn't mean that person isn't still the one that makes you happy."

I nod, understanding her point. "I know, but this is a little different than *I said something mean when I was hangry*. I married him, promised to spend the rest of my life with him, and then vanished in the middle of the night. That might be a little way past breaking my vows of 'for better or worse.'"

Cam comes out and sits on the other side of me. "What are you two gossiping about?"

My eyes roll but my mom nudges me. "No one better to ask than the best friend, right?"

Oh, now that's a bad idea if I've ever heard one. But I'd be lying if I said she doesn't have a point. He spent the whole day at the bar with him today, knowing what he said to me last night. So I know he was paying extra attention.

I turn to my brother. "Tell me what to do. Do I stay and fight for our marriage, or do I leave and let him move on?"

He's shaking his head before I even finish the question. "Nope. No, sir. I'm not getting involved in that."

"You had no issue getting involved when you told me to stay to help him."

"That was different."

My jaw drops. "How?"

"Because that was *me* asking, duh," he quips.

Ugh, he's such an ass. "Okay, fine. Then just tell me this: do you think he's over me? Like, love-is-dead, wouldn't-ever-even-consider-it over me?"

My heart balances on the edge of a cliff as I wait for his answer, and it feels like it takes ages before he lets out a gush of air. "I don't know, honestly. But what I do know is he hasn't so much as looked at another girl since you left."

*Chapter 7*

And that's all I need to hear before I have my answer.

**THE INSIDE OF THE** bar is dark, but the light coming from the upstairs window tells me he's still awake. I went to the house first. He said he was going home, so that's where I thought he would be. But his truck wasn't in the driveway and none of the lights were on. It wasn't until I called Mali that I found out he hasn't been sleeping at the house for over a year. He lives in the upstairs of the bar and only goes to the house every once in a while to make sure everything is good there.

Before I can stop myself, my fist pounds against the door. It doesn't work at first, but I'm not giving up that easily. Not when it took this much just to get me here. As I bang on it again, I don't stop until I see him come into view. He's in a pair of gray sweatpants with no shirt, and he stops to stare at me for a moment. I think he knows that I'm not going anywhere because he runs his fingers through his hair and comes to unlock the door.

"You know, for someone who couldn't bother to say goodbye, you sure seem to have a lot to say now."

I hold my head high, even though it's killing me inside. "Ten minutes."

He looks like he wants to tell me no. To fuck off and go away, shutting the door in my face for the second time in two

## Chapter 7

days. But instead, he sighs and reluctantly pushes the door open further to let me in.

I duck under his arm and step into the bar. The whole way over here, I was so worried how I would get him to hear what I have to say that I didn't think about how I would say this shit when I actually got the chance. But even if I had, it would have gone right out the window as I turn to look at him, because all I can focus on is how fucking good he looks.

My mouth goes bone dry as I stare back at him. I had that. All of that was mine. Holy shit, I've never hated someone more than the fucking stalker that forced me to leave. But as sexy as he is, the bruises that cover his chest and the road rash down his side have me wanting to nurse him back to health more than anything else.

Crossing his arms over his chest, he looks at me expectantly. "You're already down to nine. I suggest you don't waste any more time."

"Sorry," I mutter, forcing my eyes away. "That just looks really painful."

He shrugs. "I've felt worse."

Fuck. "Hayes, you have to know I never wanted to leave you."

"Oh, bullshit," he scoffs. "You don't do what you did unless you want to."

"That's not true. I—"

I go to say it, to break rule number three, but the words just won't come out. The fear that has wrapped around me like a straitjacket for so long takes over, and I can't seem to force it out.

"You what?" he presses. "Regret it? Yeah, I figured one day you would, but that's not my problem."

"Th-that's not what I was going to say," I mumble. "God, it never used to be this hard to talk to you."

## Chapter 7

"It never used to be this hard to look at you, either." He takes a step closer. "I used to fucking *love* looking at you. Craved it. But now, every time I see you, all I can think about is the night we spent together just hours before you left. And the whole damn time, you knew you were going. I thought things were finally getting better. I thought we were going to be okay. But you fucking knew that wasn't the case."

My chest tightens. "I did."

There's no point in lying. No point in denying it. He's not asking for the truth, he's telling me he already knows it. And besides, you don't randomly choose to leave in the middle of the night after making love like we did.

"Why?" He asks. "Why do all that? Why make me have hope only to destroy it the next morning?"

"I wanted one last good night with you," I confess. "Something to hold onto."

With another step toward me, his eyes bore into mine. "See, that's the thing. *You* got something to hold onto. You knew the last time we fucked was going to be the last time. But I didn't."

The closer he gets, the harder it is to breathe. I've seen that look in his eyes enough times to know what it means, and I want it. I want it so fucking bad. But I know that if I let him get his hands on me, I'll end up shattered once again and forced to pick up the pieces on my own.

Yet, even knowing that, I don't think I have it in me to stop him.

My back hits the wall, and he smirks. "What's wrong, Rochester? Don't like not being the one in control?"

"I came here to talk," I try, but my shaky voice gives me away.

He gives me a skeptical look. "I told you; I don't *want* to talk."

Grabbing my wrist, he pulls me into him and spins me

## Chapter 7

around. His touch burns as he drags his hand down my side.

"You fucked me that night knowing it was going to be the last time," he repeats. "That was on your terms. This is on mine."

The moment his mouth meets my neck, showing he remembers exactly where to go, I know I'm screwed. He sucks hard on my skin, not giving a shit if he leaves a mark for everyone to see or not, and I'm too fucked up to care. He reaches around and undoes the button on my jeans, shoving them down to my knees, along with my panties. There's no teasing, no foreplay. I feel his cock graze against my ass before he bends me over and rubs himself against my pussy.

"I don't have a condom," he tells me. "If that's a game changer for you, this is the only out you're getting."

A part of me screams to take the out. I'd probably be a lot better off emotionally if I do. But knowing he hasn't been with anyone else, thanks to Cam, I say nothing and grip the wall in front of me.

It's been too fucking long, so the moment he pushes in, I feel myself stretch around him to the point where it's painful. But unlike when he took my virginity, he's not patient or kind this time, and honestly, it's almost better that way. The two of us moan in unison, letting the sounds of our pleasure fill the room.

He pulls out and slams back in. His hands grip my hips tightly. I'm sure there will be fingertip shaped bruises left behind in the morning, but I'm okay with it. At least there will be something to tell me this really happened. That it wasn't another dream meant to torture me.

"Play with your fucking clit," he demands. "Get yourself off on my cock."

I don't even attempt to deny him. I can't. I've been so desperate for this, to the point where all I want is to obey his every word. I bring one hand down and rub circles against my

## Chapter 7

clit, but honestly, I probably don't even need it with the way his cock is rubbing against my g-spot as he thrusts into me harshly and repeatedly.

"You're going to come on my cock, and then you're going to swallow everything I have to give you," he growls.

My head falls forward, only for him to grab my hair and pull me back, wrapping his hand around my neck.

"Answer me, Laiken."

"Fuck," I breathe. "Okay."

He brings his other hand down and covers my own. "What's wrong? Still can't get yourself off?"

His fingers press mine harder against myself, and I only last a couple more seconds before the best orgasm of the last year and a half explodes inside of me. My whole body shakes against him as my pussy clenches around his cock.

"God, yes," he groans. "You always were such a good girl for me when you wanted to be."

With a few more thrusts, he throws me forward and pulls out, and I immediately know what to do. I spin around and drop to my knees, opening my mouth for him. He fills it completely as he shoves himself into the back of my throat. I look up at him, but his eyes are closed and his jaw locked. He grips my hair, fucking into my mouth for only a couple thrusts, and then he shoots everything he has down my throat. I swallow down every last drop, like it's the only thing that will keep me alive.

But I don't know if I'll even make it out of this alive.

Once he's done coming down from his high, he slips out of my mouth and looks down at me, but there's no love there like everyone seems to think there is.

He looks cold.

Heartless.

Dead inside.

## Chapter 7

He puts himself back into his pants and takes a step back. "You can see yourself out."

My heart lurches at the sight of him starting to walk away, and I scramble to my feet as I pull my pants up. "So, you'll fuck me but you won't talk to me?"

He stops and looks back at me. "Sucks, doesn't it?"

It's not that I don't understand the grudge he's holding. Trust me, I get it. And if I were in his place, I'd probably be doing the same. But we're never going to get anywhere if he doesn't tell me what I deserve to hear.

"You want to hurt me?" I keep my eyes narrowed on him. "Then tell me everything. Tell me how you felt when you realized I was gone."

He laughs dryly. "Get the fuck out of here."

"No," I bark. "Tell me how I broke you. How I ruined you. Now's your chance. Let it all out."

"Fine," he sneers. "You want to know? For a while I thought you were dead! And in some sick and twisted way, I hoped you were, because at least that meant you weren't out there somewhere, living your life as if we never fucking mattered. But that phone call confirmed it. You were out there somewhere. You really had left us behind in your rearview mirror. And that made me want to fucking die! I genuinely considered it at one point because while you may have been able to live without me, there was no part of me that was interested in a life without you."

I choke on my tears, sobbing as his words rip me to shreds, exactly the way I asked for. "But I wasn't okay. We mattered, Hayes. We've always fucking mattered!"

"You left! You walked out!" he roars, turning to walk away and then turning back. "What the fuck was the point of marrying me if you were only going to leave?"

"I didn't want to leave!"

"Bullshit! And the worst part is that I would've

## Chapter 7

understood. I'm a fucking handful, and I knew from the start that you were too damn good for me. But I tried to be the best I could be for you. You could've just told me you realized you didn't want to be with me. Yeah, it would've hurt, but it would've been better than this shit!"

"No," I sob. "You're not hearing me! It wasn't my choice to leave! You have no idea how bad I wanted to turn around and run back into your arms! It took months before I could even so much as breathe without feeling like I was dying inside! So, you're wrong! I wasn't living my life as if we never mattered because you have always fucking mattered to me! You mattered to me before you ever considered me as something other than a child!"

His chest rises and falls with his heavy breathing, and I know I look ridiculous. My face is soaked, and I can barely see through the tears. But just when I think I may have finally gotten through to him, he shakes his head.

"You have a shitty way of showing it."

He starts to walk toward the back again, and my chest cracks wide open as I collapse to the ground. This is it—the only chance I have left at saving us.

"Someone knows," I say quietly.

His head whips around. "What the fuck do you mean someone knows?"

My breathing stutters. "Someone knows about what happened that night. The person who sent me the recording of you threatening Monty left an envelope in my car. They have proof, and they said they were going to the police if I didn't leave town."

Hayes pinches the bridge of his nose. "So let me get this straight. Someone out there knows about one of the worst nights of our lives, and you just decided to keep that to yourself?"

"I wasn't allowed to tell you," I cry.

## Chapter 7

He looks at me in disbelief. "Laiken, that night wasn't just fucking about me! That shit puts all of our lives in jeopardy!"

"But they weren't threatening everyone else!" I argue. "They were dead set on *you*. On making you pay for what happened. And I couldn't let that happen. I was trying to save you!"

His shoulders sag in defeat. "That's the thing though, Lai. You were trying to save me, but the life you left me with—the one without you—that was the only thing I needed saving from."

He turns his back to me and takes a couple steps before stopping.

"Please. Just go."

**IT TAKES TWENTY MINUTES** to pick myself up off the bar floor, and another half hour to get back to my motel room. The tears kept making it hard to see the road in front of me. I considered going to Mali, but clearly, I'm only causing Hayes more pain by being here. And if there's anything I don't want, it's that.

The pain in my chest is unrelenting. It feels like the final nail in the coffin of the life I had. The one that I've always wanted. The one that made me happier than I've ever been. I know I'm never going to get over him. He's the only man I've ever loved, and I know it will always be that way. But loving someone means wanting what's best for them, and that's not me anymore.

Not for him.

I unlock the door and push it open, reaching over to turn on the light. The second it flicks on, my heart drops into my stomach. There, sitting in the middle of my bed, is another envelope—my name in a familiar handwriting scrawled across it.

*They know.*

My steps are tentative as I walk toward it, barely breathing at all. When I take it into my hands and pull the note out, my whole body goes cold.

*You were warned.*
*What happens next is on you.*

No!

Fuck! No!

Panic and terror rush through me as I frantically grab my things, throwing them all back into my suitcase at an unmatched pace. All I can do is hope and pray that it's not too late. That my leaving here will fix this.

*What the fuck did I do?*

I manage to get everything together in under three minutes, and I don't even bother closing the door as I bolt to my car. Throwing the suitcase into the back, I jump in and rush to turn the car on. The tires screech against the pavement as I peel out of the parking lot.

The urge to vomit is strong, but I can't stop. I need to get out of here. I knew I shouldn't have come back in the first place, and that I should've left that same night, but I let my feelings take over again and I fucking stayed. And now I may

## Chapter 7

have made it worse for someone who is already at rock bottom.

*What will happen if he goes to prison?*
*Who is going to be there for his mom?*
*Please God, let this keep him safe.*

I watch as I pass the *Thanks for visiting Calder Bay* sign, and it's bittersweet knowing I'll never be back. I'll call Mali and Cam when I get far enough away. And my parents, because I don't want to break them again. Our relationship is fragile enough. It'll be okay.

Or maybe it won't, because as I get a few miles outside of town, a hissing sound meets my ears. Seconds later, a sweet smell infiltrates my senses. I try to turn off my air conditioner, but it doesn't stop.

Everything starts to get hazy, as if the world is blurring around me, and I pull over. The moment my car comes to a stop, I reach for the handle, but it's too late. I can't stay awake any longer. And I watch the world fade away.

**I COME TO IN** a panic. My breathing is rapid as I frantically look around my car, but there's no one there. And then I look up and I realize it's so much worse than I imagined.

There, no more than fifteen feet in front of my car, is the same sign I know I passed—putting me right back inside the town limits. I reach down to put my car back into drive, but

## Chapter 7

my hand hits a piece of paper instead. I'm shaking as I take a minute to focus on what it says.

*You had the chance to leave, and you came back.*
*There's no escaping now.*
*Welcome to your nightmare.*

# Hayes
# CHAPTER EIGHT

For fucks sake, why can't anything ever be simple? It's always so complicated, like everything is a gray area. What ever happened to just black and white, cut and dry? I'll tell you what happened.

Fucking feelings came to the goddamn party.

I hate how she keeps trying to talk to me. How she thinks that she can just come back and everything will go back to normal, like she didn't just walk out on everyone who ever gave a shit about her. It's the most selfish and infuriating thing.

Having sex with her was a bad judgment call. I should've kept the distance between us—with a door in the middle, preferably. But after sitting at dinner, knowing she was right across the table from me, it was torture. She was *right there*. All it would take is reaching out and I could've touched her. And I had to physically restrain myself from doing exactly that.

But when she showed up at the bar, I knew I was fucked.

I needed to feel her again. To get it out of my system and make the last time we fucked on my terms instead of hers. Yeah, that plan backfired, because I want her again already.

Sex between Laiken and me was always next level. The chemistry was off the charts. There was nothing better than getting lost in each other, and we both craved it more than

## Chapter 8

anything else. When I buried myself inside of her tonight, I thought it would be different.

Less intense.

Lacking the spark that used to set us on fire.

But if anything, the tension between us only made it better.

She still listens to my every word. Still knows exactly what I need to get me off. And she let me pound into her like a punishment, taking every inch of me in a way no woman before her ever has.

A part of me wanted to come inside of her pussy. It's the one thing we've never done, and the only one of her firsts I haven't claimed as my own. But when being around someone makes you feel like you can't breathe in the worst way, getting them pregnant isn't really a risk you want to take.

And then there's the bomb she dropped on me before she left.

*Someone knows.*

For over a year and a half, I've been telling myself that all of that was behind me. Behind *us*. But I was wrong, because there's someone out there who has been holding it over Laiken's head like a guillotine—waiting for their moment to strike.

God, I wish she would've told me. I wish she would've said something instead of walking out the door and letting me believe my worst fears were confirmed—I wasn't good enough for her. I get it, she was trying to protect me, but even prison would've been better than that.

I've spent so much time trying to hate her, thinking maybe it would make being without her easier. I would lie there for hours and replay all the negative things in my head. Even the sound of her voice telling me to stop looking for her played on a loop in my mind like my head was a torture

## Chapter 8

chamber made just for me. But having her home now, it's still so fucking hard.

It's hard to be around her and not want her. Everything we had, it's still there, lingering in the background. I can still feel the electricity in the air between us. And it's so tempting to fall back into it. To fall back into *her*. But I can't. The anxiety of the thought alone is overwhelming, sending me retreating into a dark corner where no one can ever break me like that again.

If I stop being angry, I know that's exactly what will happen. I'll end up letting my guard down and falling back into everything she is. And that's not something I can risk.

I won't survive it.

Rolling over, I grab my phone off my nightstand and call Cam. If I keep lying here, thoughts of Laiken are going to eat me alive. I need to get out for a bit. Take my mind off it.

"What's up?" he answers.

Thank fuck. "You home? I need a beer."

Cam chuckles. "You're literally above a bar right now."

My eyes roll. I'm really not in the mood for this shit. "Fuck you. Forget I called."

"Shut up and come over," he says with a sigh, realizing it's a little more serious than he originally thought.

The two of us hang up without so much as a goodbye, and I climb out of bed. Hopefully Laiken isn't still downstairs when I go to leave.

*Chapter 8*

**CAM'S DOOR IS UNLOCKED** when I get there, but even if it wasn't, I have a key. Just like he has a key to my place. Mali laughed and called it our bromance, but that never surprises me. She'll latch onto anything if it means she gets to fuck with us about it.

My best friend is sitting on the couch, and I walk over to sit beside him, grabbing a controller off the coffee table. The one right next to the ice cold beer he has waiting for me. He watches me intently with his eyes narrowed to slits as he tries to figure me out.

"You want to talk about it?"

I don't even look at him as I answer. "Nope."

And that's the only thing said out loud before I crack open the beer and we start playing a game of NHL Center Ice.

**VIDEO GAMES ARE ALWAYS** the perfect distraction. You're so focused on what you're doing that other thoughts don't even have the opportunity to fuck with you. It was a big part of how I got through the first few months without Laiken.

I was barely eating, hardly taking care of myself at all, and my hair was practically matted to my head, but I was a fucking master at just about every video game around. I even got Mali to play some with me a few times, but she never has been a graceful loser, and I wasn't about to let her win.

## Chapter 8

I like her, but I don't like her *that* much.

An hour or so into the game, a knock at the door makes Cam pause it as he gets up to answer the door. There's only one person who would come over this late, but it's never unannounced. When I see who walks in, however, I understand why this time is different.

Mali drags a hyperventilating Laiken in behind her. Each breath she takes is shallow, and she's trying to let out a lot more air than she's taking in. Cam's eyes widen in a panic as he looks between his sister and Mali.

"What the fuck is going on?"

I brace myself for what's to come, my first thought being that I caused this. Fucking her and then leaving her there—that brought her to this. To the point of an everlasting panic attack. And even with as furious as I am at her right now, the sight of her speaks to the parts of me I try to keep tucked away.

"I can't get her to calm down," Mali says. "Every time I even come close to normalizing her breathing, she spirals again."

Laiken grips her chest, looking like she's experiencing the worst pain of her life.

Cam grabs her arms and positions himself so she's forced to look at him. "Lai, breathe. You have to breathe." But it's not working, and she starts to fall to the ground. "Shit. Do we have to bring her to the hospital?"

Yeah, I can't do this. I can't sit around and do nothing while she breaks down to nothing. Even if she brought me to a point just like this, I have to do something.

I jump over the back of the couch. "Move."

Cam slides out of the way as I fall to my knees in front of Laiken. She looks at me with a level of fear in her eyes that I've never seen. I grab her and pull her against me, pressing her head against my chest so she can hear my heartbeat.

## Chapter 8

"Focus on my breathing," I tell her. "You're going to pass out if you don't get enough oxygen in, and you don't want to do that. Ignore everything else and just focus on me."

The smell of her shampoo wafts into my nose and I hate the effect it still has on me. There's the biggest urge to kiss the top of her head the way I know she loves, but I stop myself from doing it. That would be too much for me.

Way too much, far too soon.

It takes a minute but her breathing starts to calm.

"That's it," I murmur. "You've got it."

If the universe wanted to torture me, it certainly succeeded. Lying in my bed all night and destroying myself with thoughts of her would have been better than this. The feeling of her in my arms, needing me as much as I've always needed her, it's a lot like walking on a tightrope—with a thousand-foot drop and a hundred starving tigers beneath me.

When she finally gets through the worst panic attack I've ever seen her experience, I feel her start to back away from me, and I have to force myself to let her go. She runs her fingers through her hair, reminding me of the way I pulled it earlier.

*Fucking stop it.*

Cam and Mali both look relieved as we all go over to sit on the couch. Laiken leans against Mali like she's the only thing in the world holding her in one piece, and I hate the fact that it's no longer me she relies on. But then again, I haven't given her any reason to believe she still can.

"Okay, without breaking out into another one of whatever the fuck that was, tell me what happened," Cam says.

Well, at least when he knocks my ass out, I'll get a few moments of peace. Then again, thoughts of Laiken have a tendency of haunting my dreams, too. All I can do is hope he

## Chapter 8

doesn't go for the ribs. There's only so much more they can take right now.

Laiken's eyes meet mine before she forces them away, and I know I'm fucked. "I don't even know where to start."

"The beginning would be nice."

Mali narrows her eyes at him for the smartass comment.

"Fuck, okay," Laiken sighs. "There's someone threatening me. They have been since before I left."

Cam's jaw drops. "What the fuck?" He turns to me. "Did you know about this?"

I can't tell if I'm relieved this isn't about me, or worried what else could have sent her into that kind of a tailspin. "I didn't until tonight. She kept that little secret to herself, as if we didn't have a right to know."

"Don't be an asshole," Mali sneers. "I love you. You're like my brother. But I'm not going to sit here and listen to you be mean to her."

Fucking of course not. Does she not realize that Laiken walked out on her, too? That not even being best friends for the majority of their lives mattered enough to her? It's like the moment Laiken came back, Mali went blind to it all and they were right back to how they've always been.

But that won't be me.

I won't give her the power to break me like that again.

Instead of apologizing, I flip Mali the bird.

"You want that shoved up your ass? Because that can be arranged," she threatens.

"All right," Cam intervenes. "We don't need you two going at each other right now. Laiken, what do you mean someone has been threatening you?"

Her breathing goes uneven, the aftermath of hyperventilating. "They know about what happened with Monty. It's why I left. They threatened to make sure Hayes

## Chapter 8

was charged with murder if I didn't." She starts to cry again. "I couldn't let that happen. There are too many people that would be devastated by that."

My eyes roll as I force myself to look away. It's not that I don't somewhat appreciate what she did for me. There's a part of me that does, but it's overpowered by a much larger part that just wants to scream in her face that she should've told me.

"Lai, your breathing," Cam reminds her, and she starts the long, slow breaths again to calm down. "That makes a lot more sense to me than you just randomly taking off, but why wouldn't you come to us? We could've helped you."

"Because I wasn't allowed," she explains. "There was an envelope left in my car with a picture in it from that night. Clear proof that Monty was dead and Hayes was involved. And on the back of it were three rules I had to follow if I wanted to keep him out of prison."

"What three rules?" Cam asks the question, so I don't have to.

Laiken lists them off like they're burned into her brain. "Leave Hayes and leave Calder Bay. Have no contact. And lastly, don't let him know that I left for any reason other than that I wanted to. I broke rules one and two the day I came back, and I broke rule three tonight—which is why I guess shit hit the fan."

He glances over at me, finally putting the pieces together as to why I needed a distraction. My brows raise for a second to confirm, and he turns back to his sister.

"Okay, what do you mean *shit hit the fan?*"

She starts to get upset again while Mali runs her hand over her back to keep her calm. "I went back to my motel room and there was another note waiting for me on my bed."

Mali reaches into her bag and pulls out an envelope,

## Chapter 8

passing it to Cam. His jaw tenses as he looks at it and then hands it to me.

*You were warned.*
*What happens next is on you.*

Jesus Christ. Who the fuck would care that much to still be watching her after all this time? Do they really have nothing better to do?

I toss the envelope onto the coffee table and take a sip of my beer while Laiken continues. "I tried to leave. I threw my things in the car and tried to go, hoping maybe it wasn't too late. That I could still just stay gone and everything would be okay."

She pauses, and I'm stuck with the pain that comes when I realize she once again tried to go—without telling me. Not that I've done anything but make her feel like she should leave. Still, the ache in my chest is there, and it's not from my bruised ribs.

"When I got out of town, some kind of gas filled my car. It was strange. Nothing I've ever smelt before. It made me feel really dizzy, so I pulled over. But before I could get out of the car, I passed out. And when I woke up, I was right back inside the town limits, with this left in my car."

Taking the other piece of paper from Mali, she passes it to Cam.

"You had the chance to leave, and you came back. There's no escaping now. Welcome to your nightmare," Cam reads it out loud. "Fucking Christ."

If I thought this was some kind of ploy or move at justifying her leaving and trying to get me back, I'd call her out on it. But there's no way she's lying about this. Not when I saw the pure terror in her eyes. Hell, I even saw it when she

## Chapter 8

confronted me with the recording a couple nights before she left. I just thought it was because of me. Because she thought I was a monster.

I never considered it was because of someone else.

"Do you have the original one with you?" Cam asks. "The one you said has the proof in it?"

Laiken shakes her head. "It's at home."

*Home.* That word shouldn't matter to me. Where she lives is her decision. But just hearing her say it like that, like anywhere but here will *ever* be her home, it strikes a nerve. As far as I'm concerned, this is the only place that will ever be her fucking home.

I stand up, unable to handle being here any longer. "I'm going to head out."

Cam's brows furrow. "Right now? You don't want to help me get to the bottom of this?"

My gaze meets his, and it's the only time I'll let any vulnerability show in front of Laiken. "I can't. Not tonight."

He nods in understanding while Laiken's head falls back against the couch as she starts to cry again. There's a voice inside of me telling me to go to her, to make everything better again, but I know I can't do that.

I can't save her anymore. She took that ability away from me. Ripped it straight from my hands as she walked out the door. There's nothing I can do for her that doesn't make me want to run for the hills.

She made her choices, and now it's time for me to make mine.

*Chapter 8*

**IT'S A LITTLE PAST** two in the morning when I finally get back to the bar. Knowing the bar probably still has the smell of sex in the air, I decided to go down to the inlet and sit for a bit. It's usually a good place to sort out my thoughts. But not tonight.

Believe me, I would love nothing more than to go back to the night before she left and beg her not to go. To stop her from leaving in the first place and promise her that no matter what life throws at us, we'll get through it. But the shitty thing about life is that there is no redo button. You can't rewind. You can't go back. All you can do is drown in the aftermath of the choices that were made, even if they weren't your own.

Sticking the key in the lock, I turn it and open the door. But before I get more than two steps in, I stop.

*Someone has been in here.*

I can't make out what it is, but there's something hanging all over the walls. I reach for the switch to turn the light on, only for nothing to happen. The power is out, and it leaves everything in total darkness.

Playing it safe, I go outside and call Cam.

"Dude, do you know what time it is?" he grumbles.

I sigh. "Yes, Sleeping Beauty, but I need you to get over here. I don't think that asshole stopped at fucking with Laiken tonight."

*Chapter 8*

His breath hitches and suddenly he's wide awake. "I'll be right there."

**I WAIT IN MY** truck to avoid the chilly night air. If I wasn't on the beach, it probably wouldn't be so bad, but the wind blowing off the ocean makes for a cold night. And at least in a locked truck, no one can sneak up on me.

When Cam pulls into the parking lot, I get out, but my stomach churns when I realize Laiken is with him.

"Why'd you bring her with you?" I ask, trying not to sound like an asshole, but I don't know if someone is inside.

He glances at Laiken, who looks down and then back at me. "She's staying at my place tonight, and I wasn't going to leave her alone. Not after what she went through tonight."

It's a reasonable explanation. I'd be shaken up too if someone knocked my ass out and moved my car with me inside of it. But that doesn't mean I'm happy she's here. Not when the danger could still be inside.

"Do you have the flashlight?" He nods and hands it to me. "Okay, you two stay out here while I make sure no one is inside."

Cam shakes his head. "No fucking way. What if someone is waiting to attack you or some shit?"

*Ugh.* "Fine. But stay right inside the door."

The three of us enter the bar and I turn on the flashlight,

## Chapter 8

going straight for the back where the circuit breaker is. At least with the lights on, we're better prepared. Thankfully, they didn't completely cut the power—they just turned it off at the master switch. And while I'm somewhat concerned for the beer we have in the walk-in fridge, I'm more worried about *why* someone was in here in the first place.

I flick the power back on and immediately hear Laiken gasp.

It's embarrassing how fast I rush back out into the front, worried that something has happened to her. And if she wasn't so zoned into everything around her, she may have noticed it. But she's too busy looking at the walls.

"Oh my God."

The walls are covered from floor to ceiling with Monty's missing person flyers. There isn't a single inch of the drywall still exposed, and if there is something hanging on the wall in that spot, they just put the flyer over it.

It's one thing hearing what Laiken has been through, and even seeing the two notes from tonight, but standing here looking at this, I know whoever this is, they're not fucking around.

Someone knows what we did that night, and now they're out for blood.

"This must have taken hours," Cam murmurs.

My eyes move around the room as I take it all in. "Unless there is more than one of them."

"Two people that know?" He shakes his head. "I doubt that. It's been almost two years. One of them would've gotten bored by now."

I run my fingers through my hair as I sigh. "Well, they definitely had something to occupy their time tonight. Help me take this shit down so we can open in the morning."

Laiken looks like she's on the verge of another massive breakdown. The fear is evident on her face, and Cam asks if

## Chapter 8

she's okay. She just stares back at him in response and then turns to me.

"I'm so sorry," she says, her voice shaky. "I never should've come back."

The urge to pull her into my arms is there, just beneath the surface, but I can't deal with that right now. There's so fucking much to unpack, and I'm sure we'll get there eventually. Right now I need to get this shit off the walls so we can open the bar on time tomorrow.

We're already fucked financially right now thanks to me. We can't afford to be closed because someone has a goddamn vendetta.

It may be a dick move, ignoring her when she's upset like this, but it was a dick move when she left, so fuck it. I walk over to the walls and start to pull down the flyers. A lot of them are taped together like wrapping paper. It at least makes it easier to remove.

Cam and Laiken both help rip down the images of one of my most hated people off the wall. Each one of his pictures feels like it's staring back at me, taunting me—like he's pointing out that he won. His death is ultimately what made Laiken leave. And I'm sure the ghost of him is basking in it.

"H," Cam calls. "There's something behind this."

I walk over and notice there's a part of another picture behind the flyers on one wall. My brows furrow as I carefully remove all the pages over top of it, only for things to get worse.

There, underneath the pictures of the crime we covered up, is a blown-up photo of us. My arms are wrapped around Laiken, with Cam and Mali beside us. We all look so happy, but it's the word painted across it in red ink that chills me to the bone.

*GUILTY.*

This was the real message. The one to show us that they

*Chapter 8*

know we were all involved. And they're not just declaring war on Laiken. It's a war on all of us.

All three of our phones go off at once, and we look confused as we pull them out, each finding a text from an unknown number.

> Let the games begin.

# Hayes
## CHAPTER NINE

My alarm blares beside me. Four hours of sleep is just not enough, but unfortunately, it's what I'm used to these days. Especially since Laiken has been back. It always seems like when I finally get myself to doze off, I'm forced awake again. As much as I hate coffee, it's become a necessary staple in my life.

I slip out of bed and leave the guest room of my own damn house. After knowing someone had been in the bar, I knew I couldn't sleep there. The last thing we want to do is let our guards down for a single second. So, as much as I didn't want to, I forced myself to come sleep here.

There was a time when I loved this place almost as much as Laiken did. It was ours—filled with our love and the promise of a future together. But when she left, the only thing I was waiting for was for her to come back, until it reached the point where it became unhealthy.

Every sound of a car door shutting had me flying to the window, hoping it was her. The creaks that come with every house were far too loud as they broke through the silence. It was all just a reminder that she wasn't here. And when I couldn't take it anymore, I finally decided to leave and sleep at the bar.

It started out as only one night, but as one month became two, and days became weeks, I accepted that I was better off

*Chapter 9*

sleeping there—where the other side of the bed didn't remind me of what I lost. The only times I come back here are to make sure everything is still in working order, and to dust from time to time. It's not like I want the place to go to shit. I just couldn't stand to be here anymore.

Even now, the emptiness is as strong as ever because while I might know where she is now, she isn't here. This house was never mine. It was always *ours*. It's just not somewhere I belong if she isn't here with me.

**MY MOM LIGHTS UP** at me as I walk into the room, carrying the breakfast we share together as much as possible. It's no secret that nursing home food isn't the best. Don't get me wrong, I'm sure they try their best and the cooks are very talented, but when it's all made in mass quantities, it's never going to taste as good.

"Stop looking at me like that," I say through a chuckle.

Her grin widens. "Like what?"

"Like I'm some kind of hero. You're going to give me a complex."

She hums, watching me put her breakfast on the bedside table and turning it so she can eat. "Honey, you've always been my hero."

I can't explain how much I wish that were true. But if I were a hero, I'd be able to save her, and no matter how hard

## Chapter 9

I've tried, I haven't been able to do that. No one has. Not even the best doctors I could manage to find, and trust me, we went through a lot of them.

I pull up the chair beside her bed and take out my bagel. "My ego thanks you for its daily inflation."

Mom snickers, rolling her eyes. "You're such a little shit."

"Now *that* sounds more like you."

We both laugh, and I love when we're in moods like this. There have been times where she's mentally not all there. Especially during treatments, she didn't seem like herself. It's like she was confused and irritated. All she wanted to do was sleep, and I understood it, but I always ached for moments like this.

It goes quiet for a moment as we eat, until my mom says something that shocks the hell out of me.

"So, Laiken's back?"

I damn near choke on my food. "How did you know that?"

She smirks, not letting her eyes meet mine. "She may have stopped by to see me yesterday."

That information knocks the wind out of me. To know that she was here, spending time with my mom, it sends a rush of different emotions through my body.

"What did she want?" I ask, trying to seem unaffected.

"To apologize, for starters." Her hand trembles as she brings the fork with more eggs on it to her mouth, dropping some on her lap that I quickly help her clean up. "She seems just as broken as you are, H."

*Fuck me.* "Yeah well, she's the one that did this, remember?"

"I know. There's no confusion there, don't worry about that. But I will say she looked genuinely sorry. I think she regrets leaving, Hayes."

If I had to guess, right now I'd say she regrets coming

*Chapter 9*

back more. We have no idea what's in store for us after last night. And I've never been so glad that my mom is safely inside of the confines of a nursing home. At least here, she's protected and looked after.

"I don't know," I murmur.

But she's not done pressing. "How do you feel about her being back?"

Looking away from her, I shake my head. "Same answer. I don't know."

My mom smacks my arm playfully. "You don't know much, do you?"

"I know that I want to enjoy breakfast with my mom," I tell her. "There's a lot going on there, and I really don't want to talk about it. I just want to be here with you right now."

That seems to resonate with her, and she nods. "Okay, but I'm here if you want to talk."

"I know," I assure her, and I do know that.

But unloading on my mom when she has much bigger problems than I do is not something I can bring myself to do. Not today, not ever.

**THE PARKING LOT IS** nearly full, but it's no surprise that the bar is empty. Most of them are locals enjoying the beach before it fills up for the summer. They'll all filter in at some point. They always do.

## Chapter 9

What *is* a surprise, however, is seeing Laiken sitting in the corner—her face practically buried in her computer. She has a notebook beside her and headphones on. When she feels someone looking at her, she turns her head and our gazes meet.

I feel like a deer caught in the headlights. I can't look away. My body won't move. I'm just stuck, staring back at the woman I once thought I would spend the rest of my life with.

To my relief, she breaks eye contact after what feels like a lifetime but is really only a few painfully long seconds.

"Oh, good," Cam says as he comes out from the back. "You're here. Mali is on her way so we can update her on last night before Riley comes in for her shift."

While he's moving onto other topics like inventory and tasting the beer we were worried about from last night, my attention is still stuck on the fact that Laiken is no more than twenty feet away from me.

"What's she doing here?" I ask, hoping that she can't hear me right now.

Not that it would matter if she could, but she's going through a lot and I'm not exactly trying to make it worse—regardless of how much she might deserve it.

Cam looks confused until I nod over toward Laiken. "Oh! Sorry, I should've given you the heads up. I think the gas she inhaled last night was some kind of anesthetic. She should be fine, but I just want to keep an eye on her for twenty-four hours. If you're uncomfortable though, we can just split the shift today."

I shake my head. "No, it's fine. I'll deal with it."

The part I don't tell him is that a part of me wants to look after her, too. With this person out there, threatening to do God knows what, it's better to keep her where I can see her. I know that I shouldn't give a shit, and I should force myself to move on like I told myself I was going to the first night she

## Chapter 9

showed up here, but I can't. Because the girl sitting over there is the same girl I fell out of my mind in love with. There's a lot in my head that I need to work through, but *that* will never change.

She's always going to have that effect on me.

It's only a few minutes later when Mali comes in like the storm that she is.

"Okay, what the fuck happened that you couldn't tell me over the phone?" she shouts.

Cam looks at her fondly. "Hold on."

He goes over and gently lets Laiken know Mali is here, careful not to startle her. She takes off her headphones and the two of them come back toward us. Laiken sits on one of the bar stools and I shake my head.

"You legally have to be twenty-one to sit there," I tell her.

She narrows her eyes at me, as if she's wondering if I'm just fucking with her or trying to be a dick, until Cam chimes in.

"He's right. Even if you're not drinking alcohol, you can't sit at the bar."

With a small, apologetic smile shot my way, she gets up and stands beside Mali. Cam slowly breaks down the events of last night, explaining it in a way that makes Laiken and me relive the moment I'd rather forget. After telling her about how Monty's missing flyers were everywhere, he pulls the rolled-up picture out from under the bar.

"This was underneath part of them," he says.

I help him unroll it and Mali's eyes widen when she sees the word *guilty* painted across it. Now that she's seen it, we can throw it away like I wanted to do last night. Not only does it feel like a threat, but it also reminds me of how great things were before Laiken left.

"So, what does this mean?" Mali asks. "This person is after all of us now?"

## Chapter 9

Cam shrugs. "That's what it looks like. We all need to be careful, at least until we figure out who the hell this is and how we're going to deal with it."

Laiken huffs out a sarcastic laugh. "You think I haven't tried that already? To figure out who this asshole is? It's impossible. They cover their tracks like a damn mob boss."

Cam's brows raise as he turns to me. "You don't think..."

I chuckle. "That Monty was secretly in the mafia? Absolutely not. He'd say the wrong thing and get himself shot." Mali snorts at my choice of words while Laiken presses her lips together. "For fuck's sake, you know what I mean."

Laiken's phone goes off, and she glances down at it. "I have to get back to work."

Cam and Mali nod and she walks back over to her computer, but I'm a little curious what *work* is. Whatever it is, she becomes completely engrossed in it.

I'm *not* jealous. I'm not. I just haven't had her attention on me anywhere near enough in the last year and a half. Does wanting her to make up for some of that by not being able to take her focus off me make me a bad person? If so, just add it to the list of sins I've committed.

I don't fucking care.

My phone dings inside my pocket, and I pull it out. My hand tightens when I realize it's an unknown number—just like last night.

> You always did have a tendency of watching her when you're not supposed to.

Yeah, fuck all that. Last night, it came in as a group text to all three of us at once. I couldn't respond without Laiken seeing exactly what it was I had to say, and I didn't want to slip up. But this time, it's just to me, and my thumbs fly across the screen as I text back.

## Chapter 9

> Who the fuck is this and what do you want?

> What I wanted was for her to stay gone, but we don't always get the things we desire most. You should know that better than anyone.

This son of a bitch. To know I'm texting the person who is the reason Laiken left me in the first place, it awakens the darkest parts of me. The part that would have killed someone if they were trying to get in between her and I. But before you go thinking that's what happened with Monty, it's not. Though I can't say I would've have been willing to do it if I came to that.

I would've done anything for her.

> How about you stop being a fucking coward and come down here so we can deal with this in person? Or are you too much of a bitch to do that? That's why you hide behind anonymous text messages and making sure you don't get caught, right? I mean, you couldn't even take Laiken on. Had to knock her out to get your way, didn't you?

The sound of my phone dinging again grabs Cam's attention, but I'm too focused on my phone to notice.

> Fuck you. You have no idea what I'm capable of. Better learn to behave like Mommy dearest says, Hazey. Wouldn't want me to take another woman you love away, would you?

I see red as my jaw clenches and I go to text back, telling them to leave my mother the fuck out of this, but before I can send it, Cam rips my phone right from my grasp. His

## Chapter 9

brows furrow as he reads part of the conversation and then he looks at me in disbelief, making me roll my eyes.

"Are you trying to get us all killed? Or have you become that suicidal that you just don't care anymore?"

I snatch my phone back and shove it into my back pocket. "Fuck off. Motherfucker had it coming."

He puts a hand on my chest as I go to walk away, preventing me from moving. "Listen, I get it. There is nothing I want more than to figure out who this is and make them regret the day that they decided to fuck with us. But they're right. We really *don't* know what they're capable of. So, as much as we want to fucking rage right now, we can't. Okay?"

Exhaling, I nod. "Okay."

"Thank you."

**MALI IS STILL HANGING** around by the time Riley walks in for her shift, much to both girls' dismay. It was amusing at first, their hatred for each other, and sometimes it still is, but right now, I'm not in the mood for any of their shit. And clearly neither is Cam, if the way he excuses himself to the back to check our inventory is any indication.

When the bar first opened, we tried to get Mali to work here. We knew Cam and I couldn't handle it all on our own, not without working ourselves into the ground. But Mali told

## Chapter 9

us no. That she loves us too much to do that. And then there's the fact that she absolutely refuses to let Cam be her boss.

I will forever refuse to ask what the look he gave her and the wink she shot back at him meant during that conversation.

"Hey, is the woman in the corner taken care of?" Riley asks.

At first, I'm confused, until it dawns on me that she's talking about Laiken. "Oh. Yeah, she's good."

Mali smirks, knowing exactly how she's going to irritate Riley today. "Don't worry, Riles. Hayes will make sure to take good care of her. I mean, he always has."

Riley glances from Mali, to me, then over to Laiken before finally settling back on me. "What is she talking about? Who is that girl?"

"No one," I spit, not trying to deal with a pissed-of bartender all day, but Mali answers at the same time I do with, "his wife."

Surprise overtakes Riley's features. "Okay, those are two *vastly* different things."

Mali narrows her eyes at me. "Don't tell me you've shoved her back into the closet with the rest of your dirty little secrets."

"Oh, fuck off with that," I tell her. "You know that's not true better than anyone."

When we were together, officially and openly, I wasn't hiding her from anyone. I would've shouted our relationship from the rooftops. I mean, I have her initial tattooed on my ring finger, for Christ's sake. But after she left, everyone kept asking me where she was. Do you know how embarrassing it is to have to tell people that not only did your wife leave you, but you don't have a clue where she is?

## Chapter 9

It's not something I'd like to go through again, that's for damn sure.

I make myself busy before I say something I'll regret, while the two of them continue their little ongoing war. Though, I think Mali is bound to win this one.

"I thought Hayes doesn't do commitment," Riley murmurs.

Mali hums amusedly. "He did for her."

They're talking like Laiken can't hear them, assuming that to be true simply based on the headphones she's wearing. But as I look up and her eyes meet mine, the sad smile she gives me proves otherwise.

"All right," I tell them. "That's enough gossiping. Don't you have enough shit to get done or do I need to create more work?"

Before Mali can throw back at me that she doesn't actually work here, Cam strolls into the room.

"What the hell did you two do that made him start sounding like a real boss?"

Riley nods over at Laiken. "Mali was just filling me in on who *she* is."

Cam looks confused. "You mean my sister?"

With brows raised, Riley turns around to smirk at me. "You're just a whole cliché, aren't you?"

I flip her off. "Back to work, before I fire you all."

"You can't fire me," Mali sasses.

"Me either," Cam agrees.

Jesus Christ, there is not enough money in the world to make this shit worth it.

*Chapter 9*

**BY THREE O'CLOCK, LAIKEN** is still laser-focused on her computer. She's only stopped a couple times to refill her water, which is when she met Riley. Judging by her reaction and the look she and Mali shared, she's already heard all about her. And I'm sure the fact that she has a thing for me was a main topic of that conversation.

Needless to say, she doesn't like her. And Laiken not being in the position to start shit, when she drained her glass, she decided against getting up for another.

The place is dead for the most part, give or take a few people who wander in for something to drink before they head back to the beach. Normally, I'd be grateful for the break, but today, it leaves too much time to think, and there's one thing that hasn't left my mind all damn day.

I fill another glass with coke and add a piece of lime to it, just the way she likes it, and carry it over to her table. She looks up at me with surprise and takes off the headphones.

"Thank you," she says.

I force a smile across my face and nod to the seat beside her. "Mind if I…"

It feels so awkward, having to ask if I can sit next to her. God, I fucking hate this. But she nods and moves her bag off it for me to sit.

"Are you okay?" I ask, realizing I haven't asked her that myself.

## Chapter 9

I've asked Cam, and Mali, and I've listened to her answer when they ask, but I haven't taken the initiative to see for myself, and that's something that bothers me.

She stretches her arms over her head. "I've been better, but I'll be all right."

"Will you?" I press.

Her eyes bore into mine, and I feel it—the vulnerability threatening to make its way to the surface. "I hope so."

It's too much, looking at her like this and being so close, and I force myself to focus my attention down at the table.

"You tried to leave again," I choke out.

The pain is evident in my voice, giving me away in an instant, but I have to know why. If she feels the way she says she does, and she really left because she was forced to, why aren't we worth more of a fight to her? It's fucking pathetic, but I need the answer.

She closes her eyes for a second. "I did."

"Why?"

"I came back because you were hurt and I was worried about you, but my being here was clearly only causing more pain, and I don't want that for you," she says plainly. "And then I got that note and I panicked."

I'm quiet for a moment as I process her words, trying to keep the anger that wants to protect me at bay. "You came back because I was hurt, but that accident was the least painful thing I've dealt with since you left."

She winces, feeling actual pain from my words. "I know. I'm sorry. God, you were probably so pissed at me that morning."

"That's the thing. I wasn't," I confess. "I was just as stupidly in love with you as I was the day before."

Looking over at me, her eyes water. "I thought I was doing what was best for you. I really did."

I nod. "I believe you, but I also know that you used to *hate*

## Chapter 9

when people made decisions on your behalf. But that's what you did that night. You made a choice for me, one I never wanted. And it sucked because I didn't just lose the girl I was in love with. I lost my best fucking friend."

Her bottom lip quivers, and I look away. I'm really not trying to make her cry. I'm just working through a ton of shit right now, and I don't have all the answers to make the pieces fit.

"There's a part of me that still loves you," I say honestly. "There's always going to be a part of me that still loves you. But right now, there's a part of me that wants to hate you, and I'm not sure which is stronger."

She sniffles, wiping away her tears and nodding. "I get that. I do."

I get up from the table and put my fist on it. "Just do me a favor?"

"Anything," she replies, and I know she means that.

"Don't go anywhere until I figure it out."

There's a glint of hope in her eyes, and the corners of my mouth raise slightly before I walk away. As I go back behind the bar, I see Riley watching me sadly.

"So, that's her, huh?" she asks. "The girl who made it so you don't believe in love anymore?"

I let myself look at Laiken for a moment before I answer, feeling the way I still crave her like an addiction that never seems to fully go away.

"I believe in love," I say simply. "I just don't believe in it with anyone but her."

*Chapter 9*

**I THOUGHT I WOULD** be relieved, listing the house for sale. And maybe I would be if Laiken hadn't come back. But as I stand here, watching someone hammer a for-sale sign into the front yard, it doesn't feel anything like I thought it would. I expected bittersweet, but all I feel is bitter.

The realtor who helped me buy this place is the same one I'm listing it through, and she's surprised to see it back on the market so soon.

"With how your girlfriend was talking about it, I thought this was your forever home," she tells me.

"She's my wife," I correct her. "And I thought so, too."

But this place feels tainted now. All the memories are stained by the one of her leaving. Even if, by the grace of God, we manage to salvage what I'm pretty sure is dead, I don't think I see our future being in this house anymore. And if we don't, there's no reason I need a four-bedroom house. Not when I'm never going to commit to anyone the same way I did with her.

Laiken was always my happily ever after.

It just didn't end happily.

*Chapter 9*

**I'M FORCED AWAKE IN** the middle of the night to the sound of banging, as if someone is trying to break in. I jump out of bed and fly down the stairs, calling Cam and telling him to get his ass here. I'm ready to rip a motherfucker's head off their damn shoulders, but as I swing the door open, there's no one there. What there is, however, is a dead raccoon pinned to the front door *with my switchblade*. My nose scrunches at the way blood drips down from the corpse.

I grab the note that's between the raccoon and the handle of the blade and rip it off.

*Peek-a-boo. I found you.*

Oh, well, aren't they fucking cute. There's a smiley face with Xs for the eyes underneath the words, probably to signify my death or something just as depraved. But the note is the last thing I'm worried about.

Cam's Jeep comes flying down the street then screeches to a halt in front of my house. He and Laiken jump out at the same time, and Cam runs across the yard to where I'm sitting on the front steps.

"What the fuck happened?" And then he sees the door. "Jesus Christ, is that a raccoon?"

I nod. "A present from our little friend."

## Chapter 9

He walks up to it, inspecting it carefully. "Hayes?"

"Yeah?" I already know what's coming.

"How'd they get a hold of your switchblade if it's always in your pocket?"

*Bingo.* "That's what I'm trying to figure out."

Laiken has her arms wrapped around herself, and the T-shirt she's wearing is one I recognize well. My favorite shirt since I was seventeen, that stopped fitting over the years, but I refused to throw it away. It's the shirt Laiken loved to sleep in. I wondered where it went after she left, and now I guess I have my answer.

*She took it with her.*

"Nice shirt," I deadpan. "Glad to see you got something of mine while leaving me nothing of yours."

Her brows furrow until she looks down and realizes what I'm talking about. I don't think she ever expected for me to find out she has it. I mean, how would I if I hadn't forced her and Cam out of bed in the middle of the night?

"I left behind more of me than you think," she mumbles.

But before I can even think of a response to that, Cam comes down the stairs and stands in front of me.

"What the fuck are we going to do about this shit? Because it feels like they're escalating already."

I shrug. "Personally, I still think they may be all talk."

He looks at me like I've lost my mind. "H, there is a fucking dead animal stuck to your door. What part of that says *bluffing* to you?"

"None of it, but what the fuck are we supposed to do?" I ask, exasperatedly. "Unless we can pull off a fucking miracle and figure out who this is, we can't do shit. So that's exactly what I plan on doing. Jack shit. I'm going to let the fire burn itself out."

His lips purse as he considers my plan. "You really think that could work?"

## Chapter 9

"Either they'll get bored that we won't play their game, or they'll get desperate and slip up," I reply. "I don't really see how we could lose."

Laiken doesn't look convinced, but I'm pretty sure she's only half paying attention. She and Mali are firecrackers—unwilling to take orders from anyone—but something tells me they'll listen to whatever Cam and I say when it comes to this.

"All right," Cam agrees. "I guess it's worth a shot."

"That's how I see it."

He looks at the house and then back at me. "Are you going to be okay here tonight or do you want me to stay?"

If he was here by himself, I'd probably tell him to crash here, but I can hardly handle Laiken being on the front lawn, let alone inside. "I'll be fine. I'll see you tomorrow."

He nods, bumping my fist with his own. "Sounds good, man. Call if you need me."

"I will."

Cam starts walking back toward his Jeep, expecting Laiken to follow, but she hesitates as she looks back at me.

"You're selling the house?"

I glance past her at the sign down by the street. "Yeah."

She swallows. "Oh."

"It's not about you," I say, then backtrack slightly. "Not completely, anyway. It's just…sometimes plans change."

It looks like she wants to fight me on that, tell me that our plans don't have to change. That we could still have the future we used to talk about. And there's a part of me that wants to hear her say the words. But she decides against it, and it's probably for the best.

The plans we made together are dead.

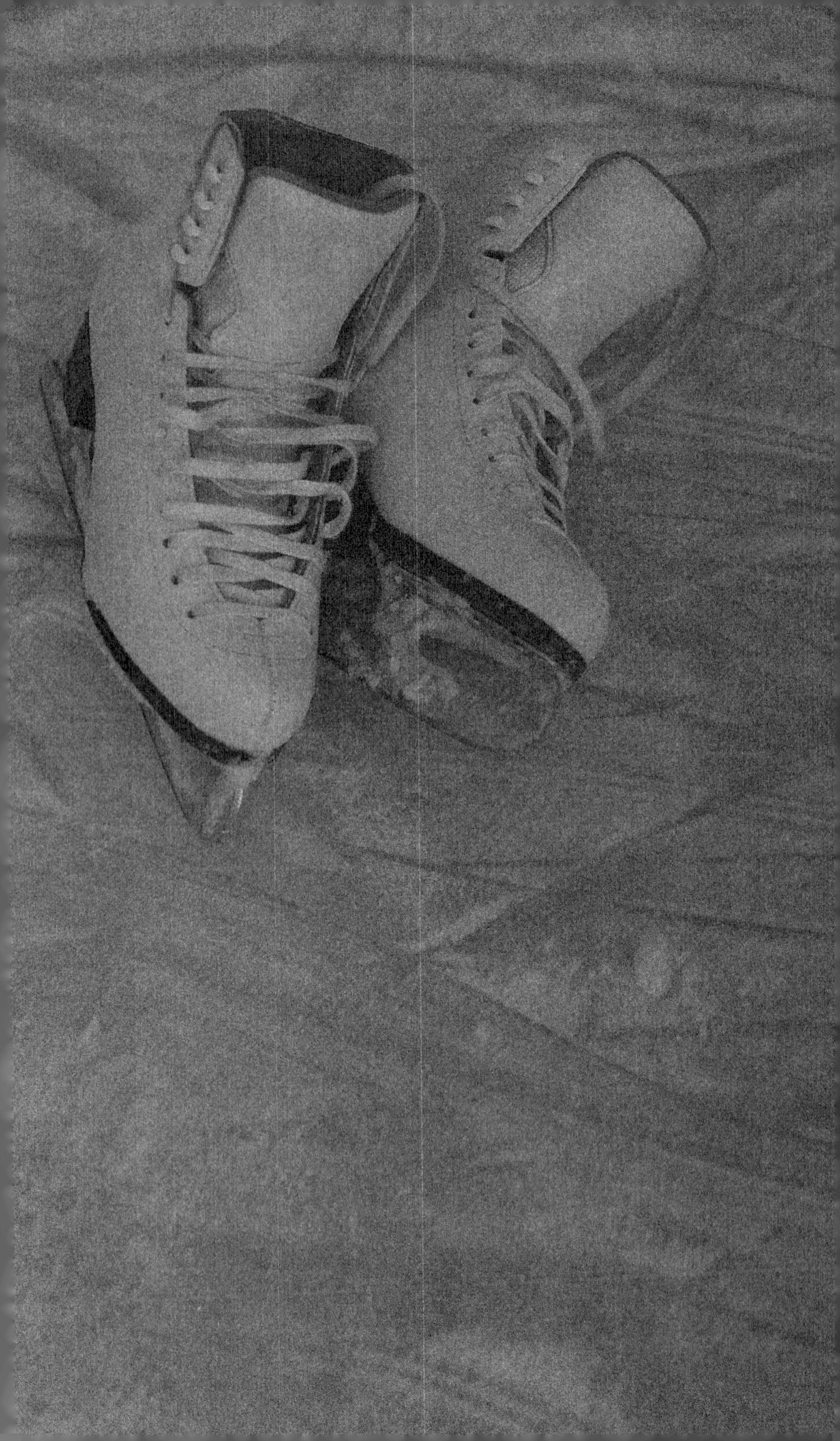

# Laiken
## CHAPTER TEN

I CAN'T DO IT. IT SOUNDS SHITTY OF ME, AND prissy, and probably even like diva behavior, but I can't fucking do it. It's just too uncomfortable. It puts me in a mood for the rest of the day as my body aches.

I. Just. Can't. Do. It.

"Cam, I love you," I tell him. "But no. I can't. If there were an award for the most uncomfortable couch in existence, it would be yours. I've slept on it for two nights and it's already fucking with my back."

He groans. "Oh, come on. How much better can those motel beds be?"

I stare blankly back at him. "The *floor* would be better than that couch."

Smirking, he shrugs. "Okay, so you'll sleep on my floor then. Glad that's settled."

No.

It's not happening.

Don't get me wrong, I love my brother, and I've really appreciated how much he's helped me lately. He's constantly looking out for me, the same way he always has, and staying with him has made me feel safer. But I can't anymore. I'll always love him. I'm genetically predisposed to love him. But

## Chapter 10

if I don't start staying somewhere else, I'm not going to like him anymore.

"I'll get a different motel room," I promise. "I won't go back to the same place I was staying."

Mali snorts beside me. "You think that's going to stop them from finding you? Hayes tried switching where he was sleeping and had a dead animal hung on his door like a redneck Christmas wreath."

Hayes narrows his eyes at her as he tries not to smile. "Your guardian angel must drink."

"Good," she replies. "I wouldn't want her, otherwise."

"Uh, H?" Cam says, lightly smacking his arm repeatedly.

"What?" he asks, confused, but as he looks behind me, his eyes widen. "Fuck."

Mali turns around to see what they're talking about, but I'm too focused on the way Hayes looks like he's mid panic. He finally lets his eyes land on me.

"You should hide," he tells me.

My brows furrow. "Hide?"

Cam huffs out a laugh. "Too late now."

The door opens behind me, and Hayes plasters a smile across his face. "Dev, you're early! I thought you weren't coming until next week."

*Oh, shit.*

"I had nothing better to do so I figured I'd move my trip up," she tells him. "Besides, I missed Mom."

"Just Mom?" he teases.

I can picture the way she's probably rolling her eyes right now. "Shut up. You know I missed you, too."

Staying completely still, I watch Hayes walk around the bar. "It's a gorgeous day outside. Let's go catch up outside."

"Hayes, it's literally raining."

Mali snorts, but I really wish she wouldn't drag more attention in my direction.

## Chapter 10

"What do you have to drink in this place?" his sister asks. "I'm so thirsty."

Hayes sighs. "You know, funny thing. Our drinks aren't actually all that great. Go figure. Let's go get something somewhere else."

Okay, how he went so long without Cam knowing that Hayes and I were secretly hooking up is a mystery to me, because he is the shittiest liar. Maybe he should take Cam's couch. They'd go well together.

"Why are you being so weird?" Dev questions skeptically.

I watch my brother give her a small smile before he cringes, and I know she's seen me. I can feel her eyes burning into the back of my head. And well, I may as well turn around so I can defend myself when she inevitably attacks me.

Slowly spinning around, I find his sister glaring back at me. "Hi, Dev."

She gives me the dirtiest look I think I've ever seen her give anyone. "Don't *hi* me. What the fuck are you doing here?"

"I came when Hayes got into the motorcycle accident," I say, but I stop when her eyes widen drastically, and she turns to her brother.

"You were in a motorcycle accident, and you didn't tell me?" she screeches. "You fucking told *her* but you didn't tell *me*?"

Hayes tries to shush her. "Please remember we're open and there are customers in here."

"It's noon."

"Which means they're still nursing killer hangovers," he points out. "And your screeching is not the best thing for that."

She rolls her eyes. "I can't fucking believe this. Does Mom know she's back?"

## Chapter 10

"Yes," he answers simply, and a part of me wonders if she told him I came there, or if he told her that I was back. "And she's supportive of whatever I choose to do about it."

Devin scoffs. "You can't possibly be thinking of getting back with her. After the way she fucking broke you like that? Are you kidding me?"

There may not be many people here, but the ones that are, are now paying attention to her. She's getting an audience, and I don't think Hayes wants our dirty laundry to be the latest drunken gossip. I know I don't.

I look to Cam for help and thankfully, he comes to my aid. "H, maybe you guys should take this upstairs."

Devin crosses her arms over her chest. "I'm only going if she does. I have some things I want to say to her."

Sighing, I stand up. "Lead the way then."

As Devin heads toward the stairs, Mali goes to come with us but I instantly stop her. "No. You already don't like her, and I'm sure what's about to come out of her mouth is going to piss you off. You stay here."

She doesn't look happy about it, but she huffs and stays in place. Hayes sighs heavily and runs his fingers through his hair as we start to follow Devin.

"What are the chances she's going to slaughter me and use my blood to paint her room?" I ask him.

He shakes his head. "She hates the color, so I'd say slim. But I wouldn't get too close. She bites."

"Fantastic."

I climb the stairs behind Hayes and notice the way he keeps himself positioned between Devin and me. I may have been kidding when I asked if she was going to slaughter me, but there's at least a part of him that's clearly afraid she'll take a swing.

"Leave, Hayes," she tells him. "This is between us."

He shakes his head. "Yeah, no. I'm good here."

## Chapter 10

She glares at him, but he isn't going to budge. "Don't worry, I won't hurt your little girlfriend."

"Technically, she's still my wife," he says, tilting his head from side to side, but Devin isn't amused.

"Some fucking wife, leaving you like that," she sneers, looking me up and down like I'm the shit on the bottom of her favorite shoes.

I take a deep breath. "Dev…"

"It's Devin," she corrects me. "Only people I care about get to call me Dev."

*Fucking hell.* "Devin," I enunciate. "I'm really sorry for how I left. It was wrong of me, and I hurt a lot of people, your brother included."

"Lai—" Hayes tries to interrupt but I stop him.

"No, it's fine." I turn back to Devin. "Seeing him like that was probably hell for you. I know it would be for me. And I'm truly sorry for that. I never meant to cause anyone pain. That was never my intention."

She huffs, cocking a single brow at me. "You *should* be sorry. You know, when you two first got together, I threatened to punch him if he hurt you. It never even occurred to me that it would be *you* hurting *him*."

I swallow down the lump that forms from her words, because she's right. Everyone was so worried about whether or not he would hurt me. Not a single person thought it would be the other way around. Granted, we were both left in pieces, but she doesn't know that, and she's not going to.

Devin has always been the type who would involve herself, and it looks like my leaving has only made her more protective of her brother. We can't have her anywhere near this shit. She could very well end up getting herself hurt. While she might hate my guts, I'd still never let any harm come to her.

## Chapter 10

"I know," I say softly. "And you have every right to hate me."

"That's good, because I do," she throws back. "You don't deserve my brother."

Now *that* hits me right in the chest because I agree with her. It's like having my worst fear spoken into existence and validated. And no matter how much I try to keep the tears down, they come anyway.

"You're right." My shoulders sag. "I don't. But that doesn't mean I don't love him with every goddamn thing I have anyway. I don't expect you to believe that, but it's true. He's it for me."

She hums. "If only you didn't have to go see what else is out there before you figured that out."

"That's not at all what I was doing, but I don't expect you to believe that either." I turn to Hayes. "I'm going to head out. Go find a new motel to stay at."

He sighs. "You don't have to."

"I do," I tell him. "I don't want to ruin your visit. And that fucking couch at my brother's is going to be the death of me." Looking back at Devin, I feel sad. I miss the time where we were friends. "Enjoy spending time with your brother."

As I turn around to leave, her voice calls out once more. "You know, if you're not going to stick around this time, you can go."

I look back at her. "I'll be around until the day he tells me to leave."

With that, I head downstairs—keeping my composure long enough grab my things and tell Cam and Mali that I'm going to go find a new motel to stay at so I can actually get some work done. Lord knows that doesn't happen here.

How can I write songs about a guy when I can't stop looking at him?

I assure them I'm fine and head out the door, but the

## Chapter 10

minute I'm around the corner and out of view, the dam breaks and a rush of emotion flows out of me. Everything Devin said was everything I deserved to hear. There wasn't a single word that I didn't agree with, except the part where she thinks I was out there looking for something better.

I wouldn't even bother with that. It would be a pointless search. I've known since I was fifteen years old that there's no better person for me than him. That's never going to change.

But I ruined it.

And if he and I can't be saved, that's something I'll have to live with for the rest of my life.

*The one that got away was because of me.*

**IT'S ONLY A MATTER** of time before the next text comes in. I manage to find a nice motel only a mile away from Cam's apartment. That way, if I need him for some reason, he's close by. It will help me feel better, and hopefully, it'll help him accept the fact that I'm not sleeping on that stack of hay he calls a couch.

I'm putting away my things, trying to make the place feel as much like home as I can, when my phone vibrates on the bed. The unknown number that stares back at me is hardly a shock anymore.

## Chapter 10

> How is it, feeling so unwelcome in your own hometown? You're probably wishing you listened to me and stayed gone right about now.

I roll my eyes and swipe out of the message, just like Cam and Hayes told me to. I don't think it'll work, icing them out like this. If anything, I think it'll just make them desperate. But they're going through exactly what I did after I left. Eventually, they're bound to come to the same conclusion.

There's no escaping this.

Instead of engaging, or letting it get to me and spending the rest of the day worrying, I crash onto my bed and call Nolan. We've exchanged a few texts since I've been here, just so she knows I'm still alive after I booked it out of the house in a moment's notice, but it'll be nice to hear her voice.

It only rings twice before she answers.

"Oh my God," she says, sounding shocked. "Is it true? Is she really remembering I exist while she's off God knows where doing God knows what? Or maybe even God knows *who*."

I chuckle, shaking my head. "You're ridiculous. I miss you."

"I miss you, too. When are you coming home?"

The question makes me laugh because I'm not lying when I tell her that I don't know, because I really don't. I *can't* leave. I tried, remember? It didn't go very well, and the idea of being knocked out behind the wheel for the second time isn't appealing enough to try again.

"I'm not sure, babe," I tell her. "Thankfully, the studio is letting me work over video chat, so at least I'll still get paid. What have you been up to?"

"Oh, you know. Hard, adult life things."

"You've spent the last few days by the pool, haven't you?"

## Chapter 10

"No," she says, then pauses. "Well, not *our* pool at least. I was by the pool at the spa though. They have this new masseuse who looks like he just stepped straight off a runway. Laiken, I *died* when I first saw him."

I gasp in mock outrage. "You're cheating on Pierre?"

She goes quiet for a moment, and I know something went wrong.

"Oh no, what happened?"

Her heavy sigh is enough to tell me I'm right. "We may have hooked up, and my dad may have fired him after he found out."

"Nolan!" I laugh. "When the hell did you hook up with him?"

She hums. "Like once or twice over the last couple months."

Damn, I'm a little impressed that I had no idea. "So, every day for the last three months then."

Her cackle echoes in the background before she brings the phone back to her ear. "You know me so damn well. Seriously, come home. I miss my roomie."

"I know, I know. I'm trying," I tell her, but that's a lie, because if it's up to me, I don't think I'm ever going to leave here again. "I actually need you to do me a favor."

"Anything," she doesn't hesitate. "You know I've got you."

I smile, even though she can't see me. "I need you to mail me some of my clothes."

"New clothes or the ones you already own?" She asks excitedly.

"The ones I already own." Nolan groans when I give her the answer she didn't want. "Stop trying to spend money on me."

"I can't help it. Spending money is my favorite hobby."

## Chapter 10

My eyes roll. "You know, most people spend money *on* a hobby, but it isn't the actual hobby itself."

She huffs indignantly. "Well, most people aren't as fabulous as I am."

*How do I always end up with the friends who are confident to a fault?*

We talk for a little over a half hour before she has to go. Apparently she has her second massage of the day scheduled with this new masseuse she's crushing on. The girl bounces from guy to guy like she's at a goddamn trampoline park. But she promises me she'll get me some of my things within the next couple days, and at least I know that she will pick me out some cute outfits. I don't have to worry there will be all sweatpants and turtlenecks in the box. Maybe she'll even make me look good enough for Hayes to want me back.

Lord knows after we fucked the other night, even with it being as angry as it was, the craving to do it again has been getting stronger with each minute I spend around him.

I need to feel him again.

# Hayes
## CHAPTER ELEVEN

Family dinners look a little differently than they used to. For the longest time, it would be the three of us hanging out in the kitchen while Devin and I tried to taste the food before my mom was done with it. Then we would all crowd around the small table and eat. As we grew up, it eventually moved to the living room—you know, once we were at an age where we could be trusted not to make a mess.

Now it's Devin and me on either side of Mom's bed, laughing at some horrible movie that plays on TV. It doesn't have the same carelessness that it used to. The heaviness of Mom's decision to end her treatments lingers in the air. But we make the most of it, because sitting around and thinking about how she's going to die is only wasting the time we have while she's still here.

"And now she's about to *accidentally* run into him," Devin predicts.

Sure enough, only a few seconds later, the main character does exactly that. My mom and I chuckle. These things are so damn predictable. Always have been. But Mom loves them, so we watch them to make her happy.

"It's cute!" Mom coos.

Devin rolls her eyes. "It's unrealistic and tells women that they need a man to make them feel valued."

## Chapter 11

I lean back in my chair and put my feet up at the end of my mom's bed. "Oh, someone's on her soapbox today."

"Don't even get me started on you," she says, glaring at me. "You've got zero sense of self-preservation if you're letting that chick back into your life."

Huffing out a laugh, I look over at Mom. "Someone saw Laiken at the bar this morning."

"Ah." She nods slowly as the pieces fall into place, and then looks at Devin. "Were you nice?"

My sister fakes a sweet smile. "I was an angel."

"Sure, if you still consider Lucifer an angel," I joke. "You ran her out of there so fast—"

She shrugs. "It's not my fault she's afraid of me."

I snort, and even Mom laughs at that one. "Dev, I've seen you cry over a broken nail. She could kick your ass all while not spilling her glass of wine. Not to mention, she has Mali. And even *I'm* afraid of Mali."

No one can blame me for it. The girl is fucking ruthless. Cam is a glutton for punishment with her, but at the same time, I can see him being the only one who can get her to listen.

"Whatever," Devin scoffs. "Don't come crying to me when she breaks your heart again. Once a bitch, always a bitch."

Pinching the bridge of my nose, I sigh while Mom scolds her—telling her she understands her disapproval, but it's my life to do as I please. And it is, but that doesn't mean I'm not terrified of her being right.

She *could* break my heart again.

And the thought of that has been enough lately to keep me from falling back into old habits with her.

"Mom, are you sure you don't want me to move home? You seem to be losing your mind a bit lately," she says.

It's supposed to be a joke, but we all know she's been itching to move home since Mom got her diagnosis. Devin

## Chapter 11

hates being so far away and having to rely on updates from me. But we also know she's best off there, where I can shelter her and make sure she only sees Mom on her good days, so she doesn't have to witness the bad.

"Absolutely not," Mom tells her. "I did not bust my ass raising you so you could throw it all away for me. You're going to keep going to college."

She huffs. "Hayes didn't go to college."

"And look how he turned out."

My jaw drops. "I'm right here!"

Mom giggles, blowing me a kiss while Devin sticks her tongue out at me.

"Besides," Mom continues. "You have nowhere to live. Sold the house, remember?"

It's a sore subject for Devin. She doesn't remember a lot of the bad memories from that house. Whether she blocked them out or she wasn't home for most of them, I'm not sure. But it wasn't a hardship for me to have it sold.

"Ugh, I know," Dev groans. "How's that going with Marc, anyway?"

Shortly after Mom learned that living alone probably isn't the best while dealing with brain cancer, Marc ran into some trouble. A business partner had been screwing him over by making some questionable deals under the table. Of course, he wasn't about to take the blame for it, so when he started feeling the heat, he pinned it all on Marc.

And he lost *everything*.

Thankfully, he was able to sign the bar over to Cam and me before it all went down, but his life was drastically changed. His house, his business, he had to sell it all just to break even. While he may have looked well off, I learned he was actually not the best with his money. He spent a lot just maintaining his lifestyle.

Mom, being the caring and good-hearted woman she is,

## Chapter 11

felt like she owed Marc. After all, he not only paid off the mortgage on her house, but he saved me from what probably would have ended up being a very dark path. So, when she told me to sell the house and give him the money for him to start fresh, I didn't argue.

"Last I heard from him, he's got a small place on the beach in Costa Rica," I answer. "He sounds good. Checks in from time to time."

Mom sighs. "I still hate what happened to him."

"Me too," I say honestly.

No one deserves to have everything ripped out from under them, but especially not someone as kindhearted and hardworking as Marc. He was so genuinely good-hearted. To know someone fucked him over like that infuriates me.

"Well, I'd say I'll live with Hayes," Devin starts. "But apparently, he's selling his place, too."

Ugh. "Devin."

Mom's eyes widen as she turns to me. "You're selling your house?"

My sister *so kindly* answers for me. "Sure is. I drove past it today and saw the for sale sign out front."

Maybe Laiken should have let Mali follow us upstairs. I'm just saying. Being knocked around a little might do Devin some good.

"Hayes Beckett," Mom says warningly. "If you're selling that house to pay for my expenses, I will haunt you for the rest of your days."

I huff out a laugh. "First of all, you're going to haunt me anyway. Who are you kidding? And second, I'm not selling it to pay for anything of yours. I just simply don't need a four-bedroom house. I'm only one person."

She looks at me hopefully. "Unless you want to give things with Laiken another shot."

## Chapter 11

Devin makes a noise of disgust. "Can I just say that I hate that you are Team Laiken?"

"Well, if Hayes wants to be Team Laiken, too, what other teams are there?"

With a dark look, she tosses a tater tot into her mouth. "Mine. Team *You Made Your Bed, Now Lie In It.*"

For the love of fuck.

Tonight should be interesting.

**WHEN CAM MOVED OUT** of his parents' house, we quickly realized we were going to need a new place for the weekly bonfires. My backyard was considered, but being as I wasn't living there and really couldn't hack looking at it, we kept thinking. And then Cam came up with the brilliant idea of building a patio with a firepit right outside the bar.

It took a while to get all the correct permits, and for the town to allow us to have the fires in the first place, but it's been a hit with all of the customers. The only problem was that Friday nights in the summer are one of the busiest at the bar.

Cue traveling bartenders.

You'd be surprised how many experienced bartenders there are that will work for tips alone if you've got a good enough place. I don't have to pay them out of my pocket, and I get a night off. It's a win-win in my book.

## Chapter 11

"You better behave," I tell Devin as we get out of my truck.

She flips her hair over her shoulder. "I *always* behave."

But I'm not fucking around. "I'm serious. These are more Laiken's friends than they are yours, and I'm not going to deal with you making a scene. You don't have to like her. I understand why you don't. But you do have to play nice."

It takes a second, but finally, her shoulders sag. "I just don't want her to hurt you again. I'd never seen you so devastated."

Sighing, I come closer and pull her in for a hug. "I know. And I appreciate you trying to protect me. But this is one decision I need to make on my own."

"Fine," she reluctantly agrees. "But if you take her back, and she fucks you over again, I get to punch her in the face."

I chuckle. "I mean, if that's the way you want to die, that's on you."

She rolls her eyes, and the two of us round the corner. The fire is already raging, and the bar is more crowded than usual—showing us that summer is approaching. Owen and Lucas are already here, but there's no sight of Mali *or* Laiken.

"Nice of you to finally show up," Owen teases.

I flip him off. "I wasn't going to come, but I figured not gracing you with my presence would be cruel."

Lucas salutes me. "We appreciate your sacrifice. Now get me a beer, barkeep."

My eyes narrow on him as I hold back my laugh. "You do realize I can still kick you out of here, right?"

The smile falls right off his face, while Owen laughs at his expense.

I've missed these guys. After Laiken left, there were a few things I couldn't really handle anymore. One of which was going to the rink. Every part of that place reminded me of her, and after I showed up there day after day, hoping she

## Chapter 11

would walk through those doors only to be disappointed, I knew I had to stay away from it. Of course, that meant quitting the team, but that was inevitable. Once the bar opened, I didn't have the time for it anyway.

Cam brings me a beer and jokingly hands Devin a juice box. Although, it backfires when she smirks and sticks the straw into it, only to spray it at him. He shrieks as he jumps back and collides into a customer, spilling his beer.

"Shit," he grumbles. "I'm so sorry, man. Let me get you a new one of those."

Luckily, the guy is understanding enough and nods, following Cam back into the bar and through the crowd. Meanwhile, I look at Devin, unamused.

"What?" she asks obliviously. "He started it."

*I'm surrounded by children.*

**I'M JUST COMING OUT** from helping with an issue they had behind the bar when Lucas's eyes widen. He looks like he's seeing colors for the very first time, and that can only mean one thing.

"Holy shit," Owen drawls. "As I live and breathe, Laiken fucking Blanchard."

*Wrong last name, fucker.* It shouldn't grind on my nerves the way that it does, but as I turn my head to see Laiken coming

## Chapter 11

toward us with Mali right beside her, everything else vanishes from my mind.

She is unmistakably the most gorgeous woman here.

Mali must have curled Laiken's hair and put just a dusting of makeup on her, even though she never needs it. But it's what she's wearing that makes me think I really *should've* skipped tonight.

The jeans she has on sit low on her hips, and the crop-top is one I've seen Mali wear before, but it looks so much better on Laiken. Then there's the thin, gold choker around her neck that I would love to replace with my hand right about now.

How the fuck am I supposed to last the next few hours when she's here looking like *that*?

I watch as she willingly walks into Owen's open arms, grinning from ear to ear. For as long as I have known Owen, I don't think there's ever been a time when I was jealous of him until now.

"Unclench your jaw," Mali murmurs from beside me. "Your jealousy is showing."

Forcing my eyes away from Laiken, I look down at Mal. "You know, before she came back, you were a lot less mean."

She smiles brightly. "False. I've been the best person you know since the day you met me."

"Oh, yeah. You're a real peach."

The back of her hand flies into me as Owen finally releases Laiken and she moves to give Lucas a hug. But as if she knows I've got eyes on her, that one is a lot shorter.

It'd be lying if I said it doesn't suck, watching them all greet her like they weren't absolutely gutted when she left. But in reality, they weren't. That was just me.

"When the hell did you get back?" Lucas asks her.

She looks over at me and looks me up and down before biting her lip, and I hate the way it makes me want to turn to

## Chapter 11

putty in her hands. "When this one decided to play bumper cars with a motorcycle."

My eyes narrow. "Rude of you to insult me when you've given everyone else a hug but me. Am I your victim of the night?"

Taking a few steps closer, she keeps her eyes locked with mine. "Do you want one?"

*Say no.*

*Say no!*

*Fucking say no!*

"I mean, if you're giving them out..."

That's all she needs to hear before she closes the gap between us and wraps her arms around me. And fuck, I'm so screwed. The last time I held her, she was in the middle of a panic attack, and it was a necessary evil. But that's not what this is. Everyone that knows us watches with bated breath as I give in and hold her close.

And then the panic sets in.

Laiken doesn't make a big deal out of it when I let her go quicker than I ever have—even before we started blurring the lines—but the look on her face tells me she noticed. I'm not trying to be an asshole. Really. I'm not. It's just that as much part of me would love to dive right back in with her, I can't.

There's just too much residual pain there.

"Nuh-uh," Lucas whines. "He had his shot. It's my turn."

Jesus Christ. I have a feeling my patience is going to be tested tonight, and not just by the way Laiken looks.

*Chapter 11*

**ALL OF THE OTHER** times we've done this, everything went smoothly. There wasn't a single issue we had to deal with. But just like with everything else lately, the universe has shown that it loves nothing more than to torment me, which is probably why we've had almost every possible problem tonight.

One keg was empty.

One keg didn't taste right.

The cash register shut down.

And my personal favorite, someone puked in the bathroom.

"Riley is getting a two dollar raise," I tell Cam.

He looks over at me and chuckles. "She's cleaning it?"

"Yep."

"That's fine. I would've given her three."

I hum, taking a sip of my beer. "I was prepared to go to five. Did you see it in there? It looks like the bathroom in an illegitimate basement rehab."

Cam smirks. "Been to a lot of those, have you?"

Instead of answering, I flip him off and go back outside. Laiken is on the phone with her back to me, but it's her words that get my attention.

"You're the best," she says. "I've got to go, but I'll text you." There's a short pause and then..."Love you, too. Bye."

## Chapter 11

It feels like all the air gets knocked straight out of my lungs. I can't breathe. Can't even fucking remember how.

"All good?" Mali asks.

She nods. "Nolan is shipping me some of my clothes. As much as I *love* sharing your wardrobe, I need my own things."

"I get it, but just so you know, mi closet es tu closet."

Laiken giggles. "That's not Spanish."

Mali waves it off. "Whatever. You're the one who only packed for a couple days."

"Okay, first of all, I was in a rush and wasn't exactly in the right mindset to pack. You're lucky I remembered to grab underwear."

"You didn't. You were stuck in your motel room after a shower and needed me to bring you some, remember?"

"Shush," Laiken mutters. "We agreed not to ever mention that again."

"I lied," Mali says with the biggest grin.

Laiken sighs. "I'm just glad I'll be able to wear some of my own clothes again. Nolan is a lifesaver."

"Yeah, yeah. Tell me all about someone else stealing you from me. It's fine. I like the pain."

My chest practically caves in on itself. With the way Laiken has been talking to me, the way she's been *looking* at me, I thought there might be a chance for us. But right now, there's only one thing on my mind.

*Who the fuck is Nolan?*

## Chapter 11

**AS THE NIGHT GOES** on, I can feel myself getting more and more irritated. Each time Laiken takes her phone out of her pocket, there's this dire urge to rip it out of her hands and see what it says. It's no secret that I've always been possessive when it comes to her, but this feels like another level.

It's not like the concept of Laiken moving on never occurred to me. The possibility of her being with someone else tormented me constantly. But seeing the way she smiles down at her phone is something else entirely.

It burns.

Literally makes me want to throw myself into the fire just to keep her attention on me and off of him.

*Fucking Nolan.* Sounds like an arrogant prick, if you ask me. He probably wears khakis and dress shoes every day because he thinks it looks *classy*. Let him come around here and I'll show him exactly what I think about him texting my goddamn wife.

As another text comes in and she laughs the same way she used to do with me, I can't handle it anymore. I fly up out of the chair so fast that Cam startles beside me.

"Where are you going?" he asks.

I don't trust my voice enough to respond so I just hold up my empty glass instead, hoping that's enough of an answer for him. The bar is clearing out a bit, with everyone either heading home because it's late, or outside to enjoy the fire, but there's still a few who hang around.

Walking around the bar, I slam my cup onto the counter hard enough for it to break. Glass falls around my fist as I mutter a few choice words.

"Everything okay?"

*Of course she followed me.*

I look up and see Laiken staring back at me. She looks worried, and when she sees the glass, her eyes widen.

## Chapter 11

Coming closer, she tries to help me clean it up, but I stop her.

"I've got it."

I don't need to owe her any fucking favors.

She sighs. "Hayes."

"I said I've got it," I snap, clenching my fist, only to feel a shard of glass cut through my palm. "Motherfucker!"

Releasing it, I shake my hand off and the glass falls back onto the bar top. Blood starts to trickle out of the freshly made cut and down my hand. Before I can tell her no, Laiken is behind the bar, grabbing a towel and pressing it to the wound.

"Clearly, you don't got it," she says tartly.

I watch as she carefully cleans up the rest of the glass and wipes the counter down to make sure she didn't miss any small pieces. When she's done with that, she turns to face me.

"Where's the first aid kit?"

I shake my head. "I'm fine."

But she's not taking that as an answer. She looks around and sees one of the bartenders we hired for the night and asks him instead. He reaches under the counter and pulls it out, handing it to her as she thanks him.

I roll my eyes the moment I see the triumphant grin on her face. Putting the kit on the counter, she takes out some antiseptic spray and a bandage. Once she's got everything she needs, she nods over to the bathroom.

"Go rinse it out," she tells me.

"I told you, I'm fine. I can take care of myself."

Not listening to a word I have to say right now, she gathers the things and grabs my wrist, pulling me along with her. The feeling of her fingers wrapping around me is so much more powerful than it should be. It's enough to make me obey her every fucking word.

## Chapter 11

I stay completely still as she turns on the water and puts my hand under it. A sharp sting shoots through my hand and I hiss instinctively.

"Don't be such a baby," she says softly.

God, I hate this.

I hate how the sound of her voice could rock me to sleep at night. I hate how she has the ability to make me feel so many things at once. And I hate how she has me wrapped around her finger, even after everything she's done.

But most of all, I hate that she's not mine.

Not anymore.

She's moved on. Found her own Prince Charming who probably deserves her a hell of a lot more than I do. But that doesn't mean a part of her won't always belong to me.

A part of her I'm never going to fucking give up.

We move into the back room for her to finish cleaning up my hand. My eyes stay locked on Laiken as she carefully dries my palm, blowing softly on it like the goddamn temptress that she is. I try my best to ignore it, but I can't. And when she finally puts the bandage into place and looks up at me, my restraint slips just a little bit more.

"So, you want to tell me why you're so pissed off all of a sudden?" She asks. "You were fine when I got here. What happened?"

I move my eyes to the floor. "It's nothing. Nothing happened."

"Because *that* sounded convincing."

Son of a bitch. Why does this have to be so hard? So complicated? Why can't we just go back to the times when all that mattered was the two of us? All I want is to go into our little bubble again and escape the world.

But she popped that bubble when she made her midnight escape.

"Lai," I say, finally looking at her.

## Chapter 11

Before I can say anything else, her phone dings again, and my jaw clamps shut. She pulls it out, looking at it for a second, and then slips it back into her pocket with a small smile. And the last part of me that could handle this dies inside.

"You know, the least you could do is not text your boyfriend in front of me," I sneer, taking a step toward her.

Her brows furrow, probably wondering how I figured it out, since she's never mentioned him in front of me. I'm assuming that's for a reason. Either she wanted to see if there was still a chance for us, keeping him on the back burner, or she didn't want to rub her happiness in my face while my life is falling apart.

As her back hits the wall, I smirk. "It's funny. I never took you for a cheater." I graze my fingertips down her arm. "Does he know the last one inside your pussy was me?"

She swallows harshly but doesn't say a fucking word. I take my uninjured hand and cup between her legs, putting pressure exactly where she wants me. A breathy moan leaves her mouth as her head falls back against the wall.

"This is mine," I growl, moving my hand slowly. "I don't care if you're here, or a thousand miles away pretending I don't exist. It's fucking mine."

She reaches up and grips my shirt, pulling me closer as she presses her head against my chest. This is one of the things I miss the most, the way I could always make her come apart so damn easily. Not taking my attention off her, I kick the door and it slams shut.

I move her back and bring my lips to the shell of her ear. "I bet he can't make you feel this way. He doesn't know how to touch you just right, but I do."

She whimpers as I release her, but when I slip beneath her waistband and get my fingers directly on her, she sighs in relief. "Fucking hell."

## Chapter 11

Her eyes meet mine, and her pupils are blown wide. There's a strong urge to kiss her right now, but it's one thing I won't let myself do. Being strong is hard enough, and while she's not the only girl I've ever made out with, she's the only one that ever mattered.

Kissing her will send me free-falling back into her and I can't risk that.

I won't.

Sliding two fingers inside of her, I groan at the way she clenches around me. "You're so fucking wet for me. I've wanted to get back inside you for days now."

She squares her shoulders and stares up at me with determination. "What are you waiting for then?"

I smirk at the way she says exactly what I wanted to hear. Bending down, I suck on the skin over her collarbone while I undo her pants. The moment I push them down, I slide my fingers across her pussy and straighten up. She watches as I suck them into my mouth, moaning at the taste of her.

"You're so filthy," she teases.

Reaching in my back pocket, I pull out a condom I brought just in case. "You love it."

It's a horrible choice of words, and I silently thank God when she doesn't answer. There's no way she could respond that wouldn't have me mentally spiraling, and right now, the only thing I want to focus on is the way she feels as I slide into her.

Laiken kicks off her pants, and I lift one of her legs to give me the right angle. In one swift move, I thrust my cock deep inside of her pussy, groaning as I bottom out. My thumb circles her clit while I fuck into her, and she gets louder because of it.

"Shh," I tell her. "Going to need you to be quiet, Rochester. Can't have everyone hear us back here."

## Chapter 11

"C-can't," she pants, gripping at me to pull me closer, but I'm the one in charge here.

"You can and you will," I growl. "Be a good girl for me and stay quiet. You know how."

Her eyes narrow, knowing exactly what I'm referring to, but as I bend down to suck a hickey into her skin, any resentment she may have had dissipates. She feels so fucking good, wrapped around my cock like this. I needed it. Needed this feeling.

*Needed her.*

"Fuck," I moan. "I want to spend every day buried inside of you like this. You pussy is the only place I belong."

She pants heavily. "Only mine."

Ballsy of her to be possessive when she's the one with the boyfriend, but okay. I'll bite.

"Only yours," I tell her, and it's not a lie.

With two hands on my chest, she eases me back and I slip out of her. She spins us around, putting my back to the wall, and bends over in front of me. I line up at her entrance and she slides herself onto me. I take my hand and slap her ass, loving the way she jolts at the feeling.

"You look so fucking good like that." I watch as my cock disappears inside of her and she rubs her ass against me. "Goddamn."

"Fuck me," she begs. "Hard. I want to feel you every time I move."

I may have to be told twice on a lot of things, but that is sure as hell not one of them. Her hand reaches under her, and she lightly plays with my balls. I grip her hips and start to pound into her. Laiken bites her lip in an effort to stay quiet, but if anyone were to press their ear to the door, they'd hear the unmistakable sound of skin hitting skin.

"Always so good for me. Play with yourself the way I like."

She shakes her head. "Doesn't feel the same."

## Chapter 11

*Good.* Call me fucked up, but I want her to need me. I want her to crave something that only I can give her. Not her boyfriend. Not herself. Just me. Something that'll have her crawling back to me on her knees when she realizes there's no one else who can do it like I can.

"Give me your hands."

She puts her hands behind her back and I hold both her wrists in one hand as I pull her up. She's completely helpless to me like this. My cock rubs against her g-spot as I reach my other hand around to play with her clit.

"Oh my God," she moans.

I smirk. "Nope. Not even he can make you feel this good."

She's already climbing. I can feel it. The way she starts to back against me while also trying to put more pressure on her clit. She's so fucking needy, and I love it. I've always loved the way she's such a fiend for my cock.

"Come for me, Laiken," I tell her. "Let me feel you explode all over me."

I press down a little harder while simultaneously slipping deeper inside of her, and that's all it takes before she's screaming my name. I let go of her wrists to put my hand over her mouth, keeping her quiet while I ride her through it. The feeling of her pussy squeezing my cock like it needs to stay filled by me is unmatched. And once she starts to come down from her high, it's my turn.

With one hand on her waist and the other on her shoulder, I bend her forward until her hands are flat on the floor and her ass is in the air. She looks so fucking good like this, and for a moment, I contemplate taking her ass again. The tight hole felt so good, not to mention being able to fill her with my cum. But I remember how intimate that moment was.

How close we felt.

It's too much for me.

## Chapter 11

The sound of her moans as I drill into her is like music to my ears. You know how people get those sound waves tattooed on them, and most are sweet things like *I love yous* and baby's first words. Well, I want that, but with the sounds she's making right now.

"This pussy is mine, Laiken," I roar. "Fucking mine."

She mumbles out a mix between an agreement and a string of obscenities. Because that's what I do to her. I bring her to the point where formulating a single sentence is impossible. Where she'd rather black out from overstimulation than have me stop.

My finger rubs gently around the part of her wrapped around my cock. "Look at you, stretched around me like this. Always so good for me."

Carefully, I slip my thumb in under my dick while my fingers play with her clit. She's so sensitive that her knees almost give in as I start to build the pressure inside of her back up.

"I can't," she says breathlessly. "It's too much."

A dark chuckle leaves my mouth. "That's funny. I must be hearing things, because it sounded like you just tried to deny me what's mine."

Her head drops forward again as I find just the right spot to bring her back to life. Within seconds, she's already chasing her high again, and this time, I'm chasing mine with her.

"You're close. I can feel it."

She presses her lips together frustratedly and nods.

"Let go," I tell her. "Don't worry. I'm going with you."

Her legs give out as she comes for the second time, doing whatever it takes to please me, and I hold her up as I release everything I have into the condom.

I stay still for a second, my cock pulsing inside of her, but once I'm done, I know I need to get out of here before I say

*Chapter 11*

or do something I regret. Because now that my sexual tension has found some relief, all I can think about is the betrayal I feel every time I look at her.

Sliding my dick out of her, I stand her up and take off the condom, tossing it into the garbage. Then I pull my pants and boxers back up and walk out the door—leaving her there, half naked, fully sated, and looking devastated.

*Just like she left me.*

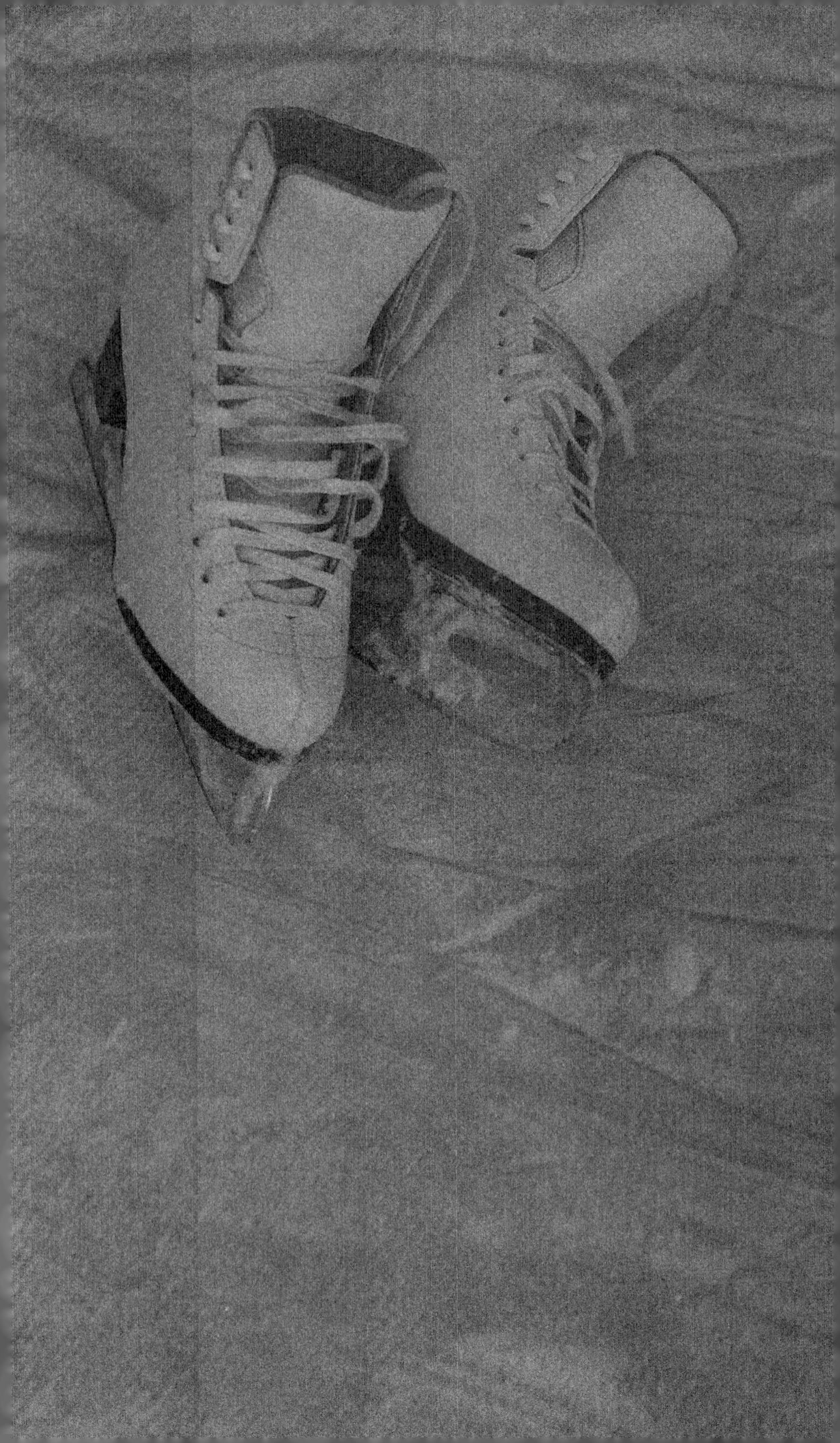

# Laiken
# CHAPTER TWELVE

I SHOULD'VE KNOWN BETTER THAN TO FUCK HIM. Just like I should've known better the first time after I came back. But I couldn't help it. Seeing him so jealous over Nolan, thinking she's something more than my overly sexual roommate with no boundary issues, it took me right back to when he would rip someone apart with their bare hands for looking at me too long. There's just something so hot about a guy being possessive over you.

I need to clarify who Nolan is. I know that. And I fully planned to when I walk into the bar to meet Mali, but the only person I see behind the bar is Riley.

Fucking Riley.

The super cute bartender who has a massive boner for my husband. Mali told me all about her and how she tried to get Mali to be her wingwoman and convince him to ask her out. If Mali didn't already hate her before that, she certainly did after. Apparently, Hayes has shown zero interest, which makes me feel a little better, but that doesn't mean I like her.

Nor do I understand why they had to hire someone who looks like *that*.

*Cam must've woken up and chosen violence that morning.*

"Where is everyone?" I ask.

She doesn't even look at me as she answers. "Upstairs."

*Strange.* I head toward the stairs when Riley stops me.

"Pretty sure you're not allowed up there."

## Chapter 12

My jaw falls open in disbelief. *Did she really just say that?* "My brother owns half of this place, and the one who owns the other half was balls deep in my pussy last night. *Pretty sure* that means I can do whatever the fuck I please."

Her eyes widen in shock, and a little in rage, but I don't give her a chance to answer as I walk away and march up the stairs. When I get up there, I find Devin and Mali looking helpless while Hayes is flipping out. Cam is trying to calm him down, but it's not working.

"What's going on?"

Devin turns to glare at me, but when Mali nudges her, she sighs, handing me an envelope just like the one that was left in my car. I pull it out to find another picture from *that* night. In it, Devin is handing Hayes a bag. I'm in the background, covered in Monty's blood and looking utterly traumatized.

"Flip it over," Dev tells me.

I do, and the handwriting that's scribbled across it is all too familiar.

> *While you're getting your dick wet in storage closets,*
> *I've got my eyes on all the people closest to you.*
> *Still want to ignore me? This is your warning not to.*

Jesus Christ. No wonder he's flipping out. This is obviously a threat against Devin.

## Chapter 12

I run my fingers through my hair. "Where did he find this?"

"He didn't," Mali answers.

"It was on my windshield when I came out of the nursing home from visiting my mom," Devin explains.

"Is everything okay?" Riley asks as she comes up the stairs.

I quickly shove the picture back into the envelope and pass it back to Devin before spinning around. "Shouldn't you be downstairs? I don't think *overstepping boundaries* is in your job description."

Mali snorts while Devin glares at me, but when Hayes flips the desk and sends everything on it crashing to the floor, he has my undivided attention.

"Fuck that!" he roars at Cam. "This motherfucker has crossed too many goddamn lines! My fucking sister? And at my mother's nursing home, no less! Nuh-uh. No. I'm not doing it."

Cam grips at his hair, tugging helplessly. It's obvious he doesn't know what else to do, and when his eyes meet mine, I can't deny the pleading look he gives me.

I have no idea if I still have the ability to do this. It's been too long since I've been his comfort. His safe space. The only one who can calm him down. And if Cam couldn't get through to him, I don't think I'm going to be much help. Not when I'm the reason we're getting these threats in the first place. But I have to try.

"Move," I tell my brother as I walk toward Hayes.

He steps out of the way and goes over to Mali. "Be careful."

My sights don't leave Hayes. "Don't worry. He won't hurt me."

Hayes is furious. His face is an angry shade of red, and the sweat that glistens across his forehead tells me he's been

## Chapter 12

at this for a while. There are papers strewn all over the ground, the mattress is pulled off the bed that sits in the corner, and now the desk is lying on its back.

"H," I say softly. He turns to look at me, his chest rising and falling rapidly. "Talk to me. What's going on?"

"What's going on is I'm going to kill the motherfucker!" he roars. "I'm going to figure out who the fuck is sending us this shit, and I'm going to fucking kill them!"

Fuck. "Okay, I get that. But how about we calm down first so we can try figuring it out without breaking anything else, okay?"

He shakes his head, the adrenaline rush speeding up his movements. "No. I can't calm down. I don't want to anymore! This son of a bitch has taken enough away from me. And now they have the nerve to threaten my sister?"

His fist flies into the wall, and it reminds me of the night things finally exploded between him and me. At least this time, he doesn't hit a nail. He simply pulls his hand out of the drywall and turns back to me with flared nostrils.

"I'm going to become exactly the monster you thought I was," he growls. "I'll rip their fucking head off and dump their body in the same place I—"

*Shit, Riley!* In a move out of sheer panic, I lunge at him—shutting him up by pressing my lips to his. His hands grip my waist as I pull him against me by the back of his neck. Riley makes a noise of disgust while Mali huffs out a laugh, but all I can focus on is the way it feels to have his mouth on mine again.

He whimpers into the kiss, tightening his hold on me and bringing me impossibly closer. Since the day I came back, I never got that coming home feeling. But right now, standing here and kissing him like this, it's so goddamn strong.

It's like remembering how to breathe or settling into a warm bed after the worst day of your life.

## Chapter 12

*It's everything.*

Knowing we have an audience, I break the kiss and he rests his forehead against my own as he catches his breath. I stare up at him but his eyes are still closed.

"Better?"

He nods, finally releasing me and stepping back as he starts to calm down. I look over to find Mali and Devin staring at me, both completely shocked. Riley isn't in the room anymore, probably back downstairs where she belongs. And Cam? Even he doesn't have a complaint.

"Well…thanks for doing *that* so I didn't have to," he tells me.

I chuckle, letting my eyes fall closed as I shake my head. But when I open them, it's time to get serious. I walk over to Devin and put my hands on her shoulders.

"I know you hate me, and that's fine. I understand that. Your feelings are valid." I tell her. "But you have to trust me when I say that you need to get out of here. Go back to college and take some summer courses. Travel the world. Do whatever you want, but you need to get the hell away from Calder Bay, at least until we figure out who is behind all of this."

She shakes her head. "I can't. I don't want to."

"I know, but you have to." I glance over at Hayes, seeing him stare out the window. "I will not be responsible for taking away another person he cares about, and I'll never forgive myself if something happens to you. As soon as it's safe, we'll tell you, but you have to go. It's the only way you're going to be safe."

Somehow, I manage to get through to her, and she sighs. I pull her in and to my surprise, she actually hugs me back. When I let go, she goes over to Hayes and hugs him goodbye. But before she leaves, her eyes meet mine.

"Keep him safe," she says. "Even from you."

## Chapter 12

I nod. "I'll do everything I can."

She goes down the stairs and I walk over to the window, standing beside Hayes. We both watch as she rounds the corner and gets in her car. She waves to us and smiles sadly just before she drives away.

Once she's gone, I sigh in relief. It's hard enough worrying about all of us, but Devin is like the little sister I never had. We weren't always super close, but when Hayes and I broke up and we were both worried about him, she was a godsend. Which is why she needs to be far away from the dangers that we're dealing with here.

I sit on the floor and curl into a ball, resting my head on my knees. "We really need to figure this shit out."

"You're telling me," Cam says.

Looking back at Hayes, he's already got his eyes on me while he plays with his bottom lip. "And *you* need to be more careful about what you say."

His brows furrow, showing us he has no idea what he did. Thankfully, Mali tells him so I don't have to. Those words are still hard for me.

"You almost said what happened with *you know who* in front of Riley."

His eyes widen in shock. "Seriously?" We all nod. "Fuck."

"Don't worry," Mali chuckles. "Laiken did a pretty good job at shutting you up."

He laughs, but we both know how awkward this is.

Last night, he did exactly what I was afraid of when we first got together. He got in, got off, and got out. I stood there, completely mortified as he walked out the door without a word before I could even get my clothes back on. And he didn't just leave the room.

He left the whole fucking bar.

By the time I cleaned myself up and went back outside, he was gone. His truck was no longer in the parking lot, and

## Chapter 12

Devin wasn't anywhere to be found either. Lucas finally filled me in when he saw me looking around like a lost fucking puppy.

I was going to tell him that he's wrong about Nolan. Correct the ridiculous false narrative about me having a boyfriend that's running through his mind. I'm sure that's what this is about. He thinks I moved on. Little does he know, there is no moving on for me.

That's something I accepted a long time ago.

Long before he even kissed me for the sole purpose of getting my ex to leave me alone.

"Can you give us a minute?" I ask Cam and Mali.

Mali nods, immediately heading for the stairs, while Cam looks skeptical.

"I guess," he says hesitantly. "But I swear to God, if I start hearing moans up here, I will deafen myself with cocktail picks."

Grabbing his hand, Mali pulls him toward the stairs. "Stop being such a drama queen and let's go."

I wait for them to go back downstairs before I look back at Hayes. "Come sit."

He shakes his head. "It's fine. We don't need to do this."

I roll my eyes and stand up as he rambles.

"I'm serious, Lai," he continues. "It's fine. You left. We were done. I get it. You don't need to explain yourself or any of that."

Taking my phone out, I scroll through my pictures, and his brows furrow as he watches me.

"What are you doing? I don't need to see some happy photo of you two. It's fine. You moved on. That's your right. I don't think it'll ever happen for me, but that's not your problem to deal with. It's mine. Can we just—"

He stops the moment I spin my phone around, showing him a picture of Nolan.

## Chapter 12

"Uh, are you trying to hook me up with someone, because that's a little weird."

I roll my eyes. "No. *This* is Nolan. *She* is my roommate."

Realization settles across his face, and I grin smugly as I watch him realize how wrong he was.

"She's hot," he jokes, trying to distract me from where I'm going.

I shake my head in amusement. "You were jealous."

He scoffs. "I was not."

"You were. You really, really were." I put my phone back in my pocket and shoot him another smug grin. "You were all *he can't touch you like I can.* Hate to break it to you, babe, but you were green from head to toe. It was like fucking the Incredible Hulk."

A growl rumbles in the back of his throat before he gives in.

"Fine. I'm jealous," he confesses. "I'm jealous of all the fucking people who got to see you every goddamn minute that I didn't. And to see you texting someone else, even if it wasn't your boyfriend, sucks because I still don't even have your phone number anymore."

Honestly, that didn't even occur to me. A group text was sent to us, which means he could've gotten it off that. But it would be just like Hayes for him to wait until he got it from me.

Not our stalker.

Not my brother.

*Me.*

So, I pull my phone back out and dial the number I've had memorized before I bring it to my ear. The ringing comes from Hayes's pocket, and I can't tell if he's amused or fed up with my shit.

"Are you going to answer that?" I tease.

He rolls his eyes, reaching into his pocket. When he

## Chapter 12

finally takes it out, he presses to answer the call. He puts the phone to his ear but says nothing as he stares back at me.

"Now you have my number," I tell him sweetly.

There's a hint of a smile on his face, but as if my mind is playing tricks on me, it disappears with a blink and is replaced by the same emotionless look I got from him last night.

"Only until you change it again."

He hangs up and walks around me, heading downstairs. And all I can do is hope that one day I'll get him to believe me when I say I'm not going anywhere. If he wants me, I'm here to stay.

It's as simple as that.

**ONE OF THE HARDEST** things I have ever had to do is talk sense into my brother. You'd think, at twenty-three, he would know that he's not the world's greatest detective. Mali and I have spent years becoming mini FBI agents, background checking almost every guy who ever looked in her direction. If we couldn't find out who this is, Cam doesn't stand a chance.

Thankfully, Hayes ended up agreeing with me and suggested he and Cam go find the hacker they used years ago, when they needed to get the sex tape Monty illegally filmed of us deleted. Cam agreed, and they both decided they'll go tomorrow morning.

## Chapter 12

I was hoping to get another chance to talk to Hayes alone. There's still so much left to say, and it feels like there's never any time to say it. But before I could, my mom called and told me that a package came for me, and I need to come pick it up *right now*. Not that I understand why—it's just clothes.

Maybe my dad is mad that I had something sent there. He's been so hot and cold lately, just like Hayes has been. One minute I think everything is okay, and the next, they both hate my guts. They say girls are most likely to marry someone just like their fathers, but I never thought it was true until now.

*Lord help me.*

As I pull up to my parents' house, I see Nolan's car parked out front. I can't help but laugh when I notice the massive box on the porch. The one big enough to hold a person. Jesus, she really is one for the theatrics. Just mailing me some outfits would have been perfectly fine.

Now, I have to worry about someone else getting caught up in all of this.

Getting out of my car, I walk up the walkway to see my mom smiling at me from the door.

"Hey. Your package is here," she says, and a giggle comes from inside of the box.

"Thanks," I deadpan. "I wonder what could possibly be inside."

As I shake the box a little, making it seem like I'm going to open it, I get a better idea.

"You know what? I think I'll just leave it here for now," I tell my mom. "I've been wearing Mali's clothes anyway, and they look cuter on me."

Nolan gasps and stands up, forcing the box open as she shoots out. "You take that back! I helped you pick most of your wardrobe!"

## Chapter 12

I cross my arms over my chest and smirk at her. "Hi, babes."

She pouts. "You ruined the surprise."

"You'll get over it," I say with a laugh as I come over and hug her, helping her out of the box before she breaks an ankle.

Seriously, who drives three hours in heels that high? Does she know sneakers and flip flops are a thing? Because if not, someone needs to tell her.

"This is a nice surprise," I half lie. "But you didn't need to drive all the way out here. You could've sent them UPS."

She shrugs. "I know, but I missed my best friend."

*Ooh.* Don't let Mali hear her say that. The last thing we need is to give our stalker *another* death to hold over our heads.

"I missed you, too." I glance in the box she was just in and notice my clothes aren't inside. "You *did* still bring my clothes, right?"

"Yes," she drawls. "They're in my car, and I'll give them to you…on one condition."

Oh God. I hate her conditions. They're always things she knows I wouldn't do normally so she needs to blackmail me into them. The last time she did this, I ended up being forced to go to a massage place that apparently rubs more than what they're supposed to, if you know what I mean.

She walked into the back, and I walked out the door to wait in the car.

I will say, though, by the time she was done, she looked very…happy. But I didn't even consider trying. I may not have much experience, but I don't doubt Hayes when he says no one else can make me feel the way he does.

It's him or nothing for me.

"What is it?" I groan.

A devious grin appears on her face. "We go out drinking."

## Chapter 12

*Okay, it could be worse.*

My first thought is to just take her to Hayes and Cam's bar, but then I quickly realize we're not allowed to drink there. Plus, if I can manage it, I'd like to keep Nolan as far away from the two of them as possible. For Mali's sake. They met when Mali came to visit me, and the last thing I want is for them to find out there was never a time where she didn't know where I was.

And well, going anywhere else isn't exactly staying safe like Cam told me to.

"How about we just go back to where I'm staying and drink there?" I suggest.

She shakes her head. "Absolutely not. I want to see where you grew up. Tell me about the place. Show me the nightlife."

"It's really not all that special…"

"Laiken," she whines. "I don't care if it's not the high-class places I'm used to. I want to see it."

I'm not sure if she just called me poor, or insinuated that I live in a dump, but I don't really think there's a good way to take that. But that's Nolan. She's like Mali in the sense that she doesn't have a filter. Except, Mali chooses not to have one, and Nolan just doesn't think before she speaks.

Or maybe she doesn't think at all.

It's a toss-up, honestly.

"I don't know, love," I tell her. "I'd really just like to sit around and drink at home so we can catch up."

But she's not taking no for an answer, looping her arm around mine and pulling me toward her car. "Nope. We'll find a quiet spot at the bar we choose. Trust. But we're going out. You *need* a night out. I can see the stress all over your face. You're developing wrinkles."

*And there she goes again.*

## Chapter 12

Seriously, if you want to stay humbled, spend some time around Nolan. Five minutes. That's all you need.

**THIS NEW/OLD LIFE** of mine needs some new rules to live by. You know, since I broke all the ones that were given to me before. And right at the top, underlined in red, should be rule number one.

*All of Nolan's Ideas are BAD!*

I tried to play it safe. I swear to God, I did. I stuck to drinks I knew had little alcohol in them, and when Nolan wasn't with me when I went up to the bar, I'd order a coke and tell her there was Jack Daniels in it. But the moment she got the lead singer of the band they had playing to buy us shots, I knew I was fucked.

See, Nolan has never had to worry about anything in life. Her dad pays for everything, down to her speeding tickets. He calls it *spoiling his princess*, but it's more like setting her up to fail in life. I think he expects her to find a rich man and marry him so he can take over her care and maintenance. But if he spent more than five minutes around his daughter, he would realize that's never going to happen.

Nolan is allergic to commitment.

I'm not kidding—she literally broke into hives once when a guy asked her to be exclusive. He was mortified by her reaction, but she cared more about the way her face looked the day before she was leaving for Bora Bora.

*Chapter 12*

So, as she keeps handing me shots and I start to feel the way the alcohol numbs out the pain of being around Hayes again, she throws them back to have fun, but I'm doing it to escape.

**THE BAR IS CLOSING** when they finally kick us out. I stumble out onto the sidewalk while Nolan follows me out—with her singing puppy dog right behind her. He obviously thinks he's going to get laid. That's what any guy would think after they paid a seven-hundred-dollar tab. But he's about to be sorely disappointed, because I'm not about to let her leave with him.

"Do you guys need a ride home?" he slurs.

I snort. "From you? I may as well lie in the street and let someone run me over. Save the paramedics the trouble of needing to pull my body from the wreckage."

He clearly doesn't like me. "No. From my driver."

Nolan gets excited, thinking he's rich, but as we both look over and see the poster child for hippie stoners behind the wheel of a banged-up van, we both realize the truth. He either maxed out a credit card in there, or he got the club to give him a massive discount for playing there.

"We don't get in the car with strangers," I tell him, walking over to grab Nolan.

His mouth morphs into a frown. "I'm not a stranger. We just spent the last five hours together."

## Chapter 12

"Yeah, still no."

He turns his attention to Nolan. "What about you, sexy? You want to come back to my place? I can show you things you've never seen before."

I take her hand, pulling her away before she can agree to go with him. "Yeah, like the easiest way to get hepatitis. Seriously, it's not going to happen, but enjoy your night."

Nolan lets me drag her behind me as she struggles to keep up. She only turns back for a second to yell *call me* back at him.

"You seriously gave that dude your phone number?"

She scoffs, rolling her eyes. "No. I gave him my dad's."

I chuckle as I take out my phone to get an Uber. "Cleaning up the streets one creep at a time."

She laughs and sits on the bench as we wait for our ride to get here. I'll have to take Nolan to get her car tomorrow, but neither of us are sober enough to drive. Especially not when I look over and see her drinking out of a flask that just came out of nowhere.

"Where the hell did you get that?"

"The bartender," she answers simply. "I bought it off him. He even filled it up for me before we left. You want some?"

I shake my head. "I'm good. Thanks."

She shrugs carelessly. "Suit yourself."

Honestly, I've already had enough to drink. I'm lucky I haven't thrown up yet. Though, after growing up with Cam and hanging around his friends, I've built up a pretty impressive tolerance for liquor. I can even go shot for shot with Hayes without tapping out.

*Ugh, Hayes.*

Everything always leads back to him, no matter how much I try to push him out of my mind. There's no escaping the feelings for him that run through my veins. And the more

## Chapter 12

he ices me out, the more I start to wonder if he'll ever be able to forgive me.

Just like that, my mood falls again.

The Uber pulls up, and I at least have enough sense to verify the car with the app before we get in. Once Nolan and I are safely in the back seat, he pulls away from the curb. I lean my head against the window and watch the town pass me by, feeling the pain of missing him start to come back again.

"You sure you don't want any?" Nolan asks, holding the flask out again.

I purse my lips, thinking about it before finally throwing caution to the wind. "Yeah, fuck it."

**BY THE TIME WE** get dropped off, I can barely see straight. The entire world spins around me as I fall out of the car and onto the grass, staining my jeans. Nolan giggles but makes no move to help me up.

Honestly, I might just sleep here.

But wait, no. The bad man might get me, and Cam said I need to be safe. Which means I have to get inside.

It takes a few minutes but I manage to get up and stumble toward the front steps, climbing them like a toddler that's still learning how to walk.

"Uh, Laiken," Nolan hiccups. "I don't think this is your house."

## Chapter 12

"Of course, it is," I slur. "I just have to find where I put the key so I can go to bed. Aw, I *love* bed. I wish I could just stay in bed all the time."

When I realize the key isn't under the mat, I pout and glare at the door like it'll open simply because I'm mad at it. But that doesn't work.

*Pretty rude.*

I bang my fist on it, at first to punish it for not opening for me, and then to try to get it to open. "Bed? Are you in there?"

Nolan is a mess of giggles and hiccups behind me. "I think we're at the wrong house."

"No," I slur. "The door is just mean and won't open. Open, Mr. Door!"

I light up at the sound of the door unlocking, but then it opens, and an exhausted Hayes stands on the other side of it.

*Why hello, handsome man.*

# Hayes
## CHAPTER THIRTEEN

OUT OF ALL THE THINGS I EXPECTED WHEN I HEARD someone outside, Laiken was *not* one of them. Laiken's eyes are glassy as she looks at me, going cross-eyed when she fails to focus. I just got home from the bar a half hour ago, and I had to keep the window open on the drive home so I didn't fall asleep at the wheel. But now, as I stand here looking at her, I feel wide the fuck awake.

"Laiken," I drawl. "What are you doing here?"

A girl off to the side giggles, and it takes me a minute before I recognize her from the picture she showed me earlier —Nolan, her *roommate*. Yeah, even if Laiken *was* into girls, this one looks a little high maintenance for her.

Laiken looks confused as she tilts her head to the side. "What are *you* doing here?"

"I live here." Jesus. How drunk is she?

Her lips purse, but she does it too much to where she looks more like a duck, then gets sidetracked for a second by the fact that she can see them.

"Laiken," Nolan mumbles. "Where are we?"

"My house!" She beams.

I pinch the bridge of my nose. Seriously, I deal with drunk chicks all night long. Why do I have to deal with them at home now, too?

"Lai, this isn't your house," I tell her softly. "This is my house. You don't live here anymore. Remember?"

## Chapter 13

She tilts her head to the side, and I wait for the moment it clicks into place.

"Oh!" she says, both looking and sounding mortified.

"There it is."

Her hands cover her face as she freaks out. "Oh my God, I'm sorry. I...I just..." She looks at me and I can see the sadness all over her face. "I just came home."

*Home.*

Fuck. She really knows how to say things that stab me right in the heart, doesn't she? All I wanted for months was for her to come home. And now she did, but it might be too late.

The damage is done, and I don't know if it can be repaired.

"Laiken," I breathe.

She shakes her head. "No, it's fine. I'll just get another Uber."

But when she takes out her phone, she starts to sway, and it falls out of her hand.

"Okay, you really need to do something about the spinning porch, because I don't remember it doing that."

I watch as she starts to lose her balance, and I'm right there to catch her. Scooping her up into my arms, I know there's no way I'm letting her get into some stranger's car right now. Not when she can barely remember her own damn name.

Leaving her friend in the doorway, I sigh and carry her up the stairs. Halfway up, I look down to see her quickly shut the one eye she was peeking with.

I chuckle. "I know you're awake."

She hums. "No. I'm sleeping. Very drunk. Very, very drunk."

"Now *that* I believe." As I get to the top, I don't even think before walking into the master bedroom and placing

## Chapter 13

her on the bed we used to share. "Do you want to get undressed?"

She thrashes her head from side to side in an overdramatic no, but then realizes what a bad idea that was and grips the covers like they'll stop the room from spinning. "I mean, unless you *want* me to get undressed."

*Still a horny drunk.* Got it. "You know, surprisingly, I'm not really in the mood for getting thrown up on."

She forces her eyes open and narrows them at me. "I would never throw—" A hiccup forces its way through, but she finishes her sentence anyway. "...up."

"Sure," I joke. "But I think what you need most right now is some sleep."

"Not tired," she tells me, but her eyes droop closed anyway.

I cross my arms over my chest. "Or you know, we could talk about how you got drunk at a bar that *isn't* mine."

"Because you"—she drunkenly flings her hand around to blindly point at me—"don't let me drink at your bar."

"You're not twenty-one yet. I could lose my liquor license."

"Or you just don't want me to have any fun," she argues.

I should leave. Go back downstairs and let her sleep this off. But I'm too interested in her drunken mumblings.

"That's not true," I murmur. "I thought we had a lot of fun last night."

She inhales for a second and holds it before letting it out shakily. "Yeah. That was fun. Until you left me there."

Okay, this wasn't the right thing to bring up. "I did."

"...Left me like I left you."

How the fuck did we go from something light and humorous to this?

There's nothing I hate more than when she brings up when she left. Every time she talks about it, her voice is filled

## Chapter 13

with regret. It's there, laced into each word. And I do believe she regrets it. But that doesn't mean I can trust her not to do it again.

I sigh, sitting on the bed beside her and letting my hand run through her hair to help her fall asleep. I take the time to admire all the little things about her, and how she looks the exact same as I remember, but also, different. She's a little older. A little more beautiful. And a lot more traumatized.

We both are.

Her breathing starts to even out, and for a minute, I think she's asleep, but as I pull my hand away, she lets out a heavy exhale.

"Please don't hate me."

The sound of her voice stabs me right in the chest. I've known that's something she's afraid of, especially after I told her that a part of me *wants* to hate her. But the truth is, no matter how much I want to, I could never hate her. It's not possible for me.

"I don't hate you, baby," I whisper. "I just hate that I wasn't enough."

But she doesn't hear any of that because she's sound asleep.

I carefully stand up and pull the blanket over her, pressing a kiss to her forehead and letting my lips linger there for a second.

When I get back downstairs, I realize I totally forgot about her friend. She's standing by the door, looking uncomfortable and intrigued all at once.

"Shit," I grumble. "You probably need somewhere to sleep, too, don't you?"

She nods and I gesture for her to follow me. I lead her to the guest room, where I planned on sleeping tonight, but it's fine. I've been sleeping on the couch for the last few nights while Devin was here. One more night won't kill me.

## Chapter 13

I push the door open and flick the light on. "Here you go. Laiken is in the room right by the stairs."

"Thanks," she tells me, as her hand drags across the bed. "You know, if you want, you could join me in here."

For the love of God. Either this chick knows absolutely nothing about me, or she is the worst friend on the face of the planet. Honestly, I'd rather not know which one it is.

"I'm all right," I tell her. "You have a good night."

She looks disappointed, but I don't give a fuck. Who the hell ends up at a guy's house that she's never met before, doesn't say more than two words to him, and then tries to get him into bed? I mean, if there was a warning sign for potential STDs, this would be it.

I shut the door behind me and roll my eyes.

*Great roommate you got there, Lai.*

**ALL I WANTED WAS** to come home and go to sleep. That's it. I just wanted a quiet night where I could shut my eyes and ignore all the things that torment me constantly until the morning. But as I lie on the couch, knowing Laiken is asleep in the bed we shared, for the first time since she left, my brain won't shut off long enough for me to drift away.

The whole night, I go back and forth between trying to sleep and giving up on it all together. What I really want to

## Chapter 13

do is go upstairs and get in bed next to Laiken, but I can't. I won't let myself. That's just downright cruel—not to mention giving her false hope, and I've been doing enough of that lately.

So, I don't.

The darkness turns to light as the sun rises in the distance, and I know there's no point in falling asleep now. I may as well go over to Cam's so we can get an early start. But I don't want Laiken to think I ran off because she was here.

I go into the kitchen, grabbing a pen and ripping a piece of paper off the notepad. I could take a page out of her book and write it on the back of a sacred memory, but I decide against it. Surprisingly, a small piece of paper works just fine.

*Who knew?*

Bringing the note upstairs, I quietly go into the room and leave it on her nightstand. She's lying on her side, holding my pillow like she needs something to cuddle with. I can't look at her in this bed without thinking of all the nights we spent in it—loving each other in the best way we know how. When she would fall asleep just because she was too worn out from sex not to.

But this is the same bed she slipped out of while I slept beside her.

The same bed she left me in as she walked out the door.

With that memory fresh in my mind, I force myself to look away and leave the room. It's better this way, for the both of us. *Safer.*

**I FULLY EXPECTED CAM** to be at the gym. He usually is every morning by five. So, imagine my surprise when I got there and realized his Jeep wasn't in the parking lot. Instead, I found it at his place. And when I used my key to get in, he was still sound asleep in his bed…

## Chapter 13

With Mali right beside him.

My eyes roll. Watching the two of them is like watching a carousel that just won't stop. It's not constant, but every now and then, they end up sleeping together. And the next day, neither of them act like anything happened at all.

I can't tell you how many times I've caught them like this, and it doesn't get any less tiresome to watch. They make me dizzier than Laiken was last night.

Going into the kitchen, I open the cabinet under the sink and find just what I'm looking for. I walk back to Cam's bedroom, careful not to make any noise at all. Then, I hold the airhorn up and press the button down.

The obnoxious noise pierces the air and they both startle awake, swearing. Cam, being used to my shit, throws a pillow at my head, while Mali groans and flips me off. She gets out of bed, wearing one of Cam's T-shirts and a pair of his boxers, and rips the airhorn out of my hand. Thankfully, I know what to expect with her and I shield myself before she's able to kick me in the balls.

"Again with this?" I ask her as she gets back into bed. "Seriously?"

"Go away!" Cam grumbles, throwing his arm over Mali and trying to pull her back down.

I click my tongue against the roof of my mouth. "Would love nothing more, but we have to go find that hacker, remember?"

He presses his face into the mattress, groaning miserably. It takes him a minute, but he finally rolls out of bed and goes into the bathroom to get ready. I stand in the doorway as I wait, just shaking my head at Mali so she knows that I'm judging her.

"Fuck off, Mr. Sex in Storage Rooms."

I can't help but laugh. "Well played."

She grins proudly. "Hayes, zero. Mali seventy-two."

## Chapter 13

Those don't exactly sound like accurate numbers, but it also wouldn't surprise me if they were.

Cam comes back out, looking a little less like a zombie as he walks over to where Mali's sitting. He bends down and kisses the top of her head, and I don't miss the way her cheeks pink because of it.

With one last eye roll meant for her, I follow Cam out the door. We make our way downstairs, and I'm just about to open my mouth when he stops me.

"No," he says. "I know what you're about to say, and I don't want to hear a word about it."

I open the passenger side of his Jeep and climb in. "That's fine. As long as you don't ask why Laiken is asleep in *my* bed."

For a second, it looks like he wants to change his mind, but he decides against it. "Deal. It's too fucking early for this."

**I REMEMBER BEING AT** this apartment. There's no way I could ever forget the way we stepped inside and closed the door before turning at least thirteen different locks, going all the way down the damn thing. So, as we stand here, looking at the door that's left partially open, I know what's inside *can't* be good.

"Do we go in?" Cam asks.

## Chapter 13

I shrug, not really knowing what other option we have. It's not like we're going to call the police. And he must be thinking the same thing I am because he pushes the door the rest of the way open.

It's a total shitshow.

Things are thrown everywhere. Computer monitors are ripped from the desk and shards of ceramic from broken plates lie all over the place. Whatever happened in here, there was definitely a struggle. Little nerd did not go down without a fight.

If we had any hopes of at least getting into his computer, that dies when we notice it's gone. All of the wires remain, but the actual tower is missing. Whoever was here must have taken it with them.

"H," Cam says, tapping my arm.

"What's up?"

I spin around to see what he's looking at, and that's when I see it. Large letters on the one wall, looking like they were written in blood.

*Hope you don't mind.*
*I needed to borrow this one.*
*But don't worry, you'll see him again soon. ;)*

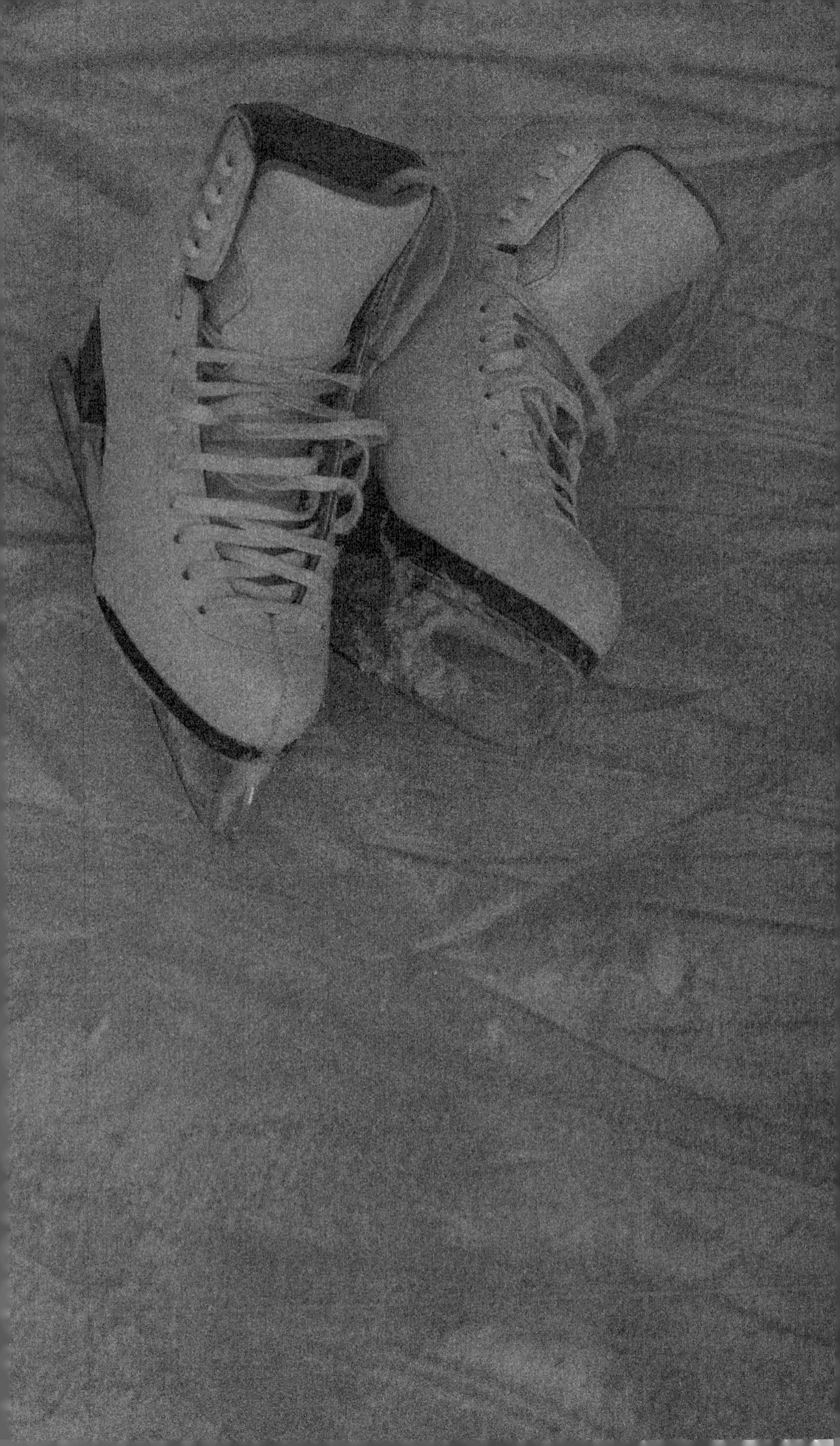

# Laiken
# CHAPTER FOURTEEN

Since the day I left, there have been plenty of moments filled with false hope... Dreams that felt real enough to make me cry when I woke up, because they weren't. But waking up in the house I shared with Hayes has to be the worst. For a good thirty seconds, I actually let myself believe that maybe it really was just a bad dream.

But then reality sets in like it always does.

I sit up, running my hand through my hair and cringing when my fingers get stuck in the knots. It takes a minute for me to remember what happened last night, but once I do, I sit there as it all replays in my mind.

*Oh. My. God.*

What the actual fuck is wrong with me? Sure, it was a drunken mistake, but it was one that should've never been made. Hayes has made it obvious that he's not exactly happy that I'm back. He's clearly struggling with it. And yet, here I am, infiltrating his space like I have some kind of right.

Footsteps come toward the door and my breath hitches, expecting Hayes to come walking in, but I let it out when Nolan knocks and peeks her head in.

"Can I come in?" she asks.

I nod. "Yeah, of course."

She pushes the door open and walks in, climbing onto the bed where I spent all my best nights in. God, being in this room again is the cruelest form of torture. I was hoping the

## Chapter 14

next time I woke up in this bed it would be with Hayes by my side.

But as I look around, the only sign he was ever in here is a small piece of paper on the nightstand beside me.

*Went with Cam to find the hacker.*
*Lock up when you leave, please.*
*H*

That's it. No heart like it used to have. No I love you that I wish I had tattooed onto my skin so I could read it over and over, reminding myself that there was actually a time where he did love me. But I can't be mad.

I didn't even have the decency to sign my name on the three word note I left for him to find.

"Is that from him?" Nolan asks.

Immediately, I start to wonder what she knows about Hayes. "Yeah. He's not here. Just said to lock up before we leave."

She nods but says nothing, and I can feel the way she's staring at me. I look over at her and sure enough, she's watching me expectantly, with chin rested on her hand.

"What?" I feign innocence.

Her eyes roll exasperatedly. "Don't *what* me. Who is he? What is this house? You used to live here?"

My head falls back as I realize I have no choice but to explain it all to her. *Fuck.* I was hoping I wouldn't have to. At least not until I knew what's going on with us. It's hard to explain something you don't have all the answers to. But I guess here goes nothing.

I take a deep breath, knowing my words are going to shock her. "He's my husband."

Just as expected, her jaw hits the floor.

## Chapter 14

I spend the next fifteen minutes explaining the story of Hayes and me to Nolan. From when I started to have a thing for him, to when we finally crossed that line, eventually leading up to us getting married and me leaving only a month later. Of course, I leave out *why* I left. I stay vague, telling her that I had to but not telling her why.

When I'm finally done, it looks like she isn't breathing. Hell, I don't think she's blinked at all since I started. I wave my hand in front of her face, but she barely reacts.

"Did I break you?" I joke.

She shakes herself out of it. "Wait a damn minute. You had a husband who looked like *that* and you *left*?"

Ugh, yep. Just rub it in. It's fine. It's not like I cry myself to sleep every night over it lately.

"Yeah," I answer, rubbing the back of my neck nervously. "I know. He's gorgeous."

"He's sex on fucking legs, that's what he is." Then, her eyes widen. "Oh...shit. I need to tell you something."

Dread washes over me as I see the way she cringes. "What happened?"

"I may have propositioned him last night and asked if he wanted to join me in the guest room," she says shyly.

It starts as a chuckle. A small laugh that just bubbles out a little. But it quickly builds until I fall back onto the bed, cackling loudly.

Don't get me wrong, Nolan is beautiful. Supermodel status if she had the work ethic to be one. But according to Cam, Hayes won't even flirt back with a girl if she tries to hit on him at the bar. There was no way he was ever going to fuck one of my friends while I was sleeping in the other room.

"What the hell did he say?" I ask as I finally start to calm down.

## Chapter 14

She pouts. "He said he was all right and to have a good night."

"Yeah, that sounds like him." Always such a gentleman.

Hayes has a way of letting girls down without them even realizing that they're being rejected until he's long gone. It's an impressive skill set, actually, and probably very useful for when he's working at the bar. There's nothing more awkward than having to turn someone down, but when you look like him, I guess you get used to it.

"Ugh," Nolan huffs. "I can't believe you're married to someone that hot and you just failed to mention it."

I look around the room once more, noticing there's nothing that shows he's been in here at all lately. Even his phone charger isn't on his nightstand. Nor are the empty water bottles I always had to get rid of when they started to pile up. It's just...lifeless.

We shared so many good memories in this room and planned to make so many more.

It was all so perfect, and now it's gone.

**WE HAD TO TAKE** an Uber to my parents' house just to get my car, and then I had to drive the twenty minutes to drop Nolan off at hers. She's following me back to the motel I'm staying at when a call from Cam comes through. I press the button on the screen to answer it through the car.

"Hey, how'd it go?" I ask.

## Chapter 14

He sighs heavily, and I already know it's not good. "We have a problem."

"I *hate* problems."

"Yeah well, the hacker is gone," he says. "Whoever is doing this shit got to him before we could."

My heart sinks. "What do you mean *got to him?*"

"There's no body," he clarifies. "But judging by the condition his place is in, it doesn't look good."

I feel sick to my stomach. Nausea kicks in as bile rises in my throat. The text messages and the threats are one thing, but if this person actually *hurt* someone, that takes this to another level. A level I'm not sure any of us can handle.

"Listen, I want you at the bar today," my brother tells me. "Somewhere I'm able to look after you."

I nod, even though he can't see me. "That's fine. I'll just have to bring a friend with me."

"Yeah, sure. Just get there when you can. I won't be able to relax until you're there."

I get it. I want to be able to look after him, too. *And Hayes.*

"I'll be there soon," I promise.

As we get off the phone, there's a feeling in the air that I can't put my finger on. It's darker than it has been. There's a stronger sense of danger that I can't seem to shake. I just hope whatever is coming, we make it out alive.

**THE WHOLE WAY TO** the bar, I drill into Nolan's head

## Chapter 14

the importance of her not mentioning anything about meeting Mali prior to her coming here. She doesn't understand it at first, but I explain that I didn't leave in the best way, and it wouldn't turn out well if either Hayes or Cam find out that she had any contact with me while I was away.

"Trust me," I tell her. "It's just something we need to keep secret."

She pretends to zip her mouth shut and lock it. "You know I live for a good secret."

We get out of the car and run inside, shielding ourselves from the rain. The beach is empty, which means it's no surprise when the bar is the same way. The only people inside are Hayes, Cam, and Mali. Thankfully, Riley isn't here.

"It's disgusting out there," I tell them as I try to shake off the damp feeling. "Nolan, this is Cam and Mali, and you already met Hayes."

Mali's eyes narrow. "She did, did she?"

I press my lips together and when she knows she isn't going to get it out of me right now, she turns to Hayes. Holding her hand out, she waits for him to shake it.

"Hi, Kettle. I'm Pot."

I'm honestly clueless as to what that's about, but it makes Hayes laugh as he flips her off—and let's be honest, I don't care what it is he's laughing at, as long as he keeps doing it.

"How do you *know* Nolan exactly?" Cam questions.

Well, shit. "She's my roommate. I've been staying with her almost the whole time I've been gone."

Nolan smiles brightly. "Yep! Saved this little duckling from a tough life on the streets."

Cam hums with a certain look. "Not that willingly leaving your home is something you need *saving* from, but sure. We'll go with it."

I had hoped that he and Hayes would understand why I

## Chapter 14

left, but let's face it—they never will. If they had it their way, I would've told them the moment our stalker first contacted me. They still think they would have been able to figure out who it is and stop them.

Clearly, they're right. I mean they've been *so* good at it lately.

Cue the massive eye roll.

Thankfully, just as things start to get awkward, the door opens and a grungy surfer I've never seen before walks in. He's got a wetsuit peeled halfway down his body and the dampness from his hair tells me that he just got out of the ocean.

"Hey, Finn," Hayes greets him.

"Barkeep!" he says excitedly. "Let me get a Blue Moon, good sir."

Hayes nods and goes to get his beer while Finn turns to my best friend.

"Mali," he swoons. "Looking beautiful as ever."

I watch as he observes the room, realizing how empty it is, until his eyes land on me. He smiles in a way that's not nearly as sexy as I'm sure he thinks it is.

"Hi," he drawls. "I'm Finn, and you are?"

Mali snorts behind him. "Oh, here we go."

"Laiken," I reply.

"Laiken. That's a gorgeous name." He comes up and leans against the table beside me. "But I guess that's fitting for such a gorgeous girl."

*Gag me.* "Better be careful. You're going to get a cavity with all that sweet talk."

"That's okay. I'm a sucker for sugar." He licks his lips, and I damn near vomit on the spot.

Hayes slams Finn's beer down on the counter a little harder than necessary, making it slosh over the sides of the glass. "Here you go."

## Chapter 14

Finn lets his eyes linger on me as he walks backward toward the bar, only turning around when he has to. "Man, you two have it made. Hanging out here with hot girls all day."

Cam scrunches his nose in disgust. "Laiken's my sister."

"Oh, my bad," he says. "Hey. If I play my cards right, I could end up being your brother-in-law someday."

Jesus Christ, I just met the guy, and he's already planning our wedding. My and Mali's eyes widen, and we look at each other. I mouth *help me,* only for her to shake her head in response.

*Bitch.*

Finn grabs his beer and takes a sip, only to swallow it with a bitter look on his face. "Barkeep, you sure this beer is okay? It doesn't taste right."

Hayes presses his lips together and hums. "Huh. Must not have rinsed all the cleaner out of the lines. Sorry about that."

Cam chuckles as he goes to get Finn another beer, and I can't help but smile because we all know that was no accident. Or at least all of us but Finn, who finally just realized Nolan exists.

"I'm sorry, darlin'. You probably feel so left out."

Nolan giggles, putting her hands up in front of her. "No, I'm okay. Really."

He shrugs, taking the new beer and drinking it happily—as if he didn't get shot down three times in a row.

Cam looks at the ingredients listed on the bottle of cleaner, probably making sure they won't be on the defensive side of a lawsuit due to Hayes's possessive tendencies. He points something out to Hayes, but all he does is shrug like it's no big deal. Cam laughs, lightly backhanding him in the stomach before putting the bottle back.

## Chapter 14

"By the way," my brother says to him, "we have to move the pool table upstairs soon, before the summer rush starts."

Of course, Mr. Surferman has something to say about that. "Bruh! I'm so fucking good at pool!"

"I'm sure you are," Mali murmurs.

He shakes his head. "Nah, for real. I could kick anyone's ass at pool! I'm legit."

Mali looks at me and smirks, and I already know where she's going with this. "Why don't you put your money where your mouth is then?"

"Good idea!" He puts his beer down on the counter, and Hayes goes to grab the cleaner again before Cam stops him. "I'll put a hundred dollars on the fact that I can win against anyone in this room."

Yeah, all right. Fuck it. It's been a while since I made someone feel like a little bitch. And this guy seems like he could benefit from being humbled.

"I'll take that bet," I tell him.

His eyes light up. "Easy, pretty. Have you ever even played pool before? I don't want to take advantage."

I purse my lips as I look over at the table. "Once or twice, but don't worry about me. I can afford to lose a hundred bucks."

Hayes chuckles, remembering the time I played against him all too well, and my attention is immediately drawn to him, only to get ripped away again as Finn whistles.

"Oh, baby. You know, I could use a sugar mama."

"Mm-hm. How about we just play pool?"

"Or we could make this more interesting," he suggests. "If I win, you have to come on a date with me."

"And if I win?" I ask.

He stretches his arms wide. "You get a date with me."

I stroke my chin, pretending to think about it. "I think I'll just stick with the money."

## Chapter 14

"Suit yourself," he singsongs.

Everyone gathers around the pool table to watch me kick his ass. Finn thinks he's doing me a favor by offering to let me break, but really, he's just signing his death certificate. Before he even has a chance to go, nearly all the balls I have are in the pockets.

Finn's eyes narrow on me. "You little liar."

"I didn't lie," I say sweetly. "I told you not to worry about me."

Scoffing, he shakes his head and takes his turn.

He's not bad, I'll give him that. I'm not saying he's good enough to warrant all of his shit talking, but I've seen worse players. Still, he's got nothing on me.

"Give it all you've got, because it's the only chance you're going to get," I tell him.

Surprisingly enough, he manages to sink a total of three balls, but he misses on the fourth. It's my turn again. I grab the pool stick and take my shot, sinking two at once. I shoot the last one in with ease, leaving me with only the eight ball.

"Oh, that's too bad," he taunts. "My ball is blocking the pocket you want, isn't it?"

I snicker and look at Mali. "What is it about guys and thinking they know everything? I mean, are their dicks that small that they need to overcompensate so much?"

Finn gestures down to his crotch. "Let's go in the bathroom and I'll show you how wrong you are."

An involuntary laugh bubbles out of me, and Cam tries to pry Hayes's hands off the counter. Seriously, leave it to him to be so possessive, even now.

"I think I'll just take your money, instead."

I point at the side pocket to call it. Bending over, I line up my shot and hit the eight ball at just the right angle. It bounces off the side, and then the other, hitting one of his balls before it spins right into the correct pocket.

## Chapter 14

*And that's the game.*

Finn stares at the table in disbelief while Hayes takes a hundred dollar bill out of the register and hands it to me. "Don't worry, man. I'll just add it to your tab."

All of us sit down around the circular high-top table and the guys join us, being as it doesn't look like anyone else will be coming in any time soon. I've got Nolan beside me, with Hayes straight across. Unfortunately, that means Finn is on the other side of me, leaving Mali to sit between Cam and Hayes.

*I wonder if she'd switch.*

"You know," Finn complains. "If I had known you were a pool shark, I wouldn't have let you take the bet."

I shrug, smiling at him. "It's not my fault you underestimated me."

"I did. I really did," he admits, then shakes his head. "It should not be so hot to be destroyed by a woman at pool."

Seriously, does he ever get any *less* cringey? Because right now, it's not looking too good.

Nolan looks at me skeptically. "Is there anything *else* I don't know about you? Because it's been one surprise after another today. First, the fact that you're married, and now this?"

*Shit. Here we go.*

Hayes hums sarcastically, looking across the table at me. "That's funny. I thought you hated keeping us a secret, Rochester."

The tension in the room is so thick, I could wrap it around my throat and choke myself with it. But it lightens slightly when Finn finally puts the pieces together.

"Wait, you two are married?"

Hayes smirks at him, and as he wraps his hand around his beer, I see it. *The L that's inked into his ring finger.* But while mine has faded a bit, his is still so damn clear.

## Chapter 14

He tips his beer at Finn with a cocky expression on his face. "Cheers."

**WHEN EVERYTHING IS GOING** so well, it's always only a matter of time before shit hits the fan. I should be used to that by now. I should *expect* it. But I don't think I imagined it would be this bad.

Nolan tries to get Hayes to make her a drink, showing him her fake ID, but before he actually makes it, her dumbass admits that it's not real. He refuses to serve her, the same way he refuses to serve Mali and me, and Nolan pouts until she realizes something else.

"Oh!" She gasps. "Are you going to be back in time for your twenty-first birthday?"

All eyes zone in on me, waiting for my answer. We were doing so well, not letting anything about me possibly leaving *again* come up in conversation. But leave it to Nolan not to read the fucking room.

"I don't know," I tell her.

She pouts. "Well, if you're still here, I want to come back for it. Remember last year?"

"Nolan," I warn.

She is walking too close to dangerous ground right now, but she's too excited to share the story and doesn't realize I'm trying to steer her away from the conversation.

## Chapter 14

"It was so funny!" she says excitedly. "We used fake IDs to get into a club, and Laiken was dancing on the table like she owned the place. I mean, she was drunk. We've all been there."

"Nolan!" I try again.

But she keeps going. "Everyone was just having a good time and cheering her on, but there was one guy who was a total pig. He tried going up to her and putting money in her waistband. But before he could get his hands on her, Mali punched him so hard across the face. They dragged her out of there kicking and screaming."

*Fuck!*

Both Cam and Hayes look like it was them she punched in the face. The one thing that was holding us all together snaps, and Mali looks like she might actually throw up.

Nolan finally catches onto what she says and tries to backtrack, but it's too late. They know. There's no way we can deny it now. Not when Hayes can see it all over Mali's face.

He gets up from the table, letting his stool crash to the ground as he storms out of the bar. It's only a matter of seconds before Mali jumps up to follow him and I go with her.

"Hayes!" She calls as she gets outside and into the rain. "Hayes, please. Just talk to me. Please!"

He throws his hands in the air and spins around. "Okay! Let's fucking talk, Mali. Let's talk about how you lied that weekend. How you said you couldn't spend your birthday here because it was *too painful* without Laiken."

I'm watching my best friend break in front of me, and there's nothing I can do as she panics.

"I'm sorry," she tells him. "I really am. I'm so fucking sorry."

Hayes scoffs. "You know, I am so fucking sick of all the

## Chapter 14

secrets and lies! Let's just air it all out, shall we? When did you find her?"

"What?"

"When did you find her?" he repeats. "Did she tell you not to tell me after you figured out where she was?"

Mali glances back at me, and that's all it takes for it to click into place for him.

"Of course," he huffs. "You never had to find her, because she was never fucking missing to you. You knew where she was the whole goddamn time."

"Hayes, it's not her fault. I—"

"No!" He stops me. "I don't want to hear anything from you. Not right now. I've heard enough out of you lately."

Mali is crying, her tears mixing with the raindrops that pour from the sky. Hayes looks at her like she's just as responsible for breaking his heart as I am.

"Was any of it real?" he asks. "Were we ever actually friends, or were you just doing your job and babysitting me for *her*?"

"It was," she tries to assure him. "I swear, H. I care about you. You're one of my best friends!"

But he's not convinced.

"Sure, you care about me. Just not enough to say anything while you watched me look for her. While you *helped me* look for her." He pauses to glance at me, and I know I'm also the target of his anger right now. "You two keep so many secrets for each other, but what about the one you're keeping *from* her?"

Mali's breath hitches. "Hayes, please."

"What? Go ahead," he taunts. "Tell her all about how you've been fucking her brother."

My eyes widen in surprise as Hayes walks away. It's not the most far-fetched concept. I mean, I'd have to be a moron not to notice the tension between them—especially before I

## Chapter 14

left. I knew there was *something* going on, but what I don't know is why she didn't tell me.

She throws her head back, turning around to deal with the mess Hayes just left behind. But instead, she's faced with much worse as she looks behind me.

"Cam," she breathes.

His voice comes out completely stoic as he responds. "Riley will be here in twenty minutes. If you leave before that, lock the door."

He goes to leave, trying to walk past her, but she grabs his arm. "No, please. Don't go. I can't lose you, too!"

"Can't *lose* me?" He shouts. "Mali, you fucking lied to me! I trusted you! Sure, I could understand why you wouldn't tell Hayes if Laiken asked you not to. It's fucked up, and I don't agree with it, but I'd probably do the same if the situation were reversed." He pauses, shaking his head. "But that's my fucking sister. You knew how worried I was about her, and the whole time you knew where she was! You knew enough to take away my pain, and you said *nothing*!"

Mali is full on sobbing at this point, and I can't help but cry with her as I feel her pain. "Please don't do this."

Cam pulls himself out of her grasp and shakes his head. "I have to go. I can't even look at you right now."

We both watch as he leaves, and once he's gone, Mali holds her face in her hands as she cries.

"Mal, I'm so sorry," I murmur.

She scoffs, turning around to glare at me. "You're sorry? *Now* you're sorry? I told you this was a fucking bad idea! But you were so goddamn insistent!"

"I know," I cry. "I never wanted this to blow up on you."

"Of course, you didn't," she says, a little softer this time. "But you've been so wrapped up in your own shit that you haven't even noticed I'm dealing with my own. What Hayes said? It's only part of it."

## Chapter 14

"What do you mean?"

She shrugs defeatedly, letting her shoulders fall. "Cam? I'm in love with him. But it's never been the right time for us, and after this, I don't know if it ever will be."

"Oh, Mal."

My heart is breaking for her. I never wanted this. She is my *best* friend. I would throw myself on a blade if it meant protecting her. But I did this. Her entire life is in pieces, and it's my fault.

She looks so devastated as she sighs. "Just take your friend and go...before she does even more damage."

Mali goes back into the bar, not wanting to be around me for the first time in our lives. Even when we were younger and we would argue, we still couldn't stand to be away from each other. We'd sit on opposite sides of the room, with our arms crossed and angry looks on our faces. But we were still *there*. And right now, she doesn't want me.

I close my eyes and tilt my head toward the sky, feeling the rain hit my face, just as my phone vibrates in my pocket. I have nothing left to give. No emotion left in me after the emotional train wreck things have been since I came back. Nothing surprises me anymore, so when I take out my phone and see a text from our stalker waiting for me, all I can do is sigh.

> Secrets never do stay secret for long, and I'm going to love watching yours explode like a ticking time bomb. ;)

# Hayes
## CHAPTER FIFTEEN

Betrayal cuts so damn deep. It goes down to the bone and makes you wonder if you can ever really trust anyone. I was finally starting to figure out if I could ever let my guard down with Laiken again, and then this bomb was dropped right into my lap.

And Mali lit the fucking fuse.

Rage and frustration pump through my veins as everything starts to fall into place. That's why she came over that morning. That's how Laiken knew I was looking for her in the first place. The whole fucking time, I thought she was just as hurt as I was. I thought we bonded over the pain of losing someone close to us. I fucking considered her as close to me as Cam is.

But I was just her pet.

The whole time, she was doing her duty to Laiken—watching me and reporting back like a good little spy. I wasn't allowed to know a goddamn thing about where Laiken was or why she left. But Laiken got to know *everything* while she was gone.

How I was doing.

*What* I was doing.

She got all the updates she wanted, while I got jack shit.

I pull into the nursing home parking lot, knowing this is the one place neither of them would ever follow me. It's the only place where I can even attempt to get my head on

## Chapter 15

straight. And besides, I need to be near the only woman who's never stabbed me in the back.

"There's my favorite boy!" my mom says excitedly when I slip in the room. "I didn't expect to see you until later."

"Figured I'd surprise you." I kiss her forehead and sit on the chair beside her bed. "What's new over in old people town?"

"Old people town," she repeats, chuckling softly. "You better watch your mouth, boy."

"What are you going to do? Sick your nurse on me?" I tease.

"Hey! I'll have you know that Theresa can be brutal when she wants to be."

Snickering, I wink at her. "I think I can hold my own."

She looks so happy as she smiles from ear to ear, but while I'm enjoying spending time with her, my mind always goes right back to everything that just happened. And a mother can tell when something is wrong, so it's no surprise when she gives me a knowing look.

"So, why are you really here?"

My brows furrow. "What? I can't come see my mom just because?"

Her smile softens. "Of course you can. You're always welcome here. But that's not why you came. Something is bothering you."

There was a time when I would've told her everything. I remember going to her house after Laiken went to the gala at Monty's house without me. I was so angry, but she calmed me down and explained that all I was doing was letting him win. She's always been my voice of reason. But since she got sick, I just can't bring myself to unload on her.

"It's nothing," I insist.

"It's *not* nothing," she replies. "I know you, Hayes. I've known you since before you were born. You don't want me to

## Chapter 15

take on your problems when I have enough of my own, but I've been doing that for years. It's part of being a mom. Let me be one while I'm still around to be."

*Oh God.* It feels like just another blow to the chest, but she's right. There's going to be a time where I don't have her for this. Why is that just hitting me now?

I let out a heavy sigh, leaning forward and resting my arms on my knees. "Mali knew where Laiken was the entire time she was gone."

Her brows raise. "Really? And she didn't say anything?"

"Not a damn thing." I shake my head. "I thought she was being a good friend, and she was—just not to me. She was just doing her damn job."

The news is obviously surprising to Mom, but the last part doesn't have her convinced. "Now, hold on. I don't know about all that."

"Why not?"

"Because Mali *is* a good friend. I've seen her around you. That kind of support can't be faked," she argues. "She might have started out doing it for Laiken, but it definitely didn't stay that way. She cares about you."

She does. Fuck, I know she does. But that doesn't mean any of this is right. I mean, she spent this whole time lying to me. Watching me fall apart, only to put myself back together and fall apart again.

How would she feel if I did this to her? If Cam was the one who vanished, and I not only didn't tell her and Laiken where he was, but acted like I had no idea. Acted like he left me, too. I thought she was a mess for the same reason I was, but she was only upset because she wanted her home. Not because she genuinely didn't know if she was dead or alive.

"What's going on with you and Laiken, anyways?" she questions, and I know she's been *itching* to ask me that.

I purse my lips, acting obtuse. "Nothing."

## Chapter 15

An amused glint appears in her eyes. "You know, there was another time when you told me there was *nothing* going on between you two. I believe it was when I found her coming out of your room early one morning. Is it that kind of nothing?"

Okay, I'll accept that she's here to listen to my problems and try to help me through them, but I draw the fucking line at talking to her about my sex life.

"Mom," I groan.

She chuckles. "What? When are you going to learn that I can see right through you?"

My head drops as I let myself think about Laiken, and how infuriated I was when I listened to Finn shoot his shot with her. I knew she would never say yes. Coming on that strong is *not* the way to go about it when it comes to her. But still, listening to someone try to flirt with her like that, I wanted to throw his ass out.

And I *like* Finn—for the most part, anyway.

"I don't know," I tell her. "I really don't."

She takes a deep breath. "You don't get over someone you loved that strongly, H."

"Yeah, no shit."

The only thing I *am* sure of is that I'm not over her. Not even a little. I still find myself looking for her in a crowded room, or gravitating toward where she is. And when she's not there, I feel off. Like something just isn't right. But when I let myself get close to her, I can't breathe. The panic sets in, and I convince myself that she's going to do exactly what she did before. I'll have her in my arms, let her back in, and then she'll be gone again.

And that's when I push her away.

"I feel like I should be though," I say. "Over her, I mean. I feel like I *need* to be."

I can see it in her face; she hates watching me struggle

## Chapter 15

like this. But she's only ever wanted what's best for me, and I have a feeling she still believes Laiken is a part of that.

"I think it all comes down to whether or not you'll be able to trust her again," she tells me. "If you can't, then trying again won't go well. But if you think you can, if it's at all possible, I don't think you should let a love like that go. It's too special."

I lean back and rest my head on the back of the chair, exhaling heavily. She's right. That's the first thing I need to focus on. But with everything that happened today, I know that's not something I can think about right now.

Not when I'm questioning if I can trust anyone at all.

**I'M STARTING TO BELIEVE** that sleep is a foreign concept to me now, and caffeine is a way of life. To think there used to be a time when I would sleep until noon if I had nothing else to do. Lately, I'm lucky if I can doze off for a few hours before I have to wake up and do it all over again.

I lean over the counter, watching the coffee slowly drip into the pot like I'm not relying on it to survive right now. Fucking gross bean juice. They couldn't have made this shit taste better? And what's taking so damn long? It needs to work on tasting extra gross? The fuck.

When it finally beeps, I pour a cup, adding an obnoxious amount of sugar because let's face it—it's necessary. To

## Chapter 15

anyone who drinks their coffee black, I salute you. That shit takes a special level of self-loathing.

As the caffeine courses through me, my headache starts to subside. I still have an hour or so until I have to be at the bar, but staying in this house has proven more difficult than I remember. Though, that could have to do with her being back and yet, not here.

A car door shuts outside, and it sounds like it's coming from my driveway, but before I can look out the window, there's a light knock at the front door. I open it to find Mali standing there, looking up at me pleadingly.

"Can we talk?" she asks.

I don't want to. Not really, anyway. I'm not sure I'm ready yet, but if I've learned anything from Laiken being back, it's that conversations like these need to be had whether I like it or not. So, I may as well get it over with.

I reluctantly step back and open the door further to let her in. "If you're going to lie some more, then go. I'd rather you say nothing at all."

She shakes her head. "No. No more lies. No more secrets. I told Laiken this morning, I'm not doing it anymore. So, ask me whatever you want to know, and I'll tell you."

Well, fuck me. This feels like I have access to the inside of Laiken's brain. If anyone knows her better than she knows herself, it's Mali. There's something dangerous about this, but I can't resist the chance to get all the answers I've been looking for.

"Okay," I say, nodding slowly. "When did she decide to leave?"

"The night you two had that blow-up argument," she answers. "When Cam and I walked in to see your fist go through the wall."

God, I hated that night. I remember thinking it was the worst argument that we'd ever have. There's nothing I hate

## Chapter 15

more than fighting with her. It makes me sick to my stomach, honestly. And that night was intense.

"Not as long as I thought."

She sighs, sitting on the couch beside me. "When we went upstairs, she told me about the text messages and showed me the proof she left in the car."

My brows raise. "Was it really that bad?"

"Yeah." She looks down at her hands and messes with the rip in her jeans. "When she told me what she wanted to do, I told her it was a bad idea. I mean, if someone is threatening her, she shouldn't be alone. But I could also see how scared she was—not for herself, but for *you*. She left on the one condition that no harm would come to you."

"And you helped her do it," I say, not asking, just throwing the fact out there.

Mali nods. "I met her at the border of town and gave her a burner phone and all the money we were able to pull together. Then I promised her again that I would keep an eye on you, and I hugged her goodbye."

The way she starts to tear up, I know remembering that moment is still hard for her. She watched her best friend leave, and she really didn't know if she was going to be okay. But being able to at least reach her and make sure she's all right is better than the hell I endured of not knowing what the fuck happened.

"Yes, I was updating her on how you were and everything, but none of it was fake, H," she says honestly. "You really are one of my closest fucking friends and I'm sorry I kept this from you. I trusted that Laiken was doing the right thing, and when nothing happened to you, I believed she was right. That we were doing what was in your best interest. But I should've told you. And I should've told Cam."

*Shit*, I didn't even think about how Cam was there, hearing the same bomb drop that I did. For her to lie to me is

## Chapter 15

one thing, but to him, this is probably devastating. It's no secret that the two of them have some fucked-up thing going on, but it all stems from love. And a lie like this has the ability to break his heart.

My own words yesterday play through my mind. The ones where I threw their secret out for Laiken to hear. But hey, we did say no more secrets, right?

"You're not going to nut punch me for outing you two to Laiken, are you?" I ask hesitantly.

She chuckles, shaking her head. "She's not mad. I mean, she literally *married* her brother's best friend. That would be a little hypocritical of her, don't you think?"

"That's fair."

I watch the smile fall off her face. "Not that it matters anyway. He'll probably never speak to me again."

If anyone knows about Cam's ability to hold a grudge, it's me. He's stubborn as hell and holds onto everything. But Mali has always been different for him. Their friendship, if that's what you want to call it, goes by a different set of rules than the rest. I just don't know if that's going to help her or hurt her in this situation.

My phone rings on the coffee table and I reach forward to grab it, seeing Cam's name on the screen. "Speak of the devil."

I answer the call and put it to my ear. "Yeah, what's up?"

"H," he says, and the panic in his voice makes the hair on my arms stand straight up. "You need to get to the fucking bar, now!"

*Chapter 15*

**MY BRAKES LOCK UP**, my tires screeching across the pavement as the truck comes to a stop in the parking lot. The second I throw it in park, Mali and I both jump out. We run around to the door, but when I go to open it, it's locked. I'm trying to find the key when Cam opens it, and the look of terror on his face is enough for my stomach to sink.

"What's going on?" I ask worriedly.

Laiken turns around at the sound of my voice. Tears run down her cheeks as she looks so hopeless. So scared.

Cam can't even say the words, so instead, he steps back and to the side—and that's when I see it.

There, in the middle of the bar, is the body of the hacker. He's almost completely buried under a pile of dirt, with his head posed to be sticking out. And I'm guessing the worms and maggots that crawl around are just for special effect.

As my jaw drops, Cam hands me the note that was lying on the table by the door.

*Let's see you get rid of this one.*

# Hayes
## CHAPTER SIXTEEN

THE WORD CHAOS DOESN'T EVEN BEGIN TO describe what's going on behind the locked door of the bar. Cam panics, muttering something about how we're twenty minutes away from having to open. He rushes to grab a piece of paper and a marker to make a sign.

Mali looks fucking terrified. She alternates between wanting to help Cam and worrying about Laiken. And she should be worried about her; I know I am. She's in fucking shock.

We all know the last dead body she saw, and the events that transpired afterward. She didn't exactly handle it well. The look on her face now mirrors the same one she had back then. I can't help but fear she's about to spiral right back into the mess she became then.

"What the fuck do I write?" Cam asks.

His hand is shaking, and his eyes are wide enough to look like he just did a whole batch of cocaine. If he writes this sign, someone is bound to think we're off doing drugs somewhere. So, I walk over and take the marker from him.

*Sorry, we're closed due to a family emergency.*

Short, simple, and just vague enough to work. I pass Cam the paper and he grabs the tape as he walks to the door.

## Chapter 16

lifting the blinds only for a second so he can stick it to the inside of the window.

The sunlight shines in and lands on the body. It shows just how pale he is. There's a grayish tint to his skin. I don't know how recently he was killed, but I'm guessing that since he's not decomposing yet, it had to be pretty recent.

Laiken won't look away from him. Hell, she's barely even blinking. It looks like a fucked up Halloween decoration, and I know that if I don't move it somewhere out of sight, she's only going to get worse. But how the fuck do you move a dead body covered in dirt, without getting shit everywhere else and leaving us with more to clean up?

I rack my brain, trying to figure it out, until I get an idea. Rushing up the stairs, I open the closet and pull the tent we used to use for events out of the closet. Marc had asked me to keep it here, in case he wanted to put on another surfing competition. Needless to say, I don't think he's going to need it now.

I pull it out of the case and struggle to remove the canvas from the metal, but it finally comes free. This should be thick enough to hold whatever *fluids* could leak out of the body and onto the floor.

Yeah, don't worry. I vomited in my mouth, too.

Cam watches me curiously as I come back downstairs and start to spread the canvas out on the floor. When it's open enough to fit the body, I grab a couple pairs of gloves, putting my own on and tossing the others to Cam. With the heaviness in the air, I ask the same favor I thought I'd never need in my life, for the second time.

"Help me move him."

He looks exactly how I feel as he sighs and comes over, cringing as he digs through the dirt to find the feet. On the count of three, we lift him. All of the blood has pooled to his

## Chapter 16

back, gravity doing its job, and the worms and maggots fall off with the dirt as we carry him over to the tarp-like fabric.

"Okay," I say, taking a breath. "Now let's get him into the walk-in fridge. At least there, he's out of sight, and it should stop this place from smelling like death until we can get rid of it."

We each grab an end and lift, straining our backs as we carry all the dead weight through the bar and into the back. It's a struggle to hold the fridge door open and carry the body into it, but we manage—neither one of us are willing to ask one of the girls for help anyway.

Once that's dealt with, I go behind the bar and grab a few garbage bags along with the dustpan. We need to get this dirt out of here. Every last speck. There could be DNA on it. And besides, no one would understand how a bunch of dirt ended up in a bar *on the beach.*

"What are you going to do? Just leave the body in the fridge forever?" Mali asks.

I roll my eyes. "No, but we can't move it in broad daylight, now can we?"

Her eyes widen at my tone, and I stop everything to take a breath, trying to bring my blood pressure down enough to think clearly. Snapping at my friends right now is *not* what we need.

"I'm sorry," I tell her. "I didn't mean to snap."

She shakes her head. "It's fine. I get it. None of us want to be dealing with this."

A sob rips through Laiken. Her hand flies up to her mouth as she tries to hold it in, but there's no use. It forces its way out and breaks her down in the process. All of this is catching up to her, and she has spent so long being strong, but she can't anymore.

"Lai," Mali says sadly, trying to hold her.

I can't focus on what I'm doing as I watch the girl that I

## Chapter 16

love fall back to exactly how she was right before she left. Cam comes over and takes the dustpan from me.

"What?"

He nods toward Laiken. "Go to her."

But I can't. "It's fine. Mali has her."

"You and I both know it's not Mali she needs right now." He takes the garbage bag out of my hand. "You're going to be useless until she's okay anyway, so there's no point of fighting me on it."

*I fucking hate when he's right.*

Getting up, I take off the gloves and throw them away. Laiken is crying in Mali's arms when I get over to them. Mali looks at me and I nod, silently telling her that it's fine. She carefully turns Laiken and passes her to me.

Her head rests against my chest, and I run my hand up and down her back. There's nothing I can say. I can't tell her that it's all right because it's not. There's a dead body in my fucking bar right now. I can't tell her she's okay because she's not okay. She's facing even more trauma. The only thing I can do is hold her close.

I sit down on one of the bar stools, bringing me closer to her level. She pulls away and looks at me. The sadness is there in her eyes. She's mourning the loss of someone she doesn't even know, and I can already tell she's blaming herself for his death.

"Don't do that," I say softly. "You did not do this. Some psycho did this."

She shakes her head. "But it all leads back to me."

"This isn't dominos. You are not directly responsible for this. It's not your fault that someone decided to make us their own personal playthings. Okay? This isn't on you."

I doubt she believes me, but she nods anyway. Using my thumbs, I wipe the tears from her eyes. I want to kiss her. Lord knows it'll take her mind off everything and put that

## Chapter 16

smile I love back on her face. But the other day, when she kissed me just to keep me from revealing a little too much information in front of Riley, it almost killed me.

The feeling of her lips on mine again was pure fire. It was like being deprived of oxygen for hours and then sucking it in straight. It's the only thing I could think about for the rest of that day and all the next, even in the midst of everything we're dealing with. But more than anything, it scared the hell out of me, because her kiss is intoxicating, and I know too well what it's like to be addicted to her.

The withdrawal is a bitch.

By the grace of God, she looks relatively okay. She's shaken up, yes, but who wouldn't be if they came walking into a place they've been a million times and saw *that* in front of them? She could definitely be worse right now, that's for sure. I guess when you go through as much as we have, you find a way to numb it all out.

"I don't think either of them should be alone," I tell Cam, referring to Laiken and Mali.

He nods as he finishes cleaning up the last of the dirt, cringing as he takes off the gloves and ties the bag closed. "I agree. This definitely takes it up a level."

Mali huffs. "As much as I just *love* men making decisions for me, I have to work. I won't be alone. There are other people scheduled with me. But I don't suppose one of you wants to sit there all day while I sell women lingerie?"

Cam purses his lips teasingly. "That depends. Do they try it on?"

*Like I said, different set of rules.*

She rolls her eyes, flipping him off and refusing to answer the question, so he moves on.

"When do you have to be at work?" he asks.

Looking up at the clock, she sighs. "Forty-five minutes, but my car is at Hayes's house."

*Chapter 16*

Cam turns to me, almost like he's about to ask me to take her, but there's no way in hell I'm taking my eyes off Laiken. Not right now. Not during this. I love Mali, I do, but this is Laiken we're talking about. And with this person's apparent obsession when it comes to her, I'm not taking any goddamn chances.

"All right," he sighs. "I'll take you to get your car and then follow you to work to make sure you get there safely."

She nods, coming over to give Laiken a hug and then looks at me. "Are we okay?"

I pull her in for a hug. "Yeah, we're good."

I'm still mad, and it definitely knocked her down a peg or two in my book, but when it comes down to it, I would've done the same thing had Cam asked me to. And he would do the same shit for me.

But let's hope it doesn't come to that.

**THERE HAVEN'T BEEN MANY** times I've been alone with Laiken since the day she came back. To be honest, I've been actively trying to avoid it. Every time we're alone, I lose all sense of self-control. Clearly, nothing has changed. But hey, at least I'm consistent.

She sits in the corner, doing something on her computer while I wipe everything down. This is the second time this

## Chapter 16

motherfucker has been in here. I don't know what's been touched and what hasn't, and I'm not taking any chances.

It's awkward being in here, knowing there is a dead body in the back. I have no idea how those mafia men deal with this shit on the regular. Personally, I'd rather do literally anything else. This is not my idea of fun, and no amount of power is worth dealing with it on the regular. But will I do it over and over again if it means keeping those I love safe? You're damn right I will.

I look over at Laiken, watching the way she nods along with what I'm guessing is music. Her headphones prevent me from hearing anything. You can tell she's uncomfortable, but she's trying to put on a brave face. And being as she wasn't even able to do that the last time, I'm hoping that means there's hope for her to survive this.

Her phone vibrates on the table, and she grabs it as if it's nothing, but then her eyes widen and her head whips over to me. I'm across the room in seconds. The texts from unknown rarely get much of a reaction out of us anymore, but this one does.

> Looks like I'm not the only one constantly watching you.

*Fuck.*

They can see us.

I spin around, looking for anything out of the ordinary. We've been all over this place since we got here, so there's no way someone is here with us. Which only leaves one option—the camera.

"Grab your things and come with me."

She nods, telling someone to hold on as she gathers her stuff and follows me behind the bar. We sit down on the floor in the only spot I know isn't recorded. It was a design flaw that I tried to fix, but now I'm grateful for it.

## Chapter 16

My head falls back against the bar. I was *trying* to keep my distance until Cam got back. At least that way, I wouldn't give into temptation and do something reckless—like fuck her in the back room again.

Jesus Christ, I'm half hard just at the thought of it.

She's so close that the smell of her shampoo infiltrates my senses. Her arm is brushing up against mine, and it's all I can focus on. She giggles, making me look over at what she's doing, and I notice she's on a video call with someone who looks like they're in a recording booth.

"No," she says.

It's obviously not meant for me, but it makes me curious, nonetheless.

After a little arguing with the girl on the screen, I get tired of only hearing one side of the conversation and nudge her with my elbow. I raise my brows and she tries not to smile as she gives in, taking off the headphones and turning them off so the sound comes through the speakers.

"Hayes, this is Ashleigh," she introduces me as she turns her computer slightly.

Ashleigh hums. "Hayes, huh? That's a pretty sweet name."

"Thanks," I drawl. "I'll tell my mom you said so."

"Oh, already talking about me to your mom, huh?"

*What the fuck is going on?*

Laiken barks out a laugh. "Now is when I should probably mention that Hayes is my husband."

I shouldn't love the sound of that rolling off her tongue, or the way she says it like she still has a claim over me. If Mali were to be here and could hear my inner thoughts, she would tell me that she does. And, well, she wouldn't exactly be wrong. Lord knows no other girl has even gotten a second glance.

Let's just say it was a very dry nineteen months.

## Chapter 16

"Oh shit!" Ashleigh gasps. "My bad. Nice to meet you, Mrs. Laiken."

I snort. "Mrs. Laiken?"

Ashleigh shrugs while Lai rolls her eyes. "Okay, can we please get on with this? We're wasting poor Greg's time."

"You're fine," a guy says through what sounds like an intercom. "I charge by the hour."

"Shit," Ashleigh groans. "Okay, let's go again."

She puts on a pair of headphones, and Laiken presses a button to mute her microphone as music starts to play. Ashleigh's voice belts out lyrics to a song I've never heard before, but it's good. Give it time and I'm sure it'll be on the radio.

The song starts to build, and Laiken looks nervous until Ashleigh nails the high note and both of them light up. When the song finally comes to an end, Lai unmutes herself.

"That was fucking fantastic, Ash," she gushes. "Greg, please tell me you got that!"

"You know I did."

"Thank you, Jesus." She takes a deep breath. "Okay, I have to go do a few things, but if you guys need me, just let me know."

Ashleigh comes over to the screen. "Yeah, you're going to enjoy that husband of yours. I get it. It's no wonder your songs are so damn good when your muse looks like that."

Everything starts to click into place while Laiken laughs and says bye to both Ashleigh and Greg. When the video call ends, she closes her computer, putting it to the side.

No matter how hard I try, I can't pinpoint exactly how I'm feeling. There's a whole range of emotions, and I think I'm getting a little bit of each of them.

"You work at a studio?" I ask, and she nods. "As a songwriter?"

## Chapter 16

"Yeah." You can tell she's trying not to smile, but the pride she feels about it shines through.

I'm not about to take that away from her. "That's amazing, Lai. You made your dream come true." She nods, looking anywhere but at me. "What's wrong?"

One shoulder raises in a halfhearted shrug. "You were supposed to be there when I did. When I sold my first song, you were the first person I wanted to tell."

I wish I was there. I really do. All I ever wanted was for her to achieve her dreams. Especially when she played such a big part in me achieving mine. But even though I wasn't there to share it with her, it's still incredible to see.

"I'm so proud of you," I tell her honestly.

She turns to look at me and she smiles, her face only inches from mine. Neither of us make a move to turn away, and I glance down at her lips instinctively. Like I said—lack of all self-control.

There's no way to tell who starts leaning in first, just that it happens. My forehead hits hers, and our breaths mix together. The tension between us crackles as the anticipation makes my heart pound against my chest. If we do this, I don't think there's any going back for me.

I'll be fucking done for.

But I'm not sure anything can stop me now as my lips ghost across hers.

...Except maybe her brother walking through the front door.

We jolt apart, even though he can't see us. And even if he could, it wouldn't matter. He'd fuck with me for it, but it's not at all the same as it was when we were sneaking around behind his back.

My eyes don't leave Laiken as I think about what just almost happened. The part of me that wants to panic is there,

## Chapter 16

pacing anxiously in the back of my mind. But while her eyes are on mine, I'm able to keep him at bay.

It's when she's gone that he wins.

"Uh, H? Laiken?" Cam asks. We both stand up from behind the bar, and he scrunches his nose. "Do I want to know what you two were doing back there?"

Laiken huffs. "Don't be weird. That fucking stalker can see us."

"I think he has access to the camera," I explain.

Cam's brows furrow as he looks up at the camera above him. As if it's no big deal, he grabs a bar stool and climbs on top of it, yanking the camera right out of the wall. Wires dangle down, and he better hope they don't touch because this place doesn't have fire-retardant walls.

"That should do it," he says, then proceeds to go around and do all the rest.

I'm not about to yell at him for it. Not when this psycho has a direct line to watch us whenever they please. But when this is all over, we're going to need to replace those, and they were expensive.

*Add it to the fucking list.*

"All right," he says to me. "Take Laiken back to your place and stay with her there until nightfall."

*Huh?* "What are you going to do?"

"I'm staying here."

A bark of laughter leaves my mouth and I shake my head. "Yeah, no. I'm not leaving you here alone."

"Yes, you are," he insists.

"What if this is all a fucking trap? The police could show up here, find the body, and you'll get arrested for a murder you didn't commit."

"Well, if that happens, it wouldn't do much good for all three of us to get arrested, now would it?"

He's completely calm, as if we're talking about the

## Chapter 16

weather or an upcoming fishing trip. But I don't fucking like this. I don't like it at all.

"H," he presses. "You've both protected me, now it's my turn to protect you. Go. When Mali gets done with work, she'll let you know, and you'll drop Laiken off at her place. Then we'll get rid of this thing."

I still don't want to, but I don't think he's going to take no for an answer. "What if they come back?"

He reaches behind him and pulls a gun out of his waistband, putting it on top of the bar. "Let them try."

**THE WHOLE WAY BACK** to my place, I make Laiken drive ahead of me. That way, I can always keep an eye on her. If that means cutting a few people off and getting the finger from an eighty-year-old lady, so be it. I even end up running a red light, and the flash of a camera tells me I'll be getting a ticket in the mail for that one.

*Thanks a lot, Lai.*

As we walk into the house we shared, things feel tense. It could be the almost-kiss Cam interrupted, or it could be the way she's looking at everything. Her eyes linger on each spot, like she can't look at it and not remember all the sexual things we've done all over this place.

I know because I do it, too.

It's one of the reasons staying here is so difficult.

## Chapter 16

I was good the night she showed up here, drunk off her ass. A total gentleman. I carried her to bed, tucked her in, and came downstairs to lie awake on the couch all night. But this time, she's not drunk.

And I don't feel like being a gentleman.

She's standing in front of the stairs as I step up behind her, pressing my front against her back. "You're thinking about it, aren't you?"

Her breath hitches. "I don't know what you're talking about."

"Sure you do," I murmur. "You're thinking about how we stood right here as I bent you over and buried myself inside of you."

Putting my hands on her shoulders, I spin us around so she's facing the kitchen.

"And when you look at that island, you picture the way I sat you on it and ate you out until you screamed."

I glide my hand down her arm, and her head falls back against my chest. Her breathing quickens. From this angle, I can see right down her shirt, and I am *dying* to get my mouth on her.

"Imagine if we went upstairs," I tease. "The things you'd remember then."

She finds her nerve and turns around, using all the force she can manage to push me away. "You walked out last time and left me standing there half naked in a storage room."

Yeah, I should've known she was going to throw that back in my face. But even with the angry look in her eyes, I smirk.

"I did," I admit. "And you walked out and left me sound asleep in our bed, hopeful for the first time in weeks."

"I've apologized for that. Multiple times."

I look her up and down, taking my time as I admire every gorgeous inch of her, but God, she's infuriating. "So, what? You want me to apologize?"

## Chapter 16

A growl rumbles in the back of her throat at the sarcastic tone of my voice. She looks like she wants to fight me, but instead, she walks closer and jumps into my arms. I catch her with my hands on her ass as her legs wrap around my waist.

"No," she says. "I want you to fuck me."

Now *that* I can do.

Pressing her against the wall, I crash my lips into hers. She drags her nails up my back as our tongues meet in the middle. I swear, I could get off just from the taste of her. She arches her hips to grind against me and the moans she lets out tells me she's just as desperate for it as I am.

There are too many layers between us. Too much keeping me from burying myself inside of her. Using my hips to keep her pinned against the wall, I slide my hands up her torso, taking her shirt and bra with them. As they go up and over her head, I discard them on the floor and immediately cover her tits with my hands.

Her back arches as she presses herself into my touch, biting her lip at how good it feels. I rub both her nipples between my fingers. Gripping her ass again, I bend down to suck one into my mouth. She mewls at the sensation, spurring me on and making my cock fill at a rapid pace.

*Fuck.* It's not enough. I need to taste her. I need the mouthwatering taste of her pussy to coat my tongue until it's bound to linger there for the rest of the night.

Putting her back on her feet, she pulls my shirt over my head while I rush to get rid of her pants. I drag my hand up her thigh, letting it graze her pussy as she kicks the rest of her clothes off.

This is how I like her.

Standing in front of me, completely exposed and mine for the taking.

I grip her waist and she jumps into my arms again before I carry her over to the fireplace. One of the reasons I bought

## Chapter 16

this house was because of her love for that damn mantel. Well, let's see how much she loves it now.

She squeals as I lift her up and sit her on top of it. "Hayes, this thing is going to break."

"I don't give a fuck," I growl.

Before she can argue further, I go for exactly what I've been craving—getting my mouth on her pussy. She lets out a moan that puts porn stars to shame as I slide my tongue over her, sucking her clit into my mouth. Her legs drape over my shoulders and her thighs press against the sides of my head.

"Holy shit," she breathes. "I've missed that mouth."

It's been too long since I've gotten to eat her out. If we could spend the rest of the night doing only this, I'd be completely okay with it. I don't care how tired my tongue would get. It would be worth it just to keep tasting her and listening to the way she screams when she comes on my tongue.

I pucker my lips and suck on her clit in the way that drives her crazy, and when I moan against her, the vibration makes her whole body jolt. She grips onto my hair and pulls me against her. Her head falls back as she gives in to the pleasure, until the mantel starts to creak.

"H, it's going to break," she says.

But I haven't had enough of her yet. "Relax. I've got you."

I shove two fingers inside of her, pumping them in and out as I bring her that much closer to the edge. She's nothing but putty in my hands. I can feel the way she's starting to lose control, and I'm fucking living for it.

"I want to eat nothing but you for breakfast, lunch, and dinner," I tell her. "Fuck you for keeping this from me."

"Fuck, yes!"

She starts to rock against my mouth, no longer caring about the stability of the mantel. All she can focus on is the way I move my tongue in circles around that little bundle of

## Chapter 16

nerves. If I'm ever dying, please let her put me out of my misery. Let her sit on my face so I can suffocate on her pussy and die happy.

"Hayes," she moans. "Hayes, fuck!"

Her voice goes up an octave, and all it takes is one deep thrust of my hand and a hard suck on her clit, and she's fucking gone.

*Just as the mantel gives way.*

The left half of it rips straight out of the wall, swinging down as only the right side holds it up. Everything that was on top crashes to the floor, but I manage to keep Laiken upright, with her back pressed into the stone of the fireplace. But we're far from done yet as she quivers against me.

I pull my fingers out of her and grip her waist to get her off the wall. She leans all of her weight forward, putting it on my shoulders, and I step back carefully before I gently set her on the floor.

"One of these days, I'm going to fuck your mouth again," I tell her.

She smirks at me, dropping down to her knees. "Why wait? Do it now."

Yeah, there isn't a damn thing in the world that could make me say no to that. I drop my pants and boxers in one go, freeing my cock and taking it into my hand. She licks her lips as she watches me stroke it a couple times, and when I line up at her mouth, she opens like the good girl she is.

"I'm not in the mood to have any mercy, so if I hurt you, you're going to need to stop me."

But she doesn't respond. If anything, that only excites her. She brings her hands around to my ass and pulls me into her mouth. I throw my head back as she sucks my dick better than anyone else ever has. Her tongue swirls around the head and then presses against the underside of my dick as I thrust deep into her.

## Chapter 16

With a grip on her hair, my hand shakes as I try to hold back, but when I see the way she narrows her eyes while looking up at me, I know she doesn't want me to. She wants the pain. She wants to choke on my cock. And fuck, I want nothing more than to give that to her.

Thrusting into the back of her throat, I pull her harshly onto me. My moan mixes with the sound of her choking on me. The walls of her throat constrict around me as she gags, and I only back off for a second so she can get a breath in before I'm going right back in.

"Fucking hell," I groan. "Look at you. You're so good for me. Making me feel so damn good."

After a couple more seconds, I let my dick slip from her mouth. A string of saliva hangs from me to her lips, and she wipes it away as she catches her breath.

"I want more," she begs. "Give me more."

I grip her chin between my thumb and the knuckle of my index finger, forcing her to look at me. "Don't be a brat. You'll get more when I give you more. But right now, I *need* to be inside of you."

She bites her lip as she moves to lie on the floor, spreading her legs for me and letting me see that pretty pussy. With my cock in my hands, I rub it up and down over her clit, watching how it makes her squirm.

"You were fucking made for me, Laiken."

Keeping my gaze locked with hers, I slide into her with nothing between us. She presses the back of her head against the floor and her eyes fall closed, overtaken by pleasure. There is *nothing* better than this. The feeling of her wrapped around me as I fuck her raw—it's fucking heaven.

The last time we had sex right here, it was the night I asked her to marry me. All I wanted was to make her feel as loved and cherished as she was. Fuck it, as she *is*. But right now, my only goal is to make sure she knows without a

## Chapter 16

single doubt that nothing and *no one* will ever be able to do this. They can't make her feel what I can because they don't know her like I do.

This pussy belongs to me, whether she likes it or not.

Pressing my thumb against her clit, I roll my hips in a circular motion and her fingers dig into the carpet as she tries to find something to keep her grounded. But that's not where I want her.

I want her soaring into sexual subspace.

Her breathing quickens until finally, she holds her breath and clenches around me. The scream she lets out is sure to alarm the neighbors, and I'm sure if they send the police, it'll look really great when they see the mantel in ruins. But I don't even make a half-assed attempt to quiet her down.

Let them hear.

More specifically, let that fucking psycho hear.

I want them to hear how she screams my name as she comes all over my cock, like she needs the entire world to know just who she belongs to.

Who she will *always* fucking belong to.

"Did you ever end up getting on birth control?" I grit out.

She shakes her head. "But fuck it. Do it anyway."

*God*, I want to. I'd love nothing more than to fill her up right now. To see my cum drip from her pussy from being filled to the brim. Fucking hell, even the thought of my sperm swimming inside of her makes me want it. But at the last second, I force myself to pull out.

My abs clench as I stroke my cock, watching spurts of white shoot out and land between her legs. It's not the same, but it's the closest alternative, and it's still so fucking hot. Her pussy is covered in my cum, and it might be reckless, but I rub the head of my dick through it and push it inside her—giving her a little taste of what she wants.

As if she wants to prove she can tease too, she reaches

## Chapter 16

down and drags two fingers through the mess I've made. I watch as she brings them to her mouth and wraps her lips around them, moaning at the taste.

*Fuck. Me.*

I crash onto the floor beside her, listening as we both breathe heavily. We should be fully sated after that, and yet, I already crave another round. This is what she does to me. Every little taste just makes me want more, until the only thing I can do is drown in her.

Fucking her at the bar was one thing. It was practically neutral ground. I was able to bend her over and pound into her, releasing all my frustrations and emptying them into her. But here, in the place where we spoke our vows and promised to spend the rest of our lives together—I couldn't do that here.

And because of that, I crossed into dangerous territory.

She rolls over to face me and rests her hand on my chest. "What are you thinking about?"

No. I can't.

I can't fucking do it.

It's too much.

"Nothing," I answer coldly, getting up to pull my pants back on.

Her eyes fall closed for a second, but before she can say anything about me shutting her out again, her phone vibrates on the coffee table. She gets up and walks over to it, stark naked, with no shame at all. She doesn't even care about the cum that drips down her leg.

"Hey Ash," she says as she answers the call. "Uh...yeah. Give me like ten minutes, okay? No problem. Bye."

"She has great timing," I muse, but the sharp look she shoots my way suggests I've overstepped.

Grabbing her clothes, she goes into the bathroom to clean herself up, and then she sets her computer up in the

## Chapter 16

kitchen. I should stay in the living room. Play video games or watch a damn movie. There's no reason I should sit at the island.

Except…it's closer to her.

So, that's exactly where I go.

**I NEVER USED TO** consider myself a bitter person. I wasn't exactly the happiest, but I don't think I was ever bitter. But sitting here, pretending to scroll through my phone as I not-so-subtly watch Laiken work, I can't help but feel that way.

Don't get me wrong, I was honest when I told her that I'm proud of her. I am. I know how much she wanted this, and the fact that she made it happen is incredible. I never doubted that she would do it. I've seen some of the things she's written, and she's really talented.

But I wasn't a part of it.

She left, and my life fell apart without her. But Laiken? She didn't just survive without me. She fucking thrived.

Maybe karma agrees with her. Maybe she was being rewarded for doing the *right thing* by protecting me, even though I never asked her to. That very well could be the case.

But there's also the possibility that I was always just holding her back.

She finishes up and closes her computer, finally looking at

## Chapter 16

me for the first time in the last two hours. "Are you just going to stare at me, or do you actually want to talk?"

"Don't know what there is to talk about," I answer simply.

Her eyes roll. "Well, you could start with why you've been watching me this whole time with a frown on your face. You're going to get wrinkles."

I shrug, tearing my eyes away from her and focusing on my phone. "There are worse things than wrinkles."

She walks around the side of the island until she's standing in front of me, leaning against the counter. "Or you could tell me what you think about every time you retreat into yourself after we have sex."

The first one. Definitely the fucking first one.

"You know, they say wrinkles show that you laughed a lot during your life," I tell her.

Some useless information I picked up from some trivia night Cam and Mali dragged me to once. I remember because Mali said I had nothing to worry about and my face would stay wrinkle free.

I flipped her off.

"Hayes," Laiken sighs. She carefully takes my phone out of my hand and puts it down. "Talk to me. Please."

My gaze meets hers, and I hate the way she's looking at me. Fragile is not a word anyone would ever use to describe me, but with her, I feel like I could shatter at any moment. After she left, I tried to put myself back together, but it was always an impossible task.

So, I faked it.

I forced a smile on my face in front of everyone who mattered, and I drank with my friends, pretending I was having a good time. But with her standing here now, staring back at me like she can see right into my soul, I know it was all a damn lie.

## Chapter 16

I'm not okay.

There hasn't been a point since she left that I was.

"I don't know what you want me to say."

"What you're thinking," she suggests. "How you're feeling."

*I'm thinking you're going to break me into a million pieces, and I'm feeling like the floor is going to fall out from under me at any possible second.*

"How long is the studio letting you work remotely?"

Her brows furrow. "We haven't really talked about it, why?"

I shrug. "Just wondering how much longer you're going to be here before you go back to your perfect new life."

"That's what this is about?" she asks. "Hayes, I'm here. Right here. Don't you get that?"

"Yeah," I huff. "I do. I also get that you have everything you've ever wanted back at your house with Nolan. The fun roommate you can go out partying with. The dream job. You've got it all."

"No," she tells me. "I don't! Because you're not there!"

"Maybe that's it!" I shout. "Has it ever crossed your mind that maybe your life is so fucking great there *because* I'm not in it? Face it, Laiken. You're better off without me."

She shakes her head. "Fuck that. I don't believe that shit at all."

"You don't have to. The proof is right in front of your face."

Turning around, she takes two steps away from me then stops. Her fingers lace into her hair and she tugs on it, groaning in frustration.

"Urgh! You're so fucking...urgh!" She lets go and rests her hands on the counter. "I'm not going to stand here and listen to you insinuate that you're bad for me! That's bullshit, and you fucking know it!"

## Chapter 16

"Who knows. Maybe I do," I say, sounding completely defeated. "Or maybe I'm just mentally preparing for the inevitable day that you leave again."

"Then why don't you just ask me to stay?" she yells.

"Because I don't know if I want you to!"

It's bullshit. A total fucking lie. Of course, I want her to stay. The thought of her leaving again makes me sick to my stomach. But I refuse to be blindsided again. It's happened too many times already.

Better to expect the worst.

Laiken looks like I just stabbed her straight in the chest. We stare at each other, knowing we're at a crossroads. She'd be smart to give up on me. I'm a lost cause. I know that. She's destined to be some super successful songwriter, and I'm meant to just be the guy she wrote a couple love ballads about once upon a time.

The sound of my phone cuts through the silence, and I half expect to look down and find some cryptic threat from someone who doesn't have the balls to say it to my face, but it's only Mali.

> Home from work. Bring Lai over whenever.

I look out the window, seeing the light fade into the darkness.

"It's time to go," I say without looking at her. "I'm dropping you off at Mali's and then I have to meet Cam at the bar."

But as I get up and start walking toward the door, I realize she's not behind me. I turn around to find her right where I left her, her eyes filled with tears.

"I don't want to lose you," she nearly whispers.

It chips another piece right off my heart, but it's fine.

I'm used to it.

## Chapter 16

I shrug dejectedly. "I didn't want to lose you either."

Spinning on my heels, I walk straight out the front door and go start my truck, because I don't have time for this conversation.

I have to move a goddamn body...again.

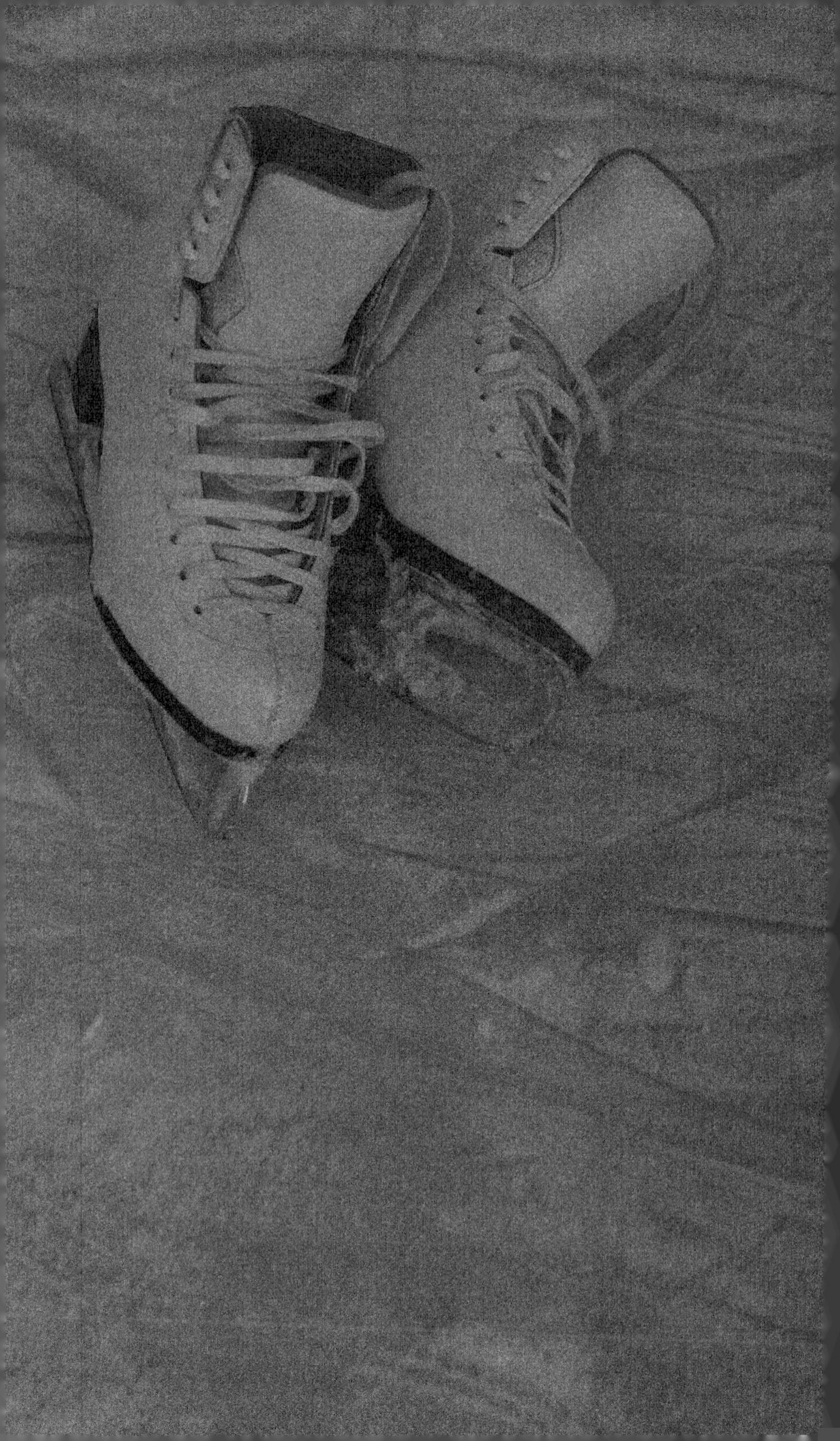

# Laiken
# CHAPTER SEVENTEEN

THERE IS NOTHING MORE BAFFLING THAN THE mood swings of Hayes Beckett Wilder. One minute he's looking at me like I'm the greatest thing to ever walk the face of the earth, and the next, he's cold enough to give me frostbite. It's like how we started, but so much worse.

It's worse because I know what it's like to have him. To *really* have him. After he told Cam about us, he was all in. For someone who had no experience with relationships, he sure did know how to act in one. There wasn't a single moment where I felt unwanted, unloved, or unappreciated. He treated me like a goddamn queen.

And now I feel more like someone he fucks from time to time.

He's struggling. I know that. It's written all over his face every time he looks at me. But I know the connection we shared is still there. It crackles in the air every time we're near each other. I just hope that ends up being enough.

After what he said to me earlier, I'm not sure it will be.

"Laiken, sit the fuck down," Mali tells me for the millionth time. "My parents can probably hear you pacing."

I'm sure she's right, but I can't help it. "What if it's a trap? What if they're being set up and they're going to get caught trying to get rid of the damn thing? I didn't torture myself for over a year just for Hayes to go to prison anyway, and for Cam to go down with him."

"Hey, conjugal visits might be hot."

## Chapter 17

Seriously? I'm on the verge of a nervous breakdown, and she's making jokes right now? Then again, this is Mali we're talking about. She's probably serious.

"You are the worst," I tell her.

She pretends to be offended as she mocks me. "Fine, don't believe me. But I think you'd look cute with a little prison baby on your hip, telling people you have to go call your inmate baby daddy."

"Stop talking."

"No can do, buck-a-roo," she singsongs. "If I don't at least somewhat distract you, you're going to stress yourself into a coronary."

Well, that's not exactly far-fetched. My limit of being calm tonight capped at a half hour, and all of that was spent sitting at the dinner table with Mali's parents. It was great to see them again. I really missed them. But when your brother and your half-husband are disposing of a dead body, it's not the best time for playing catch up.

"You know what you need? To get laid."

I roll my eyes. "Do you have a dick? Because you have sex on the brain constantly lately."

"I do!" she says proudly, reaching into her nightstand and pulling out a dildo that looks like something out of a robot movie. "His name is Linus."

"Linus? Like the fucking Peanuts character?"

She narrows her eyes at me. "No. Like short for cunnilingus."

My mouth opens and closes a couple of times before I find the right words. "Wouldn't that be Lingus, not Linus?"

"You know what? You can go," she says, like we're not in danger. "If you happen to get kidnapped, just use that emergency function on your phone. I'm sure you'll be okay. You're a tough cookie."

That's the first thing that pulls a laugh out of me since I

## Chapter 17

got here. Mali smiles contently as she grabs her phone to see if there are any updates. Thankfully, she wasn't able to stay mad at me for longer than a few hours.

*Thank God.*

I don't know what I would do if she no longer wanted anything to do with me. Functioning without her isn't something I know how to do. It's like her life and mine are directly linked together. I've said it before, and I'll say it again.

Hayes is the love of my life, but Mali is my soulmate.

"Anything yet?"

She shakes her head. "You'll know as soon as I get something."

Groaning, I throw myself down onto her bed. "This is hell. Distract me with something else."

Her lips purse before a smile breaks through. "Cam fingered me on the way to Hayes's to get my car this morning."

There is no delay between the words coming out of her mouth, and the sound of me gagging. "I said distract me, not make me vomit all over the place."

She looks so damn proud of herself, humming to herself like she didn't just overshare about her sex life with my brother. Imagine if Hayes went up to Cam and said, *hey bro, fucked your sister's mouth today.* The hacker wouldn't be the only body getting dumped tonight, that's for sure.

"So, I take it he's not mad at you anymore?" I ask.

Her expression turns skeptical as she hums. "No, he is. I just have a way of getting what I want."

Of course, she does. "In that case, got any ideas on how I can get Hayes to stop shutting me out?"

"You mean sex in the storage room wasn't the answer?"

"Har har," I mock as I flip her off. "No, asshole. It wasn't.

## Chapter 17

And neither was the sex in the bar before that, or earlier, when we fucked in the living room."

Her eyes widen playfully. "Jesus Christ. I don't know if you know this, but it's actually *not* your job to repopulate the earth."

I choose to ignore her previous statement. "It's the only way he lets me feel close to him. But it's almost always immediately followed with him icing me out. Like today, we got into an argument where he straight up said he doesn't know if he wants me to stay."

"Like in his house?"

"Like in town, or around at all."

She starts to giggle, and it quickly spirals out of control until she's a hysterical ball of laughter. "I'm sorry. It's just... you really believe that?"

I shrug. "He's given me no reason not to."

"Yes, because the fact that any time you've been alone, he can't keep his hands off you isn't an indication at all."

"Are you always such a sarcastic bitch? Am I just now seeing this?"

"Yes," she answers smugly. "It's my favorite personality trait."

I chuckle, only for it to be followed by a sigh. "I don't know, Mal. What if he decides he can't ever trust me again? What if we really are over?"

She gives me a sympathetic smile as she plays with my hair. "If you two are over, I'll be entirely convinced that love isn't real."

"It is though," I tell her. "I feel it every time I look at him. Or think about him. Or talk about him. OR think about something that has to *do* with him."

"I get it," she cuts me off. "You eat, sleep, and breathe Hayes. Tell me something I don't know."

*Okay.* "We broke the mantel above the fireplace today."

## Chapter 17

A loud bark of laughter shoots out of her mouth. "Seriously? How in the fuck?"

I giggle at her reaction. "He sat me on it and ate me out. Turns out those things aren't so sturdy."

"Damn," she murmurs. "You are one lucky bitch."

"I know." I turn to look up at the ceiling. "Now if only I could get him to love me again."

Her phone dings and she starts to get up from her bed. "He still does. He's just being an idiot. But at least he's an idiot who can get rid of a body without getting caught. They're on their way back, so let's go."

*Oh, thank fuck.*

**WHEN WE GET BACK** to the house, neither Mali nor I ask any questions. Not where they put it. Not how it went. And definitely not if they almost got caught. I think I can speak for all of us when I say that we want to put the events of today completely behind us.

Except for the mind-blowing sex. That can stay.

The four of us all head inside and the minute Hayes turns on the light, Cam's eyes widen. "Shit! I think someone was in here!"

He immediately starts looking around like a rookie FBI agent while Mali tries not to laugh. "Easy, Magnum P.I. No one was here."

## Chapter 17

"Dude, did you not see the fucking mantel?" he presses. "It's ripped halfway out of the goddamn wall."

She scrunches her nose as she looks at him. "Babe, trust me. You do *not* want to keep going on this topic."

It takes a second for the pieces to fall into place for Cam, but you can see the moment they do because he goes from worried to revolted in an instant.

"There it is," Mali says with a nod.

Hayes looks over at me with his brows raised. "You told her?"

I chuckle and nod, but it's Mali who answers.

"I'm impressed, Wilder. I didn't think you had it in you." She turns to Cam. "You need to step up your game."

"Oh, I get it," Cam whines as he stares up at the ceiling. "This is hell. I'm living in purgatory."

"It could be worse," she teases, messing with him some more. "I could tell you about how they fucked twice in the bar, too."

Cam rushes to press his fingers into his ears. "I repent, I repent, I repent!"

"Okay," Hayes stops her. "As much as I'd love to sit here torturing Cam with my sex life, we seriously have to try to figure out who the hell is doing all of this."

"Did you tell them about the text yet?" Cam asks.

Mali and I answer in unison. "What text?"

Hayes pulls his phone out of his pocket and swipes it open before he hands it to me. "I got this on our way back."

> You're getting good at that. Practice makes perfect, right?

"Jesus," I grumble under my breath, passing the phone to Mali. "I figured they'd be watching you."

He shrugs. "I'd rather them be watching us than be anywhere around you."

264

## Chapter 17

There he is—the protective Hayes that I know. It's those little things that give me the smallest amount of hope for us. Little moments where he shows me that he hasn't completely let go of us yet.

Hayes sits on the couch and subtly gestures for me to sit beside him. I go willingly while Mali takes the chair and Cam sits on the floor, his arms resting on the coffee table.

"Okay, so who is a possible suspect?" I ask.

Mali hums. "I mean, my first thought would be Monty, but he's dead." She pauses for a second and looks between Hayes and Cam. "He is dead, right? Like dead, dead?"

"Yes," they answer in unison, but Hayes keeps going. "He was on that boat with us for a half hour before we dumped his body into the ocean. He's dead, dead."

She nods, accepting that answer and moving on.

"What about Monty's mom?" Cam suggests. "Lai, you went there for lunch, didn't you?"

"Yeah, but I don't think she would even be capable of this," I reply. "She's a sweetheart, but she's a spoiled housewife."

"And a grieving mother," Hayes adds. "Is there anything you might have said or given away? Weren't you at that house when you got the text?"

"I was, but I honestly don't think it was her."

Cam doesn't look convinced. "I *honestly* didn't think that my best friend would corrupt my little sister, so forgive me if I add her to my list regardless."

I turn to Hayes, smirking. "You hear that? You corrupted me."

His eyes roll, but I can see the hint of a smile there, hiding just beneath the surface.

"You know, it might not be Monty's mom," Mali says, "but it could be one of the staff."

Now *that* is the first reasonable thing she's said all day.

## Chapter 17

"That could make sense. They'd have access to everything Monty did, and the motive for revenge."

"You really think the person doing all this insane shit is the employee of some rich family?" Cam asks cynically.

"If it were any other rich family, I'd say no," Mali explains. "But Jeremiah only hires people with bachelor's degrees and security clearances. It doesn't matter if you're the head chef or the damn gardener. That man doesn't play."

Okay, so at least we have somewhat of a potential lead.

Cam throws out the idea of Lucas because of his never-ending thing for me, but we quickly rule him out. If it were him, he would've made Hayes leave so he could have me to himself, or just had him thrown in prison.

"What about Isaac?" I suggest.

Judging by their faces, they all agree it's possible, but there's just one problem.

"He's probably the most likely suspect, but none of us have seen him in years," Cam tells me. "As far as I know, he's still in bumfuck nowhere, playing hockey."

Okay, fair enough. But me suggesting Isaac is enough to bring up his brother.

"Craig?" Hayes turns to me. "Have you heard from him at all?"

I snort. "Even *you* weren't able to contact me. You think Craig was? That I made an exception for *him*?"

He chuckles and admits defeat. "Good point."

As we try to think of anyone else who could be targeting us, a car alarm cuts through the silence as it goes off outside. We all share a look before rushing out the door. It's a neighbor's car, but as the lights flash with the alarm, they shine on where our cars are parked.

"Cam, turn on the outside light," Hayes tells him.

He goes over and reaches inside the door, flicking the light on, and that's when we're able to see it.

## Chapter 17

There's a different word spray painted on each one of our cars.

Mali's says TRAITOR.

Mine is SELLOUT.

Hayes's got LIAR.

But Cam's is the most concerning—KILLER.

"How the fuck did we not know they were right outside?" Hayes panics.

Cam sighs heavily. "I don't know. We're all pretty spent after today."

It doesn't have to be said out loud for all of us to realize that they could've been listening. Hearing every word we said as we tried to figure out who they are. Then again, when aren't they?

As I stare at the new artwork on our cars, something clicks for me. "Well, we can rule out Isaac and Craig."

"What? Why?" Hayes asks.

I nod toward the cars. "They don't know which is yours and which is Cam's. Look. They put liar on your truck and killer on Cam's Jeep."

Everything suddenly gets tense as Cam glares at Hayes. "You haven't fucking told her yet?"

"Told me what?"

Hayes sighs. "No, because there's no fucking point!"

"Okay, why don't we bring this back inside before your neighbors get a show and tell they never asked for," Mali suggests.

The four of us file back inside and Cam is clearly pissed, but he's not going to be the only one if I don't get some answers soon.

"One of you better start talking right now," I demand.

Cam looks over at Hayes. "You have to tell her."

"Why? What's the point? It's done."

"Because she deserves to know!" he yells at him.

*Chapter 17*

It's obvious that Hayes isn't going to tell me, so Cam throws his hands in the air—dropping a bombshell I never saw coming.

"Hayes didn't shoot Monty that night," he starts.

"Cam, don't!" Hayes tries to stop him, but Cam blurts out the confession before he even gets the chance.

"I did."

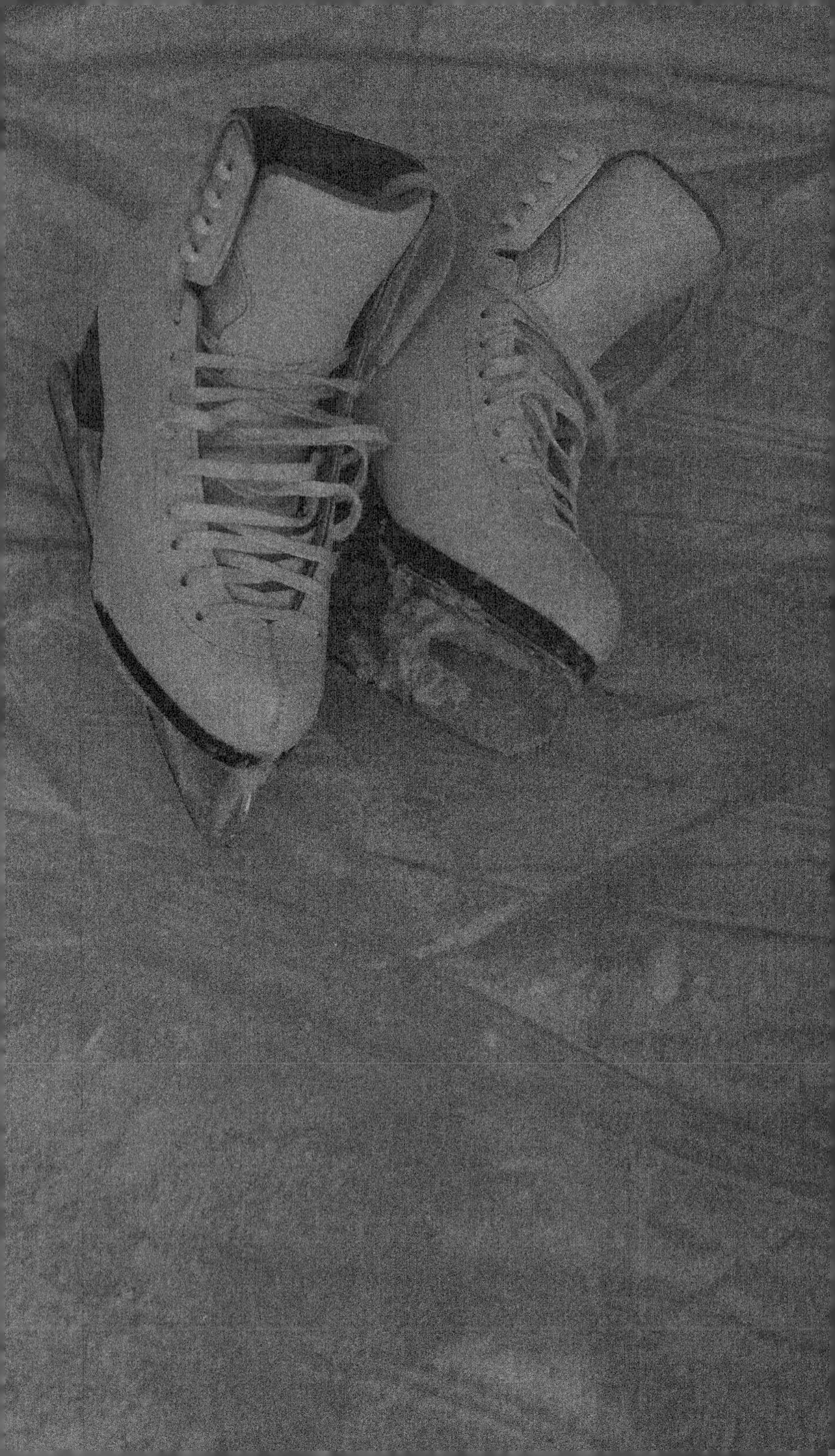

# Laiken
## CHAPTER EIGHTEEN

My jaw is practically on the floor as I stare at my brother. In the back of my mind, all the times I wondered if Hayes shot Monty on purpose play on a loop, but he couldn't have. He didn't even shoot him at all.

"What the hell do you mean *you did*?"

His eyes fall closed for a second and he winces, as if he's remembering the moment the gun went off. "It was an accident. After we got proof of the videos he took of you and Mali, we were trying to hold them over his head to get him to leave town. And at first, he acted like he was going to take the loss gracefully, but then he pulled out a gun.

"He had it pointed at Hayes first. He was rambling about how he doesn't deserve you and how you should be with someone like him. But something bit his foot, and it distracted him long enough for Hayes to wrestle the gun away from him."

Hayes goes back over to sit on the couch, resting his head in his hands, but I need to hear this.

*All* of this.

"As soon as he got it away from him, he tossed it to me, and I pointed it at Monty. Hayes was telling him that it was over, and that if he didn't leave you and Mali alone, that we were going to show you the videos and you'd never want anything to do with him then anyway. But then I heard Mali scream, and it scared me."

"And that made you pull the trigger," I finish for him.

## Chapter 18

*Fucking hell.* It makes so much sense. There was no reason for Hayes to be beating himself up over Monty's death, because he wasn't the one that did it. He just helped clean up the crime scene.

Turning to Hayes, he lifts his eyes to meet mine. "I don't get it. Why did you say you shot him?"

"He was still on probation, Laiken. And his criminal record wasn't exactly sparkly clean," he explains. "If something had gone wrong and we got caught, he didn't stand a fucking chance."

"But you lied to me!" I bellow, feeling my rage growing by the minute. "You let me believe that it was *you!*"

"I had to."

"Bullshit! You could've told me!"

"No, I couldn't have!" he roars back. "Because if shit hit the fan and we went down for it, you would've had to choose between me and your brother! I wasn't going to put you through that!"

I scoff. "So, letting me think you might have murdered someone was a better option to you?"

A dry laugh bubbles out of him. "That one was *all* you. It's not my fault you had absolutely zero fucking faith in me."

"Oh, fuck off! I knew you didn't actually shoot him on purpose! You can be an asshole, but you're not homicidal." I stop, shaking my head. "But you lied to me."

He stands up, pacing across the living room floor. "Don't give me that shit. You lied, too! You didn't tell me about the text messages, or the threats, or that you were about to walk right the fuck out of my life!"

"That was different!" My blood feels boiling hot. "If I had known you didn't actually pull the fucking trigger, I might not have left at all!"

"You think I don't fucking know that? That I haven't already thought of that?" he yells. "That tortured me for the

## Chapter 18

first three months you were gone! But even if I could go back, I still wouldn't tell you! We're married, which means they legally can't force you to testify against me. The same isn't true for Cam, though. That law doesn't apply to siblings. Hate me for it all you want, but I was protecting Cam and I was protecting you!"

"And what do you think me leaving was?" I scream, finally reaching my breaking point. "It was *me* protecting *you*!"

Cam and Mali watch with wide eyes as the argument that has been building up for the last few weeks finally explodes, and they know there's nothing they can do but let it happen. This has been a long time coming, and there is no getting through anything until we get this shit out of the way. But with the way it's going, I don't know if there will be anything left of us by the end of it.

"Fine," Hayes says after a moment, but there's venom in his tone. "Let's say those two cancel each other out. We're even on that front."

He takes a couple steps toward me, looking at me with a level of resentment in his eyes that I haven't seen before. Not even when I first showed up and came to see him in the hospital.

It's dark.

It's angry.

It's fucking volatile.

"Protecting me justifies *why* you left," he sneers. "But go ahead and try to justify *how* you left. Tell me what makes it okay that you walked out on me the same fucking way my dad did."

I stop breathing.

*Oh. My. God.*

My eyes fill with tears as I realize he's right. I did that. I never even thought about it because everything was such a goddamn whirlwind and my only thought was protecting

## Chapter 18

Hayes. I didn't tell him because I knew he would've fought to keep me here, and I wouldn't have gone.

But I didn't realize I was taking one of the worst things that's ever happened to him and repeating it.

"H," I cry.

He takes a step backward, adding more distance between us. "Yeah, thanks for that."

Turning around, he grabs his keys off the end table and heads for the door.

"Where are you going?" Cam calls out.

"To get fucking spray paint! I need to cover this shit!"

**IT'S OFFICIAL: I AM** the worst person alive. Seriously. There's a special place in hell for people like me. It's no wonder Hayes hasn't forgiven me yet. He *shouldn't* forgive me. Not ever.

I destroyed him.

I saw firsthand how fucked up he was from how his dad left. He tried to hide it, but he was devastated. Cam spent months helping him get through it. And then I went and did the exact same fucking thing.

I stay curled up in a ball on the chair, crying as I think about how much I hurt him. Honestly, if he never wants to look at me again, I wouldn't blame him. There's no justification for that.

## Chapter 18

Mali sits on the arm beside me and runs her fingers through my hair.

"He hates me," I tell her.

She sighs. "He doesn't. He's just hurt."

But that's not enough. "Well, he should hate me. I'm a horrible person. He should just divorce me and find someone better."

"Please," she says. "There is no one better than you. Well...except maybe me."

It's meant to make me laugh, but I don't think anything can accomplish that at this point. I look up at her through tear-soaked lashes.

"Did you know that it was Cam who shot Monty?"

She shakes her head. "No, but I did know he was relating the way you left to his dad."

I turn my whole body toward her. "Why didn't you tell me?"

"Because what good would it have done? Look at you. You're a mess over it. If I had told you, you would've been the same way you are now, but you would've been alone."

I could argue it further, but what's the point? It's not like it will make what I did any better. There's nothing that will make that better.

*Not a damn thing.*

**WHEN HAYES GETS BACK,** he sprays over the graffiti

## Chapter 18

with colors as close as he could find. His truck and Cam's Jeep both end up looking pretty okay—black is easier to cover. But mine and Mali's cars? Not so much.

"I'll talk to Aiden tomorrow and see if his dad can sand it down and paint it," he tells Mali.

"That'd be great. Thanks, H."

Quite frankly, the last thing I'm worried about right now is my car. My current priorities all focus around Hayes, and how I can possibly make up for what I did.

"Lai, you ready to go?" Cam asks.

He wants me to sleep at his place tonight, and he insists that we follow Mali home to make sure she gets there safely. But I'm not ready to go. Not yet.

I'm sitting on the porch steps when Hayes walks past me to go inside. I consider saying nothing, but I can't leave things like this.

"Hayes," I say as I stand up and spin around. "I—"

But he interrupts me before I can get another word out. "Don't. Please."

It feels like someone has my heart in a vise grip and is just squeezing it until it bursts. Between the defeated look in his eyes and the hurt in his voice, I'm broken inside.

Just like he is.

And it's all because of me.

"It's just, this night has been stressful enough," he explains. "I just can't handle this right now, too."

A tear slips out and I quickly wipe it away, trying to be strong. "Okay."

Standing there, I watch as he goes inside the house we used to live in together and swings the door shut behind him. My bottom lip quivers, and no matter how much I try to keep it in, I can't. I'm feeling every last ounce of pain I put him through, and I know it's going to eat me alive.

*Chapter 18*

I'm going to lose the best thing that's ever happened to me, forever.

**HAYES AND CAM DECIDE** to keep the bar closed for another day while they make sure everything is as clean as it can be and change the locks. As much as it kills me, I decided not to work from there today—giving Hayes some space.

Cam was against it at first, but I told him it wasn't up to him. That's when he changed course and asked me to at least stay somewhere safe or somewhere public. So, I work half the day at Starbucks, and the other half at my parents' house once they get home.

By the time it reaches the end of the day, I'm exhausted. Everything feels like it's catching up to me and the only thing I want to do right now is shower and change into something comfortable. Cam told me not to go back to my motel alone. He doesn't trust it. But I need something to make me feel less like a dumpster fire.

As I drive to the motel, the only thing I can think of is Hayes. I need to talk to him. To wholeheartedly apologize and tell him that if he can't get past that and he doesn't want to make us work, I understand. No hard feelings.

But I really hope he doesn't choose that.

There's no way to explain how much he means to me. Trust me, I've tried for years to put it in a song. Those kinds of feelings, with that much intensity—it would be guaranteed

## Chapter 18

to go platinum. But all the words in the dictionary don't even come close.

*I love him* doesn't feel like enough.

*I need him* isn't right either.

All the sonnets and poems in the world pale in comparison to the way he makes me feel.

As I park my car and get out, I decide to try calling him. Holding the phone to my ear, I listen to it ring as I walk toward my room.

*Hey, it's Hayes. Leave a message, or just fucking text me like a normal person.*

I chuckle as I step inside and shut the door, waiting for the beep. When it sounds, I leave a message I'm not even sure he's going to listen to.

*"Hey, H. Listen, I'd really rather not talk about this through your voicemail. It's an in-person conversation. But I can't tell you how sorry I am. I swear, I would* never *have left like that if I realized the connection beforehand. Hurting you was the last thing I wanted to do. You have to know that. You have to know that I wouldn't intentionally rip you apart like that. I lo—"*

Just before the words I haven't said since the night before I left come out of my mouth, the room erupts in chaos. Someone stands outside my motel room, smashing all the windows on the corner unit and sending glass flying into the room. And the last thing the phone records is the sound of me screaming.

## Hayes
## CHAPTER NINETEEN

I'M WALKING OUT OF THE NURSING HOME AFTER seeing my mom, when I notice I have a missed call from Laiken. *And a voicemail.* It's pathetic that I already plan on keeping it, regardless of what it says. If she ever decides to leave again, at least I'll have something else I can listen to and hear her voice.

Everything from last night runs through my head, just like it has been all day. *God*, I hate fighting with her, but lately, that's all I seem to be able to do. I'm still so fucking mad at her for leaving the way that she did. Not only did she create a new wound when she left—she ripped an old one wide open again.

I think the hardest part to deal with is that she *knew*. She was one of few people who knew how not okay I really was after everything. One of few people I didn't feel like I needed to fake it around. So, to have her walk out on me the same way he did, it fucking wrecked me.

Getting into my truck, I start it up and play the voicemail. Laiken's voice comes through the speaker and my whole body goes warm. Because that's the thing. No matter how livid I am, or how much she hurt me, she's still the girl who stole my heart right out of my chest without giving me a chance at stopping her.

"*...Hurting you was the last thing I wanted to do. You have to know that. You have to know that I wouldn't intentionally rip you apart like that. I lo—*"

## Chapter 19

My breath hitches as I wait to hear those words, not even realizing how badly I need them, but instead, I get chaos. The sound of glass shattering rings out through the phone and Laiken lets out a blood curdling scream before the voicemail ends.

*No.*

*Fuck! No!*

Panic rushes through me as I scramble to open the app we all downloaded so we could share our locations with each other. My hands shake while I wait for it to load, and the minute I see Laiken is at her motel, I press the gas pedal to the floor.

**BLUE AND RED LIGHTS** fill the street as my truck screeches to a halt in front of her motel. There are cop cars, fire trucks, and an ambulance making it so I can't get any closer. I throw the truck into park right there in the middle of the street and jump out.

I frantically look around for Laiken, but I don't see her anywhere. There are two officers coming out of the room on the corner, and that's when I see all the windows are smashed.

*That explains the glass breaking.*

My feet carry me in that direction, until the sound of Cam

## Chapter 19

calling my name stops me. I spin around to find him standing at the back of an ambulance, and when the paramedic steps to the side, I've never felt so relieved. Laiken is sitting there, with a decent sized gash on her forehead, but that's so much better than all the horrible things I imagined on my way over.

"What the fuck happened?" I ask as soon as I'm close enough.

Cam looks at Laiken, but she's clearly too shaken up to answer. "Someone busted all the windows in the room while she was inside. Glass went everywhere, and a piece of it managed to slice her head pretty good."

I exhale, turning to Laiken, but before I can say anything to her at all, Mali pushes past me and wraps her arms around her.

"Oh, thank God," she sighs. "Are you insane? What part of *don't go to your motel alone* did you not understand?"

Laiken rolls her eyes and tips her head at Cam. "Thanks, Mom, but I already got the lecture from Dad."

There's something a little weird about her referring to Cam and Mali as Mom and Dad, but it might be something I can get on board with. Right now, however, I'm only focused on one thing.

"Wait, how the fuck did both of you know to be here?" I ask.

"She called me," Cam says simply. "And I called Mali on my way over."

"And you didn't think to fucking call me?"

He glances at Mali, looking unsure. "After last night, we weren't sure you wanted to be."

"I *always* fucking want to be called when it comes to her!" I roar.

I probably shouldn't admit that, especially not in front of Laiken, but fuck it. Rules don't apply anymore, as far as I'm

## Chapter 19

concerned. And Cam should've known to at least shoot me a text about it.

"I think it's safe to say there will be no more motels for you," Mali tells Laiken. "They're not safe enough."

Cam shakes his head. "It's fine. She'll come stay with me for now."

"The fuck she will," I growl.

All three of them look at me with shocked expressions on their faces, but I don't care. That motherfucker had her alone. He could've fucking killed her. She's got a three-inch gash across her forehead, for fuck's sake. If any of them think I'm letting her out of my damn sight, they can kiss my ass.

"She's coming to stay with me, and I don't want to hear a goddamn word about it," I tell them.

Cam looks to Laiken for her approval, and he gets it when she nods. I step closer to her and put my hands on her cheeks, lifting her head so I can get a good look at the wound. The paramedics already cleaned it up but it still looks pretty bad. Which means I can only imagine what it looked like before.

"Are you okay?"

She stares up at me. "I don't know."

*Fucking hell.* She starts to get upset again, and no amount of fear could stop me from wrapping my arms around her right now.

"Come here," I say, pulling her against me while being careful not to hurt her. "We'll figure it out. Okay? You're safe. I promise."

She leans the side of her head against me and finds the comfort she's looking for in me. Not Cam. Not Mali. *Me.* Which is exactly where she fucking belongs—in my arms.

Everything feels on edge, all of us knowing exactly what could have happened tonight. If Laiken didn't understand the

## Chapter 19

importance of her not being alone somewhere before, I'm sure she does now. But I can't even say I'm mad at her right now.

I can't be.

Not when I'm just so fucking glad she's okay.

"Holy shit," Mali breathes.

Laiken's brows furrow as she slowly pulls her head off me and looks over at her best friend. "What?"

But she doesn't need to answer, because all three of us follow her line of sight across the street. I almost don't recognize him at first, standing there with hands in his pockets and an amused grin on his face. But it's him.

It's *definitely* him.

"When the fuck did he get back?" Cam asks.

Isaac sees us looking at him and he pulls one hand out to finger wave at us tauntingly. My jaw locks as my hands clench into fists.

"I'm going to fucking kill him," I growl.

But as I go to take a step toward him, Laiken rushes to grab my arm and Cam stops me with two hands on my chest.

"Are you crazy? There are like five cop cars here," he tells me. "You won't even get a finger on him before they lock your ass up."

He's right. *Fuck.* I know he's right. But I almost want to risk it. Seeing him watching the aftermath he caused, like he's proud of it…I want to slam his head into the curb and use his blood to paint the street red. But that would mean risking leaving Laiken alone, and *that* I'm not willing to do.

I keep an eye on him until he finally decides to walk away. It's not long after that when Laiken is cleared to leave by the police and paramedics. She thanks them and stands up. I wrap an arm around her and start leading her to my truck.

"Wait, what about my car?"

## Chapter 19

Mali nods for her to go. "I'll drive it there. Cam can bring me back to get mine later. Go with Hayes."

*Yeah, that girl is a godsend.*

I'm not willing to let her out of my reach right now. Not after this shit. Cam comes over and puts her things in the back of my truck, tapping the back of it twice to let me know he's done. I pull away from the scene of the crime and start heading toward my place.

"H," she breathes. "I really am sorry. I can't believe I—"

I cut her off by shushing her softly. "Not now."

My only concern at the moment is getting her home and making sure she's okay. I mentally don't have room to worry about anything else right now. None of it matters.

Just her.

**LAIKEN DECIDES TO TAKE** a shower. Apparently, that's what she went back to the motel room to do before all hell broke loose and it rained glass in there. Mali sits in the bedroom, making sure she's okay. Meanwhile, Cam and I are having a beer in the kitchen.

"It's got to be him, right? I mean, it can't be a coincidence that he's back in town when all this shit is going on."

I shake my head. "You saw the look on his face—all smug and shit. It's him. It has to be."

## Chapter 19

Cam grips the bottle tightly as he chugs half his beer. "I can't believe we were friends with that guy at one point."

"No, *you* were friends with him," I correct. "I tolerated him in the name of hockey."

He snorts. "Well, let's hope that the puck you shot straight into his balls made it so he can't reproduce."

"He won't have a dick to reproduce *with* by the time I'm done with him."

I can't believe none of us realized he was back in town. I thought for sure if he were to come back, one of the guys would have told me. But everything that's happened has been done under the cloak of darkness. For all we know, he could have been hiding this whole time—not letting anyone know he's back until he felt like exposing himself.

"Isaac is an asshole, but he's not stupid," Cam points out. "We'll have to figure out a way to get him alone. Somewhere *private*, and where his pigheaded brother isn't around to record what we do to him."

I nod. "Cornering him will probably prove to be more difficult if he only shows himself when he feels like it. And if he's keeping eyes on us, getting him to walk into a trap is probably out, too."

Cam's lips purse. "Unless he doesn't realize it's a trap."

"I'm listening."

But he doesn't explain right away. Instead, he takes out his phone and makes a call.

"Owen, hey," he says. "Remember when Morrison had me arrested and you said you wanted to help? ...Yeah, I need a favor."

## Chapter 19

**BY THE TIME MALI** starts yawning, Cam decides to go. He points out that they still have to go get her car, but we all know she's just going to sleep at his place. The same way I won't let Laiken out of my sight right now, he's feeling just as protective over her.

I'm not entirely filled in on the plan, but he seems confident that his idea might work. It's just going to take a little time. But as long as it gets me alone with Isaac by the end of it, I'm fine with being kept in the dark for a bit.

Laiken sits on the couch, looking exhausted as she stares off into space. After a deep breath, I walk over to her and put my hand out. Her eyes hold such fear as she tilts her head up to look at me.

"Let's go to bed," I tell her.

She sighs, nodding and taking my hand.

We haven't talked about sleeping arrangements. Just that it would be under my roof. But to be honest, I'm not even willing to let her in a different *room* right now. He's proven that a locked door doesn't keep him out, which means she stays near me at all times.

As we get to the top of the stairs, she turns toward the guest room, but I stop her by tightening my grip on her hand just slightly.

"What are you doing?" she asks.

I nod toward the bedroom we shared. The one I haven't

*Chapter 19*

slept in since the night she left. "You know that bed is more comfortable, and I won't be able to sleep if you're not next to me."

It doesn't take much for her to give in. She honestly looks a little relieved at the idea. But as we walk in, I feel my chest tighten at the thought of sleeping in here with her again.

"You can take the bed," I tell her, grabbing a pillow and tossing it on the floor.

"What? Why?"

I rub the back of my neck. "I don't want to make you uncomfortable."

It's not a total lie. There's a different intimacy with sleeping than there is with having sex. And the last time we were in this bed together has been playing through my mind since the day she came back.

She chuckles. "Hayes, we literally had sex *yesterday*. I don't think sharing the same massive bed is going to make anything uncomfortable."

*Shit.* "Okay."

I lean down and grab the pillow, putting it back on the bed as I ignore the voice in my mind screaming that this is a bad idea.

It's bad enough she's dressed in a pair of shorts and one of *my* T-shirts. Granted, that's my fault. I knew it would make her more comfortable after her shower, so I took the one she had lying out and switched it with mine. But I didn't hear a single complaint out of her about it.

I strip down to just my boxers and wait for her to climb into bed before I turn off the light. Once she's good, I flick the switch and walk over to slip in beside her. I never liked how big this bed is, but it didn't matter when we both slept in the middle anyway. Right now, though, I'm wishing it was a twin.

She's too far away. Sure, I could reach out and touch her,

## Chapter 19

but it's not enough. I need her body pressed against mine and my arms wrapped around her. But there's a level of anxiety that keeps me from initiating that—and I'm already on edge enough right now.

The two of us lie there, and surprisingly, the sound of her breathing and just knowing she's there is enough to settle me down. My brain goes quiet as I listen to her breaths even out. But as my eyes fall closed, I think I'm only asleep for a couple of minutes before I wake up with a jolt.

"What's wrong?" Laiken asks.

She must've felt the bed shake or heard my gasp.

"Nothing," I assure her. "I'm fine."

"Okay," she whispers into the darkness. "Goodnight, H."

"Night."

I close my eyes, willing for sleep to finally take me under, but every time it does, I'm jolted awake, thinking she's gone again. I look over at her, seeing her staring back at me with a concerned look on her face.

"I'm not going anywhere," she says as if she has a direct line to my thoughts.

I want to tell her that I know she isn't, but I can't. My mouth just won't form the words. I've never had the greatest luck, and I'm afraid that if I say it, I'll jinx it and she'll end up leaving again.

So, instead, I stay quiet—moving so I can get more comfortable and forcing myself to close my eyes.

By the third time it happens, I decide to just stay up all night, but Laiken seems to have a better idea. She sits up and runs her fingers through her hair, then comes closer. I watch as she leans over me, accidentally putting her tits in my face. It instantly makes me want her, but she's on a mission.

Pulling open the nightstand drawer, she reaches in and I hear the unmistakable sound of handcuffs. I had bought

## Chapter 19

them after our little run in with the police at the airfield, but they're getting put to a different use tonight.

As she starts to back away, I can't help myself. I reach up, putting my hand on the back of her neck and pulling her down. Her lips press against mine and we both sigh into it. There are no intentions behind it. I'm not trying to get in her pants, even though Lord knows I want to. It's just a soft, gentle kiss because I couldn't resist it anymore.

"Hayes," she sighs. "What are we doing?"

I kiss her once more, buying myself time to think of an answer, but I still don't have one. "I'm sorry."

She shakes her head. "Don't apologize. Not for that."

Rolling onto my side, I open my arms for her, and she slides down to get comfortable against me. I'm probably confusing the fuck out of her. *I'm* even confused.

"I haven't sorted it all out in my head yet," I murmur. "I don't know what's going to happen, but I know I needed to kiss you."

It's not enough, but it's enough for her. She exhales contently and cuddles closer into me before she takes my wrist and fastens one of the cuffs around it. Then, she puts the other on herself.

"There," she says decisively. "Now I can't go anywhere, and you can get some sleep."

A smirk spreads across my face as I take the opportunity to fuck with her. "I probably should've mentioned I don't have the key to those."

But she doesn't freak out like I thought she would. She doesn't even open her eyes. She just hums.

"You don't care?" I ask.

"No," she replies tiredly. "There are worse things in the world than being handcuffed to you."

That plays through my head on a loop as I fall asleep with

## Chapter 19

a smile on my face. And if it's the best sleep I've gotten in a year and a half, so be it.

**IT TAKES ABOUT A** week, but Cam's plan actually fucking works. There were multiple steps to it, and Owen's cooperation only further proved his loyalty. First, he went into a bar he knew Isaac's brother was at, but he didn't acknowledge them. He pretended to get drunk and then proceeded to shit talk Shore Break, which then led into him saying that Cam and I are assholes who don't know the first thing about running a bar.

After that, it was only a matter of time until Isaac turned up. He acted like it was just a coincidence that they ran into each other, and said he was only back to visit for a couple of weeks. Owen pretended to believe every word as he made it genuinely look like he's happy to see him again.

Earning Isaac's trust wasn't difficult. After all, the two of them used to be pretty good friends, before he went too far in this war against Cam and me. So, when Owen called Isaac and asked him to come over to play some video games, saying he ran into Cam in the store and almost punched him in the face, Isaac couldn't resist.

We stay completely quiet, staying right out of view of the door while we wait for him to get here. There are no words for how bad I am itching to get my hands on this prick.

He's the reason Laiken left.

*Chapter 19*

He's the reason Cam almost went to prison.

He's the reason Mali still won't be alone with a man unless it's Cam or myself.

Everything he has coming to him right now, he fucking deserves. He might think he's getting revenge for his friend's death, but all he's doing is giving me a reason to rid the world of another fuckhead who will only make the world a worse place by reproducing.

The knock at the door follows with Isaac's voice. "O, it's me. I've got beer."

I spin my hat around so it sits backward on my head as Owen goes to open it. He looks to us to make sure we're ready and then turns the knob. Isaac comes strolling in like he's living his best life, fist bumping Owen with one hand and holding a six pack in the other.

"What's up, my man?" he asks. "Too bad you didn't punch that prick. He deserves it."

Cam chuckles darkly. "Yeah, *too bad.*"

Isaac's eyes widen but before he can move, I grab him and throw him up against the wall. My fist slams into his stomach, and he hunches over in pain.

"Oh, I'm sorry," I feign concern. "Did that hurt? Let me help you."

I push his head down and my knee comes up, striking him in the face and breaking his nose, just like he broke mine. Blood spews out and he looks to Owen for help, but he's not going to find any.

Not when he started this shit.

Cam looks at the beer that fell to the floor when I kneed him in the face and tsks at Isaac. "That's a party foul."

He comes over, grabbing one out of the pack and hitting it against the table to pop the cap off. When you own a bar, you tend to get good at that. Anything to make your job easier,

## Chapter 19

really. Though, we'll probably have to replace the bartop sooner than we should.

As Cam takes a sip, he sighs in relief. "Nevermind. We're good."

I roll my eyes and focus my attention on Isaac. "You played your little fucking game, but it ends today."

He turns his head to the side to spit blood out onto Owen's floor. "I don't know what the fuck you're talking about."

*Yeah, I expected that.* "Do you think I'm fucking stupid? We saw you yesterday!"

"I was walking by and wondered what the hell was going on," he sneers. "And yeah, it was nice to see people getting the karma they deserve."

I glance over at Cam. "You believe this piece of shit?"

"Nope," he says, with a pop to the p.

"Me either."

Gripping the back of his neck tightly, I bounce his head off the entertainment center. He looks dizzy but I don't give him a moment to recover as I throw him back into the wall.

"If you don't fuck him tonight, can I?" Mali jokes.

Laiken chuckles. "Are you kidding? I love you and all, but I'm worse at sharing than he is."

*I seriously doubt that.*

With him a little dazed, I reach into his pocket and grab his phone. As I turn around and pass it to Mali, I notice the way they're both watching, like me kicking Isaac's ass is for their entertainment.

"Stop gawking and make yourselves useful," I tell them.

But Laiken has no shame as she smirks. "Can I gawk *and* make myself useful?"

An involuntary laugh bubbles out of me as I turn back to make sure Isaac stays put against the wall. Mali swipes the phone open, flipping it around to get Isaac's face to unlock it.

## Chapter 19

He tries to turn away, but I grip his chin tightly and force him to look into the camera.

"This will go a lot easier if you cooperate," I lie.

Let's face it, he's fucked either way.

Once Mali has what she needs, I release his chin and notice his blood got on my hand. *Fucking gross.* I use his hoodie to wipe it off, because fuck getting it on my own clothes. But then something catches my eye.

"What's that, buddy?" I taunt him, pointing to the specks of red paint on his hoodie. "What were you doing with spray paint?"

"That's old," he lies. "From when we spray painted the ice that time the lake was frozen over so we could play hockey on it. I haven't worn this sweatshirt in years."

Cam chuckles, taking another sip of the beer Isaac unknowingly brought for him. "Did you get checked into the boards too hard or something? We weren't born yesterday."

It's a little strange, seeing Cam so laid back while we deal with this. But I told him on the way here, I'm taking point on this. I want to make sure all the pain he feels is at my hands.

"There's nothing in his texts," Mali says. "But there's a burner app that's also wiped clean."

I huff out a sarcastic laugh. "Now what would you need that for?"

"None of your fucking business," he spits.

God, I love when he acts like he's the one in charge here. It makes his scream so much more enjoyable as my fist crushes into his already broken nose.

"Wrong answer."

Mali hums. "Why do you have two different calculator apps?"

His eyes widen, and he tries to push off the wall, but he's too weak to fight against me. All it takes is one press of my hand to keep him in place.

## Chapter 19

"It's a secret storage app," I tell her. "Open it."

She does it with an attitude that makes it seem like she's playing her favorite game, which only makes her that much more dangerous. Seriously, Cam is in for it if he ever hurts her to the point of no return.

"Ooh," she coos. "Isaac, you've been a bad boy!"

Isaac's head drops as Laiken gets closer to Mali. "Let me see!"

The sound of moans come through the phone, and Laiken giggles.

"Babe, I knew you had good aim, but damn," she tells me. "You really had to be spot on to hit that little thing."

My head whips around and I glare at her. "Stop looking at his fucking dick and hand me the phone."

She rolls her eyes as she takes the phone from Mali and hands it to me. "You ruin all my fun."

"Keep up that attitude and the only one who will be having fun later is me," I warn.

Cam comes over and we watch as the video plays. It's nothing he's done to us, but we already have enough proof of that. We're not doing this the legal way, so nothing else matters as long as we know the truth. What it *does* show, though, is a secret I'm sure he would not want getting out.

"Oh my God," Cam snickers, taking it over to show Owen. "You've got to see this shit."

"Well, well, well," I say slowly. "How would daddy dearest feel to know you've been fucking his wife?"

If looks could kill, I'd be on fire right now. Unfortunately for him, it doesn't work that way. But hey, like he said before —it's nice to see people getting the karma they deserve.

"I bet that trust fund and endless stream of cash would dry up real fast if he found out."

No longer needing to hold him there, I let go and walk over to Cam. Taking Isaac's phone, I send the video to myself,

## Chapter 19

Cam, and Mali. There's no reason Laiken needs it, so I leave her out. Once I'm done, I toss it at his feet.

"Fuck with us again, and I will make sure that video gets sent to every media outlet in the area while I put on a whole movie theater showing for your father. Do I make myself clear?"

He exhales, using his arm to wipe the blood off his face. "Yes."

My bottom lip juts out as I pout, coming closer and patting him on the cheek. "Aw, don't look so sad. I told you if you ever came back to town, I was going to slit your throat. You're getting off easy!"

Personally, I wanted to kill him. I planned on doing everyone a favor and ripping him limb from limb, but Laiken wasn't on board. She pointed out that we would immediately be suspects—Cam, especially, after what happened that summer. And we're not exactly professionals at getting away with murder. So unfortunately, the fucker gets to live.

Turning around, I up-nod at Owen. "Thanks, man. See you Friday?"

He grins. "You know it."

Cam fist bumps Owen and we go to head out the door when Mali stops in front of Isaac. Laiken turns around to see what she's doing.

"Mal, you coming?"

She nods. "Just one thing first."

Isaac lifts his head to look at her, and fear fills his eyes. "Mal, listen. I'm sorry. I really thought we were just having fun. I didn't—"

We all watch as she winds back and kicks him in the balls hard enough to make *me* nauseous. Isaac lets out a high-pitched wail as he falls over and curls in on himself on the floor.

"Don't ever say my fucking name again."

## Chapter 19

As if a switch is flicked, she smiles brightly and accents it with her sunny disposition, walking toward Laiken and looping their arms together.

"Let's go."

The four of us take the elevator down and walk out of Owen's apartment. As the sun hits my face, I grab my sunglasses from where they hang on the collar of my shirt and put them on. I can feel Laiken's gaze burning into the side of my head as she walks beside me.

"What?" I ask her.

She smirks, looking forward. "Nothing. It was just hot, watching you take care of business like that."

I huff amusedly, but I can't ignore the part of me that also feels a little cheated. "Imagine if you had told me when it first started. I could've ended this shit then."

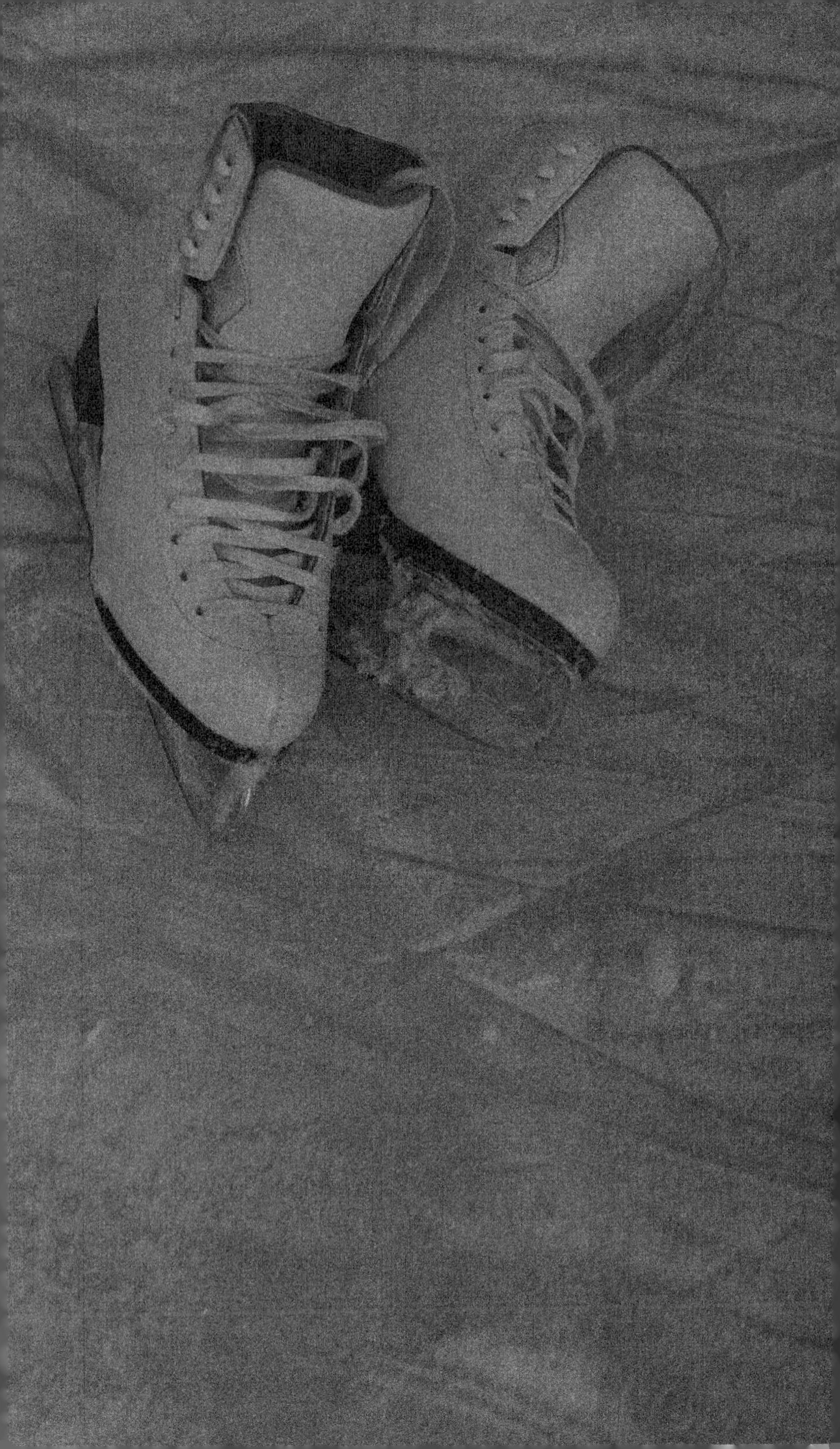

# Laiken
## CHAPTER TWENTY

It's a strange feeling, not having to look over your shoulder when you're used to doing it for so long. The fear that you're always being watched becomes a constant fixture in your life after a while and even when it stops, it doesn't fully go away. Though if I'm honest, I'm having a hard time believing it's truly over.

It all just feels too easy. Too simple. Too anticlimactic, if you will. I mean, this person went to great lengths to get to us. They knew things. Kept a constant eye on us.

*Killed someone*, even.

I'm just not sure if I believe Isaac is capable of all that. He's a garbage human, for sure. But that level of sinisterness? I've known him since I was eight years old, when he first started playing hockey with Cam. I'm not convinced.

But Mali tells me that I'm just being paranoid, and Hayes is concerned I'm suffering from a bit of PTSD. He thinks I should go talk to someone. Maybe he's right. It's not like it would hurt. Hell, they might know what I should do about Hayes, too.

After confronting Isaac, Hayes and I agreed that I would stay a few more days, to make sure nothing else happened. He was concerned about retaliation, but my mind was skirting more along the lines of *if, God forbid, we got it wrong*. But nothing ended up happening.

## Chapter 20

And I never ended up leaving.

We haven't talked about it, and it's not for a lack of trying. Believe me, I've tried. But every time, we end up arguing and then it quickly turns into getting lost in each other. Sometimes, it even seems like we argue for an excuse to fuck—like the day we got into a fight over me forgetting to use a coaster. Never in his life has he *ever* used a coaster, but that day, he was hell bent on the importance of them.

And if I purposely didn't use one later that night so we could go for round two, I won't apologize for it.

It even reached one point where I honestly wondered if this house has some weird kind of feng shui to it that makes your sex drive go wild. It would've made so much sense, except the sexual tension crackles between us even at the bar.

And at Cam's.

And in the truck.

And...well, you get it.

I've tried talking to Mali about it, but she doesn't see the problem. From how it looks to her, Hayes is just trying to let us go back to normal. Brush it under the rug so to speak, but it's not that simple for me. He's different than he used to be. And I know that's bound to happen. After everything, I'm lucky he even still looks in my direction.

But I wish I knew if there's even a chance we'll ever get back to where we were before I went and screwed everything up.

I'm sitting on the island, watching Hayes cook dinner. Well...okay, *cook* is a very generous word for what he's doing. Pretty sure whatever he's trying to make is not going to come out edible, but when I tried to help him, he told me he's got it and that he doesn't need my help.

So, I hopped my little ass onto the island and now I'm enjoying watching him ride the struggle bus to failure town.

## Chapter 20

*Is it too soon to order a pizza?*

"I think I'm going to come to the bar with you tomorrow," I tell him. "There's no one in the studio so I just have to work on writing, and I figure I can do that there."

He shrugs, keeping his eyes on the "meal" in front of him. "That's fine. Whatever you want to do."

*Ugh*, he's so frustrating. Every time I try to get a read on him, he shuts down for the sole purpose of keeping me out. It's like he wants all of me, but isn't willing to give me all of him in return.

Funny—sounds a lot like how we started.

"I don't have to," I say simply. "I could go hang out at the rink instead. Lucas told me last Friday that I should stop by sometime."

His whole body tenses. "Did he?"

"Yeah..."

"Hmm. That's interesting."

My legs stop swinging. "Why is it interesting?"

He shrugs once more. "I just didn't know he had a death wish. That's all."

A giggle bubbles out of me. "You've known Lucas just as long as you've known Cam."

"Yeah, which means I've heard almost every single time he's tried hitting on you," he growls. "But if you want to go, go ahead. I'm sure Riley will *love* some time alone with me at the bar before Cam comes in."

*Fucking checkmate.* "Wait for me in the morning. I'm coming with you."

"Whatever you say, Rochester," he says as he glances back at me and winks.

I roll my eyes. "You fucking suck."

He chuckles as he finally turns completely around to look at me. "It's not my fault you're more jealous than I am."

"Oh," I laugh. "Is that so?"

## Chapter 20

"Mm-hm." He takes a step closer.

I give him a knowing look. "Is that why you damn near poisoned Finn that one day?"

He plays it coy. "I don't know what you're talking about."

"No?"

"Nope. I just didn't rinse out the lines good enough."

Humming, I reach forward and loop my fingers into his belt loops. "You really should be more careful with that."

"I know." His lips ghost across mine. "Someone could get hurt."

Just as we're about to close the gap between us, I see smoke coming up from behind him. I lean to the side and notice the food blackening inside the pan while a burnt smell starts to radiate.

"Uh, H?"

He turns around and throws his head back when he sees it. "Mother fucker!"

I press my fist to my mouth in an attempt to contain my laughter, but it doesn't do much as he turns off the burner and realizes none of it is salvageable.

"So, is *now* when I say I told you so?" I tease.

Spinning on his heels, he pins me with a look. "This is *your* fault."

"No, no. You're the one who got distracted."

"Yeah, because you're fucking distracting!" he huffs.

But I just tsk in response. "Shouldn't have taken your eyes off it."

There's something in his eyes. It looks like a mix between frustrated and determined. And he grabs the pan before pouring the contents into the trash.

"That's it," he declares. "I'm trying again. I have enough of the ingredients to start from scratch."

Oh my God, he's trying to starve me. "Hayes."

"Nope. There's no Hayes here. Only Chef Wilder."

## Chapter 20

"Chef Wilder should stick to bartending," I joke.

"You just wait," he says, facing the fridge as I take out my phone and call our favorite local pizza place. "It's going to make your mouth water. You'll see."

I put the phone to my ear just in time for him to turn around. His eyes narrow on me, and I keep my gaze on his as they answer.

"Antonio's Pizza."

"Yeah, I'd like to place an order for delivery," I tell him, trying not to laugh at the way Hayes's jaw drops.

"Okay. What can I get for you?" he asks.

But before I can order, Hayes drops everything he's holding and comes over to scoop me up. "That's it. I'm eating you for dinner."

I squeal, realizing that I dropped my phone and the poor worker probably heard that. "Hayes! Now we can't order from there anymore!"

"What a shame," he says, obviously not giving a flying fuck as he carries me up the stairs.

*Who really needs dinner anyway?*

**I STAND IN THE** bar with Mali, watching from across the room as Hayes works the bar. Now that summer has started, Saturdays are crazy in here. During the day, it's a steady flow of people, and at night, they're swamped. As Cam passes, I call his name.

## Chapter 20

"Do you guys need help?" I ask him.

He pushes his hair out of his face, looking exhausted. "Yes, but you're not allowed behind the bar."

"Why not?"

"Because you're not twenty-one."

My brows furrow. "Neither is Mali, but you guys have let her bartend before."

He shushes me and glances around as he steps closer. "Keep your voice down. Mali did it during the off season. That's different. We're less likely to get caught then."

I shrug. "My fake ID looks real enough. Even a cop couldn't figure it out."

"Dude," Mali interrupts. "Why are you begging him to let you *work*?"

My lips clamp shut as I realize she has a point.

Cam chuckles. "Thanks for the offer, though."

I nod and watch him go back over to the bar, and then my gaze switches to where Hayes smiles as he serves someone their drink. He looks so happy, and I always love when he's like this. It always makes me want to stay in his orbit.

Playful Hayes is my second favorite Hayes.

"Ah," Mali says. "I get it now. You wanted an excuse to be near Hayes."

I scoff. "No. I was just trying to be helpful."

She gives me her best *I don't believe you for shit* look as she nods. "Sure, you were."

*Ugh.* "Fuck you. Can you blame me? I'm losing my damn mind here."

"He still hasn't given you anything to go off of?"

"Not. A. Thing. It's like he gets off on torturing me."

She goes to take a sip of her soda. "He's been getting off, all right."

"You're Satan," I deadpan.

Mali laughs into her drink. "What? I think you're the only

## Chapter 20

person I know that is having the best sex of your life and still complaining about it."

"Because that's the thing," I whine. "It's not the best sex of my life. I mean, it's amazing. I'm not saying it's not. He's insanely talented. But the best sex was two summers ago, when he loved me just as much as he fucked me. He had this way of making me feel like I was the only woman he had eyes for."

"You're *still* the only woman he has eyes for," she argues.

A heavy sigh leaves my mouth. "I know, but I'm telling you. Something's different. He's still distant and keeping me shut out, and I don't know how to fix it."

She glances back at the bar and then smiles at me. "Well, for starters, you could go talk to him. Maybe having his attention on you for a bit will help."

"For no reason? Mal, he's busy."

Grabbing my water, that's only halfway empty, she throws it back and drains the rest of it, slamming it on the counter when she's done. "There. Now you need another drink. And I need to pee."

She drags me toward the bar on her way to the bathroom and all but shoves me toward the empty seat. Hayes raises his brows at me just slightly, and I know I have no choice now.

At the last second, an idea comes to mind and I smirk, going up to the bar and sitting down—exactly what I'm not supposed to do.

"You know you can't sit there," he tells me, standing there with his hat on backward and his arms crossed over his chest as he leans back against the counter.

I pretend to look around. "Me? I'm just trying to get a drink."

He gives me a smile that has me practically ready to come

*Chapter 20*

on the spot and pushes off the counter to come closer. "Okay. What can I get for you?"

"A jack and coke."

I can tell he's enjoying this by the way snickers. "One Shirley Temple coming right up."

Glaring at him, I reach into my back pocket and pull out my fake ID. I put it on the bar in front of me and push it toward him. He lets out a breathy laugh as he picks it up and looks at it, then slips it into his own back pocket.

"You can't just keep my ID," I tell him.

He shrugs. "Sure I can. It's a false document. That's not your last name."

With a wink, he leaves me speechless as he walks away.

*My fucking fake has Blanchard on it.*

It's things like this that I swear he does to torture me. Every once in a while, he'll say something like that, and I will spend the next three days overthinking it and wondering what the hell it could mean.

Take this, for example. Is he saying he wants me to still go by Wilder? He told me when I got here that he wouldn't give me a divorce, but he was just being spiteful, and I didn't want one anyway. I'd be lying if I said I didn't worry one day he's going to come home with those papers though. I've had nightmares of him leaving them on the table and telling me he's sorry but he just doesn't think we can get through this.

"How can you talk to him like that?" a woman sitting beside me asks. "You don't get nervous and forget how to speak when he looks at you?"

It takes me a second to figure out what she's talking about, and then it hits me.

Oh, Jesus Christ.

"I've known him for a while," I answer.

She keeps her eyes on Hayes as she sighs. "Lucky. I've

## Chapter 20

been coming here almost every weekend, trying to get up the nerve to ask him for his number."

I choke on my own saliva, forcing me to cough before I clear my throat. "Oh. Well, I hate to break it to you, but he's married."

Her jaw drops. "Is he really?"

"Yep," I tell her, looking over at Hayes. "His wife is a total bitch, but he won't divorce her for some reason. I don't know."

I watch as he laughs, and I know he just heard every word. He drops a couple cherries into the glass and brings it over, placing the Shirley Temple in front of me. I look down at it and back up at him.

"That's not what I ordered."

He smiles and steps back. "Three more weeks."

The wink he shoots me makes me want to drag him into the back room. Someone raises their hand on the other side of the bar to get his attention, but just before he walks away, he stops and looks at me.

"Try not to let Mali drink that one, too."

I put my tongue in my cheek as I laugh, because of course he was watching me. He's always watching me, even when I think he isn't. But I'm not complaining. He can have his eyes on me anytime he wants.

**THE PROBLEM WITH GUYS** at the bar is that once

## Chapter 20

they start to get a buzz going, they either become complete idiots or way too ballsy. Rarely do you ever see someone with a happy medium between the two. It's usually because they're with their friends and they want to impress them by scoring a "hot babe" to go home with.

Sometimes they're fine. My issue is when they don't take no for an answer. Take this guy, for example. It was relatively funny when he had the guts to come up and ask Mali and me for a threesome. Mal even pretended to consider it for a second, until we both broke out into a laugh. But apparently, he took that as an invitation to stick around. We even try moving to another part of the bar, but he doesn't seem to get the hint.

"What are you drinking, sweetheart?" he asks. "Let me buy you something."

I shake my head politely. "No, I'm good. But thank you."

"I insist." He reaches up and twirls a piece of my hair around his finger. "Can't have a pretty girl like you going thirsty."

Taking a step back, I put distance between us. "Seriously, I'm flattered, but I'm not interested."

"That's just because you don't know anything about me yet," he presses. "Give me a shot before you rule me out."

This guy looks old enough to be my father, and I wonder if he knows he's hitting on a twenty-year-old. Then again, as long as I'm legal, I don't think he cares.

I can tell Mali is about to get involved, because she puts her glass down on the high-top table beside her. But just as he grabs my hand and tries to pull me into him, Hayes comes out of nowhere and decks him straight across the face.

The guy goes stumbling into another table, spilling their drinks everywhere and falling to the floor. Hayes shakes out his hand while Mali's eyes widen.

## Chapter 20

"Well, good to see his caveman tendencies are as strong as ever."

I sigh, looking at Hayes who doesn't seem at all apologetic about the fact that he just punched a customer in his own bar. Cam, who saw the whole thing, rushes over and leaves Riley to tend the bar by herself.

"I am *so* sorry, sir," he tells the drunk. "Let me help you up."

When the guy gets back on his feet, Cam makes sure all of his clothes are in place. But the way the man is glaring at Hayes tells both Cam and me that damage control is sorely needed.

"Handle him while I keep us out of a lawsuit," my brother grumbles to me.

I nod and grab Hayes's hand, pulling him toward the back. Thankfully, he doesn't put up a fight and as soon as we get into the back room, I shut the door.

"What the hell was that about?"

He rolls his eyes. "Don't play dumb. He was all fucking over you!"

"Yes, but I had it handled!" I say with a little more power than necessary. "H, you can't punch someone just because they tried to get with me."

"The fuck I can't," he growls.

Without taking his eyes off me, he corners me between the shelf and the wall as he turns the lock on the door.

"I will *always* protect what's mine."

My heart is racing, and I muster all the confidence I can manage as I stare up at him. "Well, if you're only going to act like I'm yours when someone encroaches on your territory, then don't. I can take care of myself."

His eyes darken as he pulls me against him. "Don't pretend you don't love it when I get possessive over you."

I stay completely still, not saying a word as he slides my

## Chapter 20

dress up and loops his thumbs through my panties, pulling them down just enough to give him access. With one hand, he undoes his belt while the other starts teasing his clit. And his pants are barely pulled down before he's stretching me open with his cock.

"Oh, fuck," I moan, but he quickly shushes me, covering my mouth with his hand.

I'm still making noise—I can't help it when he's fucking me like this with all those people right on the other side of the door—but they all come out muffled against his hand. The only thing in the room is his primal need to claim what's his, and there isn't a single part of me that's not okay with it.

Not when it feels this good.

And definitely not when he's looking at me like I'm the only thing in his life he isn't willing to lose.

---

**WHEN I WAS YOUNGER,** my mom always used the saying "you can't have your cake and eat it, too." I remember I hated it, because as long as you got a big enough cake, yeah you fucking could. But as I sit in front of my computer and log onto a work meeting to find my boss and my boss's boss staring back at me, I realize she was right.

There are some situations where you just can't have it all, no matter how much I wish I could.

"Laiken," my boss greets me. "How are you?"

I smile politely. "I'm good. And you?"

## Chapter 20

"Good, good," he says. "Listen, we wanted to talk about when we can expect you back in the studio. We understand you've had some personal issues going on, and working remotely works well for the interim, but we really need you to be in here and hands on."

A lump builds in my throat and I swallow it down. "I totally understand that. I just don't know that I have a date to give you. I thought it was going well, working through video calls. With how technology is today, I'm able to do all the same things remotely as I would do in the studio. Has someone complained about my job performance?"

He shakes his head. "No, not at all. It's more of a company image thing. We want all of our clients to feel valued and prioritized, and if our best song writer isn't in house, it takes away from that."

"That makes sense," I reply.

"I knew you'd understand," he says. "So, if you could talk to your family and try to tie up any loose ends you need to take care of, I'd ideally like to have you back in here by early next month at the latest."

My heart drops into my stomach. It's so soon. I knew this conversation was coming, but I had hoped that I would know what was going on between Hayes and me before it happened. Now I'm at a crossroads, and I have to choose...

The dream job I've wanted since I was a little girl, or the guy who has my heart in his hands but can't tell me if he's going to keep it or throw it away.

# Hayes
## CHAPTER TWENTY ONE

OWNING A BAR, YOU SEE A LOT OF PEOPLE celebrating their twenty-first birthday—especially when your co-owner went viral and they come to see him specifically. Before Laiken came back, each time a group would come in with sashes and tiaras, and the one in the middle shrieking that she's twenty-one, I would think about her birthday coming up.

I'd wonder what her plans were going to be. Who she would spend it with. What her first drink would be. Even just Mali coming to the bar would remind me of it, being as they were only born three days apart. The fact that I wouldn't be there to share it with her plagued my mind on an almost daily basis.

She's back now though, and that changes things. As long as she doesn't vanish in the middle of the night again any time soon, she'll be here to celebrate it—and I will be the one to pour her first legal drink.

"Cam," I say as he comes around the corner.

He stops and looks at me. "Yeah, what's up?"

I think about my own twenty-first birthday, and how it ended up becoming the shitshow that started this all. I don't want that for her. Or for Mali. This time, we're doing it right.

"I wanted to swing an idea by you," I tell him. "It's about Laiken and Mali's birthday."

The smile that stretches across Cam's face tells me he's in before I even tell him what it is.

*Chapter 21*

**THE FIRE BURNS HOT** in front of us. The crackling of the wood mixes with the sound of the waves crashing against the shore. I honestly think I could stay right here, in this moment, and never tire of it.

Owen and Lucas are each shotgunning a beer, racing to see who is faster while Aiden times them. Mali and Cam are off to the side and wrapped up in their own secret conversation. At first, it looks like they're arguing. But then he leans in and whispers something into her ear and any anger she was feeling goes right out the damn window as she smiles at him, shaking her head slowly. There are a few customers hanging around, but I barely even notice them.

How could I when Laiken is sitting across from me?

She's messing around on her phone, sipping from a Starbucks cup that I'm almost positive she and Mali spiked before they came here. But if I don't know about it and I didn't serve it, I can't get in trouble for it.

Innocence by ignorance.

I've been driving her insane. Not intentionally, of course. I've been driving myself insane, too. But she keeps trying to figure out what's going on with us, and no matter how much I think about it, I can't figure out what to tell her.

I wish it wasn't so complicated. That I could block out all of the anxiety that filled the holes in my life that she left behind. It's not like I'm trying to play with her emotions. I

## Chapter 21

just don't know if I can trust her again—and the six weeks she's been back hasn't been enough to show me that she's not going to leave again.

But every day, I feel like I get a little bit closer to breaking down the wall I built to keep her out.

My phone dings on my lap and I look down to see a text from Laiken.

> Stop fucking me with your eyes.

I chuckle, glancing up at her for a second to see her grin teasingly. Okay, we can play this game.

> Would you rather I actually fuck you instead?

She huffs and I can see the way she shifts in her seat in my peripheral vision.

> Yes, please.

> Right on the bar? Let everyone hear how you beg for me?

Groaning, she throws her head back against the seat and bites her lip. I look up from my phone and directly at her, raising my brows for only a second in a silent question. And when she gets up and starts walking into the bar, it's not even a full second before I'm up and following behind.

Because I'm right back to where I was—addicted to her and slowly giving her the power to break me all over again.

*Chapter 21*

**AS MUCH AS I'VE** tried to leave my mom out of my problems, there's no one better to ask about this topic than her. The answer I need from her is one that I've wondered on and off throughout the years, but never more than right now.

Right now, the answer means so much more than it ever would've before.

"Hey, Ma?" I say when I finally get up the nerve to bring him up. "Can I ask you something?"

She sighs. "No, your sister was *not* adopted."

"Dammit," I joke. "But in all seriousness, can I? It's about a touchy subject."

Looking away from the TV, she focuses all her attention on me. "What is it?"

I take a deep breath, knowing the wounds I may open have never been easy for her to heal from. They cut her straight down to the core, and it took a while before she was even remotely okay. But she got there, and that's how I knew I would too, eventually.

Until she came back.

"If Dad were to have come back after he left us, would you have taken him back?"

She goes quiet, and if I couldn't see her, I'd be worried I hurt her by bringing him up. But I can tell by the look on her face, she's really putting thought into the question.

## Chapter 21

After a couple minutes, she looks at me with nothing but resolve all over her face. "Yes. I would have."

"Because of Devin and me?"

"No," she says, a sad smile appearing on her face. "Because before he started drinking, he was the love of my life. I would've gone through anything to make that work."

"Really?" I'm honestly a little surprised. "Even after he walked out on us? Wouldn't you be afraid he was going to do it again?"

She shrugs. "Well, sure. I'm human, and that's a very valid fear. But his absence is something I still feel to this day. It fades, but it never fully goes away, even knowing he's not with us anymore. Losing a love like that leaves an emptiness behind, and no matter how hard you try to fill it or what you try to fill it with, you can't. It's a bottomless pit in the center of your heart, formed perfectly in the shape of them."

Pausing, she takes a breath and looks up at the ceiling. When she looks at me again, I know she is physically feeling the pain of every word she says.

"I would've much rather dealt with the fear of losing him again than the emptiness of not having him at all."

My head drops and I stare down at my lap. Everything she just said resonates with all the emotions I feel each day. But one thing I hadn't thought about was the last part.

This whole time, I've been wondering if I'll ever be able to trust her again. To be able to sleep without waking up in a panic just because she rolled over. But I never stopped to ask myself if I could handle not having her again. Because that's my only other alternative.

If we don't get through this, that's the end of us.

And that pain is just as bad as the fear that wakes me up at night.

Talk about being caught between a rock and a hard place. It feels like no matter what I do, I lose. All I've wanted is to

## Chapter 21

be able to go back to before she left. Before she took our perfect little bubble and popped it so she could walk out and leave me behind.

"Hayes," Mom says softly. My eyes meet hers and she gives me a small smile. "Laiken isn't your father."

"No, but she left the same way he did."

She sighs and nods once. "Okay, I'll give you that one. The similarities are there. But you're forgetting the biggest difference between the two of them."

My brows furrow as I look at her. "What's that?"

"Your father's biggest love was the bottle," she says. "But Laiken's is *you*."

**I WALK OUT OF** the nursing home with a little more clarity than I had before. When it comes down to it, there are only two options I have in front of me. And it's not a matter of if I can try to let her back in again—it's if I can handle losing her again.

Before I put the car in drive, I check my phone and find a missed call from my realtor. I press the button to call her back and put it on speaker as I start to drive toward the Blanchard's for dinner.

"Hayes!" she answers excitedly after the second ring. "I have some great news that I think will make you really happy."

## Chapter 21

I'm more focused on looking both ways at the stop sign than I am her words. "I like great news. What is it?"

"Do you remember that couple who offered you twenty grand below asking?"

"Yeah. I turned them down."

Just like I've turned down every other person who has made an offer since it's been listed for sale. Ramona hasn't hidden her frustration about it either. Then again, I probably wouldn't either if I was working on commission.

"You did," she confirms. "But they've decided they love the house so much that they're willing to give you what you're asking for it."

*Fuck.*

I fall silent at the news. When I told Cam I was going to sell the house, I meant it. We need the money to catch the bills up at the bar, and I thought that everything with Laiken was done. And even if we managed to pull off a miracle and end up okay, I thought the house was tainted by the memory of her leaving.

But slowly, over the last few weeks, we've been making new memories. Ones that cover the old like a fresh coat of paint. Right now, selling the house feels a lot like giving up. Throwing in the towel and accepting defeat.

And that's not something I'm ready to do just yet.

"You know, I thought you would be more excited," Ramona tells me.

"Yeah," I say with an exhale. "I'm sorry, but I have to say no."

A strangled noise leaves her mouth. "Hayes, I don't think you heard me right. They're willing to give you exactly what you're asking for. Not a penny less."

"I heard you correctly," I tell her. "But I just don't think I'm okay with selling it anymore."

She sighs heavily, and I'm sure she's silently mouthing

## Chapter 21

every obscenity known to man right now. "All right, but you should know that your house was listed over market value. If you try to sell it again down the road, there's a good chance you won't get anywhere near what they're offering you."

"Well, I'm hoping I won't end up selling it at all."

She's obviously not happy, having wasted hours and hours of her time for nothing in return, and I feel bad—just not bad enough to sell my house. *Our* house. Because it feels like every day, I start to get back little glimpses of a future I thought was no longer possible.

I won't lie, it scares the shit out of me, but sometimes the best things are the ones you're most afraid of.

**PULLING UP TO THE** Blanchards, I park behind Cam's Jeep. If he's here, that means Laiken is, too. She stayed at the bar so she could ride over with him while I went to see my mom.

Every visit with her is well worth it. The time we've been spending together is something I'll hold onto long after she's gone. But this one taught me something. It showed me what's most important.

I open the door and step inside, giving Mrs. Blanchard a hug just like I always do. She's just getting ready to put dinner on the table and tells me to go sit down with everyone else.

## Chapter 21

The first time Laiken showed up to family dinner, I almost didn't come in. I saw her car in the driveway and my first thought was to press the gas pedal to the floor and speed away at NASCAR pace. But there was still that part of me that wanted to see her. To sit across the table from her and sneak glances at her to remind myself that it was real. That she was really back, and I hadn't hallucinated the sight of her after crashing my motorcycle.

So that's exactly what I did, and even though my chest felt like it was on fire with every breath I took, it was worth it.

As I walk into the dining room, Laiken looks up and smiles at me. It's the one that's reserved only for me. The one that Mali calls her hazy smile. And just like that, I'm the same twenty-year-old that fell head over heels for the girl who broke all my damn rules like they never applied to her in the first place.

"Hey, you," she says happily. "How was seeing your mom?"

Instead of taking the seat across from her, I walk around the table and sit beside her. Three feet is too much fucking space in between us.

"It was really good," I reply, leaning over and kissing her temple.

Of course, that's the exact moment Cam has to walk in. He grins teasingly, and I don't even wait for him to open his mouth before I flip him off, making Laiken giggle. The sound of it sends a wave of euphoria straight through me.

As we sit through dinner, I pay extra attention to Laiken—watching the way she smiles and laughs with her family and with me. Before she left, she was broken. Just the shell of the woman I remembered. But while she was gone, she fixed herself, and it only made her stronger. And then the universe brought her back to me. It gave me a second chance at my happy ending, and I'd be stupid not to take it.

## Chapter 21

I might not trust her again yet, but after everything my mom said today, I think I want to try.

**IT'S LATE BY THE** time we get back home. After dinner, we all sat around and exchanged funny stories, reminiscing about all the crazy things we've done over the years. Though, the most shocking was when Mrs. Blanchard admitted to knowing I was climbing up the roof and sneaking through Laiken's skylight. But judging by the shock that was on Mr. Blanchard's face, she never shared the wealth of information.

*I should send her flowers for that.*

"So, what's in the box?" I ask Lai.

As we were leaving, her mom remembered that a package came with Laiken's name on it. It's a narrow box that's probably about a foot long. I racked my brain the whole way home, trying to figure out what it is, but I came up empty.

"A birthday present from Nolan," she answers.

As she tries to pick at the tape instead of just getting a pair of scissors, I pull the switchblade out of my pocket and gesture for her to pass it to me. It only takes a second for me to cut it open before I give it back. She peels back the flaps and looks inside, but then quickly shuts it again as she laughs.

"Well?" I press. "Are you going to tell me what it is?"

She shakes her head. "No. No, I'm not."

## Chapter 21

*Okay, now I have to know what's inside.*

I go to reach for the box, but she grabs it and tries to run away. Unfortunately for her, my legs are a lot longer than hers, so it doesn't take long for me to catch her. My arms wrap around her waist, and I lift her up. She squeals as I start to tickle her, dropping the box on the floor. The contents spill out of it and my eyes widen when I see the vibrating wand.

"Nolan sent you a vibrator?"

She bites down on her thumb as she nods. "It's an inside joke."

Bending down, I grab the note that fell out with it. "I take it this is part of it?"

Her eyes widen and she tries to rip it out of my hands, but I hold it up just above her reach. Even as she jumps, she can't seem to grab it.

"Laiken," I read out loud. "Try not to use this one so much it shorts out."

Lai pouts, crossing her arms over her chest. "Be lucky I like your dick. I could've hit you there. That would've gotten you to drop it."

I shake my head as I smirk at her. "Nuh-uh. You're not getting out of this that easily. What is she talking about?"

"Nothing," she lies. "She's delusional. You've met her. Total crazy person."

I pretend to be disappointed. "And here I thought we weren't keeping secrets from each other anymore."

That makes the smile drop right off her face. "That's not fair."

"Just evening the playing field," I say, flashing her an innocent smile.

She runs her fingers through her hair, trying to bring herself to be able to tell me. I wait patiently and after a moment, she starts to tell the story.

"After I left—when I met Nolan and moved in with her—I

## Chapter 21

was a bit…sexually frustrated. But I didn't even want to look at anyone else, let alone sleep with them, so I used a vibrator…a lot."

She goes on to tell me how she would close her eyes and think of me. She'd picture the first time in my truck, fucking in the ocean, the day I told her I bought the house, and especially our wedding night. And all of it should be turning me on, but I'm locked on one very specific thing.

"Wait, go back," I demand.

"To what part?"

"When you said that you didn't even want to look at anyone else."

She looks at me like she doesn't understand. "What about it?"

My mouth goes dry as I stare back at her. "Y-you didn't…?"

It's something I used to wonder about while she was gone and even more so since she came back. I knew I wasn't with anyone else. I had no interest in it. I promised all of myself to her when we got married, and those vows still mattered to me even while she was nowhere to be found. But I wasn't sure if she looked at it the same way that I did.

"Hayes," she says softly. "The thought of being with anyone but you made me physically ill. There's no one else out there for me. You're the only guy I've ever slept with, and I don't have any intentions of ever changing that."

There's something about the sound of her voice as she speaks those words, settling one of my biggest fears. I had nightmares about her being out there with someone else. When I couldn't sleep at night, I'd lie there wondering if she was sound asleep, wrapped up in another's arms. But to hear that that's not true, and that I'm still the only one who has gotten to hear the sound of her moans as she lets go…it sends a rush of dopamine right through me.

## Chapter 21

As I'm not able to put my feelings into words, I decide on a different path. Taking her face in my hands, I crash my lips into hers—trying my best to put every last ounce of emotion into it. It takes her a second to catch up, but then she melts into me as I kiss her with everything I have.

*She's still mine.*
*Only ever mine.*

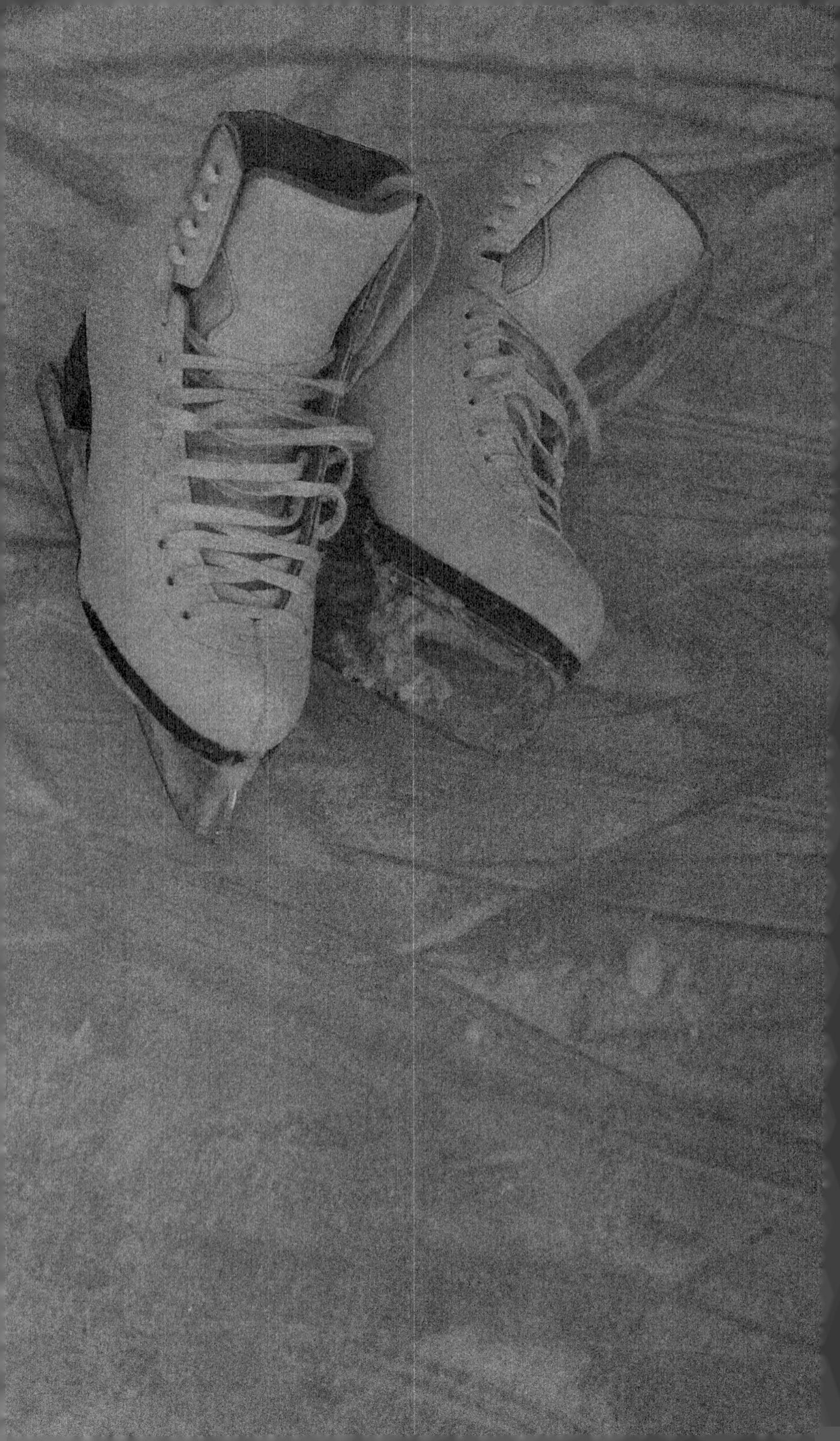

# Laiken
## CHAPTER TWENTY TWO

THIS. THIS, RIGHT HERE, IS EXACTLY WHAT I'VE needed. To feel him kiss me in a way that means something. A way that exhilarates us both. It's so intense that it sucks the air right out of my lungs. My entire body short circuits, and the only thing I can focus on is him.

The smell of his cologne.

The feeling of his hands on my face.

The way he holds me with all the care in the world.

I might not have the most experience, but I don't need it to know there's nothing better than this. I feel so close to him. And when he breaks the kiss and pulls back to smile at me, the look in his eyes is like finally coming home.

The feeling I've been missing is this.

It's *him*.

As I take a deep breath, the words I've been itching to tell him slip from my mouth. "I love you."

He smiles, opening his mouth like he's going to say it back, and I need to hear it. But nothing comes out, and fear fills his eyes. At first, I'm worried that something is wrong. A stroke. A heart attack. Do I need to call an ambulance? But then, he masks it with a smile.

"Come here, you," he says softly, pulling me back in.

I let him kiss me, but the fear that's growing inside me increases at a rapid pace.

"Hayes," I begin, but he moves me slightly so my back is against the doorway.

## Chapter 22

His hand glides down the front of me until his fingers dip under my waistband. "That vibrator isn't enough. You need this. You need *me*. And I'm going to make sure you know that."

He dips beneath my panties and presses his fingers right where I want him while he kisses my neck, but it's not the same. His words, or lack thereof, make me feel like my heart is breaking right there on the spot. I know he doesn't trust me, and he has good reason, but until now, I've never truly questioned if he loves me.

And I can't do this if there's any doubt.

"H," I say, grabbing his wrist and pulling his hand out.

The look on his face tells me that he knows exactly why I stopped him. His head drops and he focuses all his attention on the floor—unable to look back at me. And somehow, that makes it worse.

"Oh my God," I breathe, choking up.

His head lifts, and there's something in his eyes, but it only makes things worse.

"Lai, I…" But his words die out in the air once more.

I can feel my heart cracking down the center as I stare back at him. "Do you not love me anymore?"

He exhales, running his fingers through his hair. "You know I do."

"Then why can't you say it?"

His mouth opens and closes, and the longer he goes without saying anything at all, the more it chips away at me. This is the man who dropped down on one knee only feet from where we're standing right now, and sounded so confident as he told me he was going to spend the rest of his life loving me. And now he can't bring himself to form the words.

He stays quiet, silently speaking my every fear into existence.

## Chapter 22

I really did ruin this.

I *destroyed* us.

It doesn't matter that my intentions were good or that my heart was in the right place. What matters is that I hurt him to the point where our relationship, our *marriage,* may not be salvageable after all.

"I can't—" I try to speak but a sob rips right through me.

Gently moving him back, I slip out from between him and the doorway, running out the front door before he sees me break down. And the worst part may be that he doesn't even try to stop me.

This is it.

I've been avoiding coming to terms with the fact that his lack of an answer about us might actually *be* my answer, but I can't avoid it anymore. It's right in front of me. There was so much emotion in that kiss, and I let it trick me into thinking he was finally letting me back in.

But he's not.

And I'm not sure he ever will.

**I LIE ON MALI'S** bed, staring up at the ceiling. There have been a lot of nights since I left when I would feel like this. Empty. Dead inside. But then, there was still uncertainty. The question of if we would ever be together again was unanswered, and I could lie there, convincing myself we would be.

## Chapter 22

But tonight felt a lot like the end.

"I still say you're thinking too far into this," Mali tells me. "I mean, it's Hayes we're talking about. He's all *big gestures while denying he's romantic at all*. Maybe it just wasn't the right time for him, and he wants to say it for the first time again in a special way."

I huff dryly. "Or maybe he just doesn't love me anymore."

She shakes her head. "No. It's definitely not that."

"How do you know?"

"Because if it was, you wouldn't be living in his house right now. He wouldn't have all but told Cam to go fuck himself when he said you were going to stay with him. And he sure as hell wouldn't be all over you the way he has been."

She makes valid points, except for the last part. "That's not true. He knows we have chemistry, and the sex is good. He could just be using sex to mentally escape everything he has going on."

Honestly, if that were the case, I think I'd still let him. It would destroy me, but at least I'd feel like I'm helping him in some way. After the damage I caused, I just want him to be okay. It just sucks that when he is, when he finally gets back on his feet and the world stops trampling him, he won't need me anymore.

"Babes, I know you're the queen of beating yourself up and all, but don't be crazy. He loves you."

"Then why couldn't he say it?" I ask desperately, feeling the tears start to pool again. "Face it, Mal. There is a very good chance that I actually ruined this. I chose wrong, and because of it, I'm going to lose the best man I've ever known."

## Chapter 22

**I CONTEMPLATED SLEEPING AT** Mali's. I'm not really sure facing Hayes is something I can do right now. But I didn't want him to worry. One of the things he's most afraid of is me leaving again, and even though I was only a few miles away, I refuse to validate the fear of me not coming home.

I *always* want to come home.

When I walk in the door, it's late, but Hayes is still awake. He's sitting on the couch, and when I step inside, his eyes meet mine.

"You're still up," I observe, trying to keep my voice steady and neutral.

He forces his eyes away and nods. "Yeah. Just watching some TV."

It's a harmless statement, or at least it should be, but as we both look over at the TV, I notice it's off—and the remote for it is across the room. He can't even tell me that he waited up for me to come home. We're so irrevocably broken that he's lying to me just so that I don't figure out how much he cares.

"Right," I murmur. There's no use calling him out on it. Even he knows that. "I'm going to get some sleep."

Clicking the screen off on his phone, he gets up from the couch. "Yeah. That sounds like a good idea."

The two of us walk up the stairs, and the whole time I'm hoping that he'll say something. Anything. But he doesn't.

## Chapter 22

And as I reach the doorway to our bedroom—the one we shared so many sleepless nights in that were so full of love, I could drown in it—I know I can't get into bed with him.

Not when we're like this.

I turn around, finding him right behind me, and I sigh. "I think I'm going to take the guest room tonight."

A pained look crosses his face. "Why?"

The reason is on my tongue, but just like he couldn't bring himself to say the words before, I can't bring myself to say these. "You know why."

With nothing left to say, I turn and head down the hall, stepping into the guest room and shutting the door behind me.

It's so hard, being in here and knowing there was a time where we imagined this as a nursery. It wasn't something we planned to happen soon, but it was definitely something we wanted in our future.

I would let myself daydream about how it would happen. How he would hold me with so much love and tenderness as he slid in and out of my pussy. And at the end, we would both let go at the same time. His cum would fill me and we would know—our baby was made with nothing but the strongest love in existence.

**TRUE OR FALSE: THERE** is no such thing as too much sex. Depending on the person, the answer may vary. Most

## Chapter 22

men would say true. Some women would say false. Hayes would practically yell *true* before the sentence was even finished, but right now, I'd have to say it's true. Because the problem with the amount of sex Hayes and I have been having is that when I don't get it, I can't fucking sleep.

Over the last few weeks, there hasn't been a single night when I have *at least* two orgasms before I went to sleep. Even when we couldn't have sex, Hayes could tell how bad I needed it. Probably because he would feel it, too. We'd fool around, getting each other off in other ways, and then pass out in the midst of sexual bliss.

Tonight, I have to go without, and my body is *not* happy.

I roll over for the millionth time, grabbing my phone and looking at the time. It's nearly four in the damn morning, and I'm fucking tired, but it just *isn't* happening. I half consider just doing it myself, but my hand was never enough *before* I knew what good sex felt like. Now, my clit would probably laugh at me.

However...

*Nolan, you beautiful little minx, you!*

Slipping out of bed, I quietly tiptoe out of my room and down the stairs. The box with the vibrator inside is sitting on the island. I take it and sneak back up to the guest room, careful not to wake Hayes.

It takes a bit for me to get it set up. The power these things have require them to be plugged straight into the wall. But once I'm done, I slip into bed and take it into my hands. My eyes fall closed as I rest it over my panties and turn it on.

*Oh, fuck.*

Hayes was right. It's nowhere near as good at making me feel good as he is, but as it vibrates right on top of my clit, it's enough to get me off.

I imagine it's him. That he's the one holding it against me, smirking as he watches me start to come undone. He

## Chapter 22

always loved teasing me. His favorite hobby is taking me to the edge and holding me there until he's ready to let me come.

My hips arch into it, and I bite my lip to keep myself from making too much noise. I'm getting so close. A little more and I'll finally be able to fall asleep. But just as I'm about to come, the vibrator shuts off and the charger my phone is plugged into goes with it.

No power.

*Are you fucking kidding me right now?*

I click the vibrator into the off position and hide it beneath the covers before going to investigate. The light won't turn on in my room nor the hallway. I glance out the window but there's no sign of a storm.

Peeking into the master bedroom, it's dark, but I can see enough to know that Hayes isn't in bed. I turn around and start down the stairs, but just as I get halfway there, the power is restored. The microwave beeps in the kitchen as it kicks back on, and I hear Hayes's footsteps coming toward the stairs.

I quickly head back up and slip back into the guest room. There's a millisecond where I consider continuing anyway, but with him awake, I'm not sure it would go well for me. But then my phone vibrates and the text from him tells me he already knows.

> Try it again. I fucking dare you.

That motherfucker. He must have heard the buzz of the vibrator and went downstairs to shut off the power so I couldn't use it anymore.

I stare at my phone, reading his threat over and over. Each time I do, my anger grows. The goddamn *nerve* of him to think he can control whether or not I get off.

## Chapter 22

Fuck it. I'm calling his bluff.

Grabbing the wand, I turn it on and put it against me once more, but this time, I don't even try to keep quiet. If anything, I exaggerate it, moaning the same way I do with him. And it's only a matter of seconds before the guest room door flies open.

My gaze locks with his and I make no move to stop, throwing my head back and letting my mouth fall open as I feel the pressure start to build once more. I'm so fucking close. It's *right* there. But as I press it harder against me, all of a sudden, it shuts off. My eyes fly open just in time to see Hayes glare at me as he cuts the wire in half with his switchblade.

"Every fucking ounce of your pleasure belongs to me," he growls. "Get that through your head because it's not fucking changing."

My jaw clenches as I blow out a rush of air. I'm completely fucked now. There's no way I can make it work. The thing is brand new, and already useless. What is it about me and vibrators?

"Anything else?" I sass.

"Yeah, actually."

He drops the cord and the blade to the floor and comes closer, grabbing me and throwing me over his shoulder. I kick and punch him, shouting for him to put me down, but he doesn't care. He carries me into the bedroom we used to share and throws me down onto the bed.

"You sleep there!"

# Hayes
## CHAPTER TWENTY THREE

Party decor is not my forte. I'm not good at it, nor do I have any interest to be. If it were up to me, we would've hired someone to come in and make this place look the way Mali used to set up the Blanchard's backyard. But Cam quickly shot that down, telling me we have too many money issues for unnecessary expenses.

It probably doesn't help that I'm still on fucking edge. It's been three days of Laiken being distant. Not physically—she's still sleeping in bed beside me—but emotionally, she's absent. And I'd be lying if I said I didn't know why.

Hearing her say those words, it felt like I was flying. Free falling into all the things she does to me and everything she is. And I almost said them back...until I remembered what it felt like to hit the ground.

The fear that shot through my body made it impossible. My mouth physically wouldn't say the words. I couldn't even force them out. And now she thinks I've fallen out of love with her.

That couldn't be further from the truth.

I'm standing on a bar stool, trying to tape decorations to the ceiling, when I lean out too far and go crashing to the ground. Reaching up over my head, I grab the stool and throw it across the room, slightly mollified when I hear the clattering of broken pieces. Cam comes over and stands above me, looking like he's both amused and concerned.

"What did that stool ever do to you?"

## Chapter 23

I groan as I sit up, feeling the twinge in my back. "It's fucking unreliable."

Cam chuckles. "Man, really? I specifically ordered the ones with the loyalty feature on them! Those lying bitches."

It's meant to lighten my mood, but it doesn't. I don't think anything is capable of that today. Just like nothing could yesterday either. I stand up and stretch from side to side, trying to work out the newly formed kink in my back. It doesn't fix everything, but it does enough, and I go to pick up the pieces of the broken stool.

"I thought you'd be excited for this party," Cam says. "It was *your* idea."

"I'm more excited to not have to listen to them whine because we're not allowed to serve them."

Laiken is understanding for the most part, but I can't say the same for Mali. She's insufferable, or at least she was until three days ago when she finally turned twenty-one. But she agreed to wait until Laiken's birthday so they could take their first legal shots together. Before, she complained because we couldn't serve her since she wasn't twenty-one. Now, she complains because we won't let her break the promise she made to Laiken.

"That's fair," he agrees. "But that hardly warrants throwing them a party. Unless the party is actually for us, in which case, I bought the wrong color decorations."

"And here I thought you just liked the color pink." I tease.

He flips me off and goes back to hanging the letters that spell out each of their names. "What the fuck is going on with you two anyway?"

Okay, one thing Cam *doesn't* do is ask about things between Laiken and me. It's like an unspoken rule between the two of us. The Cam that's my best friend and the Cam that's my brother-in-law are separate like church and state. So, him asking can only mean one thing.

## Chapter 23

"Mali put you up to this, didn't she?" I ask, watching him intently.

He folds like a house of cards. "Ugh, yes. That girl holds sex over my head like it's the fucking key to everything."

I can't help but laugh. "You mean it isn't?"

His head falls forward as he groans. "No, it is."

Patting him on the shoulder, I shake my head. "Pocket pussies are a lot less work, dude."

"I know, but they don't swirl their tongue like she does."

Okay, there are just some things I never needed to know. He may be crazy about her, but I look at Mali like I look at Devin. As far as I'm concerned, they're nuns who have pledged to stay virgins until death. Except, Mali has no filter, so it's hard to convince myself of that most days, but I definitely don't need details.

"I'll be back."

His brows furrow. "We're not done setting up yet. Where are you going?"

"To save your sex life," I say simply.

"Ah," he nods. "Thanks, man. I appreciate it."

I grab my keys off the bar and head toward the door. "Don't thank me. Have you seen what you're like when you're sexually frustrated? This is for my own good. Trust me."

## Chapter 23

**AS I WALK INTO** Wrapped in Lace, everyone looks at me like I'm in the wrong place. It's like I've walked into the ladies' restroom. Jokes on them. Every time I'm in here, I add another thing to the list of shit I want to see Laiken in.

Mali is at the counter, helping a woman check out, and I wait for her to finish.

"I'm telling you, Louise," she says sweetly, "this will drive him wild."

"I hope so! It will make the family reunions a lot more fun."

I choke on air, pounding my fist against my chest as I cough. She takes her bag and walks out with a devilish grin on her face. Meanwhile, I turn to Mali.

"Please tell me she's not fucking her cousin or something," I plead.

She smirks. "Why? Queen Elizabeth married her second cousin and had an incredible life with him."

I stare back at her, barely blinking. "I'm starting to think there's something more behind you calling Laiken your sister despite what you and Cam have going on."

"Okay, first of all, Mr. Hypocrite, you literally call Cam your brother and you're married to his sister," she argues. "But just to ease your mind, no. She's not fucking her cousin. Her ex-husband left her for her sister. The way she sees it, showing up in lingerie and making him drool is her payback."

Well, that's a bit of a relief. I thought for sure her ringtone was set to "Sweet Home Alabama."

Mali walks around the counter and then hops up to sit on top of it. "But you didn't come here to learn about the sex life of my customers. So, why are you really here?"

I lean against the wall and cross my arms over my chest. "You can't withhold sex from Cam so that he will ask me for information on my relationship."

## Chapter 23

She huffs, rolling her eyes. "Jesus Christ. I knew he would tell you. What a baby!"

"Mali," I press. "Seriously. The only reason our friendship still works is because we *don't* talk about that shit. If you want to know something, ask me yourself."

"Okay," she says, and the look on her face tells me that I might regret saying that. "What happened the other night?"

"I'm sure she already told you."

"Well duh, but I want to hear it from you."

*Motherfucker.* "Okay. She told me she loves me, and I didn't say it back. She didn't exactly take it well."

She snorts. "I mean, can you blame her? That girl's biggest fear has been that you don't love her anymore. Why didn't you say it back?"

"I couldn't." *Yeah, this conversation is already making me uncomfortable.*

Concern fills Mali's eyes as she looks at me. "H, do you not love her anymore?"

I run my fingers through my hair as I sigh. "Of course I do."

"Then why couldn't you say it?"

"Because it feels a lot like letting her back in," I admit. "I'm just not sure I can do that. I mean, what if she leaves again?"

She shakes her head. "You don't have to worry about that."

"The fuck I don't. She already left once. Hell, she has a whole life somewhere else. How can she walk away from the job of a lifetime?"

"She's staying."

"But what if she doesn't?" I press.

Mali rolls her eyes. "She's staying!"

"You don't know that!"

"Yes, I do!" She raises her voice a little higher than mine.

## Chapter 23

I scoff. "Last time I checked, you weren't a psychic! There's no fucking guarantee she won't eventually leave again. She could realize that her new perfect life is so much better than this one, and that scares the fucking shit out of me!"

"Oh my God, you're not listening," she grumbles. "She. Isn't. Going. Anywhere."

"And how do you know that?"

She throws her hands in the air. "Because she quit the studio two weeks ago, you blockhead!"

*Wait, what the fuck?*

My jaw drops, my brain running circles as it tries to make sense of that new information. "Why didn't she tell me?"

"You'll have to ask her that," she says with a shrug. "Look, I understand not trusting her and having to work your way back to that. There's a lot of damage to be repaired. But if you keep holding her at a distance, she's going to give up, and that will be on you. I hope you know that."

It's not a foreign concept. That thought has passed through my mind plenty of times, especially how she's been acting the last few days. But I kept feeling like there was something holding me back. Like I needed something to free me from the clutches of fear and anxiety.

Mali's confession may have been exactly that.

*Chapter 23*

**I TOLD MYSELF A** long time ago that I would always do whatever it takes to put a smile on Laiken's face. And as I stand here, watching how happy she is at the sight of all her friends here to celebrate her birthday, I know that's still true. There's nothing better than the way she lights up. Except maybe the way she lights up at the sight of *me*.

"You did this?" she asks.

I had planned on letting Cam take all the credit for it. Saying it was him felt like the safer option. But standing here, looking at her while knowing what Mali told me, I'm not sure I need the scapegoat anymore.

"I may have had something to do with it," I reply.

Somehow, she becomes even happier. Wrapping her arms around my neck, she arches up on her tiptoes and kisses me softly. And as she pulls away, I find myself chasing her mouth for another.

"Thank you," she says.

I smile back at her and nod toward the beach. "Come for a walk with me?"

She tries to control her breathing, but I can tell she's nervous. Not that I blame her. I haven't exactly given her a reason not to be lately. I was going to wait until after the party, but I can't. I need to do this now.

Putting out my hand, she exhales in relief as she takes it and the two of us walk toward the beach.

"Don't get sand in places you don't want it!" Owen yells. "Hurts like a bitch!"

I chuckle, but I'm more focused on the way Laiken giggles. It's not often that I've gotten to see her so carefree like this. And I know that's partly my fault, but I'm hoping to change that.

"So, I found something out today," I tell her.

She looks up at me. "Oh?"

## Chapter 23

I stop walking, turning her to face me. "You quit your job at the studio?"

Her eyes fall closed as she sighs. "Mali, I swear to God. Nothing is sacred anymore."

"I don't get it though. Why would you quit?"

She shrugs. "They wanted me to come back to working in person, which wasn't something I was willing to do."

My heart is racing as I stare at her in complete awe. "But that job is your dream."

"No, H," she says softly, looking right into my eyes, "*You are my dream.*"

The widest grin I've had in the last year and a half forces its way through. I reach up and tuck a strand of hair behind her ear then graze my thumb over her cheek as I lean in. We meet in the middle, and the kiss we share warms me from the inside out. It's slow and delicate, like we're both just enjoying the feeling of being close to each other.

It doesn't fix everything, but it finally feels like a step in the right direction. And as we break the kiss, I can feel myself starting to let her back in—and for once, it doesn't send me into a panicked frenzy.

"I want you to know that I'm yours," I tell her. "There's still a lot that I'm working through, but I don't want to lose you. It's not going to be easy, but I want to be with you. I want the future we talked about."

Relief washes over her as she smiles back at me. "That's all I want."

I kiss her again, unable to help myself. I can't believe she gave up the job she's wanted since she was a kid just to stay here with me. Here I was thinking that she was going to leave me again to go back, and that was never even on the table.

We start to walk back to the party, but there's still a question on my mind. "Why didn't you tell me you quit?"

## Chapter 23

She takes our conjoined hands and moves so that my arm is around her and she's pressed against my side. "I didn't want you to think that I was pressuring you into forgiving me. You need to do that on your own terms, not mine."

I turn my head and press a kiss into her hair. "Thank you."

"For what?" she asks.

"Not giving up on us."

Just before we get back to all our friends, she stops and turns to face me. "It's always been you for me, H. That won't ever change."

While she was gone, I spent more time watching our wedding video than I'd like to admit. So, I immediately recognize the last two lines of her vows, and hearing her repeat them back to me now, it's everything I never knew I needed.

I crash my lips against hers, needing to be closer to hers.

"Stop being gross and get me a beer, barkeep!" Owen bellows, and everyone looks our way. Laiken giggles against my mouth.

"I'm going to ban his ass from the bar," I mutter.

"You won't. And even if you did, he wouldn't listen to it."

*Yeah, she's probably right.*

We walk back over to the bonfire, and I sit down before pulling her onto my lap. Everyone sneaks glances in our direction, probably wondering what's going on with us, but all I care about is her.

She and Mali start bantering back and forth with their little sarcastic digs they tend to throw at each other. But I'm too busy thinking of a way I can show her that I'm serious, and an idea comes to mind.

I put my hand on Laiken's leg and tap three times, just like we used to do. *I. Love. You.* Because I do love her. I've

## Chapter 23

never loved anyone *but* her. I might still be working on being able to say it again, but she needs to know that I do.

She notices it immediately and turns to smile at me. I wrap my arms around her and she leans back, putting her lips next to my ear.

"I love you, too."

**THE CLOSER IT GETS** to midnight, the more excited Laiken gets. We have it all planned out. At eleven-thirty, we push a cake out from the back and everyone sings happy birthday to both Laiken and Mali. Sparklers shoot out of it in the place of candles and they both look so damn happy. And when it comes time for Laiken to make a wish, she stares back at me, looking at me in a way that makes me come alive again.

I watch from a distance as she laughs with a few of her friends, but her attention always has a way of coming back to me. We're always focused on each other, even when it looks like we're not.

The alarm I set on my phone goes off, letting me know it's 11:59 p.m. I refuse to let anyone else be the first person to say happy birthday to her as it strikes midnight. I make my way over to her and wrap my arms around her as soon as I'm close enough.

"You're amazing, you know that?"

## Chapter 23

She melts into me, the same way she used to. *"You're amazing. I can't believe you did all this."*

I press a kiss to her cheek. "You deserve it."

It feels so good, being able to hold her like this and feel this close to her again. I missed it so damn much. She's the only one that has ever made me want to wrap my arms around her and never let go.

Glancing up at the clock, I watch as the seconds tick by and the moment it hits midnight, I pull back to look at her.

"Happy birthday, baby," I say, smiling as she lights up at the term of endearment. "I'm glad you're celebrating it where you belong."

"I wouldn't rather be anywhere else," she promises, and the best part is, I finally believe her.

Everyone gathers around as we move over to the bar, and this time, Laiken hands me her actual license even though she knows that I don't need it. Still, I pick it up and admire the way my last name still follows her first. And I'm going to make sure it stays that way.

For the first time, I hand her a drink menu while Cam hands Mali hers. Her eyes move back and forth as she looks through it, and I know exactly what she lands on when she smirks.

"Pretty Poison?"

I throw my head back as I laugh. It's her own drink, really—Malibu rum, pineapple juice, cranberry juice, and a splash of orange juice. It's been her specialty for years. And when we were coming up with the menu, the name just felt fitting. Because that's what she's been for me—a pretty poison. She runs through my veins and attacks every inch of me, making it so I can think of nothing and no one but her.

It's no surprise when the two of them whisper to each other and then look at Cam and me, smirking.

## Chapter 23

"Oh God," I groan. "I'm afraid to ask what you decided on."

Laiken smiles sweetly. "We want tequila shots, but I want mine off of you."

*Jesus fucking Christ.* My cock is already half hard just hearing her say those words. Cam and I glance at each other and I know we're both on the same page.

Neither of us are about to say no.

I pull my shirt over my head and catch Laiken shamelessly checking me out. Rolling it up, I flip it over her head and use it to pull Laiken into me.

"You do know I'm absolutely fucking you after this, right?"

She snickers as she looks up at me. "Good. I'm counting on it. Now get on the bar."

I do as she says and lie on one side of the bar while Cam lies on the other. They each lick a stripe up the sides of our necks and then pour some salt on it. Laiken carefully places a lime between my lips, and Owen comes over to hand me the bottle of tequila. It's cold as I pour it into my belly button, but it's not long before Cam's set up, too. And at the same time, they go.

The feeling of Laiken sucking the tequila from my stomach and then licking the salt off my neck is the hottest fucking thing. And when she uses her mouth to take the lime from me, I find myself jealous of a fucking fruit.

As soon as she spits it out, I pull her back down and cover her mouth with my own. Her tongue tangles with mine and I can taste the tequila that lingers there. It's fucking intoxicating, and I can't wait for the things I'm going to do to her later.

"You're such a tease," I murmur against her lips.

She pulls away and winks at me. "You love it."

"You bet your ass I do."

## Chapter 23

Laiken looks like she's high off life as she backs up and hugs Mali, excited for them to both finally be twenty-one. I can only imagine how the rest of the summer is going to be. Especially since I've got my girl back. Things couldn't possibly get any better.

But as I sit up and look across the bar, I realize they *can* apparently get worse. Because there, no more than twenty feet away, is a girl who is dressed in a familiar shirt—with an absolutely terrifying stain on it.

My chest tightens, and it feels like it's getting harder to breathe.

"Laiken," I say, not taking my eyes off the girl.

She turns to me, confused at my tone. "What?"

I pull her close so I can speak directly into her ear. "Isn't that the shirt you were wearing the night Monty died?"

Her eyes widen, and she spins on her heels. I can tell the very moment she sees it, because her whole body tenses. There's a level of fear radiating off her as we start to realize that this shit isn't over after all.

"Oh my God."

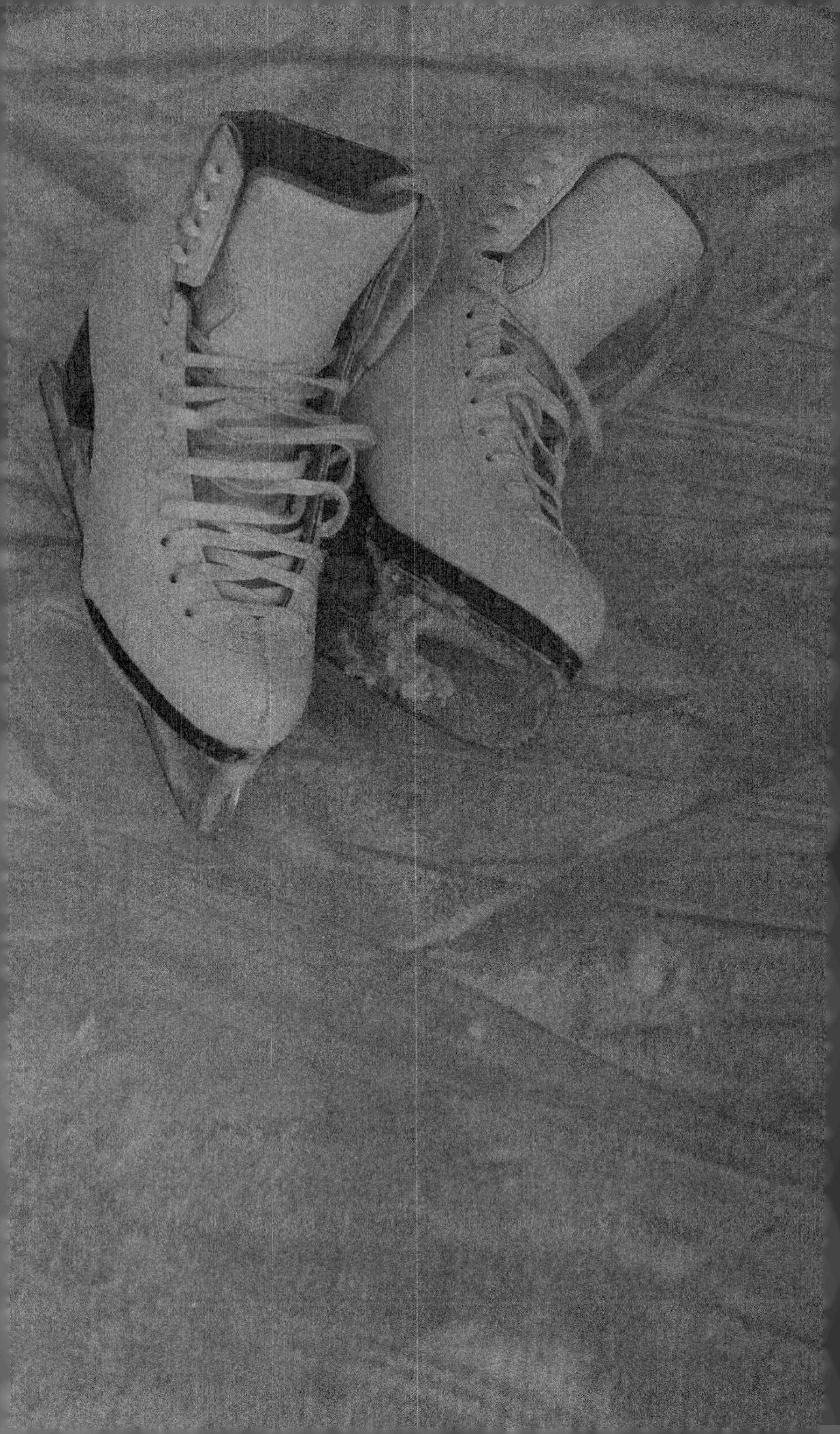

# *Laiken*
# CHAPTER TWENTY FOUR

Is it a crime against twenty-first birthdays to vomit up your first legal shot? Because as I'm staring at the shirt I was wearing the night Monty died, the same one I took off so I could try to stop the bleeding, I feel like I might. Which is such a shame, because taking a body shot off the hot bartender is a fucking epic move.

"There's no fucking way," Mali hisses. "It's got to be some shitty coincidence."

That hardly seems possible. It's the exact same shirt, complete with blood stains and everything. This whole time I thought Hayes got rid of it when he cleaned up everything else. But to my absolute horror, I was wrong.

"No," I say, shaking my head. "That's definitely my shirt."

It was one of my favorites before that night. I'd recognize it anywhere. I contemplated buying a new one, but it was understandably ruined for me after that so I decided against it.

"Unbelievable," Mali huffs. "No. We're not doing this. They are *not* ruining our birthday."

She's right. It's bad enough it ruined Hayes's. But as she starts to storm over to the girl, I'm thinking the three days she went without a drink may have made the tequila a little too strong.

"You," she demands. "Let me talk to you for a minute."

The girl looks genuinely confused, looking around to see if Mali is actually talking to her, and then agrees. Mali leads

## Chapter 24

the way, taking her into the back room, and I sigh heavily as Hayes, Cam, and I follow her.

"Where'd you get that shirt?" Mali questions.

She glances down to look at her shirt and then back at Mal. "Someone gave it to me. They bet me two-hundred dollars that I wouldn't wear it here tonight. I showed them, didn't I?"

My best friend pretends to laugh before turning serious. "I need you to give it to me."

"What?"

"I'm serious." She gestures to the shirt. "Give it to me."

Her eyes double in size as she turns to the rest of us for help. "B-but I don't have anything but a bra on under it."

Mali rolls her eyes, and grips the bottom of her own shirt, lifting it over her head. "Here. You can have mine, but you need to give me that one."

It's a win-win for her. She doesn't need to walk around in a shirt that looks like someone pulled it out of a crime scene —which is unfortunately exactly what it is. Mali and I give the guys a look and they turn around as the girl changes shirts.

"This is super cute!" she says excitedly. "Thanks!"

"You could thank us by telling us who dared you to wear it here," I tell her.

But unfortunately, she purses her lips and shakes her head. "I didn't know them. My friends and I play this extreme game of truth or dare in this app. Anyone can dare you anything. The shirt was delivered to my door."

*Son of a bitch.*

Hayes's brows furrow. "How old are you?"

The smile drops off her face, like she knows she's fucked. "Seventeen."

He up-nods at Cam who puts a hand on her shoulder.

## Chapter 24

"Sorry, little one. I'm going to need to escort you out of here."

"Man, I should've lied," she whines. "My mom was wrong. Honesty is *not* the best policy."

As Cam closes the door behind him again, I turn to Mali.

"That was sweet and all, but what are you going to do now?" I ask her.

She shrugs. "What do you mean? I'll just go out there in my bra."

Hayes and I snort in unison. "Are you *trying* to get Cam put back on probation? One guy out there even blinks your direction and he's going to go all possessive boyfriend mode. He's worse than Hayes."

"Doubtful, but I get your point," he murmurs.

Mali puts one finger to her chin. "Technically, he can't because he's not my boyfriend."

I stare back at her blankly. "Do you really think *now* is the time for technicalities?"

The corners of her lips turn upward and I know I've made my point. Mali and I look around the room for any kind of merch, but there isn't any. Just cases of beer, garbage bags, and paper towels, which would work if this was an Anything but Clothes party, but it's not.

There's no other solution I can think of except one.

"Here." I take off my own shirt and toss it to her. "Wear that."

Hayes's brows raise. "And what exactly are you going to be wearing?"

I shrug. "I'll just wait in here until everyone leaves, I guess."

It's not like I'm naive enough to believe he's going to let me go out there in my bra. He'd sooner let the girl keep the gross shirt so we could all trade back.

Hayes rolls his eyes, reaching behind his head and pulling

## Chapter 24

his shirt off. Fixing it so he can grab the collar, he puts it over my head and forces it on me. It's such a power move that it helps me feel a little less freaked out about the fact that we're back to living in our own personal hell.

"You just like when girls gawk at you because you're shirtless," I joke.

He chuckles. "You caught me. That's exactly what I wanted. I was just taking advantage of the opportunity."

The door opens again and Cam steps in, but he stops and looks around, confused. "What the fuck are you doing in here? Playing musical clothes?"

"Saving you from going to jail, buddy," Hayes says.

He looks confused until I explain. "Mali was going to go back to the party in her bra."

Choking on air for a second, he turns to Mali, but she's looking anywhere else to avoid looking at him. "Did you guys know there is a spider web in that corner?"

Cam sighs, pinching the bridge of his nose. "Couldn't have had a thing for anyone else. It just had to be her."

We all chuckle, feeling the mood lighten slightly, until all our phones go off at once. None of us move. I don't even think we're breathing. But we've tried the route of ignoring them before. It only made them more desperate.

This fire is being fed by an endless supply of gasoline. If we don't deal with it, it'll burn forever.

Taking a deep breath, I pull my phone out of my pocket and read the text.

> You're so cute to think you got rid of me. Poor Isaac. He was just in the wrong place at the wrong time. He would've made the perfect scapegoat, but I'm just not done with you yet.

## Chapter 24

Okay, now I *really* might throw up my shot—party foul be damned.

**THIS SHIT WAS SUPPOSED** to be over. We had dealt with it. There was even evidence linking it to Isaac, but as we think it over, we realize it was all things that could be related to something else. Maybe a bad coincidence, or he could've been set up. I'm just glad Hayes didn't kill him because that would've led to a whole different level of self-loathing. As for what he got, I can't say he didn't deserve it. Isaac was anything but innocent.

*"Or would you say I told you so?"* I sing as we walk into the house.

Mali pins me with a look. "All right, Carrie Underwood. We get it. You were right, we were wrong."

My lips purse. "Can I record you saying that? It would make *the best* ringtone."

She flips me off and drops her bag.

We all decided it would be best if Cam and Mali came to live with us for a bit. With this shit starting back up again, none of us should be alone. Besides, this way we're able to work on figuring this shit out every moment we're not busy. It's a win-win. We're both stronger and more resourceful.

Cam walks in with Hayes behind him and goes straight for the kitchen, coming out with a bottle of disinfectant and a

## Chapter 24

roll of paper towels. But my favorite is when he pulls the yellow rubber gloves out from his bag and puts them on.

"What the fuck are you doing?" Hayes asks.

Cam looks up at him as if it's obvious. "Don't think I don't know that you two fuck like rabbits. If I'm staying here, I'm wiping down every damn surface before I touch anything."

Hayes chuckles as I roll my eyes, realizing that sex is going to prove difficult now that my brother is going to be sleeping across the hall. I tried to learn how to be quiet once, but it's fucking impossible. Hayes doesn't quit until he's sure anyone within a mile radius can hear me.

*Fucking caveman.*

I look over at Mali to see her watching Cam with a fond smile splayed across her face. At some point, I need to ask her what's going on there. I mean, it's obvious they're crazy about each other, so why the hell aren't they together?

But that can wait.

Right now, we have work to do.

**WE'RE RIGHT BACK TO** square one, only this time, the guys are so much more protective. Mali and I are never allowed to be alone. We can be with each other, or we can be with one of them. But the option to stay home or drive ourselves somewhere? Yeah, that's long gone. It feels a lot

## Chapter 24

like being grounded, but I get it. They're just trying to keep us safe.

There's even a day where the girl Mali was scheduled to work with calls out, so Cam sits at Wrapped in Lace with her for her entire shift. Some may call it overkill, but after seeing what this person is capable of, we call it necessary.

Research goes back to the start, too. We got it wrong last time. And even though in the back of my mind I always had a feeling this wasn't over, I let myself get too comfortable in the quiet of the last couple of weeks. But that taste of my old life, the one where Hayes and I are happy together and everything is great, it's the main thing driving me to fight back.

We look into everyone that could possibly be a suspect, even Isaac, because it's not a longshot that he could be acting like it isn't him—though, that would be a dumbass move given what Hayes has on him now. But he never really did have much of a brain.

"Did you get anything on Craig?" I ask Mali.

She shakes her head. "Nope. He just got engaged to some girl he met at college. I don't think he even cares enough at this point."

*Thank fuck for that.*

"What about Lucas?"

Hayes sighs. "Nope. You were right. Just a squeaky-clean fuckboy with a thing for my wife."

I smirk. "That's twice in three days that I've been told I'm right."

Mali groans. "We have to stop that or she's going to get a complex."

"Too late," I singsong.

A part of me thought this was going to be a shitshow, all of us living in the same house, but somehow, it works. Cam goes to the gym at the ass crack of dawn every morning, so

## Chapter 24

he always brings home coffee. Mali and I make breakfast—because the morning Hayes tried, we all felt sick for the rest of the day. He can handle bagels and cereal. Nothing more.

Instead, he's responsible for making sure his mom is safe. We don't know what this person is capable of or how far they're willing to go to get what they want, so he ups his visits to twice a day. Sometimes, I go with him. She loves seeing us back together, and because she's distracted by that, she doesn't notice how stressed Hayes is.

*But I do.*

"All right," I say, closing the computer and getting up to stretch. "It's four in the morning and I'm exhausted."

"Yeah, same," Mali agrees and calls it a night.

Cam is already upstairs, passed out in the guest room he's sharing with Mali. He was assigned to look into Owen, which was simple enough. He was the least likely of all suspects, so it only took a half hour before he was ruled out.

"Are you coming to bed, babe?" I ask Hayes.

He nods but as he gets up, he grabs his laptop to bring with him. "Yeah. I can do this from bed."

Mali and I share a look and she mouths a silent *good luck* at me before heading upstairs.

*Ugh.* "No, come on," I press. "Put it down and just come to bed with me. It can wait until tomorrow."

The truth is, Hayes isn't sleeping. Like, at all. He thinks I don't see it because most days, he pretends to fall asleep when I do. But in the middle of the night, I'll peek my eyes open to see him sitting up in bed, scrolling on his phone.

Even now, I can tell he's considering just staying down here so he can continue looking into everything, but he's worn out. It's all over his face. He just won't accept the fact that it's a problem.

"Hayes," I say softly, stepping closer and resting my hand

## Chapter 24

on his chest. "It's okay. Let's just go get some sleep. We can look at it with fresh eyes tomorrow."

He stares past me, and I lightly put a hand on his cheek to make him look into my eyes. It's the only way I'll get him to agree. And when his gaze meets mine, I feel him give in as he sighs.

"Okay," he murmurs, putting the computer back down on the coffee table. "Let's go to bed."

It feels like a small win as we walk up the stairs and climb into bed. He wraps his arms around me and holds me close. It's the only thing that makes me feel comfortable anymore—the feeling of him. He's my rock, my protector, *my home.*

And when I wake in the morning to see the computer next to the bed, I know that *he* needs to be protected, too.

**THE REALITY OF WHAT** we're dealing with hangs heavily over me. Even though it's been a relatively quiet front, with only a few taunting text messages and Hayes's truck tires getting slashed one night while he closed the bar, I know that if we don't figure this out, we're in for something dark.

*If the stress doesn't wipe Hayes out before our stalker even can.*

It's Cam's day to open the bar, which means it's Hayes's day to close it. On the weekends, they do both together, but on the weekdays, one of them can usually cover it. Plus, they have Riley to help most nights.

I go downstairs and find Cam and Mali in the kitchen. "Where's H?"

"He went out to grab more milk," Mali answers. "He told us not to wake you."

Of course he did. He's always worried about everyone else, but never himself. It's something I love about him... when it doesn't put him in jeopardy. I look at my brother and

## Chapter 24

know I'm taking a risk by even bringing this up, but it's the only thing I can think of to save Hayes.

"I'm worried about him," I admit.

They both turn to look at me and it's Cam who answers. "Worried about *him*? Why?"

I shrug. "He's not sleeping. He's trying to take on everything. The bar, figuring out who is behind all of this, protecting me, and making sure his mom is okay. It's just too much."

Cam doesn't seem like it's a big deal. "Nah, Hayes is used to only a few hours a night at this point."

"No, you're not listening," I tell him. "He's not sleeping *at all*."

Now *that* starts to get through to him. "Not even for an hour or two?"

"No." I press my lips together to keep my composure, overwhelmed by how concerned I am about him. "I tried to talk to him about it, but he told me not to worry my pretty little head about it. That he's okay. But I know better than that."

Mali comes over and holds me while Cam runs his fingers through his hair. "I could try talking to him. See if he'll tell me what's up."

I shake my head. "It won't work."

"She's right," Mali agrees. "If he's telling her she's okay, he's just going to do the same thing to you. You're both stubborn asses."

His shoulders sag as he realizes we have a point. "Okay, then what do we do? It's not like we can drug him to sleep."

I look down at my lap. "I actually have an idea, but you're not going to like it."

"What else is new?" Cam drawls. "Let me hear it, I guess."

Glancing up at Mali, she nods. I already ran the idea by

## Chapter 24

her yesterday, and while she thinks I'm insane, she agrees that I do have a point.

"I need to try meeting up with them alone."

A bark of laughter shoots out of Cam's mouth. "Absolutely not. Are you trying to get yourself fucking killed?"

I roll my eyes. "Just hear me out."

"I don't need to hear you out! The answer is no."

"Cam," Mali says.

She's the only person that can get him to stop and listen. No one else stands a chance at controlling him, but she always has a way, which is why I needed her here for this.

"All she wants you to do is listen," she tells him.

He doesn't look happy about it, at all really, but he gives in. Leaning against the counter, he crosses his arms over his chest and looks at me expectantly. "Go ahead."

"Think about it," I begin. "There is only one of us that gets this asshole anywhere near us. Everything else is hidden behind text messages and done in the middle of the night. But they underestimate me. My car. The motel room. I'm the only one who gets close enough to figure out who this is, and it only happens when I'm alone."

He chews on the inside of his cheek as he processes my words. "Lai, this fucker is always one step ahead. What if they know it's a trap? You're risking your life here."

"But I won't be if you and Mali have eyes on me at all times," I reason. "Cam, he can't keep going like this. He'll make himself sick, or worse. It's not safe."

He scoffs. "And you going to meet up with a murderer is?"

I don't answer that, because he has a point, but all this leads back to me. I'm not going to let Hayes ruin himself because of it. I've done enough damage. All I want now is to

## Chapter 24

make it better. And if this gives me any chance of getting my life back, the one *with* him, I'm going to do it.

I'll do anything for it, and that includes risking my life.

Cam throws his head back. "The worst part is, I know if I don't go along with it, you two are going to do it anyway."

Mali smiles at that. "Arrogant but attentive."

He narrows his eyes at her. "Don't look at me like that. You're on her side in this. You're both assholes as far as I'm concerned."

"But you're in?" I ask hopefully.

His hands grip the counter, and his knuckles turn white. He absolutely hates this, but so do the rest of us. "Yeah, I'm in."

*Thank you, sweet baby Jesus.*

I pick my phone up off the counter and initiate the plan I've been considering since the first night I caught Hayes wide awake in the middle of the night.

> Okay, I can't do it anymore. You win. Tell me where to meet you and I'll give you anything you want.

# CHAPTER TWENTY FIVE
## *Hayes*

HAVE YOU EVER FELT LIKE YOU'RE TIGHTROPING the line between stable and epic breakdown? You know that one wrong move will send you plummeting into the abyss, but you also know that if you stop moving, you're fucked then, too. So, you keep taking steps, convincing yourself and everyone around you that you're okay, and hoping like hell that you make it through alive.

That's what my life is like at all times.

There isn't a moment when everything calms down. There isn't a time when I get to catch my breath. I'm forced to learn how to function in the chaos. It's the only option I have.

I lean against the bar, pretending to listen to Finn as he talks about the perfect swells he found the other day. I really don't have the patience for him today, especially when he asks where all the *hot babes* are at tonight, but he buys beer and Cam said that kicking him out is bad for business.

Sometimes, it's good to have him as a voice of reason. Other times, I wish I could tell him to fuck off and do what I want.

"You should've seen it, bruh," Finn goes on. "The tube was killer!"

He turns his phone around to show me a picture that his friend took, and I'm so worn out that I don't even think to stop myself before I laugh.

## Chapter 25

"Dude, that shit closed before you even went into it. It's no wonder you wiped out."

Finn rolls his eyes, clicking off the phone and putting it down on the bar. "Whatever. The waves here are shit anyway."

Now *that* is the first true thing that he's said all night. "You should head over to Cali. It's much better surfing there."

"Nah, can't," he says. "I used to live there, and I've got a few outstanding warrants out that way. If I go back, I get locked up."

My mouth goes dry. "Uh, what?"

He shrugs like it's no big deal. "Just some bullshit charges. Nothing massive."

The way he talks about it makes me want to believe him, but if I've learned anything lately it's that you believe nothing and question everything. I take out my phone and send a text to our group chat.

> Look into Finn. Apparently, he has "a few warrants" on the west coast. Might be nothing, but it's worth looking into.

As I put down my phone, I pick my head back up and see him watching me. It's a little creepy, but then again, he's not the most normal of guys. Cam thinks he's just bored and has no friends, and maybe he's right. Or maybe he's *so* bored that he needs something to entertain him.

My phone dings, and I'm expecting it to be an answer to the message I sent, but it's not. Instead, it's from the one person I don't want to hear from right now. It also rules out Finn for the most part because he's right in front of me, with his phone face down on the bar.

> It's 10 p.m. Do you know where your wife is?

## Chapter 25

I feel my stomach twist as a picture comes in. It's of Laiken, standing in the middle of a cemetery, and she's all alone.

*What. The. Fuck.*

**WAS IT STUPID TO** leave some beach bum in charge of my bar? Absolutely. But if Cam has a problem with it, he should've thought about that before he let Laiken do something this fucking reckless. I stare at the app that shows all of our locations, seeing Cam and Mali are across the street from where she is, but that's not close enough, in my opinion.

My heart is in my throat as my truck flies down the road. If a cop sees me now, I'm going to end up getting arrested, because he'll definitely pull me over for the way I swerve into oncoming traffic to get around the person driving under the speed limit. And I don't care how many lights end up behind me—I'm not stopping until I get to Laiken.

"Come on, come on, come on."

My truck tires come straight off the ground as I fly over a hill, and I nearly lose control when it lands. But that's not about to slow me down. I hear the skid on the pavement as I make the turn, and finally, the cemetery comes into view.

I slam on my brakes and throw it into park as I jump out.

She has to be around here somewhere.

## Chapter 25

The tall stones and the mausoleum in the center make it hard for me to see anything. And my biggest fear of all is that I'm going to see her phone on the ground somewhere, with Laiken nowhere to be found.

*Can't track her phone if she doesn't have it.*

"Laiken!" I roar, but I don't hear anything in response. "Fuck."

Panic rushes through me as I keep looking around, screaming her name. This is why I don't fucking want her going places alone. It's not safe! And what the hell is she doing in a cemetery, anyway? That's just asking for something horrible to happen.

"Laiken!" I scream again, and by the grace of God, I get an answer this time.

"H."

Spinning around, I see her standing there, completely unharmed. Relief floods my whole body, washing away the frantic anxiety. Despite how insanely angry I am right now, I can't stop myself from marching over and pulling her into my arms.

With her body pressed against mine, I feel my blood pressure drop closer to normal levels, but not enough to ignore what the hell she's doing out here.

"What the fuck is wrong with you?" I ask painfully. "You could've gotten yourself killed!"

She frowns, and I can see she knows how stupid this was. "I was trying to end this. You're trying to take on so much, and you claim you're fine, but I know you're not. I just want you to be okay."

I take her face into my hands and stare into her eyes. "Laiken, if something happens to you, I will *never* be okay again."

A tear slips out, and I can tell she's frustrated. We all are.

## Chapter 25

This is the last thing we want to be dealing with. But her risking her life to save mine is *not* the answer here.

Still, as mad at her as I am right now, I can't stop myself from pressing my lips to hers. She sighs into it, and her hands come to rest on my arms.

It's no surprise we've both been on edge so much. With Cam and Mali in the house, sex is pretty much impossible. We still take every opportunity we can get, but it's not the same. I miss the time when we would just spend the whole day all over each other. When we'd make our way through the house, unable to keep our hands to ourselves.

"You're going to give me a heart attack," I tell her, with a little less venom in my tone than she probably deserves. "Don't ever do anything like this again. Okay? It's not worth the risk."

She nods, with my forehead pressed against hers. "Okay, but you have to give a little, too. You can't take everything on by yourself."

I can't help but smirk. "Isn't that exactly what you were trying to do tonight?"

"No," she nods across the street. "I had eyes on me."

Looking over, I see Cam and Mali in the window of an upstairs apartment building, like a couple of horrible spies. A goddamn blind person could see them. And when I see the binoculars Cam is holding to his face, I flip him off.

*I'll deal with his ass later.*

"Lai," I deadpan. "What the fuck were they going to do if someone showed up and tried taking you? Jump out the window?"

She chuckles, realizing how obnoxiously stupid this is.

"Or maybe they'd take their eyes off you so they could come down the stairs." I snap as I have an ah-ha moment. "No, I know. They'd wait for an elevator. Really take their time."

## Chapter 25

Laiken rolls her eyes. "Okay, I get it. It was dumb."

"That's an understatement, baby," I tell her, then press a kiss to her head. "But we'll work on it."

I keep an arm around her as I start to lead us back to my truck, but we only take a few steps before I hear the familiar sounds of Laiken's moans behind us. At first, I wonder if she's hurt or fucking with me, but when I glance down and find her looking at me with the same confused expression I have, my stomach churns.

We turn around to see a video being projected onto the side of the mausoleum.

More specifically, *our* video.

Laiken and I watch in horror as I slip my cock into her, and the sounds of her moans fill the empty space.

"I thought you said you got rid of that," she says, her voice shaking.

That's the problem. "I did."

**WE RUSH HOME, WITH** Cam and Mali pulling up only seconds after us. The only place that video existed was on a thumb drive inside of my safe. I put it there after I got it and haven't touched it since. I considered watching it once when missing her got a little too difficult, but I couldn't. Not when I knew she didn't consent to being recorded.

Laiken is right behind me as I run inside and up the

## Chapter 25

stairs, going straight into our closet. My safe sits on the floor in the corner, and I pull my keys out of my pocket to unlock it. The moment the door swings open, I feel the effects of yet another loss against this motherfucker.

Right there, in the place where the thumb drive once sat, is an envelope that looks like all the rest of them.

*Never would have taken you for the amateur porn type.*
*I'm saving this for my spank bank. ;)*

**I CAN'T DECIDE WHAT'S** worse, the fact that they were in the house, or that they were there tonight, alone with Laiken. She could have been taken so easily, and the fucking dipshits across the street wouldn't have stood a chance at getting to her before she vanished.

It feels like everyone I love is in jeopardy, and there's nothing I can do about it. I'm sure it doesn't help that my mom had one of her episodes today. It happens from time to time, where she forgets what's going on due to the cancer in her brain. The doctors said it will become more frequent as we come closer to the end, and usually I can handle them, but today was hard.

When I walked in, the first thing she did was ask me where my dad is. She said she's been looking for him and can't find him anywhere. Having to remind her of what happened felt like breaking her heart all over again.

I think next time I might just tell her he's at the store.

It's bad enough that I have to worry about some psychotic asshole threatening those I care about while simultaneously worrying about the cancer that's slowly killing my mom. And

## Chapter 25

now knowing I have to add Laiken recklessly risking herself to that list, it only makes it worse.

"I can't believe you left Finn in charge of the bar," Cam says through a laugh. "I'd sooner leave Mali in charge."

"Ay!" she says, offended.

I scoff, shaking my head. "You can shove it up your ass. I would've left that place in the hands of anyone when I got the text I did. What the fuck were you thinking?"

"I was coerced," he tries, but I'm not buying it. I cross my arms over my chest and stare at him.

"What? They ganged up on me, and you know how they are."

Laiken jumps to her brother's defense, knowing he's only making it worse. "What Cam *means* to say is that we're all worried about you. You can't go without sleep, especially not with the amount of stress you're under. Your body will shut down. And what if it happens when you're by yourself? What then? You're just out there, vulnerable?" Tears fill her eyes as that fear sets in. "You can't risk that. You can't."

I sigh and hold her close. "Shh. Okay. I get it."

"Do you?" Mali presses.

"Yes," I answer sternly. She's on my shitlist, too. "I'll promise to get some sleep if you idiots promise not to let Laiken risk her life again. What the hell were you going to do if shit went wrong?"

Cam rolls his eyes. "There was a drainpipe right outside the window. I was going to slide down that."

*For the love of fuck.* "Have you ever *tried* sliding down a drainpipe?"

"No."

*Yeah, I didn't think so.* I pinch the bridge of my nose. "Don't you get it? This person is feeding off the fact that we keep hiding shit from each other. They know they're not strong enough to face us all together, so they wait until there's less

## Chapter 25

of us. And if they turn us all against each other, that's the easiest way to take us down one at a time."

"They're trying to weaken us," Laiken acknowledges out loud.

"Exactly," I say. "And each secret we keep only gives them more power."

We make a pact, right then and there, to stop keeping things from each other. I also may or may not have drilled it into their thick skulls that if they let Laiken pull some shit like this again, it won't be some psycho with too much time on their hands that they need to worry about.

Judging by the looks on their faces, none of them want to risk calling my bluff.

**I WISH I COULD** say that was the only reckless thing they do, but this is Laiken and Mali we're talking about. They're basically gluttons for punishment, and when Cam and I walk in to find a man we've never seen before sitting on the couch, I'm ready to put their asses in an adult daycare center while we're not able to watch them.

"Who the fuck is that?" Cam asks as we both freeze right inside the door. "Who the fuck are you?"

Mali rolls her eyes. "This is Henry. He's a hacker."

Cam snorts. "Henry looks like he hunts and pecks as he types. And where the fuck did you find a hacker?"

## Chapter 25

"Where anyone would. The dark web. Duh," she answers simply, as if that isn't going to make Cam and I choke on our words.

*Oh dear God.* "Cam, are you taking this one?"

He shakes his head. "I'm too weak when it comes to her. You do it."

"Fair point."

My brows raise and I tilt my head to the side as I look at Mali, noticing that Laiken sits in the other corner and stays completely silent. And something tells me the popcorn she has resting in her lap isn't coincidentally timed.

"The dark web?" I ask Mali, and she nods. "Since when do you go *there*?"

I've heard enough about it to know that's the last place she should be. I bet she didn't even think to hide her IP address, cover her camera, or close out of anything else on her computer before she accessed it. It's like Amazon for illegal shit you're not supposed to look for, and they don't call it the *dark* web for nothing. Almost everything on there is downright fucked up.

"Since someone has a vendetta against us and is better at holding a grudge than our dearest Cam over here," she sasses.

Cam doesn't even realize he just got verbally backhanded. He's too busy sizing up Henry. After a moment, he walks over and slides himself between Mali and Henry, forcing them both to move over as he sits.

"That's better," he says, pleased with himself.

Meanwhile, I look over at Laiken. When she sees me staring back at her, she freezes. Her chewing stops and her eyes widen.

"Anything from the peanut gallery?" I ask her.

She smiles sweetly. "Have I told you today that you're hot and a sex god among men?"

## Chapter 25

*Yeah, definitely calling adult daycares in the morning.*

Turning back to Mali, I exhale all the air out of my lungs. "Well, since you so kindly invited a total stranger off the dark web into my house, I may as well hear what you've got."

Mali grins triumphantly and leans forward to look past Cam. "Take it away, Henry my boy."

Cam glares at her and shakes his head slowly—a silent message that calling him anything other than his name is strictly off limits. But that's hardly what he should be worrying about as I look at *Henry*.

Our new friend from the dark web, apparently.

*If I have gray hairs, it's because I married half of this generation's Thelma and Louise.*

"Mali said you've been having an issue with someone hacking into the cameras at your bar?" he asks.

I tilt my head back and forth. "We did, until Cam ripped the cameras out of the wall."

Henry snorts. "Hardly a long-term solution."

*Okay, I'm listening.* "Do you have something better?"

"I wouldn't be here if I didn't," he says. "If you give me access to those feeds, I might be able to pinpoint who it is. In order for those cameras to feed the information to the server, they use a range of code. And when someone taps in to access it live, they add a code to the metadata. It's automatic. Most people don't even realize they're doing it."

"So, you want me to give you access to my bar's camera system because you *might* be able to find out who has been hacking in?" *Hardly sounds like a good deal.*

He shrugs. "From where I sit, you don't have anything to lose. Your buddy here already ripped the cameras out of the wall. Besides, if I can't pinpoint them, the least I can do is lock out their signal and strengthen your firewall to make it harder for them to get back in."

Well, he has a point. It's not like I plan on putting the

## Chapter 25

cameras back in until I know this has been dealt with. The irony of how it's *more* dangerous to have them is not lost on me right now. But it wouldn't hurt for the firewall to be stronger so no one else can get into it.

"Okay, fuck it," I tell him. "Mali, go grab my computer."

"Me? Why me?"

Plastering a fake smile on my face, I blink at her. "Because you have such a love for computers and the dark web."

She huffs, getting up and grumbling to herself as she goes upstairs to get my laptop. It's awkwardly quiet as we wait for her to return, and when his eyes move over to Laiken, I cough.

"Don't look at her."

He may be just doing the job Mali contacted him for, but I don't know this man. And until he shows me otherwise, he's just some fucking weirdo that met someone on the internet and came over to their house. He probably thought he hit the jackpot when they answered the door.

Seriously, I wonder if Cam is really *that* into Mali, or if he'd get over her if she, let's say…disappeared.

Mali comes back down and hands me my computer, giving me her best *go fuck yourself* smile as she does. I chuckle, opening it and putting in my password. It takes a minute to log into the server, especially since we haven't accessed it in a while. There's been no reason to. But once I'm in, I pass the computer over to Henry.

"Okay," I tell him. "Do your thing."

He takes it into the kitchen and we all follow him, standing behind as he sits at the island. I don't worry about what he might see on the feed. We already erased the video from the morning of the dead body incident. There was nothing useful on it anyway. It looked like the cameras glitched. One second it wasn't there, and the next second, it was.

## Chapter 25

My guess is they had access and turned them off before they went in, and back on when they left. Which means I can only imagine what footage they have of that. But I'm guessing that's the least of our worries, with how much they seem to have on Monty's death.

Henry presses a few buttons, and a bunch of code that looks like gibberish to me appears on the right-hand side, while the video stays on the left. He starts to play the first one and shows us how the code scrolls at rapid pace, and he's looking for a certain line of it to see when the person taps in.

He makes it sound easy, yet something tells me it'll be anything but.

**ONE VIDEO TURNS INTO** seven, and honestly, I'm getting bored of this. Either this guy has no idea what he's doing, or our little *friend* has gone through great lengths to cover their tracks.

"Okay, last one we're trying," I say, going to the video where I know they were watching because I got a text. "I know for a fact they were tapped in during this one because there's no other way they could've known I was looking at Laiken."

She glances back at me, the corners of her lips turning upward slightly. God, things would be a lot more convenient for me if I was able to stay mad at her. But I totally get what

## Chapter 25

Cam meant when he said he's weak when it comes to Mali. Laiken has the same effect.

We all watch the video together, looking for anything different in the coding we've been staring at for the last two hours, but there's nothing. Even as we see the moment Cam grabs my phone from me, which I know is when I was being watched.

"Yeah, you're not going to find anything on here," I say. "If you were, it would've been there."

Henry hums, pressing a few more keys. "It doesn't make sense. In order for them to block out this code, or remove it from every video, they'd have to be a very experienced hacker."

"Yeah, well," I drawl, "you win some, you lose some."

The only thing this has told me is why the hacker we used for the Monty thing was taken and then killed. They needed something from him, and once he was done, they disposed of him.

Or rather, made *us* dispose of him.

"Thanks for trying, Henry," I say, placing my hand on his shoulder. "I appreciate it."

I don't, really. He was relatively useless, and I feel like I wasted the last two and a half hours of my life. But it is what it is at this point.

Henry looks at me and then to Mali. "Um, there's the matter of payment."

"What?"

Mali nudges me. "You've got to pay the man."

*You've got to be fucking kidding me.* "For what? He didn't *do* anything!"

Henry gets indignant, straightening his shoulders. "I made your firewall almost impenetrable."

"From what? A kindergartener with an iPad?" I scoff. "Get the fuck out of here."

## Chapter 25

Laiken turns around with an unsure look on her face. "Babe, with everything we're dealing with right now, do you really want to be on the wrong side of a pissed-off hacker?"

My shoulders sag, and I start to consider whether or not Mali really needs the protection we keep giving her as I pull out my wallet. I mean, working a shift by herself isn't *that* dangerous, and a walk down a dark alley at night? That's child's play for her.

"How much?"

"Two-fifty," Henry answers.

I turn to glare at Mali and she quickly looks away. Pulling out half my tips from today, I count it to make sure it's right and hand it to him.

"There," I say, not masking the sarcasm from my tone. "You have a good night."

Henry happily takes it, telling Mali and Laiken that it was nice meeting them as I follow him to the door. Once he's gone, I can finally drop the fucking nice guy act. I turn around and mentally shoot daggers into Mali.

"Well, he was nice," she says.

"*He* was a fucking scam," I tell her. "What the fuck were you thinking? You don't go on the dark web and you sure as shit don't invite random people from it to the damn house! Are you trying to get yourself killed? Should we just hand you over now?"

She looks me up and down and crosses her arms over her chest. "It was a solid idea, and he was a very reputable hacker."

"He was a glorified geek squad!" I shout. "That guy couldn't hack his way into a public library."

But just like we talked about the other day, getting angry at each other isn't going to fix anything. That's what they want. We're weaker when we're apart, and if I'm pissed off at them, it puts us all at risk.

## Chapter 25

It would just be a lot fucking easier if they weren't testing my damn patience at every turn.

"It may not have been so pointless after all," Laiken calls out. "Did any of us look into Riley?"

*Riley?* Cam nods. "I did. Why?"

She hits a couple buttons on my laptop and restarts the last video we watched. "While everyone was watching the code, I was watching the video, and I couldn't help but notice her face when Hayes came over to talk to me."

We watch as I look over at Laiken and start getting her a drink before walking over to the corner. Right as I get up to her, she pauses the video and zooms in on Riley. She's glaring at us, sure, but I'm not sure that proves anything.

"I mean, with the way she wants in Hayes's pants, I don't see how this is out of the norm," Cam says, speaking the thoughts I was going to keep to myself.

Laiken nods and grabs her phone. "Yeah, but look at the background of this picture from my birthday."

She shows us a picture Mali took, from the moment it hit midnight, and Riley is in the background with the same look on her face.

"She looks like she wants me dead," Laiken says.

Mali's facial expression tells me her ego is growing as we speak. "I never did like that bitch."

I roll my eyes and focus on Laiken. "Babe, I get it. I do. And we'll keep it in mind, but I don't think it's Riley. I really don't."

"Sorry, sis," Cam says. "I have to agree. She wants him. Has for over a year now with no luck. I wouldn't expect her to ever be happy when she looks at you two. Especially when he looks at you the way he does. God, it even makes me nauseous."

I flip him off before putting my hand out for Laiken. "Come on. Let's go to bed."

## Chapter 25

She doesn't seem convinced but she nods anyway, closing the computer and coming with me. Just before we reach the stairs, I turn around to look at Mali.

"By the way, you owe me two-fifty," I tell her.

There's no denying she's not happy about it, but she understands and nods.

Laiken and I head up to our room and once we get inside, I shut the door. I finally feel like I'm able to let go of some of the stress of the last few hours. Turning around, I grab Laiken's hand again and spin her so she's facing me.

"Baby," I say, trying to keep calm.

She sighs. "I know what you're going to say, but you should know it was all Mali's idea, and I didn't know about it until he was on his way over."

"And you didn't think to let me know that some random ass guy was coming to our house?" I ask. "Come on, Lai. You're smarter than this."

Her head drops and she nods. "I'm sorry. I was just so hopeful that it would work. I mean, you guys were going to use a hacker until you realized he was dead."

"*That* was an actual hacker. One that doesn't make house calls because he's legitimate."

She winces from my tone, and I rein my anger in once more as I press a kiss to her forehead.

"I'm not mad at you, Lai," I tell her. "But I need you to be more careful. Losing you again would absolutely destroy me, and living without you isn't something I'm willing to do anymore. So, no more dark web, and no more strangers coming through that door. Okay?"

Nodding, she wraps her arms around my waist and rests her head on my chest, and I exhale because *this* is what I needed.

What I've always needed.

*It's her.*

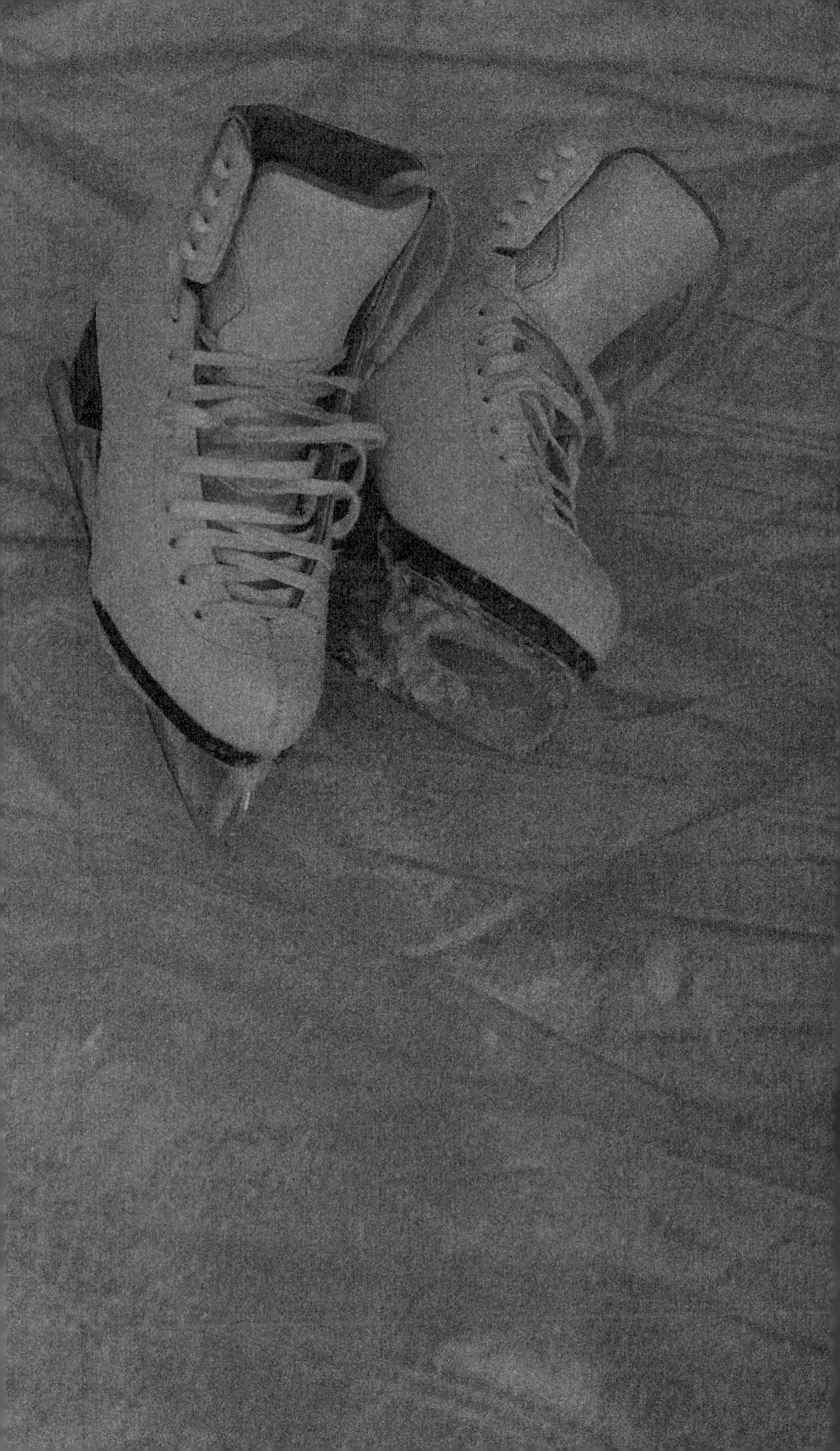

# Laiken
## CHAPTER TWENTY SIX

LET THE RECORD SHOW, I AM A TOTAL HYPOCRITE. I acknowledge that, and I own it. It was only a couple days ago that I was lecturing Hayes on the importance of sleep, and here I am, up late and doing more research as he sleeps beside me.

*Welcome to the twilight zone.*

For some reason, I can't get the look on Riley's face out of my mind. It wasn't your typical jealous glare. There was something darker to it. Something more sinister. I know Cam and Hayes are positive it's not her, but I'm not entirely convinced, and I don't think Mali is either.

So, it doesn't hurt to give something a second look.

I go through the process we created, starting with her social media. There isn't much on it, really. No pictures with friends or family. She doesn't have a TikTok, but she runs the one for the bar. Of course, that mostly consists of videos of Cam and Hayes since that's all people want to see anyway. The occasional few of drinks being made don't even have half the views. The only Instagram I can find on her is one that only has six pictures, and the last one was posted a few years ago—so that's essentially dead.

I move onto yearbook photos, work history, and other things, but it's hard because she's only a little younger than the guys. That's freshly into adulthood. There's not much to find unless you're one of those people who puts their whole life on the internet.

## Chapter 26

Which, Riley is obviously not.

It becomes clear why Cam was able to check her off the list. There isn't much to go off with her. And I have no choice but to swallow my pride and admit that they were right. It doesn't look like Riley is our stalker.

But that doesn't mean I like her.

I mean, who gives someone a dirty look for talking to her *husband*? A homewrecking ho, that's who.

The way Cam and Hayes were so quick to rule her out though, bothers me. Not that I think there's something going on. I know better. But it reminds me of how I acted when one of them suggested Monty's parents being behind the whole thing. I immediately ruled them out, and now I'm thinking we shouldn't cross anyone off the list unless they were thoroughly looked into.

I start with his mom, and of course, being the wife of a senator, there's a plethora of information on the internet about her. It takes me a couple hours, but I comb through the majority of it. It's hard because most media outlets seem to copy and paste what the other says and moves a couple words around, so each article is basically being read twice, but I don't see anything about her that jumps out at me, really.

Then I move onto Monty's dad. *Senator Rollins*. If anyone found out I was looking into him for anything, I'd have people calling for my head on a spike. He's a loved member of the community, and there aren't many people with a bad thing to say about him. But like I said, I'm not ruling anyone out based on anything but hard evidence or lack thereof.

As I'm scrolling through all of the results, I switch to the images tab and look through there. It's a lot more pleasing to the eye, and an article of anything painting him in a positive light isn't going to have a picture of him smiling on it.

Except maybe this one.

## Chapter 26

It's a picture of Jeremiah Rollins, the same one that was used for his campaign for Senator, but this one has been defiled. His eyes are colored in with red, and there are devil horns drawn on top of his head—like what you would do in your yearbook to that person you hated more than anything. Only, it's a little surprising to see this on a media page.

I click the link and let my eyes travel across the screen as I read the article.

*Looks like the jaw-dropping story on the prized potential Senator isn't going to happen after all. Our informant, who happens to be Mr. Rollins's former head assistant Theresa Hollander, says she had a change of heart. Which, in politics, means she was paid off. Oh well. We're sticking by our opinions of the politician, and if we're right, it's only a matter of time before someone else comes out of the woodwork in search of their payday.*

The whole thing seems innocent enough. Smear campaigns aren't uncommon, especially during such an important election. But as I scroll down and see an article linked to this one, my brows furrow.

There's a picture on the top of the screen of a young woman leaving an office in tears. According to the article below it, she left suddenly. From what it sounds like, they were great. The perfect team that planned to take over the business world together. But then one day, they weren't.

A part of me wonders if he got violent with her. After all, a woman at that point in her career has probably already gone through her fair share of criticism. I imagine it would take a lot for her to leave an office in tears. And if he has a violent history, maybe the loss of his son pushed him over the edge.

*Chapter 26*

It might not be the most solid lead, but it's something to go off of when we have nothing else.

**IT TAKES AN OBNOXIOUS** amount of time to convince the guys that I haven't lost my mind, and that it might not be a total waste of time to look deeper into this by going to the woman's house and asking her to talk to me. And it takes even longer to convince them that they shouldn't come with Mali and me.

I have no idea what we're dealing with here. But what I do know is that you're either a shitty person or in a really bad place to sell a story to the press. Especially when it comes to someone's campaign. From what it looks like, until things ended, Jeremiah and Theresa were a power team, and I want to know what brought her from being his right hand to almost helping attack his campaign.

*And what was the story she was going to sell?*

After a lot of begging, and the promise to keep them in the loop at all times, Mali and I finally get the go ahead. Though it also could be because I pointed out that at least I told them about it instead of just going and doing it.

Did it insinuate that I was going whether they liked it or not? Fuck yeah, it did. There's a difference between being protective and being controlling, and I am nobody's bitch.

I quickly kiss Hayes before rushing toward the door before he changes his mind and I have to go behind his back.

## Chapter 26

"Love you!" I call as I drag Mali with me.

He grumbles to himself, but I don't stick around to find out what he said.

I have a lead to investigate.

**THE HOUSE IS EASY** enough to find. When you've been looking into anyone who has so much as glanced in your direction, something like getting an address is a piece of cake. It's a cute little place, with a small porch and a garden out front. I can't imagine anything but a happy life being lived here. One where the whole inside smells like cookies baking in the oven.

"What are you going to say to her?" Mali asks.

"I'm just going to beg her to talk to me."

"And if she doesn't?"

I huff, wondering why I brought her with me. *Oh right, because the alternative was Hayes or Cam.* "I'm not accepting no for an answer."

Getting out of my car, Mali follows me. "Whatever you say, Nancy Drew."

It's clear she has zero faith in me, but what else is new? I've spent my life being underestimated, and I don't expect it to stop anytime soon. But right now, I'm determined to get to the bottom of all this—before it destroys me and everyone I care about.

We walk up to the door, and I take a deep breath to calm

## Chapter 26

myself before knocking. My heart is racing. The thought that she might shut the door in my face is right there at the forefront of my mind, but I have to try.

It takes a minute, but finally, the door opens a crack and the same woman from the pictures I saw peeks out. "Can I help you?"

"Hi," I say sweetly. "My name is Laiken, and this is my friend Mali. We were just wondering if we could talk to you for a minute? It's about Jeremiah Rollins."

"I'm sorry, I don't talk to the media," she says.

But before she can shut the door, I rush to speak again. "We're not the media. I promise."

Theresa looks skeptical as she inspects us both. "Then why do you want to talk about Jer?"

*Jer.* That's a rather intimate way to refer to your former boss. Most people would call him Senator Rollins or even Mr. Rollins.

"We just have some questions," I tell her. "Please? I wouldn't be here if I wasn't completely desperate."

I stand there, emotionally exposed to a woman I've never met before, hoping she can tell me something that will put an end to all of this. She must be able to see the terrified girl that lies beneath the surface of my strength, because she sighs and opens the door further.

"Are you okay?"

There's not really a good way I can answer that, but if being somewhat honest will get us some answers, I'm willing to give her what I can. "For now, yes, but that could change if we don't find what we're looking for. You see, Mali and I were friends with Montgomery Rollins, and because we left him at the boat docks the night he died, someone is threatening us. They blame us for his death."

Sympathy fills her eyes. "That's terrible. Montgomery drowned. That wasn't your fault."

## Chapter 26

I swallow harshly. "We'd just like to ask you a few questions. See if we can figure out who would be doing this, or at least rule some people out."

"All right," she agrees. "Come in."

As we step inside, I hear Hayes's voice in the back of my mind, lecturing me about the choice of going into a stranger's house, but that's exactly why I don't see him anywhere. If I'm going to get the answers I'm looking for, I need to make this woman feel as comfortable as possible, and what better place to do that than in her own home?

The interior looks exactly like I thought it would, with wallpaper instead of paint, and paneling going up the staircase. It reminds me of my grandmother's place when I was little. There are even some of the same knick-knacks on the china cabinet in the corner.

"Your house is adorable," I tell her as she leads us deeper into the living room.

"Oh, thank you," she replies. "It was my mother's. I stayed with her as she was ill, and when she passed, I just couldn't bring myself to leave."

"Well, I love it. It's very cozy."

The three of us sit down in the living room, and she realizes her cup is empty. "Oh, I'm sorry. How rude of me. Would the two of you like anything to drink?"

Mali and I shake our heads in unison as we murmur our appreciation for her offer. It's bad enough that I'm in her house. If Hayes finds out I ingested something she gave me, he's going to have me committed on grounds of insanity.

Theresa goes into the kitchen to get herself another drink, and when she comes back, she sits down and gives us a warm smile.

"I'm sorry for being so stand-offish," she says. "The media hasn't been so kind to me in the past."

*She isn't lying there.* "I noticed that. What was so surprising

## Chapter 26

to me, though, was how it changed almost instantly once you no longer worked for Mr. Rollins."

She nods sadly. "Yeah. I don't think people understand how brutal their words can be. Especially in such a public way, where millions are going to be reading it and believing those things about you. And the worst part is, none of it's true."

"So, is that why you were going to sell a story to the press during his campaign for senator?"

"Part of the reason. Yes." She pauses to take a sip of her tea. "I wanted to tell the truth of what happened between us and restore my reputation."

"And is it true that you were paid for your silence?"

"I'd say that's a bit of a stretch. I received money, yes, but I wasn't bribed. I hold nothing against Jer. It's his wife that did the most damage."

My brows raise in surprise. "Really? She's always seemed so sweet."

"Yes, well," she sighs. "I can't blame her for not liking me. I wouldn't like the woman who was sleeping with my husband either."

*Oh, wow.*

"You two were having an affair?" Mali asks.

Theresa nods, and I can tell by her face that she's ashamed of it, but there's also some residual feelings there. "When you work so closely with someone, it's easy to let lines get crossed. Jer was the sweetest man I'd ever met. Still is, if I'm honest. When he caught wind that I was considering selling the story of our affair, it was him that showed up. He found out that his wife had me blacklisted all over the place, and I wasn't able to get another job. He was so disappointed in her. He assured me that he had no idea, and I believe he didn't. She does a good job at portraying herself as the perfect supportive wife. He gave me enough money to cover

## Chapter 26

my bills and told me that if I still wanted to sell the story, that was my right. But I couldn't live with myself if I ruined his shot at senator."

"It sounds like you still have some strong feelings for him," I acknowledge.

She looks down at her lap and smiles, like she's remembering a happy memory. "He was the love of my life."

I've been in her position, having to live without the man you'd give anything to spend forever with. And let me tell you, it's not something I would wish on my worst enemy.

"Do you mind if I ask why things ended?" I tread carefully.

It takes her a moment to answer. We bury emotions like this for a reason, and when you need to dig them back up, they're difficult to handle.

"I got pregnant," she confesses. "Jer and his wife had been trying to have a baby for years, with no success. And there I was, knocked up because a condom broke. I thought he would be happy. I believed him when he said that at the right time, he would leave his wife for me. But she ended up getting pregnant around the same time I was, and when push came to shove, he chose her."

My jaw is practically on the floor. This woman isn't innocent by any means. She was sleeping with a married man and knew what she was getting herself into. But she was in love, and that has a tendency of blinding you to what's right.

"He gave me money for an abortion," she continues. "And enough extra for me to live on for a bit. But I couldn't bring myself to do it. I was raised to believe that abortion is wrong, and that baby was made out of love. So, I didn't terminate the pregnancy. I'll admit that a part of me was probably hoping he would change his mind, but when I saw a picture of his happy family on the front page of the newspaper, I knew there was no chance of that."

## Chapter 26

"That must've been so hard for you," I say sympathetically. "How were you able to get through that?"

She shrugs. "I was pregnant. Pushing through was the only option I had."

"So, you were a single mother then?"

"I tried to be. But like I said, Mrs. Rollins had done irreversible damage. No one would hire me, and the money Jer had given me had long since run out. I couldn't provide for my child, so I made the hardest decision of my life. At six months old, I dropped my baby off at the hospital, and I walked away."

I feel bad, coming into her house and making her relive the most painful time of her life. Judging by the way she talks about Monty's father, I don't think he has a violent bone in his body. Though, it does make me want to look further into his mom. I always thought she was the sweetest woman, but evidence shows I am not the person to trust when it comes to character judgment.

"Did you ever find them again?" Mali asks.

She shakes her head. "No. I imagine she'd be somewhere around your age by now, but I've never tried looking for her."

My heart lurches. "It was a girl, then?"

Nodding, she reaches to the table beside her and grabs a dusty, framed picture, blowing it off. "This was only a few weeks before I gave her up."

I take the picture, and my blood runs ice cold. The baby in this picture looks almost identical to the picture I saw on Riley's Instagram—even down to the birth mark on her right temple. If she's Monty's half-sister, that would give her plenty of motive to want to avenge his death.

"Actually, I'd love a glass of water if you're still willing," Mali tells her.

She smiles. "Of course, dear."

As Theresa gets up and goes into the kitchen, I use my

## Chapter 26

phone to take a picture. It's not perfect, but it'll do. Once I'm done, Mali and I share a look, and I can tell she's thinking the exact same thing I am.

**WE END UP STAYING** for over an hour, just talking to Theresa about all different topics. She's very sweet, and I get the feeling she's lonely, which would explain why she spilled so much information once she got to talking. She stays in her house to avoid the media, and she can't even meet people through work because Mrs. Rollins has done such a good job making sure she'll never be hired by anyone again. I think she was just enjoying having someone to talk to, so we stayed as long as we could.

Mali and I give her a hug goodbye, and she waves from the doorway as we get back into my car. The moment we pull away and get down the street, I'm practically screaming.

"Oh my God!"

"I know!" Mali agrees.

"Do you think Monty knew?"

She shrugs. "If he did, he never mentioned it to me. He made it seem like his family was perfect. The only thing he ever complained about was not wanting to go into politics like his dad."

I take a deep breath. "Mal, if Monty had a half-sister around our age, there's a good chance we weren't wrong about Riley."

## Chapter 26

"Yeah, but how are we going to convince the guys of that? We don't exactly have a way of proving it's her."

I reach behind my back and pull out the hairbrush I stole when we went to the bathroom. "Don't we?"

Mali's eyes light up as she takes it from me, seeing all the strands of hair attached, with a root still attached to some. "Fuck Sherlock Holmes. You're my new favorite detective."

Now let's just hope that Hayes and Cam don't give us a hard time.

**OKAY, SO THEY'RE DEFINITELY** not impressed. Hayes seems more stuck on the fact that we went inside, and Cam has gone through an entire presentation with Mali on how easy it would've been for this woman to drug her drink, even though it was water. He doesn't care that the bottle was still sealed, and we quickly realize there's no reasoning with them.

"Will you just listen to me for a damn minute?" I plead. "You need to believe us. Theresa was pregnant with Senator Rollin's baby! Which means Monty has a half-sister out there somewhere. And Mali and I both think it's Riley."

Cam rolls his eyes while Hayes looks kind of tired of it all. "Under what grounds? That they're both girls born around the same time? Those two things only rule out like half the population, and that's saying she even still lives in North Carolina."

## Chapter 26

I put my hand out for Mali's phone, using hers to pull up the Instagram photo with the caption *"only baby picture I have of myself, but at least I know I was adorable."* With mine, I open the picture I took of Theresa's baby's photo. Holding them side by side, the resemblance is uncanny.

"Tell me these two don't look like the same baby."

Hayes glances at it for a second, but still doesn't look like he's swaying at all. "It's a baby, Lai. All babies look like other babies."

This is getting frustrating. "Why are you so adamant on protecting her?"

"I'm not, but I'm also not going to accuse our only employee of being a psycho stalker who lives to torment us based on something that could just be a coincidence," he says.

"You want to talk about coincidences?" I argue. "It's not just a coincidence that there's a half-sister of Monty's out there somewhere. It can't be."

"He probably didn't even know about her," Hayes reasons. "Lord knows that guy was the epitome of only child syndrome."

Stepping away for a second, I turn around and tug on my hair. I get what he's saying. It took them a while to find someone they wanted to hire, and Riley is perfectly trained at her job at this point. And for the most part, she's been very supportive of them. She always shows up for work and gives them extra help when needed. She might be a thorn in my side, but not to them. But still, I just can't shake the feeling that I shouldn't let this go.

I take a few deep breaths and spin back to face Hayes, knowing that I have a better chance at convincing him than I do Cam.

"Babe, listen," I say calmly. "I need you to trust me here. We're in this situation because I didn't trust you when you had a bad feeling about someone. I should've listened to you about Monty from the start, but I didn't. Because of that, we ended up here and it almost ruined us."

I take a step closer to him and wrap my arms around his neck, staring into his eyes so he can see how important this is to me.

"Please don't make the same mistake that I did."

## CHAPTER TWENTY SEVEN
### Hayes

STRESS HAS A WAY OF CATCHING UP TO YOU. WHEN you go through something for so long, it's only a matter of time before it starts to break you down. And let's just say the phone call from the doctor earlier saying that they needed to up my mom's pain medication didn't exactly make matters any better.

I'm worried about her.

I'm worried about us.

And there's nothing healthy about walking down the street and wondering if anyone that looks in your direction is the person causing you so much mental turmoil.

I lean against the corner of the bar, letting my head fall back and my eyes fall closed. A part of me wonders if shit would follow me if I tried to take a vacation. Would a note show up in my hotel room? Would my rental car end up rigged to self-destruct?

As if any of that is even an option. I'd never leave my mom. Even Devin is having a hard time with it. She comes to visit any time she gets, but it's not enough. And the daily video calls just aren't the same.

It's another reason why I'm trying so damn hard to figure this shit out—so my mom and sister can have more time together. It would kill me if I had to keep her at a distance until the end of my mom's life. Sure, I'm just trying to keep Devin safe, but it's not fair to either of them.

"Everything okay?"

## Chapter 27

I jump at the sound of her voice and my eyes fly open to see Riley standing in front of me. "Shit, you scared me."

She giggles softly. "Sorry. You just look a little stressed."

"I am," I admit.

She looks worried. Genuinely concerned for my well-being. "Anything I can do to help?"

I shake my head. "Nah, but thanks. Just some personal shit."

She leans her side against the counter, looking like she wishes I'd confide in her. I think about what Laiken said—how she thinks Riley could be behind the anonymous texts and all the torment, but I still don't see it. I've known her for over a year now, and she's never given me any reason not to trust her. I'll never be what she wants me to be, but she's a great employee, and I'd even consider her a friend.

*But Laiken considered Monty a friend, too.*

"You know, I can be pretty good at personal shit if you gave me the chance," she tells me.

I chuckle. "Is that right?"

"Yep," she smiles. "I'm serious. Lay it on me."

Honestly, I don't even know where to start. I can't tell her about what's been going on, so I guess I'll just stick with safer water.

"Well, my mom is dying of cancer," I say. "So, that sucks."

She looks at me with nothing but sympathy in her eyes. "Hayes, that's horrible. I'm so sorry."

I shrug. "It's not your fault. Just been dealing with a lot, I guess."

Her bottom lip juts out as she pouts. "Isn't Laiken taking care of you? You look like you could use a hug."

*Yeah, I'm definitely not about to go down that road.* "She is. But it's hard. There's only so much you can do, you know?"

"Definitely," she says, nodding. "God, I feel so terrible for you. I wish there was something I could do."

## Chapter 27

"I appreciate it. But really, I'm fine."

Riley takes a step toward me. "Can I at least give you a hug? You really do look like you need one."

I huff out a laugh. "Honestly, I'm not really the hugging type."

"Oh yeah?" She teases. "Then what type are you?"

In all the time that I've known her, I've never seen her get this ballsy. She's not exactly subtle, but she's never come onto me so strongly. And when the door opens and Laiken walks in, I know she's standing a little too close to appear innocent.

"What the fuck are you doing?" Laiken growls. "Get away from him."

Riley rolls her eyes as she steps back. "I was being there for him. You know, like a friend."

"He's not your *friend*. He's your boss. And it would do you some good to remember that."

"Lai," I say, trying to stop her.

But she levels me with a single look. "Don't you dare defend her right now."

*The fucking hostility.* "I'm not defending her, but don't you think you're overreacting a little? We were just talking."

"Just talking, my ass," she snaps. "She's been waiting for months to get her grimy little hands on you. I just didn't think she'd actually try, knowing you're married."

Riley scoffs. "Married. Right. Because all wives leave their husbands in the middle of the night and disappear. Some fucking marriage."

"Excuse me?" Laiken shouts, taking a step closer to her. "You don't know the first thing about me *or* my marriage."

"I know you don't deserve him," she says. "I don't know why he even gives you the time of day, if I'm honest. As far as I'm concerned, you're just an ex who doesn't know when to let go."

## Chapter 27

Laiken turns an angry shade of red, and before I can even think to stop her, she lunges at Riley. Her hand grips her hair and she pulls her down to the ground. They're both swinging at each other, and Laiken is scratching the hell out of Riley's arms. But Riley is putting up a good fight.

"Fucking knock it off!" I bellow, but neither of them are listening.

It isn't until Laiken gets on top of Riley and swings with everything she has that I'm able to get a handle on her. I wrap my arms around her waist and lift her off, but she keeps a tight grip on Riley's hair.

"Laiken, let go!" I shout.

She rips some of Riley's hair out, and that finally frees my bartender as she falls to the floor, glaring up at Laiken. I spin around and all but toss her away.

"What the fuck is wrong with you?" I yell.

Her brows furrow. "Me? She fucking started this! Did you not hear what she said?"

"Yeah, I did! But that doesn't mean you can fucking attack my employees!" I run my fingers through my hair as I glance at Riley to make sure she's okay, and then focus back on Laiken. "Go the fuck upstairs. I'll deal with you later."

"Hayes," she tries, but now is *not* the time.

"I said go!"

She rolls her eyes and huffs as she turns on her heels and marches upstairs. Once she's gone, I turn to Riley and help her up.

"I am so sorry," I tell her. "I don't know what's gotten into her lately."

She stands up and tries to fix her clothes and hair. "I know exactly what's gotten into her. She knows that you can do better, and she can't handle it."

I take a deep breath, looking around and silently thanking God that no customers were in here to see that. "Listen, if

## Chapter 27

you want to head home, I get it. You can take the day, fully paid. No one should have to come to work and be attacked by their boss's wife."

Riley nods, wincing as she touches the top of her head. "Thanks, Hayes. I'll do that."

She goes into the back to grab her bag and then heads for the door, but just before she walks out, she stops and looks back at me.

"By the way, I hope after *that* you see that she should be your *ex* wife," she tells me. "You could have anyone you want. Even if it isn't me."

I nod once in understanding. "Feel better, Riley. And again, I really am sorry."

She smiles at me, and I know she isn't blaming me as she walks out. I give it a few minutes until I know she's gone and then I lock the door and head upstairs.

Laiken is standing there, facing Cam and Mali, and I walk up behind her. My arms wrap around her, and I kiss the top of her head, looking down to see Cam putting the hair Laiken pulled out of Riley's head into a bag. Meanwhile, Mali is carefully collecting the skin cells from under Laiken's fingernails.

"Did she leave?" Lai asks me.

"Mm-hm." I lean down and kiss her cheek. "I gave her the rest of the day off."

"Good. I don't want her around you."

I chuckle, knowing that she may have been fighting her for a reason, but she definitely enjoyed getting to rough her up a little. "So, what happens now?"

"Now, we bring this to the lab, who will run a DNA profile against the hair we got from Theresa's hairbrush," Mali tells me.

Cam looks over at her with his brows raised. "Another one of your dark web things?"

## Chapter 27

"You told me to stay off the dark web."

Which means it's absolutely one of her dark web things. Tell Mali to do something and she will do the exact opposite.

Once they're done collecting all of the DNA that Laiken was able to get off of Riley, I turn her toward me and look her over. I've got to hand it to her, for someone who just got into what could technically be considered their first bar fight, she barely has a scratch on her.

"You can say it," she teases. "I'm a badass."

I chuckle. "You're a crazy ass is what you are."

Pulling her closer, I press my lips to hers. She hums, grabbing the back of my neck and tugging me down. And it isn't long until Cam complains about it.

"Is that really necessary?" He groans. "Don't we all have shit to do?"

Mali giggles. "I don't know. I'm starting to think it's cute. They've gone through a lot to get here."

Cam groans loudly. "Not you, too."

He gets up and heads downstairs to unlock the door and manage the bar. Meanwhile, Laiken breaks the kiss and turns to Mali.

"Really? We're growing on you?"

Mali waves her off. "Fuck no. You're repulsive. But fucking with him is my favorite hobby." She stands up and grabs the two small baggies. "Okay, we should get going with this."

Laiken nods and turns to me once more. "I'll let you know when we get there, and I'll call you when we leave."

"You better."

She arches up on her tiptoes and kisses me quickly, but before she can walk away, I stop her. Taking my time, I press one kiss to her eye, followed by another one over her heart, and lastly, one more to her lips. It may be cheesy, but the way she giggles makes it worth it.

## Chapter 27

"I love you, too," she says.

I don't think I'll ever tire of hearing that come from her lips, especially when I had to go so long without it. The only time I got to listen to it was when I watched our wedding video. And if I have her vows completely memorized, no one needs to know that but me.

Laiken heads down the stairs first, and Mali turns to smirk at me. "You know, you're going to need to say the words at some point."

I chuckle as I roll my eyes, flipping her off playfully.

But she's right. I will need to say the words, and I'm getting there. Laiken has been so patient with me, but I want nothing more than to break down the last little bit of that wall and tell her what she to wants to hear.

*Soon. I'm almost there.*

**THERE'S NOTHING MORE FRIGHTENING** than knowing that Mali and Laiken are at some place, doing DNA testing to figure out if the person who has been making our lives a living hell has been right under our noses the whole time. When all of this started, Riley wasn't even a blip on the radar of potential suspects.

To be honest, I'm still not sure she is.

I can admit there are things that seem suspicious, but it's also possible that she really is just a girl with a crush who

## Chapter 27

turns green with envy when she sees Laiken and I together. But if that's true, that would mean I let Laiken attack one of my employees on a hunch. A wrong one at that. So, it's a bit of a conundrum.

As my phone starts to ring, I can't answer it fast enough when I see Laiken's name appear on the screen.

"Hey," I say, finally able to breathe.

Her voice sounds like honey as it comes through. "Hey, babe."

"How'd it go?"

"Good," she replies. "The results should be back in a couple of hours. Some kind of new rapid DNA test they have. Mali will get an email with them when they're ready."

Wow. "That's crazy they can do it so fast."

"That's what she said."

A bark of laughter emits from my mouth. "You better not be referring to yourself. You know damn well I can last—"

"You're on speakerphone!" Laiken yells.

"Oh, yes. Because Mali is such a saint."

Mali yells in the background. "You're the worst."

"I know," I singsong. "And yet you stick around."

She snorts. "I'm stuck with you. I don't have a say in the matter."

"She really doesn't," Laiken agrees. "We're on our way back, so we should be there in like twenty minutes."

"Sounds good, babe. I need you with me, right where you belong."

I can practically see the smile on her face as she sighs into the phone and Mali pretends to gag in the background.

"I love you so much," she says.

And I almost say it back. I could probably get it out. There's not nearly as much anxiety that comes when I think about it. Nothing like it used to be. But it's not something I want to say through the phone, and definitely not when I'm

## Chapter 27

on broadcast. I need to stare into her eyes and see the way she comes alive when she finally hears it again.

"Ditto," I decide on instead. "I'll see you when you get here."

"Sounds g—"

Her words are cut off by a gasp and a scream of Mali's name, followed by the sound of metal on metal and a lot of thumping, like the phone is being tossed around the car, before it all goes silent.

There's a part of me that dies inside. Fear rushes through me as I silently beg for her to say something.

"Laiken!" I scream. "Laiken, answer me!"

But there's nothing. Just the sound of the radio on low in the background. And my phone falls out of my hand and crashes onto the floor.

## CHAPTER TWENTY EIGHT
## *Hayes*

I CAN'T BREATHE.

My lungs are physically incapable of taking in air.

All the knuckles on my hands turn white as I grip the bar so tightly it threatens to crack under my grasp. Cam stands in front of me, demanding to know what happened, but his voice is background noise. It feels like I'm floating into the abyss, and there's nothing but pain there.

The burn of the lack of oxygen.

The stabbing of my heart trying to beat.

If I passed out now, it would be much more humane.

"Hayes!" Cam screams, taking my shoulders and shoving me up against the wall. "What the fuck is going on?"

Not knowing what else to do, he gives me a look that tells me he's sorry for this, and then he slams the heel of his hand into the center of my chest. It forces my body to take a massive inhale, finally allowing me to take in air, and the oxygen stops my brain from going foggy.

I cough, sputtering on the sudden intake, until I manage to get control of my breathing again. Dropping to my knees, I scramble for my phone and see the call is still connected, but I don't hear anything but a commotion somewhere in the distance.

"H," Cam presses once more. "What happened?"

Staring up at him, I feel like my entire world is crashing down around me for the final time. "T-they were in an a-accident."

His eyes double in size as I choke out the words, and he

## Chapter 28

immediately starts clearing everyone out of the bar. It's good that he's doing it because he's been far more professional than I would be. I'd just scream at them to get the fuck out of my bar before I throw them out.

The moment the last person leaves, we're right behind them, and we shut and lock the door behind us. We run as fast as we can to Cam's Jeep, and he peels out of the parking lot while I track Laiken's phone.

*This twenty-minute ETA better end up being cut down to ten.*

**PULLING UP TO THE** scene, I feel like I'm going to throw up. Mali's car is totaled. It's sitting upside down on the total opposite side of the street. Cops have the entire intersection shut down, but Cam pulls over onto the grass and we jump out.

I glance at the car and notice that both doors are open, which I'm hoping means that they're both okay and they got out safely. But as I see Mali standing there talking to a police officer, my fear escalates. I don't see Laiken beside her.

"Mali!" I call.

She spins around, and there's a nasty gash on her collarbone, possibly from the seatbelt. She looks like she's aged a million years in only a matter of minutes. Cam runs to her and wraps his arms around her tightly, but I'm still looking for my wife.

## Chapter 28

"Where's Laiken?" I ask her.

Her bottom lip starts to tremble. "I don't know."

*What?* "What the fuck do you mean you *don't know*?"

She's physically shaking as she starts to cry harder. "I mean I don't fucking know! Someone slammed into us full force, and I was knocked out. And when I woke up, she was gone!"

*No.*

*This can't be happening.*

I grip my hair tightly as I look around, hoping to see any trace of her, but there isn't any.

"Who the hell hit you?"

The officer she was just talking to chimes in. "Like I told your friend, the car was reported stolen earlier this morning."

"And where are they now?" Cam asks.

"They weren't in the vehicle when we arrived," he informs us. "My guess is they took off because they didn't want to get arrested for grand theft auto."

Cam and I lock eyes, and we both know that's not the case.

This wasn't a fucking freak accident.

This shit was intentional.

And now they have Laiken.

**POLICE ALL OVER THE** area are out looking for her.

## Chapter 28

There's a BOLO with her description that was broadcasted over the radio, and they've assigned every officer they have available to search. Thankfully, her parents are on vacation in St Barts, or we'd have another mess on our hands.

According to what we were told, there have been instances where someone gets into an accident and the trauma causes them to wander away because they're confused.

Basically, they think Laiken crawled from the wreckage and just walked off into the fucking sunset.

But we know the truth.

The paramedics told Mali that she should go to the hospital to get checked out, but she refused. Once they had her sign a form stating she was refusing medical treatment, she was free to go. And that's when we started searching.

She could literally be anywhere. That's the biggest problem. We tried asking the cars that were stuck in traffic if they saw the accident, but all of them said no. They only pulled up after the fact. Which means it's possible that someone grabbed her from the car and took her somewhere.

At the advice of the police, we wind up at the local ER to see if someone saw her and brought her there. I don't understand why they would leave Mali behind, but fuck it, I guess. It's the only thing we have right now. But as Mali walks away from the desk and solemnly shakes her head, I feel like I'm shattering into a million pieces.

I walk through the automatic doors and over to the wall, putting my back against it as I slide down. There's nothing like this kind of pain. It feels like her leaving all over again, but a million times worse. Because this time, I know it wasn't her doing.

She was stolen from me.

Ripped away and taken somewhere, and I don't know where the fuck to find her.

## Chapter 28

"Please, God," I beg as the tears start to fall. "Please don't take her from me. Give her back. I just want her back."

Cam comes over and kneels down beside me, putting his hand on my shoulder. "We're going to find her, H."

But how can he promise that? We don't even have a single inkling as to where she is. She could be fucking anywhere, including over an hour away at this point. And that's if she's still alive. When they took the hacker, we didn't find him until he was dead and dumped in the middle of the bar.

If they do that with Laiken, I swear, I'll die on the spot.

I meant it when I said that there's no life for me without her. Not one I have any interest in living. I made it through when she was gone because I knew she was out there somewhere. But if I know she's gone, there will be no part of me that wants to stick around.

Not without her.

Mali's brows furrow as she pulls her phone out of her back pocket. Her eyes widen as she sees what it is, and then she hands it to Cam. His eyes move quickly across the screen before his head drops and he exhales.

"She was right," he murmurs. "The DNA is a match. Riley is the half-sister of Montgomery Rollins."

Rage flows through me, and all I can see is red. My vision starts to blur as I start to black out. That fucking bitch. If she were in front of me right now, I'd strangle her without an ounce of hesitation.

Pushing myself up, I can feel my whole body shaking as I go to walk toward Cam's Jeep. "I'm going to fucking kill her."

Cam jumps into action, stepping in front of me and putting both his hands on my chest, and yet the adrenaline coursing through me still manages to move him.

"Hayes, you can't," he tells me.

"The fuck I can't."

I've never wanted to hurt someone more than right now.

## Chapter 28

This bitch has the audacity to be around me every day. To work in my bar and act like my friend, and then goes and takes my fucking wife? There is nothing worse than a scum like her, and I'm going to make sure she never sees the light of day again.

"H," Cam pleads. "Listen to me. The only reason we have an advantage right now is because she doesn't know we're onto her. This whole time, she's been the one with the upper hand, but now it's us. And if you kill her now, we might never know where Laiken is."

Fuck.

It fucking hurts.

At least when I'm angry, it masks the pain that threatens to rip me apart. But when I think about the fact that I don't know where she is, that I can't hold her and tell her she's going to be okay, I feel like I'm dying the most painful death. Being skinned alive would be more humane than this.

This pain is unforgiving.

It's ruthless and has no mercy as it takes me down.

"I can't lose her again," I say with a sob. "I can't."

Cam and I don't normally hug, but neither of us give a shit about that as he comes closer and wraps his arms around me. I know he's scared too, and so is Mali, but they both know that I'm never going to make it through this if we don't find her.

They're scared for Laiken, but they're also scared for me.

My phone dings twice in my pocket, and I rush to open it, hoping it's something about Laiken. But what I see isn't at all comforting.

Instead, it confirms my worst fears.

It's a picture of Laiken, taken from above her. She's unconscious and in what looks like a wooden box.

*They're fucking burying her alive.*

The message after is just as sinister.

## Chapter 28

> She's alive, but she won't be for long. You can find her hidden away in sacred secret places. Just hope you're not too late. ;) xx

Oh my God.

I shove the phone into Cam's hands just in time for me to turn around and vomit everything in my stomach onto the ground. The pain is excruciating. To know that she's going to die if we don't find her, and not only that, but it's going to be so damn terrifying for her.

I can't handle it.

"What the fuck is that supposed to mean?" Cam shouts.

Mali takes the phone and presses her fist to her mouth as she whimpers at the sight of her best friend. "No. They can't do this. They can't take her from us."

I force myself upright and walk over to Mali, taking my phone from her and texting them back.

> Please don't do this.
>
> I'll do anything. You can have whatever you want.
>
> My bar. My house. My truck. ME.
>
> Just tell me what you want and you can have it.
>
> This has clearly been about me. You want me to be miserable, so take me. Let her go and take me. You can do whatever you want with me, just don't do this to her.

But the answer that comes tells me they're not going to cave.

> This has always been about her.

## Chapter 28

"Fuck!" I roar, just barely resisting the urge to throw my phone across the parking lot. "Okay, think, Hayes. Think."

There has to be an answer to this. If they wanted to kill her, they would've done that and then used her body to get their revenge on us. They wouldn't have sent some cryptic riddle.

*You can find her hidden away in sacred secret places.*

Mali is racking her brain right along with me. "Is it the rink? Did you do anything there? The word *secret* makes me think it has something to do with when you two were fooling around."

My eyes widen, and she realizes it at the same time I do.

"The abandoned beach!"

**CAM GRIPS THE OH** shit handle of his Jeep, looking like he's fearing for his life as I speed down the road. He tried to get me to let him drive, but there was no way in fuck that was happening. The sooner I get there, the better chance I have at saving her. And if I let him drive, there's a very likely chance I may have literally pushed him out of the fucking car.

I rip the steering wheel to the left, and the whole thing goes up on two wheels as I turn. I almost think it's going to tip, making it the second car of the day that's ruined. But Mali thinks quick and throws herself to the other side. It falls back onto all four wheels and bounces from the impact.

## Chapter 28

Jumping out, I rush toward the sand, but it's too fucking dark to see anything. Maybe if the moon was out, it would help, but the clouds block it from shining through.

"Go turn your high beams on!" I order Cam.

He books it back to the Jeep and does as I say, lighting up the area a little better.

"Where are you, Lai?" I whisper, squinting as my eyes struggle to scan the area.

And then I see it.

My old hockey jersey.

"Laiken!" I scream, taking off and running like hell.

I fall to my knees next to the jersey and begin clawing at the sand. My hands work desperately to get to her. Cam and Mali both help me, all of us rushing to uncover the box in time, until I finally feel something hard beneath the surface.

"I've got it!" I shout.

Mali moves out of the way while Cam and I use all of our strength to grip the cover of the box and pull it open. The wood creaks as the nails give way, but nothing can withstand the sheer force of our adrenaline.

Finally, it gives way and we get the lid off. Laiken blinks up at me, almost like she's in disbelief. She's crying and she's weak, with dried blood on her face from the injuries she must have sustained during the accident.

"Thank God," I breathe.

At the sound of my voice, she finally moves, sitting up and holding her arms out to me. I wrap my arms around her and pull her to me as she breaks down, sobbing hysterically while I hold her.

"I've got you, baby," I cry with her. "I've got you."

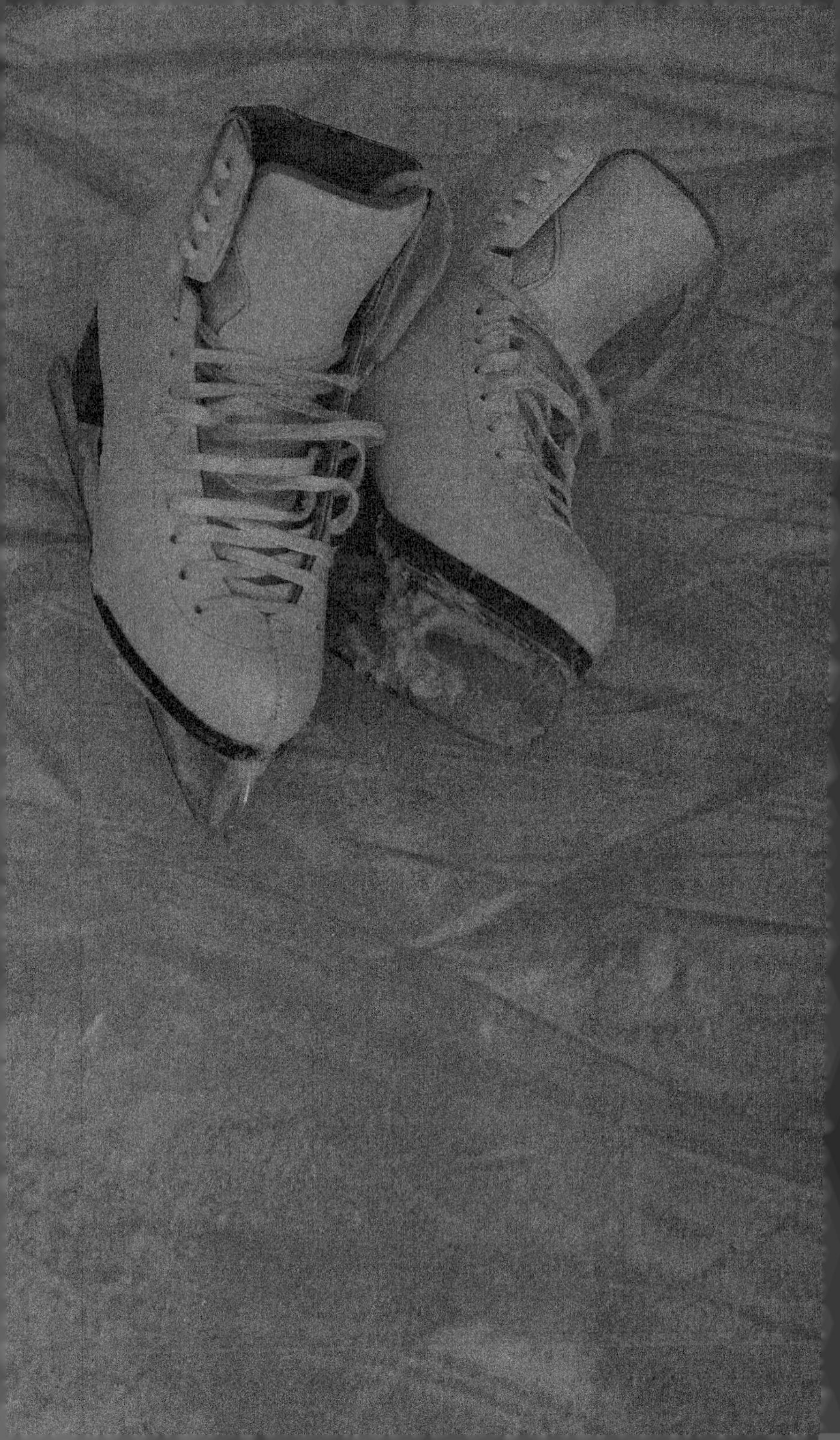

## Laiken
# CHAPTER TWENTY NINE

My dad used to tell me that fear was all in my head. That if you don't give it the power to make you afraid, it doesn't exist. But if he truly believes that, he should try being buried alive. Then we'll see just how much he thinks it's *all in your head*.

All I can remember is the crash. It felt like it was all in slow motion. The car came out of fucking nowhere and as I screamed Mali's name, there was nothing she could do.

It was too late.

The crunch of the metal was one of the worst parts, and it never seemed to end. I watched Mali go unconscious as the airbags deployed and the plastic sliced through the top of my head. And as the car rolled over and over, all I wanted was for it to stop.

I could just barely register the sound of Hayes screaming my name, but I couldn't answer. I couldn't get my mouth to function. And when I watched someone walking toward the car, I thought it was someone who was going to help. But I couldn't have been more wrong.

A van screeched to a halt next to Mali's car, and the person dropped down to their knees. Next thing I know, there's a rag being held over my mouth and nose, and no matter how hard I tried to fight it, I couldn't.

And then everything went black…until I woke up in the box.

I look down at my nails as I sit in the bathtub. The

## Chapter 29

damage to the tips reminds me of how I tried to claw myself free, but no matter how hard I fought to get free, I couldn't. I didn't know where I was. All I knew was that I was getting tired and weak. The lack of oxygen was kicking in, and I didn't have it in me to keep fighting.

So, I curled into a ball in the corner of the box and I cried, telling myself over and over again that Hayes would find me. He'd stop at nothing until he found me.

"Hey," he says softly as he pours the warm water over my shoulders. "It's okay. You're safe, and I'm never going to let her hurt you again."

*Her.*

My head whips over in his direction. "The test?"

He nods. "It's a match. Riley and Monty are related."

I feel a rush of so many different things flood through me. Terror at the fact that she spent so long around the people I care about. Sadness for Hayes and Cam that they're losing someone they thought was a good friend and employee. But most of all, I feel relief, because we finally know who is doing this.

And now we can end it.

Tears pour from my eyes as I tilt my head back so Hayes can wash the shampoo out of my hair. He works so gently, treating me like I'm fragile and he's afraid he'll break me. But surprisingly, after hearing that, I feel stronger than ever.

*Chapter 29*

**THE FOUR OF US** sit in the living room, trying to come up with a plan on how to deal with this. We know it's Riley, that much is clear. But now we need to figure out how to handle it.

She's always been smart and conniving, and the last thing we need is for her to have fail safes in place that end up backfiring on us if we hurt her. Isaac was one thing. We knew how to hit him where it hurts. But Riley is a wildcard.

I'm sitting on the chair, wearing a pair of shorts and one of Hayes's shirts. My hair is still damp from when Hayes cleaned me up. But while everyone is watching and worrying about me, I'm worried about Hayes.

He's clearly on edge, and that's understandable. But I can tell by the look in his eyes that he's blaming himself. He can't sit still for longer than thirty seconds before he gets up to look out the window.

If I don't deal with this, it's only going to get worse.

"Cam," I say softly. "Take Mali and go somewhere."

Hayes turns to me in a panic. "What? No. We need them here. We need to keep an eye on you."

I give him a warm smile. "It's okay. You've got me, remember? You've got me. I'm safe with you."

That manages to get through to him, and he calms down slightly, wrapping his arms around me and holding me close. I glance over at Cam and Mali and gesture for them to go. I know exactly what he needs, what we *both* need, and Cam isn't going to want to be in the house for it.

"You probably need water," Hayes tells me, and immediately heads into the kitchen.

I follow him and lean against the doorway. "H."

"Don't," he pleads. "I know what you're going to say. Just don't. Okay?"

But I can't do that. He needs to hear it. "This wasn't your fault."

## Chapter 29

His eyes fall closed, and his hands press down on the island. "You don't know that."

"I do," I assure him. "You didn't do this. The only thing you did was save my life."

He shakes his head. "You don't get it."

"Don't get what?"

It looks like he's in excruciating pain as he finally looks at me. "She wants to tear us apart! She's going to stop at fucking nothing until we're not together anymore! I know this, and yet I'm being selfish and holding on anyway!"

"Because I want you to!" I tell him. "I don't care *who* wants to take you away from me! We can't let them win!"

"Win?" he scoffs. "Laiken, she's fucking dangerous! Don't you get that? You were buried alive! I died a million deaths today thinking that I…"

His words fade out, like he can't bring himself to say them, but they need to be said.

"That you what? That you lost me?"

He stares back at me with an unreadable expression on his face. It's some kind of mix between pain, fear, and intense admiration. Then finally, after a moment, his shoulders sag and he stalks toward me.

His hands cradle my face, and he crashes his lips against mine. The kiss is desperate, like he's pouring every ounce of emotion into it. Like the one after I told him I hadn't been with anyone else, but stronger. More intense. More…everything.

And when he breaks it and pulls back to look at me, I can see it there in his eyes—all of the walls he built up to keep me out come crumbling down.

"I love you," he breathes. "I love you so much."

My heart leaps inside my chest as I hear the words I've been aching for. There is nothing in the world better than

## Chapter 29

this. Not a single thing that can top the way he makes me feel.

"I love you, too," I tell him quietly. "There's never been a day that I haven't."

He's been hearing me say it for a couple weeks now, and yet, it's like tonight is the first time he's believing it. His hands grip my waist and I jump into his arms, wrapping my legs around his waist and kissing him deeply. His hold on me is tight as he takes us upstairs and into our bedroom. And when he lies me down on the bed, I know he means it when he says he's got me.

He's *always* got me.

"You are everything to me," he says, kissing his way down my neck. "There isn't a thing about you that I don't love."

My head falls back against the pillow as he drags the shirt up my torso. I lift off the bed just enough for him to pull it over my head, and he drops back down to kiss my collarbone. Then over my heart.

He slowly makes his way to the center of my chest and then starts heading down. It's all soft, teasing kisses, the kind that are so light I wonder if his lips are even touching my skin at all, or if what I feel is his warm breath brushing against me.

"Hayes," I plead, needing more.

The corner of his lips raises, and I look down in time to see his tongue dart out to moisten them. "I love the sound of my name when you say it like that."

"Like what?"

"Like you're going to self-destruct if you don't get what you want."

I squirm under his stare. "Who says I won't?"

He huffs out a laugh, and while his eyes stay locked with mine, he slowly peels the rest of my clothes off, leaving me completely exposed to him.

*Chapter 29*

"Not fair," I whine. "You're still fully dressed."

It only takes a second before he's pulling his own shirt over his head, and I don't think there will ever be a day that I don't drool at the sight of him.

"Better?"

I bite my lip. "Much."

With a chuckle, he drops down and starts to kiss the inside of my thigh, nipping at my skin with his teeth. It's so intense as the little bits of pain quickly turn to pleasure. And when his thumb grazes over my clit and down to my entrance, I'm so fucking needy for it.

"So fucking stunning," he tells me as he watches me. "I can't believe you're mine."

"All yours," I reply. "Always going to be yours. That's never going to change."

He exhales, feeling the sincerity in my words. Everything I've been saying, he's finally hearing it. Finally believing it. And it's like our hearts have found a way to intertwine again, the same way they used to.

With a teasing blow over my pussy, he stares up at me and watches my reaction as he licks a stripe right up the center. My whole body tenses, and I arch my hips to chase the feeling.

"Fuck, baby," he moans. "You're already desperate for it, aren't you?"

"I'm always desperate for you," I correct him. "You've turned me into a fucking sex- addicted monster."

He smirks, bouncing his brows excitedly. "I know. It's the second best thing I've ever done."

"What was the first?"

"Marrying you."

Jesus Christ. This sweet talking, swoony motherfucker. How the hell am I supposed to grow old with him, when he's

## Chapter 29

constantly making my heart feel like it's going to burst with how much I love him?

He doesn't give me a chance to say anything back before he dives into my pussy like he's starving for it. I press my head harder into the pillow as the sound of my moans fill the room. And being as we've spent so much time needing to be quiet lately, it only spurs him on.

"That's it, baby," he tells me. "You're such a good girl, moaning for me like that."

Sliding two fingers inside of me, I clench around them like it's just not enough. The pressure he's putting on my clit is intense, but I need him inside of me. I need to feel him.

And I need to feel him bare.

"Hayes," I beg for him. "Please. I need you."

"You're getting me, baby," he promises.

I shake my head. "I need you closer."

The look in his eyes softens as he understands exactly what I mean. There's never been a time we've felt closer than when he's inside of me, holding me close as we chase the high together.

With one more hard suck on my clit, I squirm, and he lets go, standing up to get rid of his pants and boxers. His cock is so hard, it looks like just the simplest touch will make it explode. And I can only imagine how good it's going to feel to have him stretching me open when he's like that.

He takes it in his hands and leans over me, rubbing it up and down my pussy a couple times to tease me before he lines up at my entrance. His gaze locks with mine, and the two of us moan together as he presses into me.

"God, you're perfect," he breathes. "So perfect and so mine. Never going to be a day when I don't crave every inch of you."

Between the words he's saying and the way he's holding me, it's exactly what I needed. He's always been so good at

## Chapter 29

making me feel wanted and loved and cherished. And right now, I feel it all.

Knowing I'm getting close, he bottoms out inside me, stretching me open as much as he possibly can, and then uses his thumb to put just the right amount of pressure on my clit. It's a trick he learned on our wedding night, and he's been purposely holding it back until now.

Until he let me back in.

Until he trusted me again.

"Fuck," I breathe. "Yes. Just like that. Feels amazing."

He smirks down at me. "I know your body like the back of my hand, baby."

There's no lie in sight. He's taken the time to memorize me and engrained it into his mind, so he never forgets it.

My hips move with him, and I clench my pussy around him as he stays deep inside of me. I'm so fucking close. It's right there. And as I open my eyes to look at him, the way he's staring back at me with such intense, unadulterated love does me in.

One of the strongest orgasms of my life tears through me, taking me soaring off the edge and free-falling. Hayes keeps doing exactly what he was. He knows better than to switch shit up right when I get there. But once I start to come down, he begins to move.

"Hayes," I pant.

He focuses all of his attention on me. "Yeah, baby? Tell me what you want."

"I want you to come inside of me."

His motions freeze, and I know if I don't explain soon, he's going to think I'm insane. That I would bring a baby into this world while we're in the middle of what's essentially a war zone.

"I went and got the shot," I tell him. "About a month ago,

## Chapter 29

actually. But I waited to tell you because I wanted this to be special."

He expels all the air in his lungs, and he drops down on top of me. "Seriously? We can?"

I nod. "But I want to be on top of you. I want to be the one making *you* come."

A smile stretches across his face and he kisses me, grabbing my waist as he rolls us over. I bend my knees on either side of him and start to ride his cock, making sure to stay slow and calculated because we're not fucking right now.

We're loving each other in the best way we know how.

"That feels so good," he groans. "You make me feel so good, baby. I can't wait to fill you up."

My hair hangs down around my face, like it's blocking us out from the rest of the world. The only ones who exist in this moment are he and I. There's no one else who matters. We're back in our own little bubble, and I want to stay here for the rest of my life.

His fingertips lightly dig into my hips as he helps me ride him, and I can tell the moment he starts to get close because his jaw clenches. There's a look in his eyes, like he's right there, and all he needs is one more push. And as I drop down and tangle my tongue with his own, we're both done for.

Our moans mix together as he pulls me down while arching his hips up, getting as deep as he can as he fills me with his come. I can feel him pulsing inside of me as he empties everything he has, and I'm clenching around him with the same intensity as I come on his cock for the second time tonight.

When we both start to calm down, Hayes is looking at me in total awe. There have been a lot of times where I see him surprised by something, but I've never seen him speechless. He's always got something dirty coming out of his mouth.

## Chapter 29

And yet, right now, there's nothing but fondness and a dropped jaw.

After a moment, he suddenly rolls us back over, as if he forgot something. And when he sits up and starts to pull out, I realize exactly what it is. The moment he lets his cock slip out of me, I can feel his cum leak out of my pussy.

"So fucking perfect," he murmurs.

His eyes bounce between me and where he's watching his cum dripping out of me.

"There's nothing better than you. Better than this."

I find comfort in his words, letting them play through my mind over and over again, even as he gets up to find a washcloth and comes back to clean me up just as delicately as he did earlier. But when the sexual bliss fades, the fear returns in his eyes.

"I love you," I tell him as he lies beside me, trying to keep him with me in this moment.

He smiles tiredly. "I love you, too."

But while his words sound genuine, I still can't help but feel afraid. Because I know the look he has in his eyes. The one he's trying to hide from me.

*He's pulling away again.*

# Hayes
## CHAPTER THIRTY

I'll admit, when Laiken told me that she left to protect me, I thought it was bullshit. I knew that's what *she* believed, but it wasn't at all what I wanted. I wished she had told me. That we hadn't lost out on all that time together. That she would've given me the chance to do something about it before she just up and left.

But as I stand here now, I understand it completely.

Riley wants us to be miserable. She wants to rip us apart, and I know without a doubt that she will do whatever it takes to make that happen. She won't stop until we're two broken souls with irrevocable damage.

A life without her is the last thing I want, but I also won't do anything that puts her in harm's way either—including being with her.

"Hayes." Riley calls. "The keg. Did you change it already?"

I shake myself out of my thoughts and nod. "Yeah, earlier this morning."

It's so hard, standing here with her and knowing what she's done, yet not being able to do anything about it. Cam was right. We need to be calculated when it comes to her. Impulsivity won't work in our favor.

My head drops and I rub the back of my neck, feeling all of the tension piling up on me. Mali watches me intently, and if I had to guess, I'd say Riley is, too.

## Chapter 30

"Is it just me, or does he look like he's constipated?" Mali jokes.

I can tell it's killing her, too, not being able to do anything to Riley. But the important thing is not leaving any of us alone with her. Not until we get this all figured out.

And not until I get Laiken as far away from her as possible.

Riley giggles. "I think it's cute."

A strangled noise escapes from the back of Mali's throat, but I'm too fixated on the door opening and Laiken walking through it. The fact that she's even in the same room as Riley right now has me feeling like I'm going to die. It's too fucking close. She needs to be a thousand miles away from her, not in the same room.

Looking like she's been crying, Laiken walks up to the bar. "Can we talk?"

I take a deep breath, knowing this is going to break me... and her. "Not right now."

My tone comes out clipped. Dismissive. And I can barely look her in the eye when I see her wince.

"Please? Just for a minute?" she begs.

I'm so frustrated it has to be obvious to everyone in the room. "I said no."

I walk out from behind the bar and go over to clean up one of the tables, trying to put some distance between us, but she follows me.

"Hayes," she presses. "It's just a couple minutes of your time. Don't I deserve at least that?"

Spinning around, I glare at her in a way I haven't done since the first night she showed up here. "I fucking said no! I know you haven't heard it a lot in your life, princess, but it means leave me the fuck alone!"

She recoils, placing her hand over her chest as her eyes fill with tears. "You don't mean that."

## Chapter 30

"Actually, that's the first fucking thing I do mean."

Each word that comes out of my mouth physically pains me to say, but I know I need to make this believable. More than anything, I need to convince her that we're done.

"But why?" she starts to sob. "I thought we were getting better. You said we'd be okay!"

"I lied," I say with a huff. "You were right. I *don't* love you anymore. How could I after what you did to me? You expect me to forgive you for that? No."

Her bottom lip is trembling, and the tears in her eyes make me need to physically restrain myself from reaching out to her.

"Go ahead and cry," I tell her. "You'll get no sympathy here. You did this shit to yourself."

I go to walk away, but she's so insistent, she tries one last time. "Don't do this. We can fix it!"

She grabs my hand and I rip it from her grasp, knowing if she touches me, I'm going to cave. I'll make it too obvious that I don't mean a single word coming out of my mouth.

"You're not fucking listening!" I scream. "I'm not in love with you anymore! The only thing I want is for you to get the fuck out of my life!"

Standing there, looking at me like I'm a fucking monster, she doesn't move. And I need her to move.

I need her to get the fuck away from Riley.

"Go!" I roar, pointing to the door.

She chokes on a sob as she turns around and runs as fast as she can out the door. Mali walks around the bar and goes to follow her but turns to look at me first.

"You really are a fucking prick," she tells me. "I don't care how much you beg for her back after this. I'll make sure she never even gives you a second glance."

"Good," I spit.

She leaves with Laiken and I grip the bar top, trying to

## Chapter 30

exhale all of my frustration. Lai is exactly where I need her to be—anywhere but here. Riley is dangerous, and after last night, there's no telling what she might do.

"Are you okay?" Riley asks. "That was intense."

I take a deep breath, letting it all out as a heavy sigh. "Let's just say marriage isn't for everyone."

"Or it could just be that you're married to the wrong girl."

Looking up, I see the hopefulness in her eyes, and it makes me sick. She has spent the last couple months tormenting me and the people I care most about, and here she is looking at me like a lovesick puppy? Fuck out of here with that shit.

"Maybe you two only look good on paper," she says.

*Fuck that. She looks good on me.*

Running my fingers through my hair, I look around at the empty bar. "Do you think you could handle things here for a bit? I need to find a divorce lawyer. It's time I let go of this once and for all and move the fuck on."

Her grin widens at the idea of that. "Yeah, definitely. Go do what you need to."

"Thanks, Riles," I tell her.

Just as I reach the door, she calls my name and I turn to face her.

"Just know I'm here if you need me."

I nod once. "I know you are."

As I walk out, I nearly gag at even the concept of being nice to her. I have plenty of experience at playing nice when I don't want to. I spent years on a hockey team with Isaac when all I wanted to do was see a puck knock his teeth out. But being nice to Riley when all I want to do is rip her limb from limb—that was a challenge.

*Chapter 30*

**IT'S BEEN A WHILE** since I've been here. The rink was a second home to me, but when Laiken left, being here never felt right. There was always something missing. And that absence made the hole she left in my heart that much more painful. So, I avoided it—until now.

I drive around to the back and park my truck before getting out. The back door is propped open with a hockey puck, and I kick it out of the way as I step inside, letting the door lock behind me. Laiken is standing with her back to me, talking to Cam and Mali, but the moment she hears the door shut, she turns around.

It only takes a second before she's running full speed toward me and jumps directly into my arms. I catch her with ease, pressing her against the glass and holding her close as I kiss her.

"Oh my God, that was hell," I tell her. "You need to know I didn't mean a single fucking word of that."

She nods quickly, kissing me once more. "Mali told me as soon as we left."

The only way to make it believable enough was for Laiken's reactions to be genuine. She couldn't know the plan, and that was the worst fucking part about it, because as she broke down in front of me, it was real to her. And I never want to hurt her like that.

## Chapter 30

"So, the card you left on the counter for the divorce lawyer?"

"All part of it," I promise. "There is no me without you, Laiken. I may not be sure of a lot, but I'm sure of that."

She sighs in relief. "Good, because holy fuck. That felt like my insides were tearing themselves apart."

"I'm familiar with the feeling," I drawl, but there's nothing venomous behind it.

Like I said, I completely understand now why she left to protect me. I was considering doing the same thing. But she could tell, and she called me the fuck out on it so fast, I didn't even have a chance to make a decision before she was wiping the option clear off the table.

We kiss once more before I set her down. Her fingers lace with mine as we walk over to Cam and Mali.

"All good?" I ask.

Cam nods. "Everything is in place. Now we just need to see who she runs to."

When the fight between Laiken and me broke out, every move I made was intentional. Especially when I walked toward the other side of the bar. We knew that Riley would be completely entranced by it, and that gave Mali the opportunity to get her phone and plug it into hers, transferring the spyware we need over to it.

"Are you sure there's someone else involved?" Laiken asks.

Cam nods. "Killing someone and moving a body is hard. Riley wouldn't have been able to do it alone. Someone is helping her."

Mali hums. "After what Theresa told us, my money is on Monty's mom."

"The most that woman ever lifts is her pocketbook," Laiken counters.

Tilting her head to the side, Mali sees her point. "Her dad

## Chapter 30

then. Maybe they made up after he lost one kid. May as well find his back-up, right?"

"I don't know, but it looks like we're about to find out," Cam says, looking at his computer. "She's texting someone now."

> Hayes just lost his shit on Laiken. Their relationship is history.

"Can you trace the number she's texting?" I suggest.

Cam copies the number and puts it into the program the guy at the local spy shop told him about. "No. It's a burner."

*Dammit.*

"Oh, they're responding," Mali says, holding her breath.

We're all going to be on edge until this is over. The four of us stand around the small screen, watching with bated breath as we wait.

> They'll never be truly over. Not until we're done with them.

> No, it's legit. I watched it with my own eyes. He's really done with her.

> Then why are they both at the rink together right now? Don't be stupid, Riley. They're playing you. Now finish what you're doing and get here. I need your help.

*Fuck!* We need a new plan.

## Hayes
# CHAPTER THIRTY ONE

We all rush back to the bar, desperate to get to Riley. From those texts, it's obvious she's not the ringleader in all of this. She's someone's puppet. All we need to know is who is pulling the strings, and the only one who can tell us is her. But if they know her cover is blown, it's not like she's just going to show up to work tomorrow.

Our only chance is now.

Running up to the bar, we're hopeful we'll be able to talk some sense into her. Laiken could even tell her that she found her mom. Hopefully that would connect with her somehow. But as we get up to the door, we realize it's locked and all the lights are off inside.

*Son of a bitch.*

I take my keys out and unlock it. As we walk inside, we quickly recognize that the place is completely empty. But when Cam flicks on the lights, we find that the *finish up what you're doing* wasn't about working the bar. It was about what's left in it for us.

Sitting in the center of the bar are four oversized balloons —each one with an envelope attached and our names written on them. I walk over to inspect them, and that's when I see it. All of the balloons are being weighed down with fishing sinkers.

The same kind I put in Monty's pockets to keep the body down.

"Cam," I say, nodding down to the weights.

## Chapter 31

He looks down and his eyes widen. "How would they know that unless they found his body?"

"I have no idea."

We all grab our respective envelopes, and it's no surprise to me that mine and Laiken's are placed on opposite ends. Tearing us apart seems to be the most important thing in all of this. But we're stronger when we're together, and the only ones who can decide to end us are Laiken and me.

Carefully, we all open the envelopes, finding party invitations for each of us.

*A 21$^{st}$ Birthday isn't complete without a trip to Slaughter Island. Isn't that right, H?*

Looking at the date, I notice it's three days from now. There's no reason they'd be bringing us back to the scene of the crime other than this is their endgame. And what better way than a makeshift birthday party for Laiken?

After all, they did say this has always been about her.

But what I don't understand is if Laiken is what they want, why bury her alive? Why give me a chance to find her? They're obsessed with her, but when it comes down to it, this is all just a sick game to them.

"They don't actually expect us to go to this, do they?" Mali asks.

Laiken tosses her invitation onto the table. "I have a feeling if we don't, they'll force us there anyway."

She has a point, and she knows it better than anyone. Over the last couple months, they've made it obvious they have the power to do whatever they want. If we think we're safe, we need to think again, because we're never safe and we're never one step ahead.

Four loud booms echo through the bar as each balloon pops, startling all of us. I shield Laiken while Cam shields Mali. But when it stops, we turn back around to see blood dripping from every surface within ten feet of the balloons.

## Chapter 31

They must have been filled with it, like a giant water balloon, and they were designed to pop so it would create a bloodbath.

*Chances are it's fake, but as soon as we're done dealing with all this shit, I'm demanding we all go get HIV tests.*

**TRACKING RILEY'S PHONE, WE** go to her apartment, hoping to find her there. It's a small studio apartment above a realtor's office. It may not be the best area I've ever seen, but it's not terrible. Still, she has to be spending more than what she makes at the bar to live here.

We try knocking on the door, but no one answers. Mali moves Cam out of the way and pulls a bobby-pin out of her hair, dropping to her knees as she starts to pick the lock.

Cam stares down at her like he doesn't know who she is. "Okay, this shit is getting a little out of hand."

It only takes her a second to get the door unlocked, and she pushes it open before standing back up. "What's wrong? Are you intimidated by a girl that can handle her own?"

"No," he growls. "I'm just wondering how the fuck you know how to pick a lock."

She shrugs. "Whenever I was grounded, my parents would lock my phone and computer in their closet when they went to work. I learned how to pick locks so I could get to it, and then I'd put it back before they came home."

## Chapter 31

Cam purses his lips. "Okay, fair enough. Carry on."

I roll my eyes, and we all step inside. The place looks innocent enough. There's a bed against one wall with a dresser across from it. There's no TV, but it's what you'd expect from your typical twenty-one-year-old.

Or at least until Laiken opens the closet.

"Holy shit," she says.

We all gather around, staring in shock at the montage in the closet. There are articles from Monty's disappearance, his obituary, pictures of each of us that we never knew were taken, and finally, a map with each of the different places we ever went with Monty all marked out.

As my eyes scan over everything, it dawns on me that while I was devastated about Laiken leaving, I unknowingly hired the exact person that made her go. The thought of that irritates me to no end.

"Next time I tell you two I don't like someone and you don't believe me, I'm going to remind ya'll of this," Mali tells Cam and me.

I chuckle because I can't even deny it. This whole time, she was right. "Noted."

"Found her phone," Cam says, picking it up off her bed. "Don't know how we're going to find her now, though. Can't track a phone that isn't on her."

"If I had to guess, that's not a coincidence," I tell him.

Laiken looks deep in thought, and I watch the moment the lightbulb goes off. She rushes over to the bed and opens up the computer that sits on top.

"Lai-Lai," Mali singsongs. "Now is not the time to be checking your email, baby."

Laiken rolls her eyes but doesn't respond as she types something in. Whatever it is, she must be onto something because she is pecking away with great concentration. And finally, she smiles.

## Chapter 31

"I've got it!" she says, spinning the computer around to face us. "Riley wears an Apple watch, and you can track those through her Apple ID."

Right there on the screen in front of us is a little dot, moving across the water—heading straight for Slaughter Island. That must be where she was told to come once she finished up. It makes sense. They're getting things ready for the end of this.

And quite possibly, the end of us.

**WE DRIVE DOWN TO** the docks, finding Riley's car carelessly parked off to the side. It almost looks like she was in a rush, but if she knows we're onto her, that could definitely be why. She knows she can't take the four of us on. The last thing she probably wants is for us to get her alone.

Cam goes over to the car and finds the doors unlocked. There isn't much inside, but when he pops the trunk, all the evidence is right there. Spray paint cans, the envelopes and note cards, the sinkers the balloons were tied to, and lastly, a burner phone. We turn it on and find plenty of the anonymous text messages that were sent to us, but nothing sent to her ringleader.

"So, what do we do?" Mali asks.

Running my fingers through my hair, I give Cam a look and I know we're on the same page.

## Chapter 31

"We go now," he says, so I don't have to.

"Go?" Laiken repeats, sounding terrified. "As in, to Slaughter Island?"

He nods. "It's three days before they're expecting us. At least then it gives us the element of surprise. It's our only chance to catch them off guard, and possibly, before they're ready. Besides, if we wait until their plan, there's no saying whoever Riley is working with will be there."

Laiken is shaking her head before he's even done speaking. "No. I can't. I can't go back there. Not after the last time."

I position myself in front of her, holding her face in my hands and looking into her eyes. I've got to calm her down now before it gets out of hand.

"Baby," I say softly. "I know you're scared, but you have to know that I'm not going to let anything happen to you. I've got you. Okay? But we have to end this once and for all."

She still looks unsure, so I pull her in and kiss her, making sure she knows that she's always the first thought on my mind.

"You left a piece of you there that night," I tell her. "It's time we go get it back."

Thankfully, she finally nods, and I grab her hand, lacing my fingers with hers. Our marriage may not be perfect. It's troubled and has dealt with more adversity than most, but it's ours. I'm sure we'll argue, and sometimes I'll want to rip my hair out, but we're always going to be stronger when we're together.

Looking over at Cam, with Laiken's hand tightly in mind, I nod. "Let's do this."

*Chapter 31*

**HOPEFULLY LUCAS'S DAD WON'T** notice his boat is gone until after he gets back. Cam sent Lucas a text, letting him know we had something we had to take care of and it was an emergency, but that doesn't mean his dad won't call the cops for a stolen boat. What would they even call that? Grand theft vessel?

It doesn't take long for us to get to Slaughter Island, thanks to the twin motors on this baby. As we get close, we realize there's another boat here, which means Riley must be nearby. We all glance around, but we don't see her. And that only leaves one option.

*She's in the house.*

Laiken stares at the spot where Monty died, but when I press a kiss to her hair, she snaps out of it.

"Are you okay?" I check.

She looks up at me with fear in her eyes. "I just want this to be over."

"You and me both, baby. So, let's go put an end to this."

We each get off the boat and quietly make our way toward the house. You can hear the sound of someone inside, but it's hard to make out what they're doing. As we stand in front of the door, Cam pulls his gun out from his waistband and holds it in his hands.

"On the count of three," he whispers.

He counts with his fingers, and the moment he hits three,

*Chapter 31*

we storm inside. Riley's eyes widen in a panic when she sees us, finally realizing for a fact that we know it's her. Cam points the gun directly at her. She rolls her eyes and puts her hands up, looking like she's been caught.

"You have two seconds to tell me who you're working with and where they are, or I swear to God, I'll blow your brains out."

She smirks, like she knows that's never going to happen, and she looks behind us just in time for the door to slam shut. Gas quickly fills the room, and Riley throws a mask over her face, but as I try to get away, I realize I can't.

This shit is quick, taking you down with one breath, and one by one, we each fall to the floor as we pass out, hearing a familiar voice taunting us in the background.

*"How fashionably early of you. Welcome to the party."*

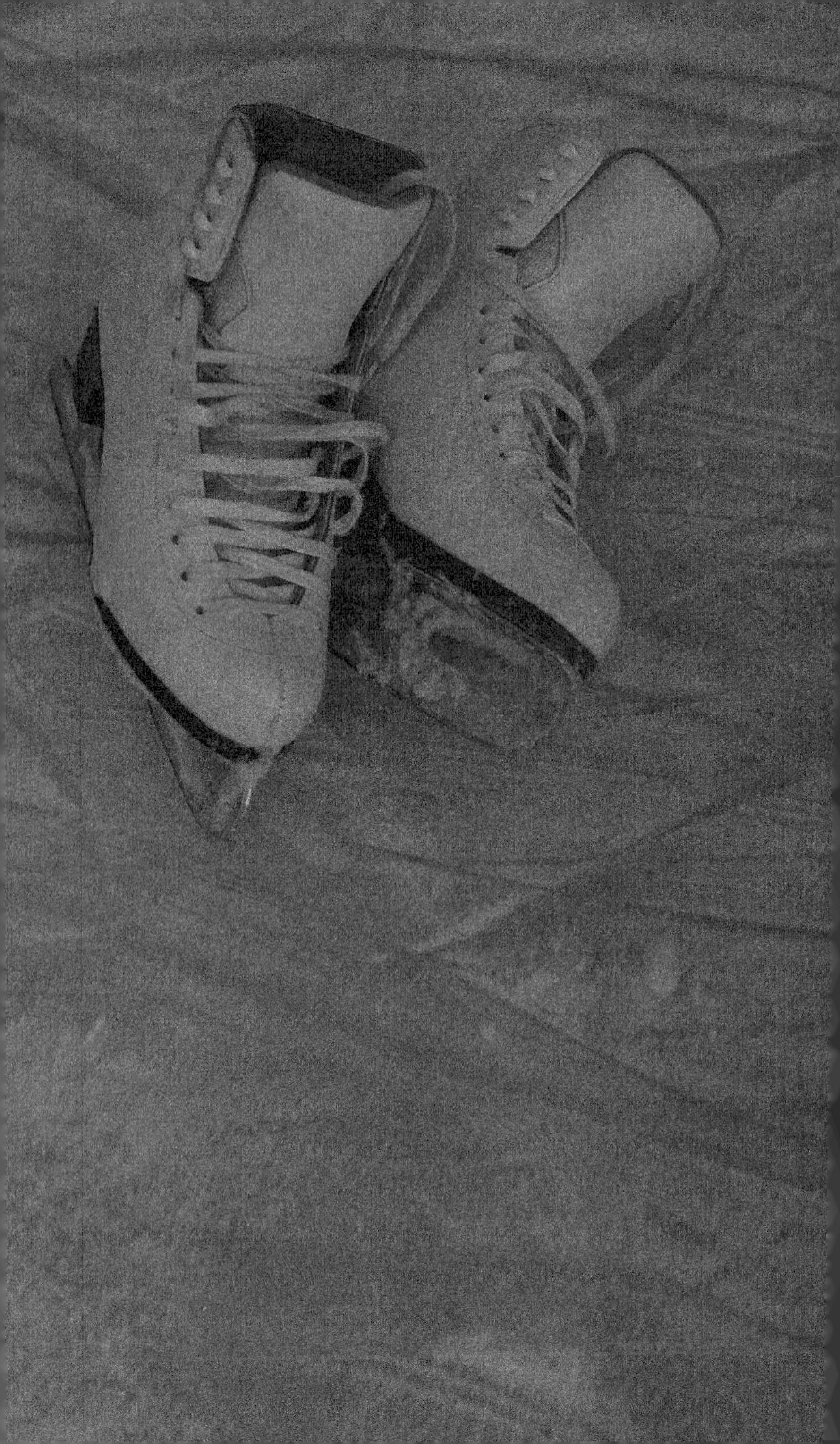

# Laiken
# CHAPTER THIRTY TWO

Everything feels foggy, like I'm just beneath the surface of the water, struggling to reach the top. My lungs burn with the need for air. I'm right there, hanging in the balance between life and death. It would be so easy to let go. It would be so painless.

But the easy road never has been the route for me.

The first thing I hear is the sound of Hayes struggling. "Get the fuck off her! You're going to fucking kill her!"

As I jolt awake, my mouth and nose are finally uncovered, and I cough violently as my lungs fill with air. My vision is blurry, and it takes a minute for everything to come into focus, but when it does, I can't believe what I'm seeing.

"There she is," he singsongs.

My eyes widen as sheer terror fills me from head to toe. I struggle to move. I'm tied to a chair with my hands behind my back, and each leg is tied to the leg of the chair. Turning to my right, I see Hayes is in the same position—looking both relieved that I'm alive and terrified because he knows we're so fucked.

"No," I breathe. "Y-you're…"

"I'm what?" Monty smirks. "Dead? Not quite."

Each breath comes out heavy. "I saw you! There was so much blood. You were—"

"Passed out from the shock of being shot in the fucking stomach," he clarifies. "Though I have to say, having my

## Chapter 32

friends dump my body instead of taking me for help? That hurt much worse."

This has to be a dream. A twisted nightmare feeding off the trauma left over from that night. But as I struggle against the rope and feel it cut into my skin, I realize that this is just as real and fucked up as it seems.

"I went to your funeral," I say, trying to make sense of it all.

He hums, swinging Cam's gun around. "Yeah. Touching little thing that was."

*He fucking knew.* I was self-destructing over the loss of him, and he was alive this entire goddamn time. "I fucking mourned you!"

"Hey!" he says, squatting down in front of me and digging the fingertips of his free hand into my thigh. "Don't act so innocent! You left me there to die!"

"I thought you were already dead," I cry. "I wanted to get help."

"And yet, you let him drag you away while I was bleeding out."

He stands up, taking a few steps away. I turn to my left to find Cam and Mali in the same position that Hayes and I are. Mali looks just as terrified as I am, while Cam is seething with rage. Riley is standing in the corner, watching all of this go down with a devilish grin on her face.

"When I heard someone coming back, I thought you came to your senses," he admits. "I thought they came to get me and were going to take me to get help. But then I heard them —talking about how they were going to dump me and let the sharks take care of it. And I realized they weren't back to get me. They were back to get *rid* of me.

"Thankfully, being submerged in water activated fight or flight. The only fucking thing that was going to save me was myself. It was rough, but I managed to swim to the buoy and

## Chapter 32

pull myself up onto it. And that was where a kind, old fisherman found me." He looks up from the floor, and his eyes are so dark. "It's too bad I had to kill him, but he was the only one who knew I was still alive. And if I was going to get my revenge, I had to be dead."

I shake my head, feeling the pain of that night all over again. "If I had known you were still alive, I—"

"You what?" he sneers. "You would have covered up your brother's crimes again? Oh, wait. No, you thought *Hayes* was the one that shot me."

"Fuck you," H growls, as if poking the bear is a good idea.

But Monty just lets out a sinister laugh. "That was the best part, if I'm honest. Hayes taking the fall for Cam gave me the perfect opportunity to make you leave him. It was just too easy."

My gaze meets Hayes's, and I can tell he's struggling against the ropes, but they're tied so fucking tight. All it's doing is cutting through his skin. There's no hope of getting free.

"It was an accident!" I yell. "No one was *trying* to kill you. Why are you doing this?"

"Because you came the fuck back!" he roars. "If you had stayed away from him, it wouldn't have had to come to this. But you just had to run to his side to make sure he was all right."

Riley looks like she's getting the utmost enjoyment out of this. "I'm so tired of the Hayes and Laiken show, aren't you?"

Monty chuckles darkly. "It's sickening, the way he can do no wrong in her eyes."

Pushing off the wall, Riley walks past Monty and over to Hayes. "Let's see how she likes this."

She throws a leg over Hayes's lap, straddling him and draping her arms over his shoulders. As she moves in to kiss him, I can feel my heart breaking. We're going to die, and I

## Chapter 32

won't have been the last person to kiss him. My lips won't be the last ones to touch his. And even as he struggles to turn away, I'm terrified she's going to succeed.

Until he rears back and slams his head into her face.

Riley grabs her nose as she falls onto the floor, in complete shock that he hurt her. Blood gushes from her very obviously broken nose, and when she touches it with her hand, her rage turns to me.

"This is all *your* fault!" she screams.

Jumping up, she rushes toward me and wraps her hands around my throat. Once again, I struggle to breathe, but this time, it's because she's strangling the life out of me. Everyone is screaming and trying to fight their way free, but all I can focus on is the look in Riley's eyes.

"He won't love me because he thinks he's in love with you!" she shrieks as she cuts off my air supply.

I can feel myself starting to give in. My vision tunnels and everything is fading, until a loud bang pierces my eardrums, making them ring. Riley's grip loosens and she falls limp onto my lap as I sputter and cough while trying to suck in air.

Monty stands to the side of my chair, looking down at the bullet hole in her temple in disappointment. He turns to me and shakes his head as he yanks her off me and drops her onto the floor.

"Why is it I'm always having to do shit for you?"

But I can't answer. I can barely even think. My trauma response wraps its arms around me and holds me close, rocking me and telling me it's all going to be okay, but I know it won't.

We're all going to end up just like Riley.

"What is wrong with you?" Mali jeers, finally having enough.

Monty looks over at her in disgust. "Don't even get me

## Chapter 32

started on you. I never thought you'd be such a traitor. Seeing you hook up with Cam broke my heart."

"I thought you were dead!" she shouts.

He stares back at her, emotionless, before he breaks out in maniacal laughter. "That's fine. I was only with you so that Romeo over here couldn't take Laiken away from me completely."

Monty goes over to Mali and squats down in front of her, slowly dragging the gun up her leg. "It's too bad I never got a chance to see what that pussy could do, though. Cam really seems to enjoy it, doesn't he?"

My brother almost knocks his chair over as he tries to get to him. "Get the fuck off her, you fucking psychopath!"

Standing up, Monty bends forward in front of him. "Or what? What are *you* going to do?"

Cam should keep his mouth shut. Lord knows we're not in the position right now to be insulting the person who just killed his own sister. But he never has been the type to bite his tongue, and of course, this is no different.

"What's wrong?" he taunts Monty. "You don't like when people make you feel less like a man?"

Monty huffs out a sarcastic laugh, looking like he's walking away, until he swings his hand with the gun and backhands him across the face with it. The force of the hit sends Cam's head flying to the side, and he looks a little dazed.

But when he cocks the gun and points it at him, the panic that shoots through me gives me back my voice.

"Don't!" I wail. "Please. Don't do this."

Tears start streaming down my face, and Monty softens as he sees me upset. He leaves Cam alone and drops to his knees in front of me.

"No, angel," he says softly, like he's a whole different person. "Don't cry. You're too pretty to cry."

## Chapter 32

I shake my head, praying to God that we make it out of here alive. "You don't have to do this, Monty. You don't. You can keep me. We can run away together, but you don't need to hurt them. Just let them go."

Hayes is turning an angry shade of red as he listens to the words coming from my mouth, but I don't care. If that's what it'll take so they can go free, I'll do it. I'll do *anything*.

He isn't buying it. "Hayes has to die. He'd never stop looking for you now."

"No," I say a little too quickly. Taking a breath, I calm myself down. "No. He doesn't. He'll leave us alone. I know he will."

Monty's eyes darken once more as he scoffs. "Unbelievable. Even still, you're trying to fucking save him. I gave you everything you ever wanted. The big house. The dream job. I made sure you were living your goddamn dream, and you *still* want him!"

"N-no," I choke out. "Nolan gave me those things."

The corner of his lips raises menacingly. "You really think you just happened to meet an heiress who didn't turn her nose up at some girl trying to get into a club she clearly didn't belong in?"

*Oh. My. God.*

There's a level of devastation you feel when you realize that everything you thought you knew was a lie. It was all Monty. Every last fucking bit of it. I believed that I lucked out. That the universe was repaying me for making the right choice and protecting Hayes. But that's all bullshit.

It was Monty.

That's why I didn't hear from him at all once I left. Why the messages stopped and the threat seemed to vanish, only lingering in the parts of me that considered going back home. He was in control the whole goddamn time.

"Yeah," he boasts. "That was all me, angel. And I can't tell

## Chapter 32

you how much I enjoyed the little show you put on for me every night with that vibrator."

*I'm going to throw up.*

He's not going to let us leave here. The man is absolutely certifiable, knowing no boundaries at all. That's why he recorded Hayes and me. Why he recorded Mali. He thinks everyone is his to do what he wants with, including taking lives.

Monty circles me like I'm his prey, grazing the tip of the gun across my shoulders. "Don't you get it, Laiken? I gave you everything you could have ever wanted."

"No!" I spit back. "You took away the *only* thing I wanted. My life with him was the only fucking thing I cared about, but you just couldn't fucking handle that."

He bends down behind me and places his lips by the shell of my ear. "No. I can't. And it's a good thing I don't have to."

Hayes is losing his shit at seeing him this close to me. "So, what? If you can't have her, no one can? That's really how you're going to do this?"

A dark laugh leaves Monty's mouth as he starts to untie me. "Oh, there is no *if I can't have her*. I'm *going* to have her. And then I'm going to kill each and every one of you." He smirks at Hayes. "I bet it'll just ruin you to know that the last person to have her was me."

"You son of a bitch!" he roars. "You keep your fucking hands off of her!"

But Monty isn't listening. He finishes untying my legs and then does my arms, freeing me from all restraints. If I thought I could get away though, I'm mistaken. Monty keeps the gun firmly pointed at my head.

"Go into the bedroom and get on the bed," he orders.

I don't move, frozen in fear as everyone around me panics. Cam is jostling so much that his chair starts to crack under the pressure. Monty rolls his eyes before slamming the

## Chapter 32

butt of the gun against his head and knocking him unconscious.

"On second thought, having him as a brother-in-law would've been hell," Monty mocks. "Now…bedroom."

My legs won't move as I stare into the barrel of the gun, wondering if letting him shoot me is the better alternative. After all, we're going to die anyway, aren't we?

But as he loses his patience, he moves the gun from me to Hayes. "I said now, Laiken!"

My whole body tenses as I fear not for my life, but his. Monty is deranged. A total sociopath. But he believes he's in love with me. I have more of a chance. But Hayes? He'll shoot him without even blinking.

And that's the only thing that makes me move.

Hayes screams for me to stop as I turn around and walk straight into the bedroom. Monty follows me in and I glance back at Hayes—our eyes locking for one final second as the door slams shut.

# Hayes
## CHAPTER THIRTY THREE

My blood boils as it runs through my veins. I fight with every fucking thing I have to get free from the confines of this chair. I don't care that the roughness of the rope is cutting through my skin or that I can feel blood trickling down my hand. The only thing on my mind is what's going on behind that door.

Laiken is going to put up a fight. She's not the type to give up easily. But he's going to win. She's already weak from whatever the fuck we breathed in and the fact that Riley almost fucking strangled her to death. He's going to overpower her, and he's going to rape her.

Unless I can get to him before that happens.

Cam is still slumped over, passed out against the chair. Mali is in hysterics as she watches him helplessly, listening to the sound of Laiken's screams.

But over my dead body will I let Monty shatter her again.

"Shut the fuck up!" Monty yells, but Laiken keeps screaming at the top of her lungs.

And when I hear Monty call her a bitch, I know she's definitely fighting back.

I just have to get myself out of this fucking chair!

Rocking against it the same way Cam did, I hear it start to creak. The wood is old. These must have been here when it was still lived in. So, if I could just get it to…

It takes all the strength in my core to lean forward enough to lift the chair off the ground. Mali watches me in disbelief as I take a deep breath, bracing myself to impact.

## Chapter 33

With everything I have, I throw myself backward. As it slams into the wall, the chair shatters—the wood splintering and stabbing into my back as I land on top of it. Pain sears through me but I don't have time for feeling anything.

It takes a second and nearly popping my shoulder out of place for me to get my arms in front of my body, but once I do, I'm able to use my teeth to get the knot to loosen just enough.

Mali lets out a wet laugh, finally feeling somewhat hopeful for once. "You couldn't have hulked out like that a little earlier?"

I huff as I force my back straight and march into the bedroom. Monty has Laiken face down on the bed, with his knees holding her legs in place. Her pants are halfway down as she thrashes around in an effort to keep him off. But the sound of her screams keep him from hearing me come in.

The gun lies on the bed behind him, and I consider taking it, but that would be too easy. Too humane for what he deserves.

No. He gets to die as slowly and painfully as possible.

With the adrenaline coursing through me, I grab Monty by the back of the neck and rip him off my wife. His eyes widen in shock and panic as I take him to the fucking ground.

He doesn't fight back, but then again, I don't give him the chance to. I grab his head and slam it into the ground repeatedly, watching as blood starts to pool under it. My clenched fist flies into his face, and I can feel as the bones break beneath the surface. But even when he goes limp, I can't stop.

His face is covered in blood. There isn't a single part of him that's recognizable. But I keep swinging. Keep pummeling into him with an unmatched force, until a gentle touch rests on my shoulder.

## Chapter 33

"Hayes," Laiken says softly. "You can stop. He's gone. He can't hurt us anymore."

But this time, I want to be sure.

I take two fingers and press them against his neck, searching for a pulse, but there isn't one.

He's fucking dead.

Finally feeling like I can breathe, I slump back and pull Laiken into me. I need to see that she's okay. That she's alive and not missing more of the pieces he wanted to take from her.

"He didn't…" I ask, not even able to say the words.

She shakes her head, gripping at me tightly. "No."

*Thank fuck.*

I run my hand over her face and watch her as my breathing starts to slow. When I can't hold back anymore, I pull her in and cover her mouth with mine. She breathes the life right back into me. There's nothing else in the world that matters.

Only her.

Only this.

Only us.

When we break apart, I glance over at Monty's *officially* dead body and then back to Laiken. "For the record, this time I killed him intentionally, and I won't fucking apologize for it."

She huffs out a laugh, looking at me in disbelief. "I won't ask you to."

I kiss her again, only to be interrupted by the sound of Mali's voice echoing in the other room.

"For the love of fuck, you two can be gross at home," she calls. "Get me the hell out of here."

*Shit, right.*

Laiken chuckles weakly as she stands up and puts her hand out to help me. I can still feel the pain in my back, but

## Chapter 33

I'll take pain with a victory over feeling nothing because I'm dead.

We go back out into the living room, and I work to untie Mali first while Laiken tries to wake Cam. She's lightly tapping his face and saying his name, but there's nothing.

He shouldn't still be out.

The moment Mali is free, she drops down in front of Cam. "Babe. Babe, you've got to wake up."

I work to untie his wrists, watching as his arms fall to their sides, and dread fills me from head to toe. My eyes meet Laiken's, which are starting to fill with tears, and Mali begins to cry.

"You are not allowed to fucking die on me, Blanchard," she scolds between sobs. "I swear, if you don't wake the fuck up, I'll make sure everyone you've ever known thinks you have a tiny dick!"

In the best timing known to man, Cam stirs, finally coming to. Laiken and I exhale in relief. He must remember where we are because he jolts in a panic and looks around. Mali still has tears streaming down her face as she lets out a wet laugh and puts her hand on his cheek.

"Hey, Sleeping Beauty." His head whips around like he's looking for the rest of us, but Mali focuses him back on her. "Don't worry. Hayes saved your princess ass."

His head drops in relief, and he takes a couple breaths then looks up at Mali. He grabs her face and only hesitates for a second before kissing her impatiently. When he breaks the kiss, she rests her head on his shoulder and he holds her close as he looks at Laiken and then back at me.

"Monty?" he asks.

I nod toward the bedroom. "Dead."

He snorts. "That's what you said the last time."

I blow out a rush of air and stand up, taking Laiken into

## Chapter 33

my arms and holding her close. There's never going to be a time where I let her go. There can't be. We need each other, and maybe that's unhealthy and codependent, but I don't care.

She's my entire fucking world.

Looking around, Cam finds a pack of matches and a can of gasoline in one of the cabinets. It's new, which means Monty planned on burning this place to the ground once he was done with us.

Little did he know he'd be burning with it.

After dousing as much of the house as we can, including both Monty's and Riley's bodies, Cam takes out one of the matches and goes to light it. But just before he does, Laiken puts her hand out.

"He took so much from me," she says. "This started with me. Now, it's going to end with me."

He glances at me, but I don't stop him. There isn't a doubt in my mind that she knows what she's doing. Laiken has been through so much and somehow made it through it all. She may have broken at times, but she never let herself stay that way. If this is what she wants, I'll give it to her.

Taking the match, she sparks it against the side and looks into the flame.

"Enjoy hell, assholes."

She drops it onto the floor beside Riley's body and steps back as the decaying wood instantly catches fire. It spreads rapidly through the house, and the four of us walk out together. My arm is draped around Laiken's shoulders, with Cam's around Mali's. Laiken leans into me as she and Mali loop their arms together. We all managed to make it out alive, but we'll never forget the way we felt when there was a possibility that we wouldn't.

Standing in the water, I clean the blood off my hands. Cam waits for me, and when I'm done, we push the boat into

*Chapter 33*

deeper water. We both climb on board and the engine rumbles as it comes to life.

Mali stands beside Cam as he drives, with her head resting on his shoulder, but Laiken is watching as the house burns in the distance. I wrap my arms around her from behind. There's nothing better than holding her close, especially after I was convinced that I was going to lose her.

"It's really all over?" she asks.

I nod, pressing a kiss to the top of her shoulder. "It's all over, baby. Except us. You're stuck with me for the rest of our lives."

She spins around in my arms and smiles fondly up at me. "I love you."

Looking down at the girl who surprised me at every turn, I can't believe there was a time I wanted to deny myself this. But she fucked all my rules then the same way she does now. And I wouldn't change it for anything in the world.

I kiss her forehead before saying the words that aren't nearly enough, but they're the only thing that comes close. "I more than love you."

# *Hayes* EPILOGUE

*One Month Later*

THE AIR FEELS LIGHTER THESE DAYS, LIKE IT'S easier to breathe. It's been quiet and uneventful, which is *exactly* how I want it. We've been filling our time with mundane things like work and grocery shopping, and after the hell we went through, I've got to say, it's refreshing. I never used to think that the simplicities of a domesticated life would appeal to me, but I was wrong.

Then again, Laiken always keeps things interesting.

I look out the window as I see a moving truck pull up, and I step out onto the porch. Two guys hop out and open up the back. I turn around and shout into the house.

"Lai," I call. "It's for you!"

Her brows furrow as she comes out from the kitchen. "Huh?"

As I nod for her to come outside, she looks confused until she steps out onto the porch. One of the movers comes up with a clipboard and smiles politely at her.

"Are you Laiken Blanchard?" he asks.

She cocks a brow at him. "It's Laiken *Wilder*."

He nods. "Of course, my apologies. I have a few boxes

## Epilogue

here from a Miss Nolan Brentwood. Does that sound familiar?"

"Unfortunately," she says dryly. "Where do I sign?"

The mover shows her where to initial and sign, and when she's done, he hands her a letter with Laiken's name written in Nolan's handwriting. She scrunches her nose at it but takes it anyway, opening it while the guy goes to start retrieving her boxes out of the truck.

A few days after we nearly lost our lives, Laiken was finally ready to confront Nolan. I sat in the living room and watched Laiken pace as she laid into her. Nolan admitted to everything, but claims she knew nothing other than that she was someone who needed to be looked after. Still, the trust there was destroyed, so when Laiken told her she never wants to see her again, I didn't blame her. And when Nolan asked if she wanted her things packed up and mailed to her, Lai was so done with it all that she said she didn't care.

*"Do whatever you want. It's not my concern anymore."*

Looks like she decided to ship it to her anyway.

"For what it's worth, I really did value you as a friend," Laiken reads out loud with a scoff, before crumbling it up in her fist. "Well, it's worth nothing, bitch."

I chuckle, watching her go down the steps and tell the movers that she wants all the boxes on the porch. After everything, it makes sense that she would want to go through it before bringing it into our house.

As I see she has this handled, I go back inside to continue finally fixing the mantel. Laiken has been on me about it, telling me that it's always been her favorite part of the house. What she *doesn't* know, however, is that I'm reinforcing it to make it stronger.

I hear the name Rollins come through the TV and I pause, grabbing the remote to turn it up just slightly as the news anchor starts to report on the story.

## Epilogue

*"After a month-long investigation, police are finally closing the case on a fire that took place on a small island off the coast. Investigators say that Montgomery Rollins, who had disappeared and was presumed dead, was living there for two years out of the house that had been abandoned for over a decade. During what authorities believe was a lover's quarrel, a female who was at the house with Montgomery struck him fiercely and repeatedly in the head and face, killing him before lighting the house on fire and shooting herself. According to sources, even Montgomery's own parents didn't know he was still alive and had believed their son was dead. We reached out to Senator Rollins for comment, but he declined."*

The idea of Riley and Monty being lovers grosses me out. Then again, it wouldn't surprise me. Monty was a sick fuck. I don't think there's anything I'd put past him.

"What are you watching?" Laiken says as she walks through the door.

I press the button to turn off the TV, smiling back at her. "Just that they're closing the case on Monty. Everything okay?"

She glances out the window and nods. "Everything is perfect."

It only takes a couple steps before I'm in front of her, pulling her into my arms. "Good. But as soon as they leave, I'm taking you somewhere."

"Do I get to know where?"

"Do you ever?"

Her lips press together as she pouts. "Fine."

As she goes to walk away, I reach out to grab her, spinning her back into my arms and kissing her so fast it catches her off guard. Her whole body melts into me as her lips move against my own, until I finally break the kiss to look at her.

"Happy Anniversary, baby."

*Epilogue*

Her smile brightens, lighting up my whole damn life. "Happy Anniversary."

**THE SUN SHINES DOWN**, warming us as we drive down the street. Laiken's hand hangs out the window as she lets the wind run between her fingers. I find myself glancing over at her a lot lately, just to admire how beautiful she is. When she came back, I was so angry, and trusting her again proved difficult, but we were always going to hold on until it happened. I don't believe there was ever another alternative for either of us.

As if she can feel me looking at her, she turns to me and grins. "What?"

"Nothing," I tell her. "Just glad you're mine."

She looks down at her finger, where the tattoo of my initial is newly touched up. A week after finally putting an end to the nightmare, the two of us went to the tattoo shop and sat across from each other, not looking away for a second as we reaffirmed our love for each other with the buzz of a tattoo gun.

"There will never be a day that I'm not," she promises.

And I know she's never meant anything more.

I pull into the parking lot of our special beach, the same one that was taken from us the night Monty and Riley buried Laiken alive here. Laiken's breath hitches, and she looks at

## Epilogue

me with fear in her eyes, but I put the truck in park and turn my entire body to face her.

"If you want to leave, we can," I tell her. "But if you think it's something you can get through, I'd really like to get out of the truck."

She takes a deep breath as she stares back at me. "They're gone."

"They're gone," I confirm.

It's a thing she's needed to do lately, especially when the nightmares caused by the trauma creep up on her at night. But she's so damn strong, and all I can do is be in awe of her as she puts her hand on the handle and opens the door.

I hop out and walk around the truck, taking her hand in mine. We go slow as we walk onto the beach, until I stop and turn to her. Her eyes narrow slightly as she looks up at me.

"What are we doing here, H?" she asks.

My head turns as I look around, surprisingly feeling a little nervous. "This place was so special to us, and it was just one of the many things that were stolen from us. But I plan on changing that. They don't get to take away this place or the incredible memories we have here. So, I'm taking it back."

I drop down on one knee and pull the ring out of my pocket. The same one she put on the island next to the words *I'm so sorry* before she left. Her breath hitches as she recognizes it immediately.

"Two years ago today, I married you in the middle of our living room in front of our closest family," I say, with all the love I feel for her pouring out in my words. "Now I'm asking you to marry me in front of everyone we know and love, here, on our special beach."

Laiken's smile stretches from ear to ear as she giggles. "You're such a caveman you have to marry me twice, huh?"

*Epilogue*

I huff out a laugh as I stand, grabbing the back of her neck. "You know it, baby."

As I pull her in, she goes willingly, and the two of us meet in the middle. I move my mouth gently against hers. It's slow and it's calculated, which is exactly the kind of kiss that tells her everything she means to me.

"So, is that a yes?" I ask once we stop for air.

"Of course, it's a yes," she answers. "But I have one condition."

*Condition?* We're literally already married. It's hardly the time for bartering, but I'll entertain her. "What is it?"

"It has to be soon because I want your mom to be there."

Just like that, her words warm me from the inside out. Leave it to her to always be thinking of me. What I want. What I need. I'm always the first thing on her mind, and it shows in everything she does.

"Every time I think I can't love you any more than I already do…"

She brightens a little more and throws her arms around my neck, bringing our lips together again.

**THE FIRE BURNS HOT** in front of me, reminding me of the day we won. After something so horrific, some people will try to avoid anything and everything that could trigger the memory of what they went through. But not us. We're

## Epilogue

stronger than that. Letting them take this from us would only be letting them win, and the four of us? We're a little too competitive to let that happen.

All of my friends, all the people I care about, they're all here—drinking and enjoying the good life. They may drive me insane sometimes, but that's what friendship is. I watch as Cam lectures Mali on the proper way to roast a marshmallow, only for it to catch on fire. Mali giggles as he blows it out and then presents it to her like it's the best thing in the world. She pulls it off the skewer and looks at it skeptically, blowing on it just before she smushes it all over his mouth. Cam stares back at her in shock, but I wouldn't expect an apology out of her if I were him.

Not for that, or anything else.

"Hey," Laiken says, coming to stand beside me.

I sigh in relief, feeling everything somehow get even better now that she's here. "Finally. I missed you."

"You literally saw me an hour ago," she teases.

Turning toward her, I give her an incredulous look. "Woman, I miss you when you walk away for five minutes. Don't act like this is news to you."

She laughs and rolls her eyes playfully, but as she looks at the fire, I notice the envelope in her hand.

"What's that?" I ask her.

Her brows furrow for a second until it dawns on her when she looks down. "Oh!" She hands it to me. "It was in one of the boxes Nolan sent."

Opening it up, I pull out the first note that Laiken received. The one that was written on the back of a picture. And when I turn it over, I can see why it had the ability to make her leave. The photo looks like a still frame from a video. Monty must have still had the hidden camera on the boat, and it was able to capture footage as I pushed it away.

It's definitely incriminating—a clear shot of Cam and me

## Epilogue

lifting what we thought was Monty's dead body up off the ground. Laiken was right. If this had gotten into the hands of authorities, I wouldn't have stood a chance.

Putting it face down on the envelope, I lean forward and toss it into the fire. We watch as it burns, just like the bodies did, and we know there's nothing that can hurt us now.

I wrap my arms around her while the last thing that holds us to Monty turns into ash, pressing my lips against her cheek. "I think, deep down, I always knew you'd end up back in my arms."

"You did?" she asks, tilting her head to the side to look at me.

"Yep." My eyes lock with hers and I smirk. "After all, I'm your pipe dream."

Laughter bubbles out of her, and I bask in the sound of it.

Luck has a way of rarely being on my side, but I think that's only because I must've spent it all on her. Laiken Rose Wilder is the best part of my day. She's my present, my past, and my future, and because of that, I'll never regret a single thing. All the times I stumbled and thought it couldn't get any worse, only to be proven wrong—it was all worth it because it brought us here.

I will spend the rest of my life being incomprehensibly in love with her. And if there's a life after this one, I'll go to the ends of the earth to find her again, because her soul and mine are two halves of a whole.

*There's no me without her.*

# THANK YOU FOR READING!

I hope you enjoyed the finale of Hayes and Laiken's story. If you did, I would greatly appreciate it if you could leave a review. :)

## WHAT ABOUT CAM AND MALI?

Keep an eye out for their book.
It's coming, and it's going to be a wild one. ;)
xoxo

## BONUS CONTENT

I've loved writing Hayes and Laiken's story so much that I just had to add some bonus content. And who can really only stop at one? Certainly not me. Enjoy :)

-

Didn't get enough Hayes and Laiken?
Read the Extended Epilogue.

Craving some more pain?
Read the night Laiken left in her POV.

*Bonus Content*

Need to know more about Riley?
Check out this bonus content.

# Who is she?
## THAT GIRL, KELSEY CLAYTON

Kelsey Clayton is a USA Today bestselling author of Contemporary Romance novels. She lives in a small town in Delaware with her husband, two kids, and two dogs.

She is an avid reader of fall hard romance. She believes that books are the best escape you can find, and that if you feel a range of emotions while reading her stories - she succeeded. She loves writing and is only getting started on this life long journey.

Kelsey likes to keep things in her life simple. Her ideal night is one with sweatpants, a fluffy blanket, cheese fries, and wine. She holds her friends and family close to her heart and would do just about anything to make them happy.

For inquires: management@kelseyclayton.com

For social media links, scan below:

# Books by
# KELSEY CLAYTON

**The Pretty Poison Trilogy**

A Dose of Pretty Poison

A Drop of Pretty Poison

A Shot of Pretty Poison

**Malvagio Mafia Duet**

Suffer in Silence

Screams in Symphony

**Haven Grace Prep**

The Sinner *(Savannah & Grayson)*

The Saint *(Delaney & Knox)*

The Rebel *(Tessa & Asher)*

The Enemy *(Lennon & Cade)*

**North Haven University**

Corrupt My Mind *(Zayn & Amelia)*

Change My Game *(Jace & Paige)*

Wreck My Plans *(Carter & Tye)*

Waste My Time *(Easton & Kennedy)*

**The Sleepless November Saga**

Sleepless November

Endless December

Seamless Forever

Awakened in September

**Standalones**

Returning to Rockport

Hendrix *(Colby & Saige)*

Influenced

# SIGNED PAPERBACKS

Want a signed Kelsey Clayton book?
You can purchase them on her website.
Check it out.

Printed in Great Britain
by Amazon